Connie Monk grew up in Reading and, following her marriage, lived in the Thames Valley area until 1974, when she moved to Ringwood in Hampshire. After she and her husband retired to Shaldon in Devon she began to write and her first novel was published in 1984. She has since written over fifteen novels. Two of her books, *Jessica* and *A Field of Bright Laughter*, were nominated for the Romantic Novel of the Year Award.

THE SANDS OF TIME

When Tamsin Yelland is thrown upon her own resources, she takes a job as private secretary to Charles Hardcastle. It is through Charles that Tamsin makes the acquaintance of suffragette Lucinda Murray and her handsome son, Alexander. In the challenging early days of flying, Alex is determined that nothing will stand in the way of his aspirations to become a leading figure in aeronautics — not his mother's politics, and certainly not his growing affection for Tamsin Yelland. Working for local aeronautical firm Proctors, Alex has become owner James Proctor's protégé. But James doesn't always approve of Alex's treatment of women — especially Tamsin, who is clearly a young girl in love.

CONNIE MONK

THE SANDS
OF TIME

Complete and Unabridged

CHARNWOOD
Leicester

First published in Great Britain in 1999 by
Judy Piatkus (Publishers) Limited
London

First Charnwood Edition
published 2001
by arrangement with
Judy Piatkus (Publishers) Limited
London

British Library CIP Data

Monk, Connie
    The sands of time.—Large print ed.—
Charnwood library series
    1. Aeronautics—Great Britain—History—Fiction
    2. Suffragists—Great Britain—Fiction
    3. Love stories
    4. Large type books
    I. Title
    823.9'14 [F]

    ISBN 0–7089–9216–1

Published by
F. A. Thorpe (Publishing)
Anstey, Leicestershire

Set by Words & Graphics Ltd.
Anstey, Leicestershire
Printed and bound in Great Britain by
T. J. International Ltd., Padstow, Cornwall

This book is printed on acid-free paper

We can make our lives sublime
And, departing, leave behind us
Footprints in the sands of time.

(William Longfellow)

1

1900

'Grandpa, we've picked an enormous lot of strawberries for market. Me and Albert and his sweetheart, we did the picking.' Tamsin crept into the bedroom where Justin Herrinshaw lay. At six years old, she'd never come face to face with death. Illness was something like measles or influenza or mumps — she'd had mumps last year and remembered how funny she'd looked. Those sort of illnesses she could understand: they had a name and people seemed to know how long it would be before they were better. But what ailed her grandfather wasn't like that. During the last week, the doctor had been coming each day and always talking to her mother in a secret sort of whisper.

'That's the way.' Justin mustered up his strength to answer her. 'Knew my little helper — ' and a stop for breath ' — knew you'd see to them.'

She had to bend close to hear him.

'Just till you're better. Then we'll do them together, like always,' she made herself say it, as if in voicing what meant so much to her she could make it a reality.

He moved his hand an inch or two in her direction, a hand that only a few weeks ago had been hardened with work. Now it was soft to

1

touch, cold and clammy, the pale skin too loose for the bones. She took it in hers, climbing to sit on the edge of the bed.

'Mum says I shouldn't come and see you. She says I'll be a nuisance. I'm not one, am I?' A question that didn't need an answer. She knew she could never be a nuisance to him. But she wasn't prepared for the way his mouth trembled as if he was going to cry. It made her tummy hurt. She didn't know how to help him. When she bent forward and put her face on the pillow next to his it was partly because she wanted the comfort of his nearness. More than anybody in the world, she loved him. 'My little helper': that's what he'd always called her and, from when she'd taken her first staggering steps, she had followed him on the field of his smallholding. With him she'd dropped the seed potatoes into the furrow as Albert walked ahead, leading Brutus and the plough; she'd learnt not to cry when the spikes from the gooseberry bushes scratched her as she'd filled her punnets; she'd helped him pick the broad beans, the peas — and the runner beans too, if they grew low enough for her to reach. In bad weather, she'd still pulled on her coat and followed him, spending hours in the potting shed where he'd light a paraffin stove and fill the place with smoke from his pipe. Sitting on upturned boxes, they'd found time for more than work: there were word games to be played or paper models to be made.

Now all that had changed. It was nearly nine weeks since Justin had finally been unable to carry on and had been forced to send for the doctor. She wouldn't let herself be frightened; young though she was, she sensed that to give in to fear would be to fail him. She had to believe — really believe — that he would soon be working in the field again and everything would be normal; that was the only way she knew to help him. Even so, it was for her own comfort as much as his that she rubbed her smooth cheek against his end-of-day stubble. But the touch of his yellowish skin, so taut over the bones of his face, did nothing to reassure her. And how funny his breathing sounded; not quite a snore and yet a sort of rattle. Was he asleep? His eyes were half closed. Perhaps she ought to creep away and let him take a nap.

'Night night, Grandpa,' she whispered into his ear. 'I'll come and see you in the morning.'

She was disappointed that he didn't answer, but she gave him a goodnight kiss anyway.

'My duckie . . . ' Did he really say it or did she imagine it?

Gently, she slid off the bed, but even then she didn't go out of the room. Instead, she tiptoed to the window and looked out at the yard and the field beyond. All the animals had gone, all except the chickens. Mr Chilvers from Sandy Hill, their neighbouring farm, had collected them. Albert had told her that one day when her grandfather was well again they would bring them back, but she had suspected he'd only said it because he'd found her crying in the pigsty that still smelt of Snowy.

Tamsin had never lived anywhere else. Her

3

mother, Mavis, had been married for less than six months to David Yelland, a fisherman, when his boat had been wrecked on the rocks off the Cornish coast and he'd been drowned. Already pregnant, she had returned 'to keep house' for her widowed father at Gorsemoor, his smallholding in the New Forest. In the neighbourhood, Mavis was looked on with affection and respect: such a lovely young woman, ready to listen to other people's troubles, ready to visit the sick, help the aged, and with never a sign of self-pity for her own plight. She wasn't blind to the looks of appreciation cast in her direction, nor yet deaf to the murmured admiration; it was from knowing that she was looked on as 'beautiful' and 'brave' that she drew her own strength. As for 'keeping house' for her father: certainly she took the trap to Fordingbridge or Ringwood to do the shopping, just as she dusted, made the beds and sometimes even pushed a mop around; but it was Mrs Jenkins, mother of seven, who came each day to Gorsemoor and kept the wheels of the household turning, just as it was Trudie Maggs, Albert's sister, who helped in the yard and the dairy. It was the usual thing for the womenfolk of a farmer's household to rear the chickens and look after the dairy, but Mavis preferred the arrangement as it was. She arranged the flowers in St Michael's, the church she attended each Sunday morning; she whipped up the occasional sponge cake to take when she was visiting the sick but mucking out the cowshed or turning the handle of the butter churn had never been her job and she saw no reason to change things.

Tamsin knew that downstairs there was a visitor, one who came quite frequently lately. When she'd gone off to help gather the strawberries, she had suspected he must be coming; she could tell because her mother had set a jug of flowers on the table in the seldom used parlour and had been sitting in there with her sewing. Not even just sitting, but somehow looking as though she were arranged in her chair just as carefully as the flowers were in their jug, with the lengthening rays of the sun highlighting the gold of her hair. Busily picking the berries, enjoying being with Albert and his sweetheart, Tamsin had forgotten why she'd been especially glad to escape. Coming home, she'd flung open the door from the yard, eager to report how many punnets they'd filled ready for tomorrow's market in Ringwood. Voices from the parlour had reminded her: the preaching man was there. So she'd taken off her boots as quietly as she could and crept up the stairs so that they wouldn't hear her on her way to her grandfather's room.

★　★　★

Arthur Hillbright glanced at his pocket watch, sighed and stood up.

'I fear I must leave you, my dear. My train is due in less than an hour and I have to walk to Ringwood.'

'With Father as he is, I'm frightened to leave him alone or I'd take you to the railway in the

5

trap.' She dreaded his going. Lately, her life had revolved around his visits.

She felt like a young girl consumed by adolescent love instead of a woman of thirty, a widow for nearly seven years. He was her first thought in the morning, her last at night. Did he feel the same for her? If he didn't, why did he arrange to preach in the area so often? Why did he come out of his way to visit Gorsemoor? Always so correct, never saying a word that might be misconstrued: could it be that he felt protective of her plight, here alone with the responsibility of a dying father?

'If you care for me to see your father, I just have time. We will pray together that he may be relieved of his pain.'

Her deep blue eyes told him of her gratitude, quite the loveliest eyes he'd ever seen. Indeed, he'd never known a woman so utterly lovely — so desirable. And that was the root of his trouble. She aroused feelings in him that he'd fought against all his days, fought and overcome. Lust was evil. And what could it be except lust that throbbed in his veins, that haunted his dreams and woke him in the night craving for the warmth of her nearness, taunting him with images of her soft, pale body? In the past, when he'd been driven by thoughts of carnal desire, he had found the willpower to fight, to kneel and pray for strength to turn aside from the devil's temptations. A man of such outstanding appearance, women of all kinds had been more than ready to dance to his tune. But for Arthur, love — physical love — outside marriage was the way to eternal damnation. Mavis was a widow. He could make her his wife, she would be his . . . his today, tomorrow, willingly she would be there for him . . . beautiful Mavis . . . her pale body . . . warm, loving. And that's where he floundered. Was it only this craving to possess her body that drove him to thoughts of marriage? Until now, his whole life had been given to God. Was he failing his God? Was he giving way to the need of frail flesh? Night after night, on his knees, he'd wrestled. There were times when he believed he hated Mavis, saw her as the devil's advocate trying to come between him and his God.

All those thoughts crowded into his head as he followed her up the stairs to Justin's bedroom. Reaching the top, they turned to pass two closed doors (which one would be *her* room? The thought was there before he could stop it) just as the third was flung open and Tamsin collided with them.

'Tamsin! How many times do I have to tell you? You are *not* to worry your grandfather. What are you doing in there? How long have you been there?'

'Mum, come and see — Grandpa — I can't make him hear — Mum, funny rumbling noises — not now — ' A whole sentence seemed to be beyond her.

'What have you done?' It wasn't a question, it was an accusation.

Arthur had pushed past them and gone to the bedside, where he was holding Justin's wrist. With a restraining hand on Tamsin's shoulder,

Mavis stood rooted to the spot, watching him.

'The Lord in His mercy has taken his soul.'

'Gone . . . ?' Hardly more than a whisper.

'No! No, Grandpa!' Tearing away from her mother, Tamsin was across the room in a second and on the bed, Justin's cold hand in hers. 'Wake up, Grandpa. It's *me*! Please hear me, Grandpa.' In her heart, she knew he couldn't.

'Hush, do.' Mavis half lifted and half pulled Tamsin off the bed and stood her on the ground. 'You shouldn't have been in here. I've told you before, your grandfather needs — needed — to be quiet. Now he's gone.' She bit her lip, looking appealingly at Arthur.

'I *was* quiet.' In the frenzy of her misery, Tamsin's small fists pounded her mother. 'And he did want me, he did, he did. Grandpa!' Uncontrolled and hysterical, she screamed his name, as if even now he might hear her.

'Stop that!' Arthur's sharp tone was accompanied by a light smack on her wrist. 'It's the only way,' he excused his action to Mavis. 'Go along downstairs, Tamsin; this is no place for a child.'

He was surprised she didn't argue. Her screams had died down into occasional snorts as she turned to the door. Small and forlorn, she went slowly down the stairs and out through the kitchen into the yard. Giggling sounds from the sheds told her that Albert and his sweetheart were loading up the cart to take to Ringwood in the morning. She didn't want them to see her. She wouldn't be able to tell them, to say that he wasn't going to be there anymore. Dead. She'd never be his helper any more . . . she put out her tongue and licked the salty tears. The door of Snowy's sty was undone, so she slipped inside. Even though it had been cleaned, it still smelt piggy; sitting in the corner, with her eyes closed, she could almost pretend it was all like it used to be.

★   ★   ★

Willingly, Mavis let Arthur take control. That night, he didn't go back to his lodgings in Winchester. It was so easy to persuade himself that Mavis ought not to be alone in the house with the body (alone, except for the child, and she didn't count).

'Mavis, my dear, I don't believe your father was a regular church attendant?'

'That doesn't mean to say he wasn't a good man.' Immediately she was on the defensive.

'Of course he was. I just thought it would be a comfort for you if I were to conduct his service.'

'Yes, it would. But would the Rector allow it? I mean, you aren't ordained in the Church of England.' But the thought of Arthur sharing her sadness, being part of the loss, was a comfort, just as he'd known it would be.

'It would be in the chapel — '

'Then, no. He wouldn't like it.' She cut into his sentence, speaking before she gave herself time to question.

'My dear, his spirit is on a higher plane. He is above such pettiness.'

'I know that, Arthur — and I know it would be a comfort to hear *you* helping me through the ordeal. If he could speak for himself, he would probably agree with what you say. But it's because he *can't* speak for himself that I have to see he's taken to St Michael's.'

Surprisingly, Arthur was glad of her stubbornness; it showed him a side to her he'd not seen before.

★ ★ ★

Next morning, Tamsin went into the village to school at the usual time.

'Don't you want your skipping rope?' Mavis passed it to her as she kissed her goodbye.

Tamsin took it, but how can you skip when your tummy is knotted up with unhappiness?

'I've taken it upon myself to ask Albert's sister — Trudie, do you call her? — to sleep in the house with you until after the funeral.' Arthur's voice cut across Mavis's thoughts as she watched the disconsolate stoop of Tamsin's shoulders as she started up the lane to the village. 'You'll be all right, my dear? After all this is cleared up, I mean. You have a good helper in Albert — '

'I can't stay here. Father only rented Gorsemoor. It paid its way but then he worked all daylight hours in the field, he went to market . . . I can't do what he did . . . must find a way to keep Tamsie and me. Twice this has happened.' She looked at him, with those glorious eyes full of pain. 'I'd only been married five months when David was drowned. But then I had a home to come back to. Now, Pa gone . . . I dare say he had a few pounds, enough to find Tamsie and me a room somewhere, buy us enough to live on until I can find work. I shall look for something with — '

'You think I could see that happening to you?' Was this his God's way of guiding him? Was it the Devil's way of tempting him? No, no: what had the Devil to do with Mavis, when she was surely the dearest, kindest and most Christian of women?

'But you won't see it, Arthur.' She caught the corners of her mouth between her teeth to hold her lips steady, but there was no disguising how near her voice was to breaking. 'In less than a month you take up your new ministry. You'll have a chapel of your own — no more preaching in village halls or under the open sky . . . no people like me who wait for your visits . . . '

Her words petered into silence. Why was he standing so still, his head high, as if he were listening for something? She listened, too. But there was nothing. How strange he looked, staring ahead of him: yet there was nothing on the wall to put that exaltant light in his dark eyes.

Dropping to his knees, he gripped his hands together until she could see the white of his knuckles, his eyes tightly closed.

'Arthur? What is it, Arthur?'

'Did you feel nothing?' His eyes were open now and his hands reaching to take hers. 'Like a rushing wind, choirs of angels, voices that speak to my soul.'

'Arthur?' There had been times when she had felt he had been lost to her, moments when he'd

11

been preaching and had been moved by the fervour of his own words.

'Marry me, Mavis. Tell me you'll be my wife. When I take up my ministry in Brackleford, you'll be my side, my helper in my parish work. Come with me, my comfort and my love. I've wanted you for so long: I've fought against the temptation of my desire. But the Lord has shown me what He wants of me. Don't you see, my love? All this is part of His glorious pattern. This is His will. For you and for me there is work to do. I will preach the Word; in your compassion and understanding you will do His bidding.'

Kneeling before her, his dark eyes shining with passion (for her? For his mission?) she knew she had never seen a man so perfect.

'How can I say 'yes' to you, even though it's what I want more than anything in the world? But Arthur, I was very ill when Tamsin was born. They said it was a miracle I lived; they had to take her from me by surgery. They told me then that it was impossible for me to conceive again. I didn't care: I had no husband. You should marry a woman who can give you children.'

'It's *you* I want. If our love can't give us the blessing of children, then we will be all in all to each other. In everything there is a purpose. Promise you'll be mine: let me love you, let me cherish you.'

She slipped from the chair to kneel just as he still did, only inches from him. She could smell the perfume of his brilliantine; she could feel the warmth of his breath as she raised her mouth to his.

'Yes, I'll marry you. I'll work with you. I'll go with you to the ends of the earth.' Brave words, for the Berkshire town of Brackleford was hardly that.

★ ★ ★

'Tamsie, I want you to listen.' Mavis sat down and drew the little girl towards her. Both of them were conscious of Arthur standing close by and Tamsin's glower in his direction told him as clearly as any words that she resented his being there. 'You've never had a father — '

'Had Grandpa. Didn't want a father.' Not a promising beginning.

'All children need a father. They need to be part of a proper family. You've always had love, but one parent can't take the place of two.'

'Had Grandpa . . . ' She knew she was losing the battle even before she understood what she was fighting for.

'Of course you did and he was a loving grandfather. But we can't bring him back. We have to be happy for him that he has been taken to paradise.'

Tamsin squirmed uncomfortably. She wished her mother would let go of her hands and she wished Mr Hillbright would go away. She wished — she couldn't help it, even if her mother thought it was wicked of her — she wished more than anything that her grandfather was still there. She shut her eyes and imagined the happy feeling of being in the field with him.

' . . . a home of our own. As soon as the

13

wedding is over, we shall all go straight to Brackleford. You'll be just the same as all your friends. You must learn to call him 'Father'. Now I want you to give him a kiss and tell him how happy you are.'

Snatching her hands away, Tamsin stood still. He seemed to loom over her, a threat to all she knew. Like a cornered animal she looked from one to the other, then turned and fled.

'Arthur, I'm sorry. So ashamed that she could behave like it.'

'My dear, we must give her time. She's no more used to having a father than I am to having a daughter. But we both have you, and you will draw us together.'

Over the months before her Grandfather's death, Tamsin had studiously avoided Arthur. He'd had very little contact with her and saw her simply as a pale-faced, skinny child (in fact, he often marvelled that a woman as lovely as Mavis could have produced her), and assumed that she would be obedient to her mother's will. Mavis knew better. She wasn't misled by Tamsin's frail appearance: she knew it hid a will of iron. Loving them both, being the one to try to draw them together, cast the first cloud on her horizon.

★   ★   ★

Gorsemoor was half a mile outside the village, but in no time the news spread that Mavis Yelland was to marry the preacher, the man whose godlike good looks filled the dreams of many a local woman, be she a young hopeful, an

14

ageing spinster or a 'taken-for-granted' wife. Interest in the couple — and no one would be the first to suggest the interest was anything but good-natured, for who would doubt the morals of the gentle widow or the upright preacher? — was mixed with respect for Justin Herrinshaw as the pews at St Michael's filled for his funeral. Already widowed, Mavis had been able to dress herself appropriately for mourning without having to do more than stitch a fresh piece of veiling to her hat, so she had spent the intervening days making a black outfit for Tamsin. As she'd turned the handle of her sewing machine, she'd been grateful to her father for his gift of it. But when the time came to set out for the funeral she looked at the child and, not for the first time, felt a stab of disappointment. Appearance had always meant so much to Mavis, and nature had been on her side. If only Tamsin had inherited *something* from her: but there was nothing. A mother with deep waves in hair that was the colour of burnished gold; a daughter with fine, straight locks so light that they were almost colourless. (Like moonbeams, Justin used to say, but then Justin had thought everything about his 'little helper' was perfect.) Mavis's eyes were a deep violet blue; Tamsin's seemed undecided. They took their colour from what she wore: if she were dressed in blue, they were blue, in green and they'd appear green, grey and they'd forget all about blues and greens. Out of keeping with her pale hair, the fine lines of her eyebrows looked as though they'd been put in with dark brown crayon and

15

the strange-coloured eyes were fringed with thick dark lashes. On the day of the funeral, her black attire accentuated her pallor and the shadows under her eyes.

'It fits nicely.' Mavis did her best to find something encouraging to say as she viewed the woebegone figure.

★ ★ ★

Three weeks later, in the local chapel, Mavis and Arthur were married. Without the luxury of a honeymoon, they travelled that same day to Brackleford and the start of their new life.

The day had been full of new experiences for Tamsin. She wanted the day to be over, yet she wanted things to keep happening so that she wouldn't have a chance to remember the sound of the door shutting behind them as they'd left Gorsemoor. She'd run from her mother's side and, despite her new frock, she'd climbed up the gate to lean over and look into the field. Looking at it had made her tummy hurt even more, but she couldn't leave it without saying goodbye. Her bantam run was empty: Mr Chilvers had had all the chickens, too. The buildings that used to be part of her every day looked different, already neglected and only one stage from derelict.

After that had come the wedding itself, watching and listening to the vows, promising that they would love only each other. If Grandpa had been there, it wouldn't have hurt, but it was like Mum saying that no one mattered except beastly Mr Hillbright: not *her*, not Grandpa, not all the things at home. Now it was just *him*, and she was promising to 'keep herself only to him' for ever. Then there had been lots of good wishes while people talked to what they called 'the happy couple'; then she'd been hugged by Trudie and Mrs Maggs, her hair had been given an affectionate tug by Albert — and they'd been bowled away to the railway station. Somehow, that had made things easier. She'd never been on a train before and she'd pressed her face to the window, making sure not to miss anything. She'd listened to the rhythm of the wheels and pretended they were trying to talk to her. When at last they'd reached Brackleford, there was plenty to take her interest. It was bigger than Ringwood or Fordingbridge; she'd never been to a busy town like this before.

Outside the railway station, two men had been selling evening papers, each trying to shout louder than the other. A tramcar rattled along its track, attached by a pole to overhead wires; a man was playing a barrel organ, turning the handle while a monkey sat on top of it, scratching in its search for fleas. There was so much to watch as the station cab took them the short ride to the Manse that she almost forgot how miserable she was.

Later, though, supper over, she was sent to bed. That's when the memories flooded back and, just as it had when she said goodbye to the field, her tummy felt as though it were tied in knots.

It had been a day of emotion for all of them, the end of the known and accepted way of life. Mavis was already in bed by the time a nightgowned Arthur padded barefoot from the bathroom. A bathroom was a luxury previously unknown to her — and she hadn't had the courage to try to use the geyser that he'd proudly told her would supply their hot water. The day had been warm and sticky. It had been no hardship to freshen up from just the cold tap; she'd soon got warm again in the comfort of a feather bed.

'Hello.' She greeted him unnecessarily, her mind a sudden blank.

He knelt at her side of the bed, reaching for her hand. 'Was I a long time? So many prayers, so much thankfulness . . . '

'For both of us,' she told him.

'I will never fail you: with all my heart I pray it.'

She laughed softly, fluttering her fingers almost teasingly on his well-trimmed moustache.

'You've never failed anyone in your life. Sometimes I wonder how I came to deserve you. I just want to be worthy of you, to be all that you want.' She held back the bedcovers invitingly and, getting up from his knees, he sat sideways on the edge, facing her.

'You're all I want. You've had a husband, you've loved before — '

'Long ago. I want to be yours, just yours.'

As if a spring had snapped in him, he moved

18

onto her, breathing hard, his eyes closed as his hands forced up her nightgown and touched her nakedness. Tonight, he wouldn't fight his desire: she was his to love. Tonight, tomorrow, always. His hand moved over her thigh. As he touched the warm wetness of her, he gave way to the Devil whispering to him that if he'd not always fought temptation there could have been women before this. Tonight, his joy and excitement wouldn't have been tempered with fear that he'd fail her.

'Help me,' he whispered aloud to his Maker.

Believing he spoke to her, Mavis guided him. Always restrained, always correct in thought and word and deed, that was the Arthur she expected. Rather than exciting her, his uncontrolled passion made a stranger of him. With her nightgown pushed almost to her neck, his hands explored her; the dreams he'd repressed for years were encapsulated into those few short minutes. Even his voice made a stranger of him. David's love-making had been silent, tender; Arthur's was wild. In each breath he groaned, grunted and finally, when he could hold back no longer, his climax came with a cry of triumph.

Mavis held him close, her own happiness coming from the knowledge that she was the woman chosen to be his wife. Their union had been all he'd yearned: hers was the power, hers was the glory. She gently moved from under him and, in minutes, they both slept. Yet later — how much later, she didn't know — when she half woke and moved her hand, expecting to touch him, he wasn't there. Then, by the light of the

19

waning moon, she saw him getting up from where he'd knelt by the bedside. Some of her own satisfaction evaporated, but she wasn't awake enough to feel resentment. Climbing back into bed, he reached to draw her close.

'Our Lord gave you to me; He made you mine. An earthly partner, a gift above all gold.' Still not fully awake, she heard his whispered words, his hands telling her that his imagination was already carrying him back — carrying him forward.

When she'd drifted contentedly into that first sleep, her last thought had been one of thankfulness that hers was the power. But was it? Lying beneath him, she felt that power was one thing she lacked. But did it matter if he accepted her as a heaven-sent gift, sent to make his life complete and share his mission? She was his wife, she would be his companion, his helpmeet — all that and his love, too. Even so, as he worked himself up into a climax of passion, the thought jumped uninvited into her head that she hoped he wouldn't feel duty-bound to climb out of bed again and say 'thank you': if anyone should be thanked, surely it was *her*?

★   ★   ★

Tamsin had rebelled often enough at having to go to St Michael's with her mother every Sunday morning (although it had been different at Christmas or Easter; then, Grandpa had always come too, and it had felt like a proper outing) but now she remembered the pretty country

20

church with nostalgic affection, the shafts of tinted light as the sun shone through the coloured glass, the wooden pews and that smell of old stone, old wood, flowers, a 'shut in' sort of smell that she would have been able to recognise even with her eyes closed. How different from the plain building of the chapel, with its whitewashed walls and rows of wooden chairs, its upright piano where each week hatchet-faced Mrs Harker would clip her wire-framed spectacles on her nose and sit to pound out the hymn tunes.

Next door to the chapel was the Manse. Grudgingly, she agreed that it was a pretty house, with its bow windows and glazed porch; but it looked as though it was pretending to be somewhere else, somewhere away from the dust and smells of the centre of town. To start with, she found it a novelty to watch the tramcars sway and rattle their way along their tracks every ten minutes or so, from their terminus in Millsham, on the residential eastern boundary of the town, to Wemberton on the residential western boundary. Brackleford's prosperity came from the centre — 'its heart' Arthur liked to call it, for that's where the chapel was. Shops, the railway station, a timber yard, a brewery, bakeries, tailors with their workshops, an abattoir, a shoemaking factory, a new brick edifice, on one wall of which was painted *Model Laundry* — all the industry was in the centre of town, and most of the poor housing where the workers lived, too. Immediately opposite the Manse was Perkins' Pickle Factory and, weekday or Sunday, day or night, the stench of boiling vinegar with a hint of onion lingered in the air.

'We'll soon get so used to it that we shan't even notice,' Mavis told Tamsin, in a voice that was just too bright to be natural. 'Remember the pigs at Gorsemoor? They didn't smell very pretty, but it didn't worry us.'

Tamsin's only answer was a scowl. She didn't want to talk about Gorsemoor — not the pigs, not her bantams, not the fields, not that warm safe feeling of working with Grandpa. All those things were locked safely in her heart but she was frightened to remember.

Arthur, new father or not, believed that looking after children was for women; his mind was on a higher plane. His lack of interference might have been expected to please his rebellious stepdaughter, but such was her state of angry insecurity that she saw it as a sign that he wasn't interested in her; and that was only one small step from believing he didn't want her at the Manse at all.

She hated the way her mother appeared to hang on his every word, eager to please him, grateful when he told her of parish work he wanted her to do and anxious to earn his praise.

'This afternoon, I'd like you to spend an hour with Mrs Freeman; she's lonely, you know. I told her you'd call.' That on a day when the rain lashed unceasingly against the windows. 'Then Mrs Chadwick could do with a visit. She lost her first child at birth, I'm told. This second one is due and the woman has no stamina, no courage. Fear! Of all the earthly sins, surely there's none greater. I told her she should gird herself with prayer and faith: there's no other way of destroying the demon fear. But I don't think she so much as listened. Go and see her, Mavis, my dear. And, on the way home, perhaps you'll look in at the chapel and make sure the lamps are filled.'

Tamsin's glare was a silent 'Why don't you look at the lamps yourself? Just because you preach it doesn't mean you're *God*! Anyway, even He wouldn't be so bossy.'

'Yes, dear, of course I will.' Why didn't her mother ever tell him she had something else to do? But no, she gave him that smile, as if they shared a secret. 'Don't kick the table leg, sweetling, there's a good girl.'

'I paid a visit on some new people this morning. In Tannery Lane. I'd been told the furniture wagon came yesterday, so I made up my mind to be the first to welcome them.'

As usual, Mavis's gaze was full of admiration. 'Will they be coming to the chapel?'

'She — not they. No, she has no intention. Clearly, I wasted my time. And if Reverend Burrell calls on her he'll face the same brick wall. Mrs Murray, she calls herself, but there's just herself and a child — a child whose red hair is a sign he's in the hands of the Devil — and no ring on her finger. Mrs!' Tamsin couldn't see why he said it in that cross, sneering voice. 'Have you ever seen a widow with no ring on her finger? A dangerous woman.'

'Oh, no! Arthur, there's no one beyond your redemption. Would you like me to call?'

'I forbid it. I'll not have you mixing with a creature of her sort. A woman full of fight, a rebel. We read enough about those in our newspaper. Brackleford can do without her sort. The voice of a lady couldn't disguise her belligerence, her resentment. A most uncomfortable meeting.'

★ ★ ★

Living at Gorsemoor, she'd had no near neighbours, but loneliness had been unknown to Tamsin. There had always been things to do: looking after her bantams, helping in the field, learning to help Trudie in the dairy — important things, as she thought of them. At the Manse, everything was different: she was one child living in a household of the sort of orderliness Gorsemoor had never known. It even made a stranger of her mother and made it impossible for her to ask to have someone from school home to play. The good part about attending Miss Searl's school each morning was that it was at the Millsham end of town and entailed a ride in the tramcar. That was fun and made her feel vastly important, travelling with people who were off to start their day's work. But by half past one, she was home again, often having to amuse herself ('And mind you don't make a muddle!') in the house alone.

On a Saturday at the end of October, she went off with her skipping rope, pretending it was just as much fun here as it had been in 'the lane at home', as she still thought of her old play-ground. Mr Dunn, the greengrocer on the other side of the chapel bade her, 'Hello, young lady,' as she went on her twirling way, and that cheered her up no end. Adventure called, so she turned from the main road into Tannery Lane, somewhere she'd not explored before. It was rough and rutted, not much good for skipping, but there were a lot of conkers on the ground. She'd collect them and pick out the best to put on strings and take to school on Monday.

'Hey! You can't pinch those. That tree's ours.'

Her fingers tightened on her spoils as she was confronted by a boy who rushed out of the first house of the terrace that fronted the lane, a boy with a shock of auburn curls and light brown eyes that defied her to challenge his authority. The small patch of ground to the side of the house was hardly worthy of being called a garden; on it stood a solitary horse chestnut tree.

'I picked them up in the lane. I wasn't pinching.' She stood her ground.

'Give 'em here.'

Small she might be, but Tamsin wasn't the sort to be brow-beaten.

'Won't! They weren't on your tree, they were out here on the ground — so they were for anybody.'

'I'll give you a Chinese burn.'

She had no idea what he was offering in exchange, but she was sure it was something she wouldn't want.

'I'm not swapping; I'm keeping these. Finders keepers.'

Without a word, her assailant was as good as his threat. Grabbing her wrist in both his hands, he twisted it, just like she'd watched Mrs Maggs wringing the washing. Her mouth shot open involuntarily as she gasped and let go of her treasures.

'I warned you! That's what happens to girls who steal my things.'

'*I never steal! Don't you dare call me a stealer!*' Twirling her rope, she brought it sharply across his bare leg, triumphant yet frightened at the way tears of pain sprang to his eyes.

They looked at each other wordlessly, he with a weal on his leg, she with the marks of his fingers still on her wrist.

Wiping the back of his hand across his nose and eyes in one go, the boy sized her up. There was something like respect in his expression.

'Where do you go to school? A shrimp like you, I suppose you're not old enough.'

'Course I am, I'm six. I can read better than you, I bet. Girls always can.'

'I've never seen you at school.'

'I go to Miss Searl's.'

'That's for cissies.'

Before she could think of an answer designed to knock him off his perch, a woman followed him out of the house.

'Alex, you have more conkers on the tree than you want. Bring her in and let her pick some up.' The voice was deep, authoritative. For a second, the boy she called Alex looked ready to argue, then he changed his mind.

Tamsin snatched at her dignity, perhaps taking

a lead from the tall woman with the voice like brown velvet.

'The ones I picked up outside will be plenty, thank you very much. I don't need to be given any.'

The woman's voice had sounded as though she'd brook no argument, but her dark eyes were smiling, looking as though the answer pleased her. Into Tamsin's mind flashed the memory of Arthur's description of the couple who'd moved into Tannery Lane, the woman he refused to let Mavis visit and the boy whose red hair showed that the Devil had already put his stamp on him.

'Come in anyway, if you like,' Alex mumbled. 'You can see my rabbit.'

'I'll just pick up my conkers.' She accepted his olive branch, then she followed him through the little two-up, two-down villa.

By the time she set out for home she knew meeting Alex and his mother, Lucinda Murray, had made this a special day. She hugged her secret to herself. They were *her* friends. And if Father, as she was trying to school herself to call Arthur, thought they were wicked, then it just showed how stupid he was!

When, the following Friday he read aloud an account from the *Brackleford Standard*, she assumed an air of uninterest. Lucinda Murray had held a women's rally in the town; finally the police constable had had to move her from the Town Hall steps and restore order.

'Disgraceful!' Arthur flicked the newspaper scornfully, to emphasise his view. 'We can do without women of her kind in this town: I said so

27

from the day she came. A rabble-rouser! No better than that Pankhurst woman.'

Inside her, Tamsin was bubbling with indignation. Why had it been right for him to collect people around him when he'd preached in the streets, and yet not right for Mrs Murray? Her vocabulary didn't stretch to such words as 'bigot', but her senses knew the meaning of it.

★ ★ ★

It wasn't in Tamsin's nature to let anyone ride roughshod over her. Alexander Murray was two years her senior, often arrogant and dictatorial; he nicknamed her Shrimp, lest she was tempted to overlook his superiority. Despite these things, games with Alex were always an adventure; none of her friends at school were half as much fun.

It was a bitterly cold Saturday morning, the following January, when Tamsin and Alexander were in the Dylans' Wood. It was one of their usual haunts; to get there they had to walk — or usually run — the length of his lane then, beyond the old tannery, climb a stile and skirt the edge of a field of cows, then climb a five-bar gate. No one ever seemed to come to the wood except them; it was a magic place where they became Robin Hood and Maid Marion, a Cavalier and a Roundhead or simply competitors, seeing who could climb the higher. On this occasion, they'd brought an old sack and were collecting fir cones and twigs brought down in the previous night's gale or any larger pieces of wood they could find to burn on the Murrays' fire, when he said something about the house they used to live in with his father.

'My proper father died, too,' she told him cheerfully, hoping it would help him sound less gloomy.

'My father didn't die. He cluttered off with Mrs Sherbourne. You wouldn't know her; she lived where we used to be.'

Tamsin pictured a man on a charger swooping up some unsuspecting married lady and galloping off with her. 'Gracious . . . '

'We used to live in a house with Mrs Hunter — she was our cook — then there was Jenny, Alice, Emmie, and 'young Flo'; that's what everyone called Flo, because she was only thirteen. They all worked in the house; then there was Mr Granger and Bert in the garden.'

'Gracious . . . ' she repeated. Then curiosity got the better of her. 'So Mrs Murray isn't married any more. She was but she isn't now?'

'Of course she's married. Men can do that sort of thing. If Mum had run off with some man, then Dad could have divorced her — divorced is what they call it when two people stop being married. I don't expect you knew that.' She didn't, but she wasn't going to admit to her ignorance.

'So why didn't she do that?'

'Divorce Dad? Because she's a woman, stupid. Women aren't allowed. It's different for men. But women, it's their job stay at home and see everything is comfy.' He threw the words at her as if to remind her that she, too, was of the inferior sex.

29

'But that's just plain stupid! A man is married just as much as a woman.'

'You sound like Mum.' His tone told her just what he thought of women's stupid ideas. 'She's always on about what she calls injustices. Don't you reckon we ought to have stayed there? Probably we wouldn't have been turned out.'

'I think she was brave and right. You ought to be jolly proud of her.'

'Suppose I am, really. But it's a rotten little house — and we never used to have to collect wood.'

'Well, I know what I'd rather — I'd rather keep warm with wood I'd collected.'

Alex looked doubtful, but he didn't argue.

★　★　★

Mavis's involvement with Arthur's work left Tamsin with freedom as long as she always came home to time, so unknown to them her friendship with the Murrays went on. Even though Alex had plenty of boys to play football or swim with in the stream by the mill, she always hoped he'd be free when she called for him. She had more fun with him than with any of her other friends but it was Lucinda Murray who became her secret idol. She must have been about eight on the day she called at the house, glad that he was there to answer her knock. She heard his mother pounding on the piano in the little parlour accompanying herself as she sang.

Land of Hope and Glory,
Mother of the free,
How shall we extol thee,
Who were born of thee?

Then, seeing Tamsin, and with even greater gusto in her deep contralto voice:

Truth and right and freedom,
Each a holy gem,
Stars of solemn brightness
Weave thy diadem.

'Truth and right and freedom, Tamsin we'll fight for it. We'll never put down the sword until we reach our goal.'

Tamsin nodded, her pale strange-coloured eyes lit with the wonder of something she didn't understand. Truth and right and freedom . . . the goal was uncertain, she wasn't sure how she'd recognise it; but of one thing she was determined, she meant to be as brave and as strong as Mrs Murray.

The die was cast and, even when the Murrays moved away from Brackleford as suddenly as they'd arrived, metaphorically she still carried the banner; she always would.

31

2

As Tamsin learnt to accept the new order so, gradually, memories would catch her unawares and, instead of running away from them, she found they gave her a feeling of security. No one and nothing could take them from her.

With the passage of time, it happened naturally that it was she who became responsible for the garden. Mavis's pleasure came from arranging the flowers it produced, but never from getting soil in her fingernails. Arthur felt that for him to spend an afternoon tidying his own garden would be to give way to the luxury of relaxation and, therefore, something he couldn't permit himself; always there were those among the faithful who needed his counsel and those of the unfaithful whose souls it was his duty to save. So, as soon as Tamsin was old enough to wield a pair of shears, it became her responsibility to keep the back hedge trimmed: just as it did to take up the weeds, prune the roses and in the autumn to plant out the bulbs. Neither Mavis nor Arthur were really interested in what she did with the patch of ground and, by the time she was ten, she had dug up a few yards at the far end of their typical town garden to grow vegetables. For her, this proved to be the route back to her past. With each successive year, she encroached a little further onto what had been grass, planting fruit bushes and even a few

32

strawberry runners. A town garden, never free of the sounds of the busy street, the rumble of trams, the clip-clop of horse and carts — and never free of the smell of vinegar from Perkins' pickle factory across the road. For her, though, it had the power to carry her back to the field which to the eye of a young child had seemed enormous.

Turning the soil to plant her early potatoes, she imagined Albert leading Brutus and the plough while she and her grandfather followed, dropping their potatoes into the furrow. Leaning on her spade, she smiled.

'Have I dug deep enough?' she asked him silently.

Whether he was telling her she had or she hadn't, she couldn't be certain: but as she closed her eyes, she could see him clearly and hear his 'That's the way, duckie.' No wonder she smiled as she trod her spade into the ground, then put all her energy into turning the soil.

Her vegetables were always greeted by her mother and father (as she'd grown used to calling Arthur) with praise. This did have its downside, for it meant that he was always able to tell Mavis of someone more deserving than they were themselves: 'These peas are splendid, Tamsin, young and sweet. I wish you'd find enough for a good serving for your mother to take to Mrs Perkins when she calls this afternoon,' or 'The first strawberries of the season! Can you put a few in a bowl for George Derwent? We're so fortunate to grow them, while for him they must be a luxury he can ill afford.'

In truth Tamsin didn't mind picking for other people; her own satisfaction was in the growing as much as the eating.

Her first resentment and jealousy of Arthur had given way to acceptance. She even tried to make herself love him, but the best she could rise to was a sneaking respect — albeit mixed with irritation — that he consciously tried to put other people before himself. No, even that was an exaggeration of the truth, as she so often reminded herself: the other people who had to be considered didn't include those in his own household. She couldn't understand how her mother could accept it so tolerantly. For herself, her mind was made up that as soon as she was old enough, she would set herself free.

Growing up in those early days of the century she knew when the time came to leave Miss Searl's school she would be expected to stay at home: 'Ease your mother's burden' as Arthur described what she saw as the straitjacket of her future. That seed of rebellion sown so long ago by Lucinda had made firm roots and grown. It wasn't just; it wasn't even sensible. If she'd been born a boy, it would have been expected that she should want to do more with her life. Arguments got her nowhere.

'If you had some burning ambition — to teach, to look after little children — '

'How can I know what I want, when I'm not given the chance to find out?' Which was her way of saying that the one thing she wanted was freedom, space to test her wings and fly. There was nothing unusual in a girl staying at home, learning how to run a house so that she was ready when the day came that some young man made her his wife. Perhaps that suited some girls, but it didn't suit her. Each day she read the newspaper, there wasn't a suffragette demonstration reported that escaped her. What if she packed her bags and joined their ranks? Yes, but it wasn't as simple as that: they all had homes. And, in any case — although she wouldn't give Arthur the satisfaction of hearing her admit to it — even though she supported their objective, she didn't always agree with their method. But the longer she hit against the brick wall of opposition at home, the more she came to believe that sometimes protest was the only way.

It was a day when she'd been reading about how a party of women, foremost of whom was Lucinda Murray, had broken up a political meeting where the local MP. had been speaking. If Mrs Murray had no fear, then neither had she! Once again, she brought up the subject of finding work; once again, it met with the same answer.

'There's plenty for you to do in the home,' Arthur told her.

'I'm wasting my life.'

From her tone, Mavis knew a battle lay ahead. She marvelled at Arthur's patience as he answered.

'Look at it logically, Tamsin. What experience would you have to offer people in times of trouble? Far better that you take your mother's burden. She is my right hand and she enjoys the part she plays. Isn't that so, Mavis, my dear?'

'You know I do. Take today, for instance, Tamsie: I have a visit to make to poor bedridden Mr Hopkins. His wife does so appreciate my going in to help her change his bedding. It's a hard job for one alone. You know, it wouldn't be at all the thing for a young girl to do — the poor man would be embarrassed. Then, this evening, I'm staying with Evie Dunn while her husband is on the late shift at the railway, as she's near her time, she's nervous to be alone. But what confidence could she draw from *your* companionship?' Then, looking towards Arthur for support, 'Perhaps you might take a Sunday School class?'

'I said work — proper useful work. I intend to look for a job.'

'Nonsense!' Clearly Arthur expected that to be the last word on the subject. 'There can be no more important work than training the young. However, let's hear no more on the subject, if you please.' He wouldn't bring himself to say so, but the truth was he doubted if her influence on the young would be all he desired.

At Miss Searl's school, Tamsin had learnt reading, writing and basic arithmetic, and enough lacemaking to be able to produce a none too expert set of doileys. On the wall was hung an embroidered picture, the product of two years of tedious Wednesday afternoons. Her French stretched as far as the ability to write a letter to some imaginary aunt, thanking her for a birthday present and hoping the weather was fair, her Latin was of the *amo, amas, amat* variety. In short, she had very little talent to take to the labour market. There was work to be found in domestic service, but that wasn't where her dreams lay; and in any case, Arthur and Mavis might approve her learning to care for the Manse, but the idea of her going into paid service was out of the question. Arthur had a position to uphold in the town; he wasn't prepared even to let himself imagine what people would say if the daughter of the minister's household went into service or rushed to some factory at the sound of the hooter.

She was determined that, in the end, she would wear them down. It was a cold January evening, a few weeks later, when a visit from Reverend Claude Houghton, an old colleague Arthur hadn't seen for some years, sowed seeds of change. A thin man, older than Arthur, with a complexion like dried and yellowing parchment: yet there was about him a suppressed energy. Tamsin foresaw an evening of evangelistic ardour so, as soon as she could escape, she took a book and disappeared to her bedroom, where she wrapped herself in her eiderdown for warmth and settled down to read until she heard the visitor being seen out. Going back downstairs, she sensed a change in the atmosphere; something of his vitality still remained.

'Let me tell her! I just can't believe it — and yet I feel it has always been waiting for us.' It was extraordinary to hear Mavis so excited; Arthur's expression was full of affectionate satisfaction as he looked at her.

'Yes, you tell her, my dear. It's a momentous decision and yet, as you say, it's as if our work here has been in preparation for what's ahead.' His smile encompassed them all. 'One family . . . one future', it seemed to say.

So Mavis told her their plans, expecting that, when Tamsin heard, she would gladly relinquish her silly argument about taking some unsuitable job of work. Not for the first time, she was wrong. Dear as Tamsin was to her, she didn't begin to understand this stubborn battle for independence.

★   ★   ★

'Your father is certain this is our pre-ordained course. He's right: you and I both know he is. Oh, I wish you could feel the same excitement as I do. Our lives have been so easy, so comfortable. Don't you see, Tamsie? This is our God-given chance to repay. Reverend Houghton's health has forced him to come home to England's kinder climate. Africa — people who need to hear the Word your father will take to them, people living in darkness without the Light. How thankful I am that you are grown up, old enough to come with us and be part of the Mission.'

Tamsin had never known her mother show her feelings so openly; it was frightening how the net was closing on her. She used the first argument that came into her head.

'How do you know they want to listen to him telling them that if they don't believe what he believes, they're on the path to damnation?'

'Tamsin!' Mavis was shocked and hurt. 'That's an unkind way to speak of your dear father.

38

Never let him hear you say such a thing! And how can the poor souls know, if they've never been shown the Truth? Reverend Houghton will come here to Brackleford for the year we're away.'

'Anyway, you aren't a preacher, I don't see what — '

'What I can do? Oh, there's so much.' She had found Tamsin finishing making her bed; now she sat on the edge of it, her lovely blue eyes so earnest that it almost hurt to look at her. 'You know, Tamsie, what I do truly believe?' Tamsin shook her head, knowing she was about to be told — and sure it would be something she'd rather not hear. There was something unsettling in this rare display of passion from her mother, who was usually so controlled and allowed no hint of emotion. 'I believe everything in this life works for a pattern. When David — your first father — was drowned, I could see no reason. It wasn't until I knew Arthur that I began to understand, to see that it had been my years living back again at Gorsemoor, trying to ease my own loneliness by helping other people, that made me able to take my place at his side here. More than a decade in Brackleford — don't you see what I'm saying? I've sat with the dying, helped the midwife bring babies into the world, supported the bereaved: oh, a hundred and one things I've been given the strength to do. And surely all of them preparing me for *this*.'

'But anyway — ' Tamsin fought her corner ' — that's you: it's not me. I've not done any of

39

those things. If you believe in things working to a pattern, then try and see my pattern. If you and Father are going away — where you can be useful, but I can't — then this pattern you're so sure about must be telling us that this is the time for me to look for work and stay behind.'

'As if I'd be able to go, knowing I was leaving you! And you could *make* yourself useful: you could help the children. There are no schools for them. You could teach them to do their sums, to read. Just think — no schools, no chapel where they can meet and listen to the message Arthur will bring them.'

'How do you know that isn't the way God meant for them? Are they saying 'Come and teach us to read and write in English', 'Come and tell us all about your religion so we can think like you do' — '

'That's a wicked, wicked way to talk. Never speak such blasphemy! We have a duty to spread the Word, all of us: you and me too. Why do you have to be so difficult? Oh dear.' Her pretty face puckered as she bit her lip in an effort not to cry. 'I wanted it so much, all of us to go there and work together. We're lucky to have been born where we are. The world is vast, millions of people less fortunate than we are. Don't you see, Tamsin? To turn our back on this heaven-sent opportunity is to deny the Truth.'

Tamsin had never seen her mother cry.

'Of course we have a duty, Mum. *Truth and right and freedom*, the words of 'Land of Hope and Glory'. Remember Mrs Murray? She said that's what we have to fight for.'

40

Nothing could have banished Mavis's tears more swiftly.

'That dreadful suffragette woman who used to live in the town? I've read about her in the newspaper often enough. How can you liken the nonsense she talks with the work we have to do? I wonder you even remember her. I suppose you've been reading about that dreadful scene she created in the Town Hall. 'Land of Hope and Glory', indeed. The land would be better off without her sort and their disturbances, bringing discontent into the homes. Anyway — ' Mavis squared her shoulders, thoughts of Lucinda Murray having put her once again in control of her emotions ' — if your father and I say you are to come with us, then you're to come, and that's an end to it. Why should I forego my chance — my destiny — just because you're frightened to face a little discomfort? Oh, sweetling, think again. Be brave: we shall support each other. Use your time there for a purpose and you'll come to understand the pattern.' She spoke with more confidence than she felt as she looked at the stubborn set of Tamsin's mouth. At seventeen, despite still having the appearance of a skinny child, Tamsin had a will of iron.

To Tamsin, nothing of their scheme had any bearing on the sort of truth and right and freedom that ought to be fought for nearer to home. Surely there were enough destitute on the streets of their own country, enough beggars, enough barefoot children, enough men who had to sink their pride and go to the Parish for help rather than see their families starving? Those were the injustices and wrongs that had to be righted. But where should one start? Was Mrs Pankhurst right: would giving women a vote make any difference?

When Mavis had gone downstairs, Tamsin leant out of her bedroom window. The pungent smell from the factory hung on the air. Inside the ugly brick building, women would be working, hour after hour, day after day, to eke out some sort of living. While they were there, where were their children? Yes, she'd been lucky: her mother was right. As if to illustrate her point, a ragged little girl, surely no more than four years old and followed by a thin, long-tailed mongrel, walked past. When Tamsin had been that age, she'd been at Gorsemoor, surrounded by love, never doubting that that was what it was like for everyone. Life wasn't fair. The little girl waited while the dog lifted his leg against the vegetable boxes outside Mr Goodwin's shop; he showed his gratitude by leaping up at her, tail flailing. In a lull in the street noises, Tamsin could hear her laugh. Truth and right and freedom . . . Perhaps none of those things gave automatic happiness, but that little girl deserved a better hand than she'd been dealt.

How Tamsin could make a difference, she had no idea, but of one thing she was certain: she had no intention of burying herself in the middle of some far away continent, trying to force her way of life on people who hadn't asked for it.

★   ★   ★

42

The next day was Friday and as well as the *Times*, the *Brackleford Standard* was delivered. Mavis handed the two papers to Arthur as they sat down to breakfast.

'Thank you, my dear. A little luxury we shall soon have to forego, eh?' But his tone implied that he was more than ready to shed anything that came under the heading of luxury. 'You're feeling better this morning, I hope?'

'Yes. A good night's sleep works wonders for my poor head.'

Did Tamsin imagine some underlying tension?

'Go through my clothes, my dear. Anything that can be spared put to one side for me to take to the Casual Ward. We shan't need winter garments, but there will be those here who will be glad of their warmth.'

Mavis' expression told Tamsin the undercurrent must have been in her own mind.

Arthur didn't attempt to look at the papers until the meal was over, not simply because he considered reading to be disrespectful to the others at a meal table but because he enjoyed the satisfaction of depriving himself. Only when they rose did he go to his study, taking both papers with him. So, like it or not, Tamsin had to wait until she heard the front door close and knew he had gone on his morning round of visiting before she seated herself at his desk and opened the *Brackleford Standard* to scan the columns headed 'Vacant Appointments'.

'Please, let there be something I can do, something that even *they* can't object to. The trouble is, I need somewhere to live. I don't know what I'm looking for but I'll know it when I see it. Please let there be something.' It didn't enter her head that whoever it was she pleaded to might be connected with the vengeful deity Arthur put such store by.

Moving her finger slowly down the column, she read the list — then her expression changed. 'Thank you. I knew there'd be something: I knew you'd help me.' She tore a piece of paper off Arthur's notepad and jotted down the address.

A few minutes later, wearing her tweed cycling skirt and jacket and with her velvet beret pulled on firmly, she found Mavis sorting out the bureau.

'Mum, it's such a glorious day I thought I'd go for a bicycle ride. There ought to be primroses in the woods at Farley Hill. But it'll be too far to get home in time for lunch, so it's all right for me to make a sandwich, isn't it?' Rarely did she say where she meant to go when she rode her bicycle into the country; wasn't she being just a little too eager to set up a smokescreen? How she hated the need to be underhand; she felt it must be obvious she had something to hide.

But Mavis paid no real attention; she was too busy sorting out old letters, filling the waste-paper basket so that she left the house in order.

'When you get home, Tamsie, you ought to make a start on your drawers and cupboards. You heard what your father said at breakfast: we shan't need winter clothing. In a year's time, you might have shot up. Parcel up what you don't think you'll be needing and Arthur will take it to the orphanage. Some of the girls are quite as well grown as you are. Bigger, I dare say. Primroses? Yes, that will be lovely. We must make the best of the spring flowers, for we'll be gone before the first of the roses.'

Not much more than an hour later, cycling past the woods of Farley Hill, Tamsin had another nudge from her conscience. On the way home — whatever the result of her day — she must spend time gathering some flowers; her mother was looking forward to them. Then, turning to the right, she followed the sign pointing to Oakleigh, a sprawling village. Before she came into view from any houses, she back-pedalled to stop, then hopped off her bicycle and laid it carefully on the grass verge. In her pocket was a small mirror, a comb and a collection of hairpins she'd taken from the glass jar on her mother's dressing-table. By her age most girls had already put their hair up but, because hers was so fine, she found it easier to let it hang loose. If she arrived with it hanging down her back, she wouldn't stand a hope. It was important to appear trim and efficient. After five minutes struggling with it, and trying to see the result in the pocket mirror she'd lodged at shoulder height in a hawthorn bush, she was almost ready to give up. Thin and fine, it refused to stay in the pins . . . perhaps if she just pushed it up underneath her beret? Yes, but she might be asked to take off her hat, and think how stupid she'd look! The only answer was to comb it through, plait it as tightly as she could, then wind the plait around her head like a coronet.

45

That way, the pins promised to hold it in place and, satisfied at last, she once more pulled on her velvet beret. Satisfied? She tried to tell herself she was, but there was no hiding from the fact that she looked more like a runaway child than a young lady seeking a responsible position. She looked down disparagingly at her thin frame, trying to push out her almost non-existent bust. It was no use wasting time here; if she didn't get on, he'd be in the middle of eating and wouldn't see her at all. He'll either like me or he won't, she told herself — and then, to God, a Fairy Godmother, a Guardian Angel, to any or all — please make him like me, make me be just what he's looking for. With head high, she hopped on her bicycle and pedalled into Oakleigh to find Elm Road and finally came to the gate bearing a sign 'Westwood House.'

Built fronting the narrow pavement, it was a Georgian house, absolutely symmetrical with its porch supported by two stout, stone columns. She liked the way the March sunshine made the windows sparkle, seeming to welcome her.

'Here I go, then!' She crossed her fingers for luck, not even uncrossing them as she took hold of the hanging metal bell-pull and heard the jangle from somewhere inside the house, then footsteps coming across the hall.

'Good morning, Miss.' If the plump uni-formed maid of about her own age wasn't fooled into seeing her as worthy of 'Madam', what chance did she have?

'I've come to see Mr Hardcastle.'

'Who shall I say it is?'

'Miss Yelland. I've come about the position he advertised in the *Brackleford Standard*.'

'You have?' The girl looked at her in disbelief; clearly she wasn't what was expected. 'You wait in the hall, Miss. Does he know you're coming?'

'No. The paper only came out this morning. I didn't waste time writing.'

The young maid bit the corner of her mouth, looking uncertain what to do. 'Trouble is, the master don't never see anyone without an appointment. Always says he's not to be disturbed, you see.'

For one moment, they were as uncertain as each other.

'I tell you what,' Tamsin suggested hopefully, 'you go in to him, say I'm here and I've told you he's waiting for me.' Then, with an impish smile, 'After all, so he is.'

'Right-o. You just wait here and I'll see how it goes.' Then, glancing uneasily over her shoulder to make sure they were alone, she added quietly, 'He can get in an awful pother, though, not that it's my place to say so. But best you know what to expect.'

Standing alone in the hall, Tamsin awaited her fate. Perhaps she ought to have read all the advertisements. There must be other people she could work for, people who didn't get in an awful pother. The maid had seemed timid and frightened of putting a foot wrong; the thing was to let this Hardcastle man see that she wasn't scared of him. She watched the door through which the girl had disappeared.

As the maid re-emerged and scurried back

47

across the hall, Tamsin was confronted by an elderly man leaning heavily on two sticks and looking as though he bore a grudge against the world.

'Expecting you? Not to my knowledge I'm not, young madam.'

Not a promising beginning.

'Not expecting, sir.' She stood very straight hoping to add an inch to her height. 'What I said was that you were waiting for me. It won't be a lie; if you give me the chance you'll be glad I'm there to help. Truly, I'll work really hard.'

To her own ears she sounded silly, childish — and, from the way he looked at her, she knew she did to his, too.

'You'd better come in here,' he told her, but there was nothing welcoming in the invitation. 'If we stand here talking, every ear in the house will be listening.'

She followed Charles Hardcastle into the untidiest room she'd ever seen. Books were left open on chairs, even one on the floor; the papers strewn over the large table gave the impression of having been dropped there from a great height — and given a stir for good measure. In an attempt to hold on to her flagging optimism, she conjured up a half-formed image of Arthur's mission and the part she would be expected to play in it. She wouldn't let them force her into it. This was her life; if there was a pattern, then she would be the one to design it.

'You'd better tell me about yourself. That doesn't mean I shall find you suitable — I'd been expecting someone with experience, a male — '

'Being a girl doesn't mean I couldn't help you just as well. When I was at school, a lot of the boys were dunderheads; all they thought about was getting out to play football. Oh, I'm not saying there aren't clever boys — of course there are — but don't you think they'd be following some sort of profession, not be prepared to take a job like this?' She looked at him seriously, her wide eyes unsure today whether they were blue or green, as they took the colour of her tweed cycling suit. 'I don't mean to be rude, but I do think that if a boy is clever, he has so much more opportunity than a girl.'

'And you consider yourself clever?'

She felt her face grow uncomfortably warm. 'That wasn't what I meant. But I like books; I like words.'

'And what about plants? A dreamy girl who wants to spend her life reading is no good to me.'

'Well, to be truthful, I only know the things we grow in the garden of the Manse, and a lot of that's vegetables. But it's me who looks after it.' In her mind she was suddenly in a field on the edge of the New Forest; she was picking gooseberries helping her grandfather to fill a basket ready for market. Remembering him, her confidence grew. 'I used to help my grandfather in his market garden . . . ' She knew it wasn't relevant, but saying it gave her spirit a lift.

'The Manse?'

So she told him about the proposed mission.

'There's no greater experience than travelling

the world. Yet you want to stay and write about my travels, see it all at second hand.'

She considered what he said; he could almost feel her weighing his words as he waited.

'I don't see it like that. The work I'd do here would be mine. I mean, it would be up to me to do it as well as I possibly could. But on the mission, I'd be just a tool for Father to use. And I can't do that, I really *can't*. I wouldn't be being honest. If you don't give me this job, then I'll just go on looking until I find another. I know that taking care of the garden at home isn't a bit like your expeditions, but I'd learn.'

★ ★ ★

Cycling home, Tamsin prepared herself for the battle ahead by gathering a large bunch of primroses from the wood at Farley Hill.

'Lovely.' Mavis looked up briefly from sorting out a pile of her own clothes for Arthur to take to the workhouse at the other end of town. 'You see to putting them in water, dear, I want to get on.'

'Mum, I've lots to tell you — '

'Run and do the flowers first. Then see to the table for supper; I've been so busy, I really could have done with you at home to help. Don't forget you have your clothes to sort out, this evening.'

'But, Mum — '

'Tell me about it at the table. I don't know if I'm coming or going — I can't think for you as well as myself. Arthur has made the reservation:

50

we're to sail in less than three weeks. I don't think even *he* understands what has to be done before the house can be handed over to another minister. No, pretend I didn't say that. Of course he understands, and what I do is nothing compared with his own preparations.'

Accepting that this wasn't the moment, Tamsin waited until they were all at the supper table and Arthur had carved the cold beef before she dropped her announcement into the silence.

'I went further than Farley Hill,' she began.

Had they been listening? Neither made any comment.

'I went all the way to Oakleigh. Have you ever heard of Charles Hardcastle? He's a botanist: he's travelled the world bringing back new plants to introduce to the country. But he can't do it any more; quite suddenly, he's become very crippled. Not an accident or anything — arthritis.' When, still, neither of them answered, she made a conscious effort to continue her tale in a positive, 'not to be interrupted' voice. 'He's compiling a book. He has a machine, a typewriter, but his hands are too stiff for him to use it.'

'Oh dear, that's sad.' Mavis's pretty face clouded with sympathy.

'He wants someone to live there to help him. He has a good domestic staff, a housekeeper, maids, and a gardener who acts as a coachman, but he needs help with his botanical work.' How impressive it sounded! She looked from one to the other, ready to combat any objection.

'How do you know all this?' Arthur put down

51

his knife and fork and gave her his full attention.

So she told them, making her voice sound far more confident than she felt. She had accepted his offer of work for a salary of £2 a month and promised to move in, the following Monday. When she finished speaking, she waited, gathering every argument ready to fire.

'I can't believe what I'm hearing!' With his meal half eaten, Arthur pushed the plate away; his quiet voice was no disguise for his anger. 'Time and again I've told you and still you've argued to go your own wilful way. But this is beyond all else, your arrogant disobedience past belief. Before you go to bed tonight, you will see to it that you write to this man and tell him your parents forbid your going to him. The arrangements are made; our passages are booked. Now we'll have an end to all this nonsense. Not another word.'

'I'm not coming with you. It may be what you want for your future; it's not what I want for mine.'

Mavis looked from one to the other, her eyes brimming with tears. 'Don't! Please don't quarrel. Tamsie, why do you have to be so difficult? Can't you give just one year to doing what we want?'

'She can and she will,' Arthur snapped; then, seeing Mavis's distress, looked at her more kindly. 'I'll not have you upset. We've had the last word on the subject, so put it out of your head.'

'I can't. And neither can you, no matter how much you pretend.' Mavis knew it was true; she could tell from the nervous way he drummed the fingers of one hand against the back of the other as he clasped them on the edge of the table; she could tell by the nervous tic at the corner of his mouth. She knew the signs and she knew it meant he wouldn't sleep, even though for both of them every minute of the day had been crammed with preparation and excitement.

'You go on to bed,' he told her. 'I shall only be a few minutes. Tamsin will clear the meal away before she sees to the letter she has to write.'

The scene had been as difficult as Tamsin had feared and even now it wasn't resolved, for Arthur believed he'd had the last word. But her mind was made up. There was nothing very appealing about the job ahead of her at Westwood House, nothing except that she would be working her own passage, knowing the money in her purse was what she'd earned and the clothes on her back what she saved up to pay for. She wouldn't be part of Arthur Hillbright's entourage: she would be her own person.

* * *

Upstairs, Mavis hurried to get into bed, even though she knew she wouldn't be able to sleep. She hated these scenes with Tamsin and lately there had been so many. She hated them on their own account and, even more, for what they did to Arthur. They made him tense, keyed up . . . and she knew the way he'd look for escape from his tension. If she kept her eyes closed when she heard him coming, perhaps he'd try not to wake her. Dear Arthur, so caring of her:

53

when he'd seen she was upset by the argument, to protect her he had suggested she should come up ahead of them. That was the thought she must hang on to. She loved him dearly; she respected him above every living person. She could work by his side till she dropped from exhaustion and be exhilarated with the satisfaction of being his partner.

She closed her eyes, as if to escape from her thoughts. In the early years, it had been different; when he'd made love to her, she had believed she was blessed above all women to be the one he wanted. It had never entered her mind to refuse him, although she'd not been able to understand what he got so excited about; and, as his passion had mounted to its climax, she had felt that had been reward enough. It was Tamsin's fault that she so often finished the day with arguments echoing in her mind. It had been the same ever since she had given up school: what with wanting to take paid employment; then all this nonsense about equal rights for women, expecting them to be paid as much as the menfolk, even agreeing with those dreadful suffragettes that women ought to have a say in ruling the country.

No wonder she couldn't give her mind to Arthur's demands. At the end of the day, what she wanted was to lie by dear Arthur's side, to know they were loving companions. Why couldn't that be enough for him, too? It wasn't fair that she had to feel guilty, making the pretence of a headache or a troublesome back to ensure an early sleep. She always rebuffed him gently: not for anything would she hurt him and he must have realised how tired she was by the end of each day, especially with all she had to do to get ready for their wonderful mission. Willingly she worked for him all her waking hours; wasn't she entitled to peace at night? Hark! He was coming. Would he believe her if she kept her eyes closed?

'It's no use her arguing,' Arthur didn't wait to shut the door before he picked up the argument where it had been left.

'If she really doesn't want to come with us . . . ' Pretence of sleep had flown out of the window.

'Want? Want? Are we put on this earth to do only what we want? If we leave her behind, we are failing her. She has to learn that there is more satisfaction in serving others than in seeking her own pleasures. Why does she want to find work? I'll tell you why. As balm to her own sense of achievement, that's why. Earn her own money, spend it on vanities for herself. And how long do you think she'd stay with this elderly man Hardcastle, with his peppery temper and arthritis? Long enough to find a situation with more money, more sop to her self-esteem.'

'Arthur, darling, don't sound so cross. I hate it so when you're cross.'

'Cross? With you? You know I'm not.' Still that nervous tic by his mouth, even if under the cover of his nightshirt there wasn't evidence enough that he wasn't ready to sleep.

'All this arguing, it's really upset me, given me such a nasty fit of nausea.' To back up her lie, she forced what sounded like a suppressed belch. 'Forgive me,' she apologised. 'Oh, I do so hate disturbances. Suppose she comes with us and we have these sort of scenes? I don't think I could stand it.'

'Confound the girl! We're both upset.' Pushing his nightshirt almost to his waist, he swung his legs into bed, easing her towards the middle. 'Forget her,' he whispered urgently. 'This is our day, our sailing fixed, our work waiting there for us.' Already, he was pushing up her nightgown, his breath rattling in his throat in the way she'd come to know so well.

'No! I told you I don't feel well. Not tonight, Arthur.'

'Yes, yes: you can't leave me like this. Tonight . . . last night . . . last week . . . you can't keep denying me . . . you've got to let me.' Even as he spoke, he forced himself into her.

The scene downstairs must have given her extra strength. Taking him by surprise, she threw him off her.

'I said 'no'! Don't do it. All I can think about is Tamsie. If we go without her, what will become of her? If we make her come, will she destroy our wonderful year?'

For a moment, he lay panting at her side, fighting for control. When at last he spoke, his voice was tight, as if his jaw was set. 'Forgive me: I'm ashamed. We're both upset.'

Apparently, she was satisfied; she kissed him with affection then turned her back and settled for the night, all thought of nausea forgotten. For Arthur, it wasn't so easy. What was the girl doing downstairs? Was she writing her letter? How dare she defy him! She was a child still. Child? No, she was more than that, she was almost a woman. Like a bud bursting into bloom . . . Restlessly, he turned onto his back. How could Mavis sleep so peacefully, when his body was alive with need? Lust . . . the temptation of the Devil . . . Lord deliver me from temptation, deliver me from temptation . . .

★ ★ ★

Downstairs, Tamsin had cleared the meal, tidied the room for the night and put the guard in front of the fire. She was reaching to turn off the gaslight when she heard a movement behind her.

'Father! Is something the matter?' Why else would he come down in his dressing gown, even without slippers on his feet?

'Yes, a great deal's the matter. Is that letter written? I'll not allow you to make trouble between your mother and me. You're on her mind all the time.'

'Of course I'm not. The thing that's uppermost in her mind is this year you're both planning. And of course the letter isn't written. Honestly, Father, I'm not trying to be difficult but I'm ready to stand on my own feet. You see me as a child still — but I'm not.'

He sat on a straight-backed chair, his unfastened dressing gown falling open and his nightshirt just covering his knees. She was

57

surprised by the hint of what was under the nightshirt; her knowledge of the male form went no further than paintings in the local art gallery or statues of naked men with muscular legs and tiny genitalia. The truth must be very different and somehow kept camouflaged under formal attire.

'You're a good girl,' he told her unexpectedly, something in his tone making her uncomfortable. 'I know I'm not always easy.'

'Rubbish,' she floundered. 'Perhaps you're right and I'm selfish.'

'No. I've not been much of a father to you.' Putting his arm around her waist, he drew her closer. 'It's not that I haven't loved you; you know that, don't you?'

'Silly.' She felt uneasy, there was something unsettling about this new side to his character. He looked different, vulnerable, sitting there with his feet bare and his hair ruffled. She didn't pull away from him, but she wished he wouldn't hold her quite so close, his face touching the curve of her breast. But he was her father; she mustn't let him think she minded.

When she did move away from him, she was aware that straight away he was on his feet and close behind her. 'Father, please try and understand — 'What in the world was he doing?

Taking her by surprise, he ripped open the catches at the neck of her blouse. With one arm, he imprisoned her against him while the other hand explored her young breast, his fingers finding and tugging at her nipple.

'Stop it! Let go of me!'

He didn't seem even to hear her. They were so near the fire, her toes were against the brass fender. When she wriggled to get away, he forced himself closer, pressing against her in rhythmic jerky movements, a soft deep sort of moan with each exhalation of breath. In the mirror about the fireplace she looked at his reflection, his eyes closed, his mouth half open. His movements quickened, he pulled her nipple harder, he pressed closer . . .

'Father!' He couldn't be doing this to her!

'Oh, God . . . oh, God . . . ' With all his force, he pushed her to one side; thankfully she stumbled across the room. 'Get out! Go! Go!'

From the other side of the room, she turned towards him, half expecting him to be chasing her. Instead, he'd fallen back into the chair, holding his dressing gown closed in front of him; his body shuddered and trembled, and his face was contorted. What should she do? Almost before the question formed in her mind, he sagged forward, as if every bit of strength had left him. Suddenly, something that had been half understood was clear to her.

Arrogant and bigoted though she'd often thought him, she'd trusted him. He'd been her father since she was six years old. But, in that moment, she felt nothing but loathing and revulsion.

She was glad of the contempt in her voice as she told him, 'My mind's made up about that job. I'll leave you to explain to Mum.' She knew he must recognise the threat in her cold words.

From his slumped position on the chair, he

tumbled to his knees, his head bowed to the floor.

'Dear God . . . forgive me . . . forgive me . . . '

She left him to make peace with his conscience.

3

Tamsin preferred not to know how Arthur explained to Mavis his change of heart. It was hard enough to make herself meet her mother's worried and trusting gaze and give no hint of the contempt and anger she felt for him.

'Your father says I may tell you he has agreed to consent to your staying behind. But, Tamsie, I know it worries him as much as it does me. To please me — just one short year — is it so much to ask?' The pleading expression gave way to a smile of suppressed excitement. 'Just think of the adventure. You're grown up, now; the two of us could share a new way of life. Dear Arthur, he says I must give you your head: I mustn't try to dissuade you.'

The memory of his hot hands, the sickening image of him falling to his knees in weak and trembling despair, filled Tamsin's mind.

'No, Mum. I've given Mr Hardcastle my word.'

'He'd understand your mother's need — '

'You'll be too busy to miss me. And this is something for you and Father to share, a special year.' Something to share! The thought revolted her. How did she manage to make her voice sound so loving and understanding?

'Yes. Yes, that's what he says. Perhaps sometimes he must have felt jealous — jealous? No, he's too good a man for such an ignoble sentiment — but he must have felt shut out, the only male. A year will soon pass, sweetling; that's what I'll keep telling myself every time I find myself wishing you were with us.'

★ ★ ★

So, the following Monday, Arthur borrowed the governess cart from Mr Wilberforce, one of the better off among his flock, and he and Mavis transported Tamsin, her boxes of clothes and favourite possessions — and her all-essential bicycle — to Oakleigh and passed her into the safe keeping of Charles Hardcastle. Fortunately, it was one of his better days, so the thought of leaving her in his charge didn't worry Mavis as it might have done, could she have seen him when his arthritis imprisoned him in pain.

It soon became evident why he needed an assistant who lived in the house.

On his 'good' days, he would be at the breakfast table at eight o'clock, and from there they would go straight to the workroom, as he preferred to call his study. Except for just long enough to eat a midday meal, they would work until late supper, after which he would retire to his own room, good humoured and satisfied with his labours. That Tamsin was less so didn't occur to him. Surprisingly, he found her company congenial — or, if not congenial, at any rate undemanding. As she scribbled down his dictation, usually a mixture of longhand and her own abbreviations (and always printing Latin names just as he pronounced them), it didn't occur to him that she was out of her depth. Her expression told him nothing; her concentration was completely on what she did. After he'd gone to his room, she would work far into the night, transcribing what she'd written, looking up botanical spellings (thankful for even the smattering of Latin she'd been taught at Miss Seal's school, for at least she knew the rudiments of pronunciation), then with two fingers and grim determination typing out her notes. During her first week, she had two such days. The others were more difficult. Almost as if she were personally responsible for the burning pain in his joints, he threw out his sentences in a voice filled with what sounded like hate but was, in truth, bitter resentment.

The first time he made no appearance, she spent her day in the study, listening for his step, dipping into his many books in the hope of making some sort of sense of the work that was foreign to her. At the forefront of her mind was something far more personal, but even here her imagination could conjure up no clear picture. At that time, she'd been at Westwood House for three weeks, and the previous Sunday she'd cycled back to the Manse for a last goodbye to her mother. When she'd arrived back at Oakleigh, Charles had been watching out for her. He'd seemed interested to hear all she could tell him about the mission, and he'd talked about his own voyages. Listening to him had helped erase that unfamiliar feeling of finality she'd felt as her mother had stood at the gate, watching her cycle away. By now, where would they be? Would they have sailed yet? She'd never seen a port, couldn't imagine what it would be like on board ship. Would her mother still be excited at the prospect of her adventure?

Making an effort to use her time wisely, Tamsin opened a book; then, with elbows on the table and her chin in her hands, brought her concentration to bear on the origins of the orchid. Latin names seemed to her as dry as dust — a far cry from the feeling of the warm earth on her fingers as she'd groped amongst the plants to gather her stawberries or pull up the weeds. Into her mind came the memory of kneeling in the huge field at Gorsemoor. Had it really been huge, or was it just that she'd been small? She recalled the safe, happy feeling of working with Grandpa, so sure that he was glad to have her there; she relived the secure feeling of being with him; nothing had dimmed it over the years, any more than the pride she'd felt in being useful to him, being his helper. Those things were bright in her memory, and the sound of his voice, 'That's the way, duckie.' What would he make of all these learned books? The corners of her mouth twitched into a smile.

Next morning, again she ate a solitary breakfast and went to the study, sure that when she heard Charles Hardcastle's step it would be a warning of a difficult day ahead.

'No use you waiting for the gov'nor, Miss Yelland.' Barnes opened the door just far enough to put his head around it to speak to her. 'He sent me to tell you, he won't be coming down today. He says if you've nothing waiting to type

64

up on that machine, then you'd better take the day off.'

'I'm sorry he's not well. Are you sure he doesn't want me to come to his room for dictation?'

'Just you keep clear of him. It's more than I can do to persuade him to sit up and take his food, so he'll not be in a state to give you work to do on that typewriting machine. No, best you hop off and make the most of your time. Once he's about again, he'll likely want to be making up for the time lost. He says the best thing is for you to ride back to Brackleford, take the opportunity to say another goodbye to your folk.'

At the suggestion, Tamsin felt strangely alone. Charles had appeared to be interested when she'd told him which day her parents were setting out, but clearly not interested enough for him to remember. She thought of the Manse as she'd seen it the previous Sunday. The strapped trunks had been standing in the hall, the rooms stripped bare of pictures and ornaments, everything stacked in the attic except essential furniture, so that Reverend Houghton could put his personal stamp on his home for the next year.

Except for that one Sunday, she'd worked every day she'd been at Westwood House. Her mind was made up that she wasn't going to be beaten, so she'd taken notes on a subject she didn't understand, typed them on a machine that was new to her and spent every available hour keeping up with the work Charles expected of her. It was hard to dispel her suspicion that he'd purposely been testing her, seeing how far she'd go before she broke. Well, she'd not let him beat her!

But one thing was sure: if she spent the whole day poring over books, what she'd learn could be no more than a drop in her ocean of ignorance. The sun was shining; freedom beckoned.

Her bicycle shared the coach house with Charles's elderly carriage, one that hadn't been on the road for years. He had no interest in visiting in the area: 'Lot of silly chatter with people who haven't enough to do with their time' was his opinion of local entertaining. Until he'd so suddenly fallen victim to arthritis, he had accepted engagements around the country giving talks, but even then he'd travelled by train and had always been taken to Oakleigh Halt by the local cabby. For more than a year he'd not left the house and, short of a miracle that's where he'd remain.

Shutting the coach house door, Tamsin wheeled her bicycle onto the road. She couldn't get away fast enough, to be free of the atmosphere that pervaded the house. Did it stem simply from the uncertainty of Charles Hardcastle's humour: did that colour the mood of the whole household? Below stairs, Mrs Jenkins's view of life was every bit as jaundiced as his was above. Her sharp voice still echoed in Tamsin's memory.

What harm could there have been in asking that she might make herself a sandwich to take on her ride?

'I beg your pardon, young madam?' The

housekeeper had looked at her in disbelief at the suggestion, pulling herself to her full height and looking down her long nose.

'I don't mind what I put in it. But I have the day off, you see, so I'm going for a ride.' Until that point, their paths had never crossed and Tamsin tried to believe she was imagining the unfriendly manner.

'No one comes into my kitchens expecting to help themselves to my food. Cut yourself a sandwich, indeed! You'll have to wait until Edith has finished kneading her dough, then I'll see what I can let her use. Nothing better to do with your time than gallivant off out! Just remember, in future, I don't want you coming down snooping around in my kitchen. The master never does it and I'll not have it from some chit like you.'

From behind her back, Kitty had thrown a look of sympathy. After more than six months, she had grown used to Mrs Jenkins and her sharp tongue but she wished she'd warned Tamsin how carefully you had to tread.

'I won't wait, then, thank you all the same, Mrs Jenkins,' Tamsin meant her words to carry a ring of dignity. 'I'll find somewhere to buy a bun.'

'No need to take that tone. I said I'd let Edith put you up something when she'd got the dough put to rise.'

'No, I won't trouble you.'

'I suppose now you'll go tittle-tattling back to the master that we didn't feed you.'

'I never tittle-tattle. And anyway, I think I'd

rather go to a baker's shop and choose what I eat.'

Anyone looking at the scene would have recognised in Tamsin the small child who had stood her ground with Alex as, clutching her conkers, she'd told him, 'I never steal. Don't you dare call me a stealer.'

Then, without glancing at the other servants, who'd stopped what they were doing to listen, she turned and left them before anyone could guess how hard she'd had to bite the corners of her mouth to stop it trembling. She'd wanted just to get away, to be free of the atmosphere of the house.

To the left, the road led to Farley Hill, her old familiar ride. Today she meant to turn to the right; she needed to discover new ground. But first, she had to go back to Hodge's Bakery, one of the few shops that surrounded the village green, for she had no idea how far she'd have to go to find another baker.

Mr Hodge's white-overalled, rotund figure and his shiny florid face helped to restore her spirit.

'Morning to you, Missie. And what can I sell you?' he beamed.

'I expect it'll have to be a bun — or perhaps two. It's for a picnic. I'm going for an all-day cycle ride.'

'And a right nice day for it, Missie. If it's your dinner you're looking for, what about one of my pork pies? Eat a treat cold, they do. Better than buns, wouldn't you say?'

'That would be lovely. Better than taking

68

sandwiches.' It seemed to score a point against Mrs Jenkins and made her feel she had found a friend in the jolly baker.

'Going somewhere special?'

So she explained that she meant to explore the district.

'I know from here to Brackleford, but not the other way. Where would you suggest?'

'Interested in aeroplanes, are you?'

'I did see one, once. And I've seen balloons. Why? Is there going to be an aeroplane flying somewhere?'

'My brother Ken, he works at Proctor's. Never did want to go into the business. Our father — gone on to the better world this last five years — he was the baker here first. He taught me and Ken right from when we were nippers. But was Ken interested? Not a bit of it. Mechanical things, that's where his interest lay. Dare say he was brainier than me, that's likely why I was happy to carry on from old Pa and he wanted to strike out for himself. Any road, he's at Proctor's Engineering — an engineer, if you please. Sounds pretty fine, don't it?'

To please him, she nodded her agreement. 'But you were telling me about an aeroplane?' she prompted.

'Ah, at Proctor's. Mr Proctor, he's the real brain, of course. Draws it all out on paper, Ken tells me about it. Just perfect it has to be, every nut and bolt of it, just the right measurement and weight, all that's important. What is it our Ken calls it? Aero — aeronautics, ah yes, that's it, aeronautics. Then they make the plane like

69

he's done the design: build it right up, you understand, there in those sheds. Any road, like I was telling you, today there's a new one ready to be taken up for a fly. Go that way towards Proctor's and you'll have a chance to see something I've never seen, even though our Ken had a hand in the making: an aeroplane pushed out onto the grass then being tested to see it flies proper. Our Ken sets great store in these flying machines, but to me it don't seem natural.'

'I expect people said that when the railway trains first came — and motor cars, I'm sure they said it about those.'

'Ah, and still do. Noisy, smelly things. As for aeroplanes, enough to frighten the poor birds out of the skies. How about this pie, then, m'dear: this one do you? Done to a golden brown, just the thing for a picnic.'

With her pie in a brown paper bag in the basket on the front of her cycle, he saw her on her way, pointing out which lane led from the green towards Proctor's. Life was suddenly full of promise.

★   ★   ★

When Mr Hodge had talked of sheds, she'd imagined farm buildings, or sheds like those she remembered at Gorsemoor. But this must be the right place; the painted board told her this was *Proctor's, Aeronautical Engineers*. These buildings were quite different, large and brick-built. She propped her bicycle against the surrounding hedge and leant over the five-barred gate to peer

70

across the field, trying to see what was happening on the other side of the enormous open door. People were coming out, standing in a group; she could almost feel the excitement as they waited. Then she saw the plane. It was being wheeled onto the field, coming towards her. Disappointed, she saw it turn so that it faced in the opposite direction towards the full length of the open field.

She wanted to be closer. It couldn't hurt if she climbed over the gate and walked around the edge of the field until she came towards where everyone was waiting. Now a tall man was climbing to get into the plane, a man wearing a leather helmet and goggles as if he were going to ride a motor cycle. Imagine actually driving an aeroplane! Imagine the moment when it left the ground behind! Her heart was hammering with excitement; she even forgot she was trespassing as she hurried towards the workers who were clustered outside the wide doorway. Never having seen a flying machine before, the propeller was a mystery to her. Someone was bending down, grabbing it with both hands. Just like she'd seen men turn the starting handle at the front of a motor car, so he spun the propeller and, as if by magic, the engine fired. 'Chocks away!' and it was moving, bumping uncertainly over the uneven grass as it went, gathering speed. It had to rise high enough to fly over the trees beyond the next field. Supposing it didn't! Supposing . . . her mouth was dry; whether from fear or excitement, she didn't question.

She saw the man in the plane raise his hand in

71

a 'thumbs up' signal to the watching crowd; she heard the young man who'd spun the propeller shout: 'She's off! Good luck, sir.' There could have been nothing familiar in the voice, so what was it that made her take her gaze off the plane and look at him? Could it be *him*? In the morning sunlight, his auburn hair shone just as it always had — Alex — She started to wave. Perhaps she was mistaken . . . The thought died as soon as it was born.

The aeroplane had cleared the trees and was continuing to climb as the young man turned to go back inside the sheds. That's when he noticed that someone was trying to attract his attention and, instead of following the others indoors, he came towards her. As he got closer, his pace quickened.

'Alex! I knew it had to be you! The hair, that's how I knew.'

'And you, you're just the same. Still a shrimp.' His delight was in his smile and in the twinkle of his tawny-brown eyes. When they'd played together as children, she'd been quick to defend herself, and nothing had changed. Small she might be, but she meant him to realise she was as much part of the working world as he was himself.

'Someone told me I'd see a flying machine. That's why I came. I'm working in Oakleigh.'

'Struth,' he laughed. 'The little shrimp a working woman. What are you doing? A children's nursemaid?'

She was suddenly proud of the part she played in compiling Charles Hardcastle's notes into what was to become a learned book. Holding her head high, she told him about it — knowing she exaggerated her efficiency and usefulness while saying nothing of how often Charles left her in no doubt of her failings. She suspected Alex listened to her with no more than one ear, sharing his attention between her and the machine that soared and swooped over the neighbouring farmland.

'Just look at that!' he muttered, half to her and half to himself. 'Everything we expected.' Then, struck by another thought: 'If you're not in a rush, I'll bring my sandwiches outside to eat. I'll want to be on hand when he brings her down to land, but after that we could ride out to Hinds Hill; it's only five minutes away.'

She nodded, her eyes alight with pleasure at the prospect. Alex had been her special friend ten years ago; in childhood, his two years' seniority had made him more than an ordinary friend. He'd been her secret hero. Even if she hadn't let herself admit it when she'd set out that morning, looking back at the start of the day from this point, she knew just how deep had been the misery she'd refused to allow to surface. And just when she'd been miserable and lonely, he had come back into her life. Suddenly neither Charles Hardcastle's carping, Mrs Jenkin's sharp tongue nor even the fog of understanding she tried to find her way through as she worked, had any power to hurt. Being with Alex would be just as it always had.

* * *

Even before they came to the end of their quickly eaten picnic, she knew the years between couldn't so readily be discounted. They were no longer the carefree children they'd been.

'Do you live with your mother? I read about her in the newspaper sometimes. It's years since I saw her, but I'll never forget. You must be proud of the way she fights for what she knows is just.' In her mind, Lucinda Murray was still firmly on a pedestal.

Ignoring her championship and not answering her question, he told her: 'I'm in digs, have been ever since I came to Proctor's. He's a great chap, James Proctor. That biplane you were watching: it's his design, you know. Nothing he doesn't know about aeronautics. But more than knowing, he's a practical man. A great pilot. I've been up with him, a couple of times.' Tamsin's wide-eyed look of wonder was just what he wanted. 'Better than banging the keys of some typewriting machine, writing about plants none of us have ever heard of,' he teased, revelling in her undisguised admiration.

'To *you*, they may be no more than that, but then Mr Hardcastle finds the same thrill in discovering a new species of plantlife as you do about the design of a flying machine.' She didn't intend to let him dismiss her work so casually. 'When we think a subject is boring, it's usually because we're ignorant of it.'

'Yes, ma'am. Beg pardon, ma'am.' He held out his hand palm upwards, inviting a smack. She felt laughter welling up; first her eyes then her mouth picked up the message. 'I said you'd not altered . . . You've still got your dimple.' He pressed his finger into the cavity that appeared as if by magic in her left cheek when she laughed.

He would never have done that ten years ago! And neither would she have felt this surge of unfamiliar excitement.

By this time, his sandwiches and her pork pie had been devoured and he was folding up the wrapping paper and putting it in his pocket.

'So when am I going to see you? You haven't some handsome swain hanging around, wanting to take up all your time?'

'Of course I haven't. Mr Hardcastle has first option on my time. And he's ill in bed, I told you, so I'm free all day today.'

'Trouble is, I'm already booked up for this evening. You wouldn't want me to let a lady down, would you?'

'I certainly wouldn't.' She made her voice as bright as his. 'You didn't tell me you had a sweetheart?'

'One for every day of the week, that's the best system. Which day can I book you down for?'

'Quite a Casanova!' came her laughing reply. But pride made her glad of the excuse of the uncertainty of Charles Hardcastle's working pattern. A girl for every day — and he saw Tamsin as just one of them. It must be because their friendship went back so far that she wouldn't let herself be bracketed with his other admirers — and she had no doubt that they would fall into the category of admirers. As a child, she'd taken his appearance for granted but, remembering, she realised now how

75

good-looking he had always been. Now she saw him as a handsome man (no more than twenty or twenty-one, but from her viewpoint that made him a man), his auburn hair springing into waves, his tawny-brown eyes clear and bright, his teeth strong, even and white, and his hands strong too. She wanted to imprint the image of him on her mind — more than that, she wanted this short midday break to last so much longer than it could.

Holding out both his hands, he pulled her to her feet. 'Time's up, shrimp. I must go back. But, I say, hasn't this been good? I'll be in touch.'

She nodded. Had it really meant as much to him as it had to her? No, of course it hadn't. He did a job he loved; he had a sweetheart for every day of the week; he took his freedom for granted.

'Don't look so solemn,' he told her. 'Pity I can't come with you, this afternoon. Mind you don't get lost.' Then, taking her by surprise, he lightly kissed her left cheek. 'That's for your dimple.' Before she could find a reply, he was on his bicycle and heading back towards Proctor's. As for Tamsin, she sat down again on the grassy slope of Hinds Hill, reliving every minute of the last hour. The thrill of her afternoon of freedom had evaporated but she'd come out to explore, so explore she would.

Determined to rekindle her pleasure in a day with no one to please but herself, she went on her way, following signposts and taxing her navigational ability so that she arrived back in

Oakleigh in time for supper. But long before, that, she'd come to regret not having sunk her pride and let 'Casanova' find a slot for her in his round of pleasure.

Next day, Charles was a little more mobile; with difficulty, he was able to get down the stairs. Work was his way of winning his battle against infirmity, but unfortunately it did nothing for his good humour; he needed a whipping boy and Tamsin filled the bill.

★　★　★

She had heard Alex's 'I'll be in touch' as a hollow promise and when a week went by, followed by another, with no note from him, she tried to put it out of her mind. When they'd been children, he had never called for her at the Manse (and as well he hadn't, for a friendship with the son of *that woman* would have been stamped on with a firm foot), always it had been she who had gone to the little villa in Tannery Lane. But that had been different; she'd been aware of his two years' seniority and, although she wouldn't have let him know it, she'd been grateful that her hero accepted her company. Now, it was different: she wasn't a child and, when her next few hours of freedom came, she cycled past Proctor's airfield without a glance; she wouldn't let him think she was hanging around in the hope of the crumbs he could spare.

★　★　★

The household staff worked weekday and weekend alike, with one whole Sunday off a month and a half day during each of the other weeks. It might not have been much, but at least they knew when their freedom would come. Tamsin had accepted the conditions; she'd known from the start that she would work when she was needed and have time to herself when she wasn't.

It was a warm Sunday morning in July and she knew with one glance at Charles's face that trouble lay ahead. He'd taken breakfast in his room, descended the stairs with 'ohs and 'ahs,' that warned her that he was in no mood for stoic endurance, and come into the workroom without so much as a reply to her 'good morning'.

'Pass me what you've printed up from yesterday. Let's see what sort of a mess you've made of it.'

'I checked the plant spellings. I don't think you'll find any mistakes.' She'd sat at the typewriter long after he'd gone to bed, laboriously making sure her two fingers punched the right keys. He glanced through the work, not so much reading it as looking for something to criticise; then he almost threw the sheaf of papers back at her.

'Mr Hardcastle, if you aren't satisfied with my progress, would you like me to look for another position?' It took all her courage — one thing she'd never been short of. It wasn't his anger she feared; it was the prospect of being without a job, without a home and almost without a penny.

'What?' he snapped. 'What the devil's the girl

78

talking about, now?'

'I asked you if you wanted me to go. If you advertised again, you might find the sort of young man you hoped for, one with a more suitable background.'

'Are you telling me you want to throw in the sponge? Too much for you to cope with, is that it? If so, come straight out with it: don't pussyfoot around trying to put the responsibility on me.'

'I didn't say I wanted to leave, I asked if you'd be happier with someone who didn't make mistakes.'

'Yes, of course I would. Who wouldn't? But you said yourself, anyone worth his salt wouldn't waste his time on the sort of job you do — or make a fist of doing.' For a second, he saw her expression alter; she drew back as if he'd hit her. But only for a second, before she looked him squarely in the eye. 'Don't let me have tantrums! Tears, looking for sympathy, expecting to be given quarter because you're a girl!'

'Why should I?' His manner put the mettle straight back in her. 'There's nothing inferior about being female — if you ask me, women can put up with things a lot more stoically than men can.'

His elbows on the table, he slumped in his chair. She was ashamed; she'd hit below the belt and wasn't at all sure what was coming next, so she waited quietly.

'Yes,' he said after a minute. 'I know what you're telling me — perhaps you're right. I hope you never have to find out how you'd behave.

Not a joint in my body that isn't alive with pain.' It was the first time he'd spoken like it and, in an instant, she made a move towards him, her eyes full of sympathy. 'No, no,' he stopped her. 'I've no excuse, I've no business to vent my spite on you. You're doing very well, if I'm man enough to be fair about it. Just get on with — ' He stopped speaking at the loud peal of the bell at the front door. Visitors were unheard of at Westwood House at any time — and certainly never arrived unannounced on a Sunday morning.

'Whoever it is, I'm not seeing them. Go out and tell that stupid Kitty to say I'm not available. Say I'm out — say I'm dead — more's the pity I'm not. Just get rid of them. Get along, or she'll be there before you.'

Just in time to waylay the young maid, Tamsin whispered her message, then returned to where Charles was sitting tapping his fingers impatiently on the table.

'It's all right,' she whispered, closing the door quietly. 'She understood.'

'Come along, then. Stop wasting time.'

Tamsin made a supreme effort to forgive him; she tried to tell herself he wasn't so much full of hate as full of pain . . . but the shaft of sunlight streaming across the table didn't make it easy. She could hear the eight-bell peal from St Peter's church by the green and saw a family dressed in their Sunday best hurrying past the window.

'Excuse me, sir.' Kitty opened the door just far enough to put her head round, her face a picture of worried misery. 'Sorry, sir, but it's Miss

Yelland he's after. He won't go away, Miss; I told him you were working.'

He'd come! It could be no one else.

'It'll be Alex, Alex Murray. He's an old friend. He said he'd call — and, of course, he doesn't work on Sundays. People don't.' Already Tamsin was halfway to the door.

'Wait! All right, Kitty, you may go. This person, you say, is an old friend. You'd better bring him in here. Let me have a look at the kind of company you keep.'

'That's ridiculous! I choose my own friends.'

'In my house, I have a right to know who comes calling. Just have this young man — is he young, or some old family friend? — have him come in and show himself. Just remember, young miss, fool that I was, I made myself responsible for you when I took you off your parents' hands.'

'If you care to meet him, I'll ask him in. But even you won't be able to find fault with him.'

Charles raised his eyebrows. Briefly, she believed she suspected something akin to a twinkle in his eyes.

'Mr Wonderful, is he? So that's the way the wind blows. Just go and bring him through.'

'The wind doesn't blow at all. I've known him since I was six years old. I can easily talk to him outside in the hall.'

'Just stop fidgeting about and do as I say. At this rate, it'll be dinner-time before we get any work done.'

She closed the door behind her when she went out to greet Alex — for that it must be Alex, she

81

had no doubt; she knew no one else to come calling — and Charles was left alone.

Reaching across the table, he took up the work she'd sat late into the night finishing. What was the matter with him that he could vent his spite against life on her? Warped, that's what's the matter with me, he told himself. My mind's become as miserable as my body. What sort of a life is it for her here? And does she complain? Never. Not that she's cowed — like that silly Kitty. No, she's brave enough, and works harder for me than I deserve. I'll have to talk to this chap, see what sort he is. With her people away, I can't have her getting in with the wrong company. But would she? I doubt it. She's no fool, even if she looks as though she ought still to be in the schoolroom.

'This is Mr Hardcastle, Alex.' He'd been so wrapped up in his own thoughts, he hadn't heard the door open. 'This is my friend, Alex Murray.'

'I'm pleased to meet you, sir. Tamsin tells me she has to work. What a sin, on a glorious Sunday. I came hoping to collect her to support me at cricket.'

'Is it more of a sin to spend the Sabbath working than knocking a ball?'

'I believe it is, sir, on a day like this.'

'Humph. So you think I overwork her, is that what you're trying to tell me?'

'I think everyone deserves a few hours of freedom. You should hear my mother on the subject.' When Alex smiled like that, no one could take offence at his words. 'Fair treatment for workers, equality for women, votes for all — '

'One of that Pankhurst brigade, is she?' There was no doubting what he thought of the suffragette movement.

'Lucinda Murray. I dare say she's right, but she rubs a lot of people up the wrong way. I keep telling her — but she won't listen.'

'She won't do her cause any good pussyfooting around, frightened of upsetting anyone. Only way to get anywhere is having the courage to stand up and be counted. So what do you say, Miss Yelland? What's your opinion? Let's hear you.'

He glared at her, much the same as he had when he'd thrown the sheaf of papers back across the table at her — defying her to be crushed, yet ready to pounce on her if she lent her support to Lucinda's battle.

'I believe she is right. She's been my hero almost as long as I can remember. But, Alex, you ought to go. I told you, I'm working today and the morning's nearly half over already.'

Charles gave her a smile that was almost a sneer.

'Working on a Sunday? Working when it suits *me*? It's to be hoped some of her supporters have more backbone, more gumption. You'd better let this young man of yours take you out of my way, or I'll get his mother coming to lay the law down.'

If he expected her to look at him with gratitude, he was disappointed.

'If I have a battle to fight, I'm capable without anyone's help. Under the terms of my engagement, I agreed to work whenever you needed me. And that's what I mean to do. Alex, you'd better go — '

'What you do with your day is no concern to me.' Charles struggled to his feet. 'I thought I'd be able to concentrate for a few hours. Hadn't bargained for all this rumpus.' Just for a second, as he leant heavily on his sticks, he let his armour of irritability slip; his eyes were closed. He looked just what he was: a man aged ahead of his years by pain.

'There's no rumpus, Mr Hardcastle. Alex is going; I'm all ready to start work.'

'So you may be, young woman. But I'm not. Take her away to this stupid ball game. And just see to it that you take care of her. No family to watch over her: seems the responsibility lands on me, whether I want it or not.'

'Have no fear, sir. I'll treat her like my own sister.'

'Now, open the door for me. Next battle is those dratted stairs.'

Alex opened the door, his smile letting no hint of sympathy show as he watched Charles shuffle past him.

'Put your hand on my shoulder for the stairs, I'm more stable than a stick.' Then, out of Tamsin's hearing, 'And thank you, sir.'

'See to it she enjoys her day. Works all the hours God sends.' He frowned, as if to wipe out his words. Getting soft, that was his trouble. 'If she were more up to the job, it wouldn't take her so long.' When his eyes met Alex's, he looked away, ashamed of his disloyalty. 'That mother of yours: I've read about her. She's got spunk.'

★   ★   ★

Who would have believed a day that had started so badly could turn out as that one did?

Tamsin didn't mean to waste a second so, while Alex fetched her bicycle from the coach house, she rushed up to her room, already unbuttoning her long skirt. It took no time to change into her cycling suit, and pull on her beret, then back down the stairs and straight out of the front door to find him waiting in the road, holding the handlebars of their machines, one in either hand.

'That way? But where is the cricket match? Isn't it on the Green?' she queried, surprised to see they were facing in the opposite direction.

'It's on the field at Proctor's. Our eleven is playing a team from Merchant's, the firm who build farm machinery out on the Reading road. Some of the chaps have been rolling the pitch every day for a week. It doesn't start until two o'clock but Miss Halliwell — where I live — said to bring you back to the house so that we can eat before we go.'

Tamsin would like to have asked him if all his companions were given the same treatment, but swallowed the question, preferring to give the impression that she'd already forgotten he'd boasted of a 'sweetheart for each day of the week.' Today, none of them mattered; she wanted nothing more than the unexpected gift of being where she was. Why was it that being with Alex made her so happy, so in tune with life? Even when he was serious, he was never solemn. Yet he

85

wasn't flippant. He was dependable, interested in his work, ambitious: so did she imagine that he saw life as a prize to be enjoyed?

'You get on all right with this botanist chap? You mustn't let him tread on you, Tammy.'

'No one treads on me. I'm sorry for him that he's having a bad day but, if he had to have one, I'm glad it was today. If he'd been fit to work, I wouldn't have come.'

'You underestimate the power of my charm,' he laughed. 'I'd have persuaded him; he'd have given you the day off.'

'I told you: I wouldn't have taken it. I don't want favours. I persuaded him to take me on. I wasn't really a bit what he was hoping for. So, you see, it's up to me to see I do better than my best. I don't want allowances made for me. I'm still slow at using the typewriting machine; it takes me all my time to keep up with what I have to do, even though I usually stay up late catching up. I'm not awfully good at it, yet. One thing I don't want is favours.'

'Women!' he teased. 'You're another just like Mother.'

As they rode, she turned to him to beam her pleasure. 'Now that's the sort of compliment I like!'

He smiled back at her, his mind not on his mother, not on Tamsin's pleasure at being likened to her hero, but on that dimple in her left cheek.

About a mile beyond the buildings and field of Proctor's, he led the way onto the drive of a house. 'Here we are.'

'You mean, you lodge here?' It was hardly the sort of establishment she would have expected to take boarders!

'Miss Halliwell is a friend of my boss. He put me on to it. Prop your bike with mine and I'll take you to meet her.'

They could see no one in the garden and were just turning to go indoors when they heard a voice calling.

'Coo-ee.' It came from someone working in the vegetable garden.

'Ah, this way.' He steered Tamsin towards the voice.

'Who's that? Wouldn't it be more polite to take me to meet your Miss Halliwell first?' Even though they were too far away for the odd-looking woman to hear, Tamsin found herself whispering.

'That's who it is, silly. Don't take any notice of how she looks. That's her gardening togs.' He chuckled as if he were seeing her afresh. 'When she wants, she can look like a duchess. Come on.' Taking Tamsin's hand, he quickened his pace as they crossed the grass towards the gate in the trimmed hedge that divided them from the kitchen garden and the spectacle of Naomi Halliwell. She wore heavy boots, the sight of which carried Tamsin's mind instantly to Gorsemoor. She'd never consciously thought of the sort of footwear her grandfather used to wear in the fields, yet the memory was suddenly as clear as though it had been yesterday. Naomi's grey woollen dress owed nothing to fashion, whether of that time or earlier; any hint at shape

87

came from the hessian apron wrapped around her long, straight waist. The bodice was fastened with buttons that would have been more at home on a man's jacket, except that the top one was missing and the neck fastened by a brooch, its large sapphire set in a surround of diamonds that flashed in the sunlight. The ensemble was topped by a misshapen felt hat she might have borrowed from a scarecrow. But, even before she spoke, it was her bearing that set her apart from the attire which would have passed unnoticed in a gypsy encampment — except for the brooch, worn as casually as if it were of no more value than a safety pin.

'I winkled her out; here she is. Tamsin, this is Miss Halliwell, who keeps me fed, watered and thoroughly spoilt. Tamsin Yelland, an echo from my past.'

From the way his eccentric landlady looked at him, it was apparent he could do no wrong. Then she wiped her hand on the coarse and much-used hessian and extended it to take Tamsin's in a firm grip.

Immediately, Tamsin liked what she saw. 'It was kind of you to say Alex might bring me here.'

'Fiddlesticks! Kind, nothing! Anyway,' Naomi smiled, showing a wide gap between her two front teeth, 'I like to know what he gets up to, like to know his friends.' Ah, so perhaps she had vetted them all. At the thought, Tamsin felt a prickle of resentment. 'He tells me you work for the Hardcastle man. Don't envy you, girl.'

'You know Mr Hardcastle? I find working for

him interesting,' Tamsin answered with more loyalty than truth.

Naomi gave a guffaw, in keeping with her get-up. 'I dare say it might be interesting living on the edge of a volcano, too. Yes, of course I know him. Before the Lord gave him his comeuppance, we used to rub shoulders locally. Not now, of course. I did call on him just the once, when I heard of his predicament . . . ' and with something between a laugh and a snort, 'yes, just the once. I'll clear all this clobber away,' she indicated a wheelbarrow half filled with trimmings from the hedge, shears, hoe and a ball of twine, 'then I'll get scrubbed up. If you take Miss Yelland to the house, you might look into the kitchen as you go past and say we'll be ready to eat in half an hour. That'll give me time to get the garden out of my fingernails.'

'Can't we clear up for you?' Tamsin offered. 'I wish we'd come earlier. We could have helped with the hedge.'

'Good idea.' Naomi untied her hessian wrap, its removal taking all semblance of shape from her figure; tall, broad-shouldered, as straight as a board. 'I'll look in on the kitchen.' She watched Tamsin start to rake up the remaining clippings, then Alex scoop them into the barrow. It would take an exceptional girl to be good enough for him, but she considered that in this one he'd shown a certain degree of common sense. So she left them and went to make herself presentable for the lunch table. Not quite to the promised standard of a duchess, but at least she would pass unnoticed in a group. The effort she'd made was a sign of her approval.

From the first moment, Tamsin had liked the fact that Naomi was sufficiently natural to appear eccentric. Now she was dressed in more conventional attire, it was easier to assess her age: probably about fifty, and no beauty, with her large wide-apart teeth and her pale leathery complexion. Her hands were long and strong, clearly capable of hard work. An honest woman, one not to be beguiled by pretence.

The meal over, Alex changed into his cream flannels and striped blazer; then Naomi came out to see them on their way. When she shook Tamsin's hand in farewell and waved away her thanks, they were all aware that they'd come a long way in the last two hours.

'If you think of it, you may give my regards to Charles. Cantankerous creature that he is, he probably doesn't deserve them.'

'I shan't tell him *that*,' Tamsin laughed, 'but I'll give him your message.'

'Good luck, Alexander. Make sure that Proctor's see that other lot off.'

* * *

It was a day of firsts. The first time of visiting Lambton House; the first time of meeting Naomi Halliwell; the first time of meeting James Proctor, the employer Alex held in such esteem. Much later, when she looked back on that May day, she might see it as the time that set her future from her past, but that was something she had no means of knowing. The team from

90

Merchant's arrived in ones and twos, some walking and some on bicycles, and it was while they were assembling that Alex introduced her to James Proctor, the tall man she'd watched take the machine up on its test flight. Unlike Naomi, he didn't make a vivid impression. Alex clearly looked on him as one stage down from a god but, if she thought of him at all, it was that he appeared to be a kindly enough person, quietly spoken, treating everyone with the same courtesy. His appearance didn't strike her as outstanding: brown hair, blue eyes, a pleasant-looking man.

And there her interest ended; her eyes were back on Alex.

4

In July Mavis's first letter arrived.

Tamsie, sweetling,

I thank God we are on terra firma again, although even now the ground in this strange land seems uncertain under my feet. I cannot begin to tell you how dreadful the voyage was; there were moments when I longed to die. You don't know the lonely tears I shed. No, that is a wicked, unkind thing to say, for how could I be lonely when my dear Arthur was so unfailingly kind and caring? The voyage made me realise how far I fall short of his unwavering trust. He accepted every miserable hour with such stoicism; he prayed aloud for me to be given strength to accept and to see my temporary discomfort as a small price to pay for the opportunity we'd been given to serve.

Now we have landed, our luggage is already coming ashore and we are to set off on the next part of this long journey. I am ashamed of the weakness I try so hard to overcome, the moments when I find myself in tune with your stubborn refusal to be part of our mission: moments when, just as you did, I fear the hardships that may lie ahead. Pray for me, Tamsie, pray that I may be all that Arthur deserves.

When we reach our destination, I will write again, for I know you will be anxious to know our situation.

It was a great disappointment to me that you were unprepared to share our work. Indeed, I know we shall miss many of our home comforts; your father, with his never-failing compassion made me see that if it wasn't the Lord's will to give you the strength to face sacrifices, we must learn to accept.

I cannot write more now as Arthur is waiting. Now that we are ashore, he is anxious to be on with the next stage; he is keyed up with something far deeper than excitement. I am not clever with words; if only you were here you would feel for yourself the intensity of his desire to end the frustration of this interminable journey and to set out on what we are called to do.

As soon as I can, I will let you have our address so that you can write to me but until then and always, I am

Your loving Mother.

Reading it, Tamsin felt a pang of loneliness. Where was the mother she remembered, the gentle woman who had delighted in making pretty gowns, combing her lovely golden hair to enhance her beautiful face, absorbing admiration as a sponge absorbs water? Always she had been a kind woman, willing to visit the sick, bring a cheerful word to the troubled. That was why everyone had loved her; in bringing happiness to others she had found her own. But where was the happiness now? Rather than a pretty gown to flatter her slim figure, she was seeking sackcloth and ashes. It made a stranger of her. And of course it was silly to be disappointed that in her letter she showed no interest in things at home, Tamsin told herself. What would have been the point in enquiring how she was getting on in her work for Charles Hardcastle, when there was no address for her reply? And her father . . . intensity of his desire. She shuddered, images she'd fought to forget springing alive.

Since her first chance meeting with Alex, they had met as often as she was free. But her freedom so often didn't coincide with his. The warm weather did nothing for either Charles's health or for his temper; as often as not, it was midday by the time he forced himself to leave his room. But, once started, he would expect them to work until the last light faded. She tried to concentrate on what she wrote, but her mind had a will of its own.

Alex made no secret of the fact that he was never short of willing female company: sometimes he'd talk about Edith, the rector's daughter; sometimes Margaret, whose father ran the bakery; then there was Evelyn, who worked in the local laundry; and Muriel, the daughter of a fellow employee. Did he enjoy telling her about them, in the hope of encouraging her to stand up to Charles and refuse to work in the evenings? Was he trying to make her jealous? Or did he simply put her in a different category from the others? After all, he must ask each of those to go out with him because he was attracted to them.

So what about her? Was she no more than part of his childhood? Did he still think of her as the child who had loved to be his shadow, who'd collected wood with him to take home for his mother's fire? Did he still think of her as she'd been during the long hot spell when she must have been about seven, the summer when she'd stripped off everything except her knickers and, under his guidance, learnt to swim in the millstream? He wouldn't have known how half the thrill of what she did had come from knowing how scandalised they would have been at the Manse if they could have seen her. She still remembered the feeling of daring as she'd gone home each day, gloriously conscious of her lack of underwear, carrying her wrung-out knickers in her pocket to be hung to dry on the springs of her bed so that they wouldn't be seen. No, he hadn't understood her thrill then, any more than he knew what it meant to her to be with him again, more than ten years later.

She told herself it was because she'd had no experience of young men that he was so important to her. But what was the use of telling herself, when she knew that couldn't have been more than half the truth? If she were like him — if she had a sweetheart for every day of the week — none of them could give her this feeling of choking happiness, making her heart beat like a drum and her mind refuse to focus.

Whenever she was free around midday, she would pedal to Proctor's and sit on the five-barred gate of the airfield (that was what Alex grandly called it) and wait for him to come out to eat his sandwiches. That's where she was when she heard the noisy engine of a motor car, surprised when it came to a halt just behind her.

'Does Murray know you're coming, Miss Yelland?' James Proctor's voice surprised her.

'He knows I come if I'm free. He'll be out soon, I expect.'

'No, that's why I stopped to speak. He and I are catching the afternoon train from Brackleford; we're going to the West Country for a day or two.'

'He's not gone yet, though?' She wanted to hear about it from Alex, not from this quietly spoken almost-stranger. 'I haven't seen him for a few days; that's why he hasn't told me.'

'He didn't know until last evening. I dined at Lambton, that's when I suggested he might like to come with me. The name won't mean anything to you, but Captain Clayton is having his Bleriot machine conveyed to South Molton; he's to give a display at the agricultural show. I'd already arranged to go. Then it occurred to me, Murray would benefit from the trip.'

He was right, the name of neither the plane nor the man meant anything to her, but she didn't intend to admit to it.

'I'm sure he will.' She made sure her voice was composed and her disappointment well hidden.

Why should the sight of her touch James as it did? He brought his thoughts into line before they had a chance to take hold. He told himself she was a delightful child, with those eyes so wide and solemn. Clearly she thought a good deal of Alex Murray — and for her to be good enough in his eyes for Alex was indeed merit.

'I have great hopes for Alexander Murray,' he found himself explaining, more sensitive to her feelings than she suspected. 'Perhaps he reminds me of myself at that age. To him, what he does here is more than just an interesting job of work. He has vision. He feels as I do myself. Flying is the future; we're only on the brink.'

With unconscious grace, she turned; instead of sitting sideways, looking at him over her shoulder, she swung her legs effortlessly over the gate and faced him.

'That day I first came here, it was because someone told me you were going to test a flying machine. I'd seen one up in the air once before, but nothing like that day. I'll never forget it, just watching it leave the ground behind. It must be the most wonderful — no, more than that — what do you feel when you know you're rising up into the air, over the trees?'

'As you say, wonderful can't describe it.' His pleasant face creased into a smile that brought crows'-feet to his eyes. 'I feel thankful, too! Confirmation that what I put on the drawing board was right. I'll let Murray know you were here, shall I? I told him not to come in, this morning. I'm on my way to pick him up now and we'll go straight to the railway station.'

'Thank you for stopping to tell me.' With all the politeness of a well-behaved child.

'Do I take him any message?'

'What sort of a message could compete with your Captain Clayton's Bleriot — is that what you said it was called?' Disappointed though she was, she was conscious of James Proctor's eager anticipation for the days ahead. It was impossible not to smile at him. He slipped the car into gear and raised a hand in salute. And as his gaze lingered on that deep dimple in her left cheek, his thoughts leapt to Alex, a young man with undoubted potential — and just as surely with a magnetic personality, as far as his female acquaintances were concerned.

Cycling home to Westwood House, Tamsin already felt the void of Alex's absence. The sun still shone just as brightly, she told herself, and just listen to the birds. It's lovely for him to be going to this place in Devon. And anyway, she answered the unacknowledged hurt that wouldn't be pushed from her mind, he must have had far too much to do this morning to find time to come over to tell me he was going.

He was away for almost a week, surprising Tamsin by sending her a postcard from Devon with a picture of open moorland on one side and three lines of scrawl on the other telling her, *The trip has come up to our highest hopes. Wonderful machine. Alex.*

Reading it for the third time, she let her imagination carry her on an impossible trip; she saw Charles Hardcastle free of pain and she accompanying him on the expedition to Peru his physical limitations had made impossible. 'Trip magnificent,' she would write in a casual card to Alex. 'Found wonderful and fascinating orchids unknown even to Mr. H.' In Peru? She didn't know. And what did it matter? There was no substance in a dream. Orchids in Peru or anywhere else weren't the reason for it: simply the image of Alex reading her words and knowing she lived an exciting life independent of him.

But the truth was that, as the weeks turned to months, he became ever more the pivot on which her thoughts revolved. When winter came, there was small appeal in eating a picnic at midday; the evenings were dark and her spare time continued uncertain. Seeing each other less frequently made no difference; her dreams were all of Alex.

Letters arrived every few weeks from Mavis, letters that did nothing to bring her presence close. She didn't paint a word picture of their surroundings, but she never failed to stress Arthur's dedication.

Our time here is going quickly. Of course, I look forward to us all being together again at the Manse. It worries me that you are so far away, making friends with people who are probably not suitable. This Murray boy, you say he is the son of that dreadful woman. Tamsie, sweetling, do be careful. I feel so torn — I want to be here with your dear father, to be his helper and, please God, his comfort, too. But you are so young to be alone. What sort of a mother am I that I could leave you perhaps to get into the clutches of that wicked woman? Wiser by far if you stop seeing her son. Arthur recalls that he was an unpleasant child, in fact Tamsie he *forbids* your friendship with him. Is there not a nice girl nearby you can have for a companion? Be sure you attend chapel regularly — or church as we used to when you were small. Guard against the temptations the Devil is always waiting to put in your path.

Her letters were always in the same vein: no mention of the happy times they'd shared in the past, no hint of humour, no hint of warmth; always talk of duty, of trying to walk in 'your dear father's' footsteps. So Tamsin kept her own counsel. By the time her parents came home, her job with Mr Hardcastle would be coming to an end. When the typescript was finished, he would want an illustrator to work with him; her own part would be done. But she had no intention of going back to the Manse. She hadn't fought for her independence only to lose it again. She vowed she would *never* live in the same house as *him* again. It sickened her to think of what had happened: his hot groping hands, his contorted expression as he'd slumped shuddering in the chair, and how always after that night he avoided meeting her eyes. Until then, she'd accepted him as well-meaning but tedious, joyless, often stupid in what she considered his narrow-minded arrogance; now even those memories were besmirched. Ahead of her, there would be more arguments, but she wasn't to be dissuaded. Once they were home, she would be able to get near to her mother again; and once Mavis met Alex (and here Tamsin let her imagination run riot) she would fall under his spell.

Christmas came and went, a period when

Charles was able to get downstairs each day to work. So the festival passed almost unnoticed at Westwood House. January found him less mobile and, despite the cold, Tamsin cycled each day to Proctor's and Alex never failed her; no matter what the weather, he would eat his lunch 'on the hoof', as he called it, since it was too cold to sit on the winter-damp ground.

In February, Charles rallied. For more than a week, he had been downstairs and working each day. Feeling better, he was more cheerful and talkative.

'Excuse me, sir,' poor Kitty timidly opened the door of the workroom, 'but a lady's come calling. I was outside doing the knocker, see, that's why you wouldn't have heard. She says her name's Miss Halliwell. And sir, I'm sorry sir, but she says she means to talk to you. I did tell 'er you wouldn't be seeing no one, but she's still waiting there.'

'Naomi Halliwell. Fancy her visiting again.' Then to Tamsin with what, remembering what Naomi had hinted of her one and only visit since the onset of his illness, she saw as a mischievous twinkle, he added, 'After the way I treated her last time, I wonder she still talks to me.'

'I did try, sir, I did say you wouldn't — '

'Don't stand there blethering, girl. Bring her in.'

'In here, sir, or in the morning room?'

'God give me strength.'

Tamsin saw Kitty's worried face quiver; it was the effect Charles always had on her. 'I'll go and get her, shall I?' She was on her feet and rewarded by a look of gratitude from poor, plump Kitty.

'Ah,' Charles remembered, 'of course, you know her. Likely enough, it's you she's come to see. Go and get her in — and, Kitty, stir the fire up before you disappear. Make the place look a bit more cheerful.'

Kitty would rather have escaped to the kitchen; Mrs Jenkins's bossiness she could cope with, but the master turned her into a trembling wreck. She scurried past him, then knelt in front of the grate and took up the poker.

'Give it a good raking: do it as if you mean it. Pussyfooting about like that, how can you expect to set it flaming?'

'Still the same silver-tongued Charles!' Naomi laughed as Tamsin ushered her into the room. 'No, don't stand up, my dear. My word, Tamsin seems to have got you sorted out. I've never seen you work in such order.'

'She's doing very well. I take it it's her you've come to see?'

'In part. Actually it's both of you.'

'All right, Kitty. If that's the best you can do, you'd better leave it alone before you put it out altogether. Go on, off you go.'

Which she did, her bottom lip caught between her teeth and her face red with misery and embarrassment.

'You really are a dreadful old man.' Naomi said it with more affection than he deserved. 'How do you put up with him, Tamsin?'

Tamsin laughed. 'I'm more used to him than poor Kitty is.'

'All bluster and no substance, is that what you make of him?'

Under cover of pulling a chair nearer to the fire for Naomi, Tamsin watched him. Would he explode into the sort of angry outburst she had become accustomed to? His brows were pulled into a frown — but it didn't disguise the twitch at the corner of his mouth. It seemed he enjoyed Naomi's assessment.

'More than a year since you paid me your last visit. Christmas greetings or some such rot, I seem to recall.' If his mouth had tried to betray him into a smile, his voice certainly didn't.

'What an old Scrooge you are.' Naomi laughed. 'Stop wallowing in self-pity and make yourself sociable. If you carry on like you do much longer, you'll find you've forgotten even the rudiments of good manners.'

'Humph. Miss Yelland, just pull the bell, will you? We'll get that silly girl to bring the Madeira through.'

'I'll fetch it for you.'

'At least you might manage without dropping it! Three glasses, mind.' Charles called as she left them.

'You're lucky with that girl, Charles. I hope you treat her well.'

'Well enough. Don't know why I let her persuade me to take her on: no experience, precious little knowledge. But you're right, I'm lucky she's stayed with me. Plenty of spirit. I like a person with spunk.'

'And that brings me to the reason for my visit. I'm having a small dinner party — '

'No, no, no, don't waste your breath. You know I've done with visiting. What energy I can muster, I don't mean to use on a lot of empty table talk.'

'And I don't blame you, Charles. There's nothing more dull. But this won't be. There will be only six of us, and that counts you and me. There's a young man living with me at Lambton: Alexander Murray. You'll remember, you've met him; he's a friend of Tamsin's.'

'Tamsin, you call her. To me, she's always been Miss Yelland; I won't have easy familiarity in the house.'

'To me, she's Tamsin. From the first time Alex brought her to the house, I took to her, but I don't have to tell you about her. Alex will be there, he and Tamsin will be company for each other. The other is James Proctor, a man I think you'll find interesting. He may not know an orchid from an edelweiss, but then you wouldn't be able to put a flying machine in the air. Clever man, make no mistake, and a brave one too. Aeronautics may be his subject, but you won't find his outlook narrow. I've known James for many years — used to push him out in his bassinet, more than thirty years ago. Then the sixth is Alexander's mother. Sharpen your wicked tongue on her as much as you like; she can take it and give as good as she gets.'

'Humph. She's not the only one,' he grumbled. But, this time, there was no disguising the smile in his eyes as he looked on his visitor. Today, she had made an effort; her appearance could rightly be likened more to a duchess than a scarecrow. 'Ah, here's the wine. And some biscuits, I see. You pour, if you will, Miss Yelland.' Then with a quick, sly look at Naomi, 'Tamsin.'

Tamsin threw him a smile that told him she approved.

'This Mrs Murray,' he said, 'she's one of that Pankhurst woman's set, isn't she? If she lives in the area, how is it her son is with you at Lambton?'

'James Proctor thinks highly of him. It was his idea he came to me while he looked for somewhere to live, but we took to each other. The arrangement suits me well; he's a charming young man to have in the house. As for his mother, Lucinda Murray: no doubt you've seen her name in the local paper. She's always looked on this district as her own. For the time being, she is living with me, too. I find the situation very agreeable: she's a woman with more than her share of common sense, wide interests, high ideals (whether or not you agree all of them) and no fear. I promise you an evening of scintillating conversation. And about time, too. Charles, you're much too intelligent to shut yourself away, concerning yourself with nothing but reliving your last trip and bemoaning the fact you can no longer do what you did. Life goes on.'

'More's the pity.' Like a petulant child, he pushed his glass away from him. 'And what use do you think I should be amongst these scintillating conversationalists? What would a mind that dwells on yesterday be able to contribute? Humph? Humph?'

'If you come in the guise of your friend Scrooge, nothing. If you come as the man I used to know, then, my dear Charles, the evening will be the richer for your presence. And as for Tamsin: she, like Alex, is a breath of fresh air.'

'All very well for you.' He glowered. 'How did you get here today? In your trap? On your bicycle? Do you imagine I can hoist myself into a carriage?'

'Charles, my dear, I'm not asking you to. I shall send Burgess with my auto; you will travel in style.'

★ ★ ★

And so they did. Tamsin possessed no gown suitable for a dinner party. She was thankful for her knowledge that the only other two females were to be Naomi Halliwell and Lucinda Murray, both of them women she knew to have minds above the fripperies of fashion. She wore what had been her 'best' gown at the Manse, sea-green silk with a long flowing skirt, belted at the waist, a V-shaped collar and an oyster-white tie. As an afternoon gown, it would have been dressier than she had cause to wear, but for the evening it left much to be desired. If only she were tall and elegant; if only she could pile her pale hair into what her mother had always called 'a woman's crowning glory'. Fine and straight, it defied the pins. She was on the verge of despair as she tried to overcome its stubborn refusal to be anchored. From her room, she could hear the 'ohs' and 'ahs' as Charles made his way downstairs. It had to be a choice of her normal daily tight plait pinned around her head, or her fine hair left to hang as it had all her life until she'd come to Westwood House. She decided on the latter, holding it back off her pale face with an off-white band. No wonder she scowled at her reflection; she might have stepped straight out of an illustration in *Alice in Wonderland*, the book she'd had for her tenth birthday.

Meeting Lucinda again after so many years did nothing to boost her self-confidence.

'Alex said you hadn't changed.' Lucinda took her hand. 'A pity the years haven't left us all so unscathed.'

She spoke no more than the truth. Tamsin felt a pang of disappointment. Lucinda had been so clear in her memory, tall, graceful, willowy, yet as strong as tempered steel. For more than ten years, that was the image she'd carried. The truth was different. Height was something that time couldn't change: she was still tall. Strength was still there, too, but now slender gracefulness had given way to something harsher. Even her hand was hard as it gripped Tamsin's. She'd fought her battle — indeed she meant to go on fighting it until she was rewarded with victory — but she hadn't come through unscathed. Her face was thin, lined in advance of her years; where once she had been willowy, now she was thin and angular. There was a harshness about her.

But to Tamsin, she was still a hero. 'I've often read about you in the newspaper. I've been so

107

proud to think I knew you.'

'Knew me when you were a child. You're a woman now, Tamsin. There's work for every woman of like mind.'

'It's not just the vote — it's far more than that.' Tamsin's eyes (sea-green, this evening) gazed at her earnestly.

'How right you are.'

Alex interrupted them. 'Enough putting the country in order. This evening, you must both try to behave yourselves.' His tone was teasing, his eyes were laughing. But they both knew he was right. A dinner party was no place for one of Lucinda's tub-thumping tirades.

Naomi had chosen her guests well. By the time they reached the second course, conversation flowed and bore no resemblance to the social small talk Charles so hated. It was Tamsin's first glimpse of the man he must once have been, interested in a world beyond his own subject. That alone would have set the evening apart but, above all else, it was her consciousness that she and Alex were being bracketed together — 'the young ones'. Unjust to James Proctor, perhaps, for in years he was far nearer to them than to the other three around the table; but he fell into the other group easily enough, sharing their views on most subjects and airing his own in that easy pleasant way of his when he saw things from a different angle.

' . . . to Lloyd George's credit.' Taking her eyes off Alex, Tamsin caught the end of what Lucinda was saying. 'It takes away some of the fear of being off work because of sickness. Not that it's a

108

gift from the state. Twopence a week isn't a huge contribution from the government. Yet the fourpence that the worker has to pay can mean a lot to a man with hungry mouths to feed.'

'Then, of course, there is the unemployment contribution,' James put in. 'The same again for that. But it's a safety net. Seven shillings a week isn't much for a man with a family if he is thrown out of work, but at least it's better than the Poor Law.'

'Employers don't like it, you may be sure of that.' Lucinda glowered around the table, her manner defying anyone to disagree. 'Let the worker pay, let the government chip in with its measly twopence, but it's the first time the employer has had to think of the welfare of his workers.'

'I believe you misjudge him. I know many employers — ' James was one himself but he didn't point this out ' — and I believe you misjudge the general feeling. Although, with a big staff, threepence for sick benefit and threepence for unemployment for each man on the payroll could come to a sizeable sum from the firm's profits.'

'My heart bleeds for them!' Lucinda scoffed. 'And even now, in this new Utopian era, if a man is thrown out of work he only gets this bountiful seven shillings a week for just three months in any one year. There's precious little pleasure in the struggle of making do on a pittance. Believe me, I've tried it.'

'That's what gives you the drive to fight so hard for what you know is just.' Tamsin's eyes shone with admiration.

Alex had a hero of his own. 'When the Insurance Act became law, at Proctor's we were all given an increase in wages.'

'I have a small staff, people I know and trust. No one could expect large industrial companies to act as I was able to. And my motives weren't entirely altruistic.' James added, with a laugh, 'When you know you have good people working for you, you want to make sure you keep them.'

'Better for profit than losing them.' Lucinda barely disguised the sneer in her voice.

That was the moment when the pedestal on which Tamsin had held her all these years began to rock. She could see that Alex was annoyed that his mother should want to fight her battle when she was a guest and among his friends — friends, with the exception of Charles Hardcastle, whom he felt fitted well into her assessment of employers. But it wasn't the look of irritation Alex turned on his mother that gave Tamsin this feeling of disappointment. She wasn't even sure what it was: it had to do with James's gentle manner.

'That's what I like.' Charles turned to Lucinda, with a rare smile. 'A woman not afraid to speak her mind. Not that I agree with some of the rubbish you shout about. But at least you shout: you stand up to be counted.'

'But how seriously do people listen? How much do *you* take note of what we see as just and right? Or do you glance at the newspaper as you eat your breakfast porridge — 'Ah, those suffragettes have been causing trouble again.

110

Been put inside to cool their heels. Pass the marmalade.' '

This time, he laughed, something that Tamsin had never known. The occasional smile, and that but rarely, but never a laugh.

It wasn't until they'd left the men to their port and Naomi was raking a blaze into the drawing room fire (for she didn't believe in ringing the bell when she was perfectly capable of doing a job herself) that Lucinda once more went into the attack, this time aiming her shafts at Tamsin.

'It's a cause you believe in; why not put your shoulder to the wheel? Afraid of upsetting that puritanical father of yours?'

'I never have been. And he and my mother are in Africa on a mission.'

'So, I'll give you some pamphlets to distribute. I'll give you some reading. Women have as much right as men in the running of the country. You're a minor, still, of course, but never too young to start to think — '

'Mrs Murray, I *do* think. There is much that is wrong, but this new Act has helped those who are hard up. And it's right to say so, to give credit instead of using it as a springboard to attack employers and sneer at what you call the Government's 'measly' contribution. It would be fine for women to have the opportunity to vote, but that's a national thing and you'd still get the same parliamentarians. Even if you had women in the House, who's to say the people in your local town or village would feel the benefit?'

'So you'll bury your head in the sand, the same as everyone else.'

111

'When I was little, I remember we used to sing a hymn at Miss Searl's school,' Tamsin told her earnestly, even forgetting Naomi, who made no attempt to add an opinion. 'I don't remember many of the words, but I know it was about 'you in your small corner and me in mine'. And it's there I want to make a difference. If every village, every parish, put in the right reforms, spent their money wisely, looked after their own, then on a broad base the problems would vanish.'

'Local Government, you mean? What have you there except men, men full of their own importance?'

'And here are three of them,' boomed Charles's voice as he preceded the other two into the room. 'As arrogant and bigoted as any, I dare say, but putty in your hands when you decide what you want of us. Wouldn't you say so, Naomi, my dear? What's it to be? Perhaps a rubber of bridge?'

'You see?' Lucinda took up his suggestion, but this time she laughed softly, her voice reminding Tamsin just why in her mind she had always likened it to brown velvet. 'What's it to be, he asks; then promptly tells us.'

'I appear to have lost my manners with my mobility. Forgive me. You don't care for bridge, Mrs Murray?'

'On the contrary, I enjoy it.'

At Naomi's enquiring look, James nodded his agreement and, more at home than the others, drew out what appeared to be an occasional table placed against the wall, then opened the top to expose its green baize.

'Can you two amuse yourselves?' Naomi gave Alex and Tamsin their freedom. 'Watch, if you like, of course: but I expect you'd rather see what music you can find on the phonograph. You know where everything is; look after your guest, Alex.'

So they found themselves in what was known, for want of any other description, as 'the den'. It was permanently comfortably untidy, a room where Naomi would leave whatever she'd been doing on the table, knowing it wouldn't be touched — be it sewing, letter-writing, marquetry (something at which she was particularly skilled), paying monthly accounts or trimming a hat. The fire was always lit first thing in the morning and kept banked up all day. A piece of furniture that had been created as a dumb waiter stood against one wall, an item made many years before the phonograph that stood on it complete with a box of cylinders.

'I never expected to feel grateful to your Mr Hardcastle, but we have him to thank for this. What would you like to hear? There are waltzes, a soprano who sounds too dreadful to be true — '

'Let's have waltzes. If we rolled the rug back, we could dance.'

Since she'd left Miss Searl's classroom, she had never danced, but the thought of being whirled around the room in Alex's arms was like a dream come true. But soon the reality held more wonder even than the dream.

Alex took her hand with an exaggerated bow.

They twirled to the tinkling music of the phonograph, and she felt as light as thistledown. Instead of the homeliness of Naomi's den, she was in a glittering ballroom in the arms of her lover; she wanted the moment never to end. At arms' length they moved delicately in the traditional style of the Viennese waltz until, without warning, she found herself pulled closer. Still they danced, but now his body was hard against hers; his cheek was rubbing against her head.

The music moved on without them, forgotten as surely as her imaginary ballroom.

'How could my shrimp have done this to me?' he whispered seriously, yet with that familiar teasing laugh only just beneath the surface. 'With a sweetheart for every day of the week, how could she have made me fall in love with her?'

She pulled her head away so that she could look up at him, her solemn eyes speaking to him as clearly as any words.

'Don't tease me, Alex.' Did he know just how much his words had meant to her?

'I'm not. I'm telling you the truth. We're not the same people as we were ten years ago, but it's because of those times we spent together as children that we recognised each other that day on the airfield.'

'It must have been Fate that made me see Mr Hardcastle's advertisement and persuade him to take me on. Tell me again, Alex, what you just said.'

'I'm in love with you. People would say we're too young — '

'I'm eighteen, now; I'm not too young to know. I think about you all the time, Alex. When I have to work in the evening, you don't know how hard it is to concentrate. All the time I write down what he tells me, I am listening, hoping the doorbell will ring and it'll be you coming to see whether I am free. You're the first person I think of when I wake up in the morning — '

'And you're the first for me, and the last at night.'

She wound her arms around his neck, then raised her face to his and felt his lips lightly kiss the corner of her mouth. She wanted more than that; she turned her head so that his mouth covered hers, and willingly parted her lips. She was drowning in uncharted waters. When she felt his hand on the small mound of her breast, another memory sprang into her mind, but only for a second. Immediately it was pushed out by something she had never known, an overwhelming hunger to be so close to him that they were one: one body, one soul. He wanted it, too. She moved against him in a silent message that was beyond any words she knew, a message of her recognition of and joy in his desire. The tinkling music had stopped, but they hadn't noticed.

Suddenly, they were brought back to reality by the sound of a crash from across the hall, followed immediately by voices: Naomi's, Lucinda's, James's. It was no ordinary crash. Their moment was gone.

'Don't try and move him,' they heard James say, as they rushed to see what had happened.

Charles Hardcastle lay sprawled on the

drawing room floor. The first thing they noticed was a gash on his forehead where he'd caught it on the corner of the card table as he'd fallen.

'He's knocked himself out.' Tamsin supposed he must have tripped.

'I think it's more than that. I'll go for the doctor; put a rug or something over him and see he stays warm. I'll be as quick as I can.'

'Bless you, James.' Naomi threw him a quick look of gratitude as she went off to fetch a rug.

Despite Lucinda's determination to fly her banner, the atmosphere around the dinner table had been congenial, and Tamsin had never seen Charles in such good spirits as he'd been at the prospect of a foursome for bridge. But the evening that had started so well was to have a very different ending.

Fortunately, Dr Boothby was at home when James reached his house by Oakleigh Green, so it was no more than a quarter of an hour before they heard the motor car returning up the drive. By that time, Charles had regained consciousness, although his only sounds were muffled moans of pain and despair.

'If you ladies will leave us, perhaps you'll be good enough to stay, Mr Proctor,' the doctor said, after no more than a cursory, 'Good evening'. As for Alex, he hovered undecided for a second and then followed the ladies.

The examination confirmed what Dr Boothby had feared at the first glance: Charles had broken his hip. The wound on his head would soon heal, but the hip was a very different proposition. For more than a year, he'd

116

alternately raged against and fought against his inability to walk as he had once been able; in the future he would be confined to bed or, at best, lifted out to sit in a chair.

The four waiting by the fire in the hall heard the verdict.

'Bed rest is the best we can do for him. Femur, tibia, ankle: if only he'd fallen in such a way that one of those had suffered the injury, then I could have set it and put him into splints. But a hip . . . no, I'm afraid the outlook is bleak.'

'Will bed rest help it to heal itself?' Naomi asked, with more hope than expectation.

'He is a fighter, but that would need a miracle. His only way to gain any sort of independence will be with the aid of crutches — and that not for some time and not without a great deal of pain for a man in his condition. The next thing is, how is he to be transported home? You have no telephone, I take it? Mr Proctor will drive me home and I will make a call to the hospital. But I fear it will be some time before they get the ambulance out here for him. A late night for you, my dear Miss Halliwell.'

'Never mind me. The poor man must be got to bed. I have a room with a bed aired.' Then, to Lucinda, 'I wasn't sure which was better to give you. Fourtunately, I had two rooms aired and we'll soon get a fire going in the grate.'

'We ought to ask him, Miss Halliwell.' Tamsin had come to know him very well in the eight months she'd been at Westwood House and the one thing he would never tolerate was anyone else doing his thinking for him.

117

'We'll ask him tomorrow. He's in no state to argue, tonight.' Lucinda had only met him that evening, but that didn't prevent her assuming control. 'How do we get him upstairs? Strap him onto a table leaf, perhaps?'

'I'll have a word with Proctor,' the doctor said. 'He lifted him for me, just now. I dare say, with this young man's help, he can carry him up the stairs.'

Tamsin looked at Alex with pride as he followed the doctor into the drawing room, those wonderful moments in the den alive in her mind as she saw his straight back and thought of the power in the arms that had held her. A moment later, the four men emerged: first Doctor Boothby, who went ahead up the wide, shallow stairs, followed by Charles, whose upper body was cradled by Alex and his legs by James.

Soon after that, Tamsin was driven back to Westwood House, this time by James.

'Thank you for bringing me. It's very kind of you to come out of your way.'

'What will you do, Miss Yelland? Are your parents due home soon? Alex has told me about their mission.'

'I think they expect to be home in the spring. But I don't live at the Manse any more. When my work for Mr Hardcastle finishes — and it was nearly finished, even before this evening — then I shall do something else.' Something else! Her heart sang. Desperately sorry for Charles though she was, this evening it was impossible for anything to dampen the joy that filled her. Alex loved her. He would be her future. He said they

118

were young — but they weren't too young to love. No matter how many other girls he spent his time with, it was *her* he loved.

'Well, don't worry tonight,' kind James was telling her. 'You have friends here; and I hope you look on me as one of them.'

'You're very kind.' But you don't know: I have a love, a precious love.

That evening saw a change that was to be far-reaching. Over the next two or three weeks, Mrs Jenkins continued to reign supreme at Westwood House, but now she had no master to serve, for he was still at Lambton and Barnes installed there to look after him. Tamsin was busy making a fair copy of her previous work, leaving gaps where he had marked so that there was space for the illustrator to work.

'Disgraceful!' Mrs Jenkins glowered at her underlings as if they were personally responsible for what she saw as 'that chit of a typewriting girl's' lack of morals. For how else could she think of her when she shut herself in that workroom every evening with her young man? Curtains closed (and she knew they were, because she'd made it her business to walk round the side of the house to see), door firmly shut. Disgraceful! And someone said her people were preachers! Instead of trying to teach those Africans how to walk the straight and narrow path, that mother of hers would be better spending her time at home keeping an eye on the little minx.

Tamsin had never been happier. With Charles away, it never occurred to her to shirk her work, but always at the top of her mind was the thought of the evening, the time Alex would come.

'This is nice,' he said as he drew her against him where they shared the single armchair by the fire in the workroom. 'Tammy, when your people come home, what do you say to my asking if I can take you off their hands?'

'You mean . . . ?' It was too wonderful to be put into words.

'You don't want me to go on bended knee to ask you, do you?' he laughed.

'You mean you want us to be married?' This time she managed it. 'You know what I'd say. Oh, Alex, I love you so that I can hardly think of anything else. Married. You and me, always together.'

'You're crying . . . '

'No, I'm not.' She smiled, seeing him through a haze of tears. 'It's just I'm so happy. I've prayed so hard for you to love me too. So happy.'

His mouth covered hers, he tasted the salt of her tears.

'As soon as they come home, I'll get their permission — '

'And if they won't give it, then we'll run away to that place in Scotland, Gretna Green.'

'I can't expect them to give it the moment they meet me.' Then, with a chuckle, as he planted more of a smack than a kiss on her forehead, 'I'll just have to work my irresistible charm on them. Then I'll buy you a ring. I'd like to have the money for the sort of diamond you deserve, something you'd be proud of.'

'I'd be proud of a curtain ring if you gave it to me.'

'Never change, Tammy: promise me you'll still say that when we're old and grey.'

It was wonderful beyond belief. The fact that she knew her mother would oppose their plans couldn't cast so much as a shadow; if Alex loved her, then nothing could stand between them. In the meantime, she wrote telling her parents — not that what *he* says can make any difference, she told herself, not admitting that it was he who coloured her mother's thinking.

I know because you disapprove of his mother you don't want me to be his friend. But, when you meet him, you will feel quite differently. He is an engineer at Proctor's Aeronautics and Mr Proctor thinks extremely highly of him. So highly that he has found him lodgings with a very good friend, Miss Naomi Halliwell, who lives in a very grand home and is also a friend of Mr Hardcastle. In fact, that's where we had been invited to dine when poor Mr Hardcastle fell and broke his hip. Alex is completely accepted in their circle, and Mr Proctor tells me he has great expectations of his future.

That should lay the foundations for her mother looking kindly on him! Each day she watched for the post — and each day she knew she was more in love with Alex. If her mother refused to give her consent, Tamsin would run away with him; they would defy everyone. But how could her mother fail to give her consent? She would fall under his spell, just as surely as everyone else did.

After that one letter, Tamsin decided not to write again until she had a reply. The weeks went by; no letter came. Arthur's period at the mission was due to end in May. If she didn't hear soon, there wouldn't be time enough for her to follow up her first letter with a second, either joyously happy that she'd not met an obstacle or using all her wit to bring her mother round to her side. It was just before Easter when Kitty came into the workroom. No timid knock, now that Charles was out of the way: indeed no knock at all.

'Here's a letter just come for you, Miss Yelland. Second post.'

'From Africa? Thanks, Kitty. I've been waiting — '

'Not the usual handwriting. I've got to know your Ma's hand.'

Taking the envelope, Tamsin immediately recognised the writing. It was a year since they'd left Brackleford . . . why should he write now, after so long?

Dear Tamsin,

It is my painful duty to tell you that your dear mother has been taken from me. I try to find solace in the sure knowledge that she is in better Hands than ours. Indeed, I pray with a full heart that I may be given the strength to carry on alone now that she has left my side.

The last year has not always been easy for her, although she took heart from the work she was able to do, the support she unfailingly gave me. I do not need to tell you where her own grief and loneliness lay: before we came, she begged you to forgo your own selfish pleasures for one short year and, had you felt able to sacrifice your comforts and your familiar surroundings, perhaps I would not now be robbed of my dear wife. For months, she has found the climate trying; the food has not agreed with her. I tried my utmost to sustain her; never for one day did I leave her in doubt of my need of her here with me. But the lack in her life was for a woman of her own sort to understand her physical hardships. I have no need to spell out to you who it was she pined for. Now it is too late. She had become a shadow of her former self, but her heart for her work never faltered.

Some ten days ago, weakened by an ongoing stomach upset and lack of food, she took a fever. The kindness shown to her here from the people we serve was certain evidence that our mission had not been in vain. Love for our fellow men and putting service to others before our own selfish wishes: that is the way of the road we have always striven to tread. I prayed constantly that she would not be taken from me. Now, I pray for acceptance of the Lord's will.

This will come as a shock to you. Had you done as she wanted and been here with her, you would have been aware of how over the months her strength had been failing. But she put the service of others before her own comfort. Heaven is her reward. I try to be thankful, for her sake, that the pain she was called on to endure is over. It is not easy.

You must be aware of my suffering. Before I knew her, I found complete satisfaction in the work that had been entrusted to me. Now I must find the strength to put these years behind me, to be the man I once was. But I know my own weakness; I know that to return to Brackleford alone would be too painful. So I shall remain out here. Perhaps all this has been the Lord's way of showing me the path He has set for me.

One day, perhaps, we shall meet again, but my vision cannot reach so far.

I remain your affectionate Father.

With the two sheets of paper on the table before her, she stared unseeingly into space. Mum ... not coming back ... dead ... snuffed out as suddenly as a flickering candle. A thousand memories crowded into her mind — and in not one of them did Arthur have a place. Her mother standing in front of the mirror, her head turning this way and that as she admired the effect of a freshly trimmed hat; the sound of her voice saying the name that only *she* ever used, 'Tamsie sweetling'. It was that that brought the scalding sting of tears to Tamsin's eyes.

* * *

As James had said to Tamsin, in Alex he saw much of himself at that age — keenness to learn,

124

keenness to move forward, always inspired by the excitement of flying and the vision that air was the transport of the future. But vision was powerless without knowledge and James was proving to be as good a teacher as he was a flyer. Most days, there were hours spent together in his drawing office where he was working on the design for a wider-winged variation of the model under present construction.

'You know the formula, so you work out the lift.' Something he'd already done himself, of course, but he meant Alex to move independently through each stage.

'Air density times square of the speed, area of the wing, lift coefficient for angle — ' Alex muttered, concentrating on the mathematics as he took his place at the desk, his whole mind focused. It was James who, rather than watch his work, wandered to the window.

'Something must be wrong . . . ' His voice cut across Alex's concentration.

'Where? That's the right formula — '

'No, not that. It's Tamsin. Something must have happened.'

At this time of day? There were two hours to go before the midday hooter. Alex came to James's side.

'Leave this,' James said. 'Go out and see her. And, Alex, don't rush her. This can wait until tomorrow.'

Reason told him she wouldn't have come here halfway through the morning without serious cause. But it was more than reason that made James so aware of her unhappiness.

5

'Something's the matter.' It wasn't a question: he knew it from her silence even if her eyes hadn't been sure evidence of recent tears. 'I'll get my bike and we'll go to the hill.'

'You can't. It's only about eleven. I just wanted to see you — to know — '

'Of course I can come. What's more important? You, or being ruled by the works hooter?'

This time, she smiled: not a smile that dented her cheek with that dimple, but at least one that for a moment banished her look of dejection. Better not to question her here; whatever it was that had upset her, she would hate to let the men in the workshop see how miserable she was. So, before she had time to answer him, he went to the shed where the bicycles were kept. He supposed Mr Hardcastle must have sent for her to tell her her job had come to an end, he knew she was well on with making a fair copy of the text and already an illustrator had been interviewed at Lambton. Alex was rarely angry but, as he imagined her being casually dismissed, despite having no home to go to, he felt a choking rage for the man Naomi Halliwell and his mother both seemed to think so much of. Indeed, he didn't imagine for a moment that it was on his own account that his mother had been back to the house on two occasions since her original visit when Charles Hardcastle had had his accident.

They didn't talk as they cycled the short distance to Hinds Hill where, just as they always did, they propped their bikes against a clump of gorse bushes and set off up the slope to the treed summit.

'You can read it.' She took the crumpled letter from her pocket and passed it to him when they reached the edge of the wood.

Whatever he'd expected, it wasn't this. Young though he'd been at the time, he remembered his dislike of the preacher who had called on his mother — a dislike that had magnified in his mind with the years.

Tamsin watched him as he read; she saw the way his mouth tightened into a hard line.

'I knew she wanted me to go with her,' she told him. 'Was just one year so much to ask? That's what she said. But I couldn't: not with him. I *couldn't*. Now he says that if I'd been with her — '

'The rotten sod,' half under his breath, Alex said. 'Don't you see, Tammy? He's trying to ease his own conscience by making you feel guilty. He's known for ages the place didn't suit her, he says so in the letter — or perhaps it wasn't even the place. Perhaps there was something wrong with her that needed proper medication, the sort of treatment she couldn't get out there. What sort of a man would put other people before his own wife? Anyway, you can't make me believe all those poor natives were overjoyed to have him breathing fire and brimstone at them. Oh, don't,

Tammy: darling Tammy, don't cry.'

His arms were warm and strong; he held her close.

'Didn't even know she wasn't happy there, that's what's so awful. Why couldn't she have told me, and told me she wasn't well? All she ever wrote about was how wonderful he was and how she tried to be good enough for him.'

'Perhaps that's the way she really felt about it all; perhaps she honestly couldn't see he was selfish. You're not on your own. You've got me. I wish she could have known about us.' All the same, a silent voice whispered to him, now there would be no one to stop them being together. For all his grand talk about working the magic of his charm on the unknown Mavis, it must surely be a lot easier to have the way clear for them.

'He said he forbade me to see you. She told me that the last time she wrote. As if I'd take any notice of what *he* said.' Although trembling sobs still caught in her throat, she laughed as she said it, clinging to him.

The ground was soft and damp from winter, but they were oblivious to it.

'Is he your legal guardian? Do I have to get his permission before we can be married?'

'No. I called him Father, but he was just Mum's husband. And I shall do what I like with my own life; I'm certainly not asking for his approval.' And, this time, her laugh had a sound of triumph about it. 'Not that he'd give it — not to you. You know what he said, when he came home from visiting your house in Tannery Lane? He said — ' and, with her mouth pulled in a

128

tight line and turning down at the corners, she mimicked Arthur's voice ' — 'There's just the woman and a child — a child whose red hair is a sign that he is already in the hands of the Devil.' ' She wriggled closer. Somehow, repeating Arthur's words made her more truly Alex's. 'Isn't it funny how you remember some things so clearly? I didn't know you then, but I felt you and your mother belonged to me simply because he disliked you so much. Then, the day you accused me of stealing the conkers from your tree — remember? — I knew who you were by the colour of your hair. Even though I was so angry at being accused of stealing, I was sure I wanted you to be my friend.'

'More than your friend, Tammy. All that's years ago: we were just kids. We're grown up, now. You're the woman I want to share my life with. It won't be the sort of ring I'd like to afford for you, but it would mean just the same. It would show everyone that, when we can, we shall get married.'

'I don't care what sort of a ring it is. I've told you that. An engagement ring is a symbol; it says that we want to be bound together.'

'I'll go back to the house and fetch my money, then we'll ride straight into Brackleford. There won't be time to have anything to eat; we'll have to live on love.'

Was it wicked to feel so happy, when that letter from her father was screwed up in her pocket?

★　★　★

129

Barnes brought the message from Lambton that Charles was coming home. It was as if Westwood House stood to attention at the prospect. With only twenty-four hours' notice of his arrival, the staff were thrown into a bustle of anticipation. Mrs Jenkins, secretly displeased that she would no longer reign supreme, insisted that the silverware must all be cleaned, the china in the cabinets washed. That Charles was to be confined to his own room made no difference; there must be no sign that she'd allowed things to become lax in his absence.

An ambulance had been engaged to transport Charles home.

From the morning room window, Tamsin watched for his arrival. Not many motor vehicles came through Oakleigh so, as soon as she heard one approaching she went to open the front door. Most days, she had cycled to Lambton to show him what she had done and to check that she had left gaps for illustrations in the right places but, apart from that, it had been up to her to organise her timetable as she liked. So she was surprised just how pleased she was to see him coming home. Often cantankerous (and more often than ever now, of that she was sure), but she was glad to think of him back in his own place, giving his own orders as to how his own home should be run. She hurried to open the gate wide for him to be carried in.

'I'll go ahead, Charles, make sure they have a clear passage.'

The 'brown velvet' voice!

'It's all quite clear, Mrs Murray. I've moved

the things on the landing out of the way.'

'Sensible child. You come ahead with me: show me which is his room so that I can see he'll have what he needs within reach.' On Barnes's account, Tamsin resented her authoritative tone; he'd been indispensable to Charles since the onset of his crippling arthritis! 'You wait and see he is carried carefully, Barnes.'

Tamsin led the way back through the house and up the wide, shallow stairs.

'It was kind of you to come with him, Mrs Murray.' Instinctively, she tried to rekindle the flame in the torch she'd carried for Lucinda Murray all those years. 'Miss Halliwell had an engagement, I suppose?'

'No, she was doing something to that vegetable plot she spends so much time on — digging, planting, I didn't enquire. Naturally, I came. It was I who made the arrangements for him to be brought home. Not that he wasn't well cared for at Lambton — Naomi is most generous with her hospitality. Indeed, I think she likes her house turned inside out to accommodate other people. Yes, his things seem well placed near the bed.' And with that, she focused her attention on Tamsin. 'Alexander tells me you have lost your mother. I'm sorry. She must have been a brave woman, a woman prepared to sacrifice her own comforts for something she believed in. Whether her beliefs were misguided is neither here nor there. And what about you, Tamsin? Have you given any thought to my suggestion? Your work for Charles is coming to an end; there's plenty for you to do in the cause of women's suffrage.'

'You haven't said anything about Alex and me.' Tamsin held out her left hand, displaying the ring with its chips of diamond around an opal. 'He must have told you we are going to get married.'

'He told me you had accepted his proposal. There is more to life, Tamsin. Don't rush into marriage without sampling something of the world. I don't mean partying, frivolous living — '

'In Oakleigh!' Tamsin laughed.

'The world exists outside Brackleford and Oakleigh. Come to London with me. Let me introduce you to women who see life as something more than knitting by the fireside, cleaning the step, cooking the food, bearing a brood of children inflicted on them to satisfy their man's carnal appetite.'

The pedestal rocked dangerously; any second, Lucinda would come crashing to the ground.

'I may be selfish, I may be stupid — that's what you probably think of me — but whatever I do with my life, the most important thing is that I share it with Alex. No one can know what is right for someone else. You didn't like being married; you've found your own salvation. Then there's Mum: I couldn't understand how she could bear to have Father for her husband, yet all she wanted was to know he was pleased with her. I thought that was wrong. But for her, perhaps it wasn't. You've made me see that what's right for one person wouldn't be right for another.'

'So you want to be like your mother, to devote your life to pandering to Alex's selfish whims.

You disappoint me, Tamsin.'

'Don't you want to think that I'm going to be your daughter?' As she said it, she seemed to hear her mother's voice warning her against 'that woman'. But that wasn't really her mother's own opinion: how could it have been, when the two of them had never even met? Her mother's satisfaction had come from being everything that *he* wanted, from echoing his thoughts, from 'pandering to his selfish whims' — that's what Lucinda Murray would say, and she'd be right.

'There is no one I'd rather have for a daughter. But I know Alex: I've seen it all before. He'll use you and he'll put himself first, just as his father did before him.'

'You're wrong. We'll prove to you just how wrong. And Alex isn't selfish, he's — '

'Never mind that, now; they're coming up the stairs with Charles. While I see he's comfortable, you go down and order tea. He and I will have it together.'

'Now who's pandering?' There was no smile in Tamsin's voice. 'He's used to getting his own way. He'll make circles around you.' She wasn't so much criticising Charles as wanting to hit out at Lucinda.

'Oh, no,' Lucinda laughed softly. 'No one will do that. But one thing I respect in a person is courage, and Charles has plenty of that. Run along down and tell them we'll have tea in ten minutes.'

Although she officially lived in a shared house in London, Lucinda had spent a good deal of time over the previous few weeks at Lambton.

133

Since Alex had finished school and taken his first job — fetching and carrying in an engineering works and determined to learn — they hadn't lived together, so he had no illusions that her frequent visits were on his account. Naomi welcomed her guest with her usual open-handed hospitality, just as she welcomed Charles. But if she harboured the idea that it was for her company that Lucinda came so frequently, she was to realise her mistake once Charles was back at Westwood House.

'It beats me,' Alex said to Tamsin. 'I thought she looked on men as her natural enemy put on this earth to thwart her.' The way he laughed as he said it showed that he might be amused by her behaviour, but he wasn't concerned.

That disappointed Tamsin. Despite the way Lucinda's pedestal rocked, it never managed to throw her to the ground. She wished Alex and his mother cared more for each other; it disappointed her that they didn't. They tolerated each other — probably they even understood each other — but, in some ways, that made their relationship harder to understand than if there had been open hostility.

'Mr Hardcastle has had the best guest bedroom given to her; he calls it 'Lucinda's room'. But, Alex, I'm glad she spends so much time there. You can tell there's nothing new in their liking each other's company; it must have been the same at Lambton.'

'However will the suffragettes manage?'

She didn't like the way he said it: as if he'd seen all her campaigning as a joke. 'Mr

134

Hardcastle respects what she does; he's behind her all the way.'

'Don't look so cross, Tammy. You know what I think? I think when people get so wrapped up in some commitment or other that they get filled with hate for people who don't agree with them, then they do more harm than good. If Mum wants to march about with a banner, good luck to her. Just so long as she doesn't want to lecture me on the injustices her sex have to suffer.' There was a twinkle in his eyes as he said it; Tamsin knew he was testing the ice, seeing which side of the fence she would jump. 'And you know what else I think?'

'No. But I know that you're going to tell me.' There was a smile in her voice; she was as surely under his spell now as she had been when they'd played together in Dylan's Wood. But there was a difference: then, they had been children. She felt the grip of his fingers on hers and found Lucinda's battles receding.

'I think — no, I know — that for you and me, all those things Mum gets so excited about are irrelevant. Never mind governments; never mind causes. We'll make our own lives.'

Standing in front of him, on the edge of the wood on Hinds Hill, she wrapped her arms around his neck; she pulled his head down towards hers. Her answer to what he said was in the way she parted her lips as his mouth found hers and, standing on just one foot, wrapped her other leg around his, pulling him nearer.

'Oh, Tammy . . . if only you knew . . . '

But she did know. His unfinished sentence

held all their longing, all their certainty, and all their need to find a full and joyous expression of the love that filled their hearts and minds.

'I do know, Alex,' she told him, her eyes wide and earnest. 'I want us to be together more than anything else in the world. Let's be married soon. Perhaps Miss Halliwell would let me come to Lambton: it's a huge house. I'd not get in her way and I think she quite likes me.'

'No. It's not what I want for you. We'll have our own home. Nothing much, to start with, but I'll work hard.'

'Perhaps one day Mr Proctor will make you his partner. Honestly, Alex. He has great expectations for you; he told me so himself.'

Alex pulled back a few inches, the better to see her expression. 'He did?'

'And I know he's right.' She caught her bottom lip between her teeth. 'Sometimes I'm so happy, so excited, so — so — *sure* about the future — that I'm frightened. If something happened, I think I'd die . . . '

'Don't say that.' He put his hand over her mouth. Then, in a characteristic change of mood, he took her hand. 'Come on, let's go to Lambton.'

'Does Miss Halliwell know you're bringing me?'

'She says you're always welcome. Anyway, it's my home.'

She loved his assured way of talking; she loved the purposeful way he set off down the hill; she loved . . . she loved everything about him on that glorious afternoon of early spring. Uninvited, the memory of Arthur sprang to her mind; she heard the echo of his voice telling her she should kneel and thank God for happiness beyond anything she deserved. His God? A god of vengeance who frowned on fun and had no compassion for sinners? Oh, no, that wasn't the God who had filled her heart with love. Just look around at the beautiful spring day, listen to the birds, feel the warmth of the first sunshine of spring. That was her God, and she *did* thank him with all her heart and she prayed she would always be everything that Alex wanted.

Another image, this time her mother. Hadn't that been all she'd wanted from life, just to know that she'd never failed her precious Arthur?

'Come on, what have you stopped for?'

'Just thinking,' she answered. And, in those thoughts, she took a giant step forward on the path of understanding.

At Lambton, they expected that on such a glorious Saturday afternoon they would find Naomi in her scarecrow garb, amusing herself in the garden. When there was no sign of her, they went indoors.

A note in her large bold writing greeted them from the hall table.

Alex, I told the staff they were free as soon as they'd cleared breakfast. Tomorrow being Mothering Sunday, we have to manage without them, so I thought they could make a whole weekend visit to their mothers — as I am myself to mine. You knew I wouldn't be here, but I ought to have thought sooner and

warned you you'd have to fend for yourself.
There's plenty of food in the larder. I shall be
home about teatime tomorrow. Naomi H.

'You didn't say she wouldn't be here.'

'Forgive me?' Confidence put a teasing note in
his voice. 'Of course you do.'

'Did you think I wouldn't have come?' Why
else should he have acted out that charade of
looking for Naomi in the garden? But, of course,
even he hadn't expected the house to be empty
of everyone.

'I was frightened to take a chance.'

Their voices seemed to echo in the stillness of
the house. No one would be coming . . . the
afternoon stretched ahead of them . . . the
evening stretched ahead of them . . .

'Let's find something to eat.' Food was the last
thing he wanted, but he needed to put a brake
on thoughts that were bounding out of hand. It
helped to concentrate on carving thin slices from
the cold beef he found, while she pulled the
kettle of warm water from the back of the range
and raked the fire that had been left banked up
to smoulder slowly. When they'd eaten, and
without waiting for the 'watched pot that refused
to boil', they went out into the garden.

But what were they doing, wandering hand in
hand across the lawn, admiring the army of
tulips that stood tall among blue swathes of
forget-me-knots, gazing at the early blossom on
the fruit trees, turning to Naomi's well-dug
kitchen garden? There was an unreal quality
about the afternoon.

'I feel like Alice in her wonderland — 'Tamsin knew he would understand what she was telling him — 'knowing there's a door waiting for me to turn its handle, calling to me; yet I don't know what I'll find . . . '

'You don't?' Even though he spoke so softly, she couldn't miss the urgency in the question as he turned her to face him.

'I want to be with you, close to you . . . I want . . . '

His mouth covered hers; through the cotton of her blouse she felt the warmth of his hand on the curve of her small breast. Instinct was her guide as she opened the fastening and drew him to her. For one brief instant, as his fingers found her hardened nipple, she remembered Arthur and her sick revulsion at what he had done. Now she could see beyond the closed door that beckoned her, she was moving towards it; every nerve in her body was alive.

They moved back towards the house, going in through the kitchen door. This time, even the sound of the kettle singing on the range didn't register with them.

'Ought I to feel guilty, as if I'm doing something bad?' she asked him as he led her up the stairs to his own room. 'I don't — and I'm not. I've never felt so right about anything.' Then, as he reached to turn the handle of his bedroom door. 'The door to our magic kingdom . . . '

'I do love you.' Abracadabra . . . open sesame . . . no magic words could have cast such a spell. There was something ritualistic in the way they took off their garments, not a frantic scramble. He was only slightly above average height, but his body was perfect, and he was strong. Again came the memory of Arthur, but it was almost as if the episode had happened to someone outside herself. Reason might have made her glad of the understanding she had gained; but reason had no part to play. As she and Alex faced each other, each knowing where they were heading and neither with the experience to know the way to their goal, the only thing to mar her total joy was regret for the failings of her thin frame. Briefly, she saw herself in the mirror: small breasts that seemed to her hardly to make her a woman at all, thin arms and legs. He was so perfect. With all those girls so eager to be his sweetheart, how could he possibly love *her*?

'My own shrimp.' He held his hands towards her.

Instinctively, she folded her arms across her small chest. She felt ashamed. All her life, her friends had been more robust than her. She'd been the last of her group to show even the smallest sign of puberty; one after another, her classmates had boasted in loud whispers when they'd first menstruated, but she had had to wait so long that when at last it had happened, her friends had long forgotten their pride in the event. So she had said nothing.

'I wish I was different.' He was so beautiful, his physique so magnificent. 'I wish I had a huge bosom and big hips; I wish — '

'No. I've imagined you like this; I've thought of you till I've gone crazy with longing to see

140

you, to touch you.' His hands were warm; they caressed and explored from her breast down her flat stomach, over her narrow hips. As they came to her groin, she felt his fingers; her eyes closed and she wanted these moments to last for ever. Of one accord, they moved towards the bed; with instinct, love and urgency guiding her, she found herself caressing him just as he was her.

'It's what you want? You're sure it's what you want?' he whispered, by now lying above her.

'Yes, oh, yes. I want us to love; I want us to be like one.'

'Help me, Tammy. It's my first time, too.'

All spoken in hushed voices, as if they were frightened of breaking the spell that bound them. His finger moved deep into her. Surely it must be easy. She was small; she was a virgin. Nothing was easy. For one moment, he wondered how any young girl could possibly be raped! Then at last he entered her.

Lying beneath him, she felt she was being torn apart, and yet she exulted in the pain.

'I'm hurting you,' he panted.

'No, yes, no. I love you so much.'

It was too much for Alex. He'd brought her up to the bedroom with wild pictures in his mind of lovemaking that would last all the afternoon, all the evening, every wonderful minute they were alone. Now, in a wild frenzy of abandonment he reached his climax.

'I hurt you,' he breathed. 'I didn't want to hurt you. Tammy, you're crying.'

She gritted her teeth hard together, as if that would stem the tears that rolled down her face.

'Not crying,' she gulped. 'Just so happy, so happy I can't think straight. Not crying.'

He held her close. He longed for the words to tell her what these moments had meant to him. With a string of eager girls ready to be his sweetheart, with all the private knowledge he had of his own body, with all the dreams, there had been nothing to compare with what he had shared with Tamsin.

But had he shared?

She wept for joy, but she hadn't experienced that wonderful moment of release that had been his, something different from anything he had ever known. Often, alone in the privacy of his bed, drifting into sleep, waking in the night, or half roused in the early dawn, he would follow the needs of his healthy young body; he would find release from the clamour of his desire, but always to be faced with cold and lonely reality. This time, he had been buried in the loving warmth of Tamsin's body, and he had heard those words: 'I love you so much.'

'I never dreamt it could be like that ... wonderful ... ' He laughed; she heard something of his usual spirit returning with his breath. 'Feel weak as a kitten. Want to be strong. Want to love you again — and again — and again. But look at me! Delilah.' His eyes were closing.

Pulling the counterpane over them, she held him in her arms.

* * *

142

His strength returned. Before the hour when, each day from Monday to Friday, the hooter would sound at Proctor's, he had rallied. If he were frightened that the second time couldn't compare with the first, he need have had no fears. There was a difference, but that difference was in Tamsin. If anyone had mentioned the word orgasm, she wouldn't have known what they meant; but then she wasn't guided by words, simply by instinct and by a driving force that drew her towards something, she knew not what. Beneath him, she thrashed and strained, pulling him nearer, nearer. She wanted to shout — perhaps she did shout — she seemed to be lifted out of herself, transported to some wonderland shared just with him.

'Couldn't have stopped.' No tears this time: rather a breathless laugh as they collapsed side by side. 'If King George himself had walked into the room — couldn't have stopped.'

'Nor me.' He gasped for breath. 'When God made — ' another gasp ' — men and women — ' and another ' — He knew what He was doing.'

She wrapped her arms and legs around him, glorying in the nearness, the intimacy. It went far deeper than his physical presence; it brought home to her how alone she had been until he'd come back into her life. Always? It was a long time since she'd consciously been aware of those distant days, days that in retrospect seemed always to be warm — whether from the sun or the comfort of the hearth. 'That's the way, my duckie,' came the echo of that voice from long ago.

'What are you thinking? Why are you smiling?' His tone implied that he knew the answer.

'Not about *you*,' she chuckled softly. 'I was about four years old, helping my grandfather in the field. But perhaps I was thinking about you, too. Being with him gave me the sort of warm, complete feeling I have now — us being together. I'd forgotten it. Not excitement, not even joy — just, oh, I don't know, but it must be how a cat feels when it stretches as it lies on the hearthrug, purring without seeming to wake.'

★   ★   ★

Convention demanded that she be back at Westwood House in time for their evening meal. She had no feeling of guilt about what had happened, but being home late would entail questions, lies, excuses: somehow casting a shadow over their precious hours.

The next day was Sunday, a day when often Tamsin was expected to work. But this weekend, Lucinda was occupying Charles's time, so she was free. Any other Sunday when she'd managed to escape, she and Alex had looked for nothing beyond a wintry cycle ride. But their relationship had moved on; Lambton was empty and waiting for them. After yesterday's sunshine, the fickle weather had changed; Tamsin had battled against the wind as she'd ridden from the village, the threatening clouds scudding across the sky. Since then, the rain lashing against the window had only seemed to emphasise the warmth and intimacy of where they were.

144

'Hark,' Tamsin whispered. 'Isn't that someone downstairs?'

That was the first moment that guilt had cast a shadow. They lay very still, hardly breathing, as they listened. Yes, someone was coming up the stairs.

'Alexander? Are you home?'

Naomi!

'I got soaked,' he shouted. 'I'm having to change my things.'

Naomi's brows puckered into a puzzled frown.

Making as much noise as he could as he opened and closed drawers, he dressed while Tamsin lay very still, the covers drawn almost over her head.

'I'll get her to the kitchen, grind some coffee for a drink,' he whispered, with his mouth almost to her ear; then with his irrepressible grin, added, 'that'll make a row. I'll keep her talking so that you can dress and creep off. She'll never know you've been.'

Slamming the bedroom door behind him, he went down the stairs, whistling jauntily.

'Did you have a good time?' Tamsin heard him call to Naomi as he reached the hall. 'I got soaked — and perished. Can I make us some coffee? Let's go in the kitchen; I haven't done the fire in the drawing room yet. My next job — honest!' With that laugh that she could never resist.

Silently, Tamsin pulled on her clothes, then opened the door a fraction to listen. Yes, they were in the kitchen. If she carried her shoes, she could go out through the side door. But she'd

145

have to pass the kitchen window to reach her bicycle! Bent nearly double and pressed close to the wall of the house, she managed to avoid being seen. She felt cheap, soiled. Naomi had always been good to her, made her welcome. Now she'd abused Naomi's hospitality and cheated her. For she had no illusions; she knew that if it were known how she and Alex had used the empty house she would never be invited to Lambton again — and probably he'd be turned out, too! She knew how Naomi, Lucinda, Charles — and James? But what had he to do with it? — would see it. How dare they? What did any of them know of the miracle of loving with all your heart and soul? Naomi, a spinster whose world was Lambton, where she'd been born; Lucinda, whose views on marriage were warped; Charles, whose heart was given to the study of flowers and who was embittered by physical restrictions; James? She believed Alex had said that ages ago he'd been married but his wife had died. But, in her present mood, James was victim of her anger as surely as the other three. And Mother? No, don't think about Mother. She must have known about love, but she would still have been disgusted. Yes, but that was because of *him*, because of his priggish, sanctimonious, self-righteous . . . Anger needed a target, and who better?

The wind gusted, speeding her on her way, while the rain lashed. She didn't want to imagine Alex, sitting in the warm kitchen of Lambton, drinking coffee with Naomi, probably telling her some concocted story of how he'd spent the time she'd been away, smiling at her, charming her . . . That wasn't *her* Alex.

In fact, at the same moment that Tamsin leant her bicycle against the inside wall of the coach house (with stealth that almost equalled her and Alex's), Naomi was checking in her own coach-house-cum-garage, where Albert Higgs — her one-time coachman, now turned chauffeur — was leathering the Renault.

'Still busy?' Like a child caught with her hand in the sweet jar, she spoke with exaggerated jollity. 'That motor car never lacks attention.'

'That it doesn't, ma'am. Real little beauty, she is. Were you wanting me for something? Somewhere else you need taking?'

'No. I just thought you might still be here. There's hot coffee in the jug on the range; I'm sure you can do with it.'

'I'll not be above five minutes, ma'am. And I'll do the scuttles, see they don't run low, with Edith off home to see her ma.'

But Naomi had had a very different reason for looking in the coach house. When she'd arrived home, two bicycles had been propped against the wall. Now there was one: just Alex's.

'Did Tamsin have to work this morning?' she asked as she went back into the house. 'Poor child, the first Mothering Sunday with no mother to go and see, or send a greeting to.'

'No. My mother's staying at Westwood House, this weekend, so Tamsin was off her lead. We did set out for a ride; she wanted to see if there were any primroses still out in Farley Woods. The rain started so suddenly we scurried for home — but,

147

of course, I had further to come than she did. That's how I got so wet. I've brought my trousers down and hung them over the guard at the range.' No need to tell her that they'd been made wet from the water in the washstand jug in his room.

And she said nothing. No need to remind him that there were no wet wheel marks leading to where his dry machine was propped against the wall, any more than there was to mention that where there had been two bicycles now there was only one. That poor child would get soaking wet pedalling back to Westwood House.

★ ★ ★

On that Sunday morning, both Alex and Tamsin had known that their relationship had moved on and would never be quite the same. But time alone was inevitably time out in the open, with the brief spell of spring weather gone.

'James Proctor had me in his office when we were just going home, last night,' he told her as they they walked up Hinds Hill the following weekend. 'You were right, Tammy — you know, what you said about him having great expectations for me. Well, I knew it really; at least, I knew he'd always been pleased with my work and had been keen to explain things — talk things over, you know.' If he spoke to impress, then he succeeded. Wide-eyed with admiration she gazed at him. 'I'm to have my own office, right next to his. There's a drawing desk and somewhere for me to sit and work. You understand, there is a lot of mathematics in aeronautical engineering.'

'More than just sums, you mean?'

'Sums!' he scoffed. 'Mathematics is something apart from that: you work on mathematical formulas — formulae,' he corrected himself. 'He's taught me such a lot: probably as much as he ever learnt at college. And he trusts me. For ages he's been talking about the designs to me, then getting me to work things out. Just testing me, I expect, making sure I got the same answers as he did himself. Anyway, I was telling you, I've got this room right next to his: there's even a communicating door. He used to use it as a storeroom. As from Monday, it's to be mine. Of course, I shall still need to be on the workshop floor some of the time, just like he is, making sure things are right.'

'Alex.' She gripped his hand. 'I'm so proud. Didn't I tell you, one day he'll make you a partner? I bet you my best Sunday bonnet to a penny that's what he means to do.'

'Since when have you worn a bonnet?' he chuckled.

'That's what I remember — what was her name? I can see her so clearly — Trudie someone, I can't remember her surname — she used to help at Gorsemoor, when I was little. That was what I remember she used to say. Just you see: in a few years' time it will be Proctor and Murray.'

'It will, Tammy. I'll work so hard, we'll have a home as good as Lambton, one of these days.'

'It must be grand to know you are good at

something, that someone has expectations for you.' There was a note of wistfulness in her voice as she remembered the battles she'd had to fight to overcome her own inability simply to type what Charles Hardcastle had dictated.

He drew her close, but not so close that she couldn't read his teasing expression.

'You want me to tell you what you're good at, is that it? If this ground wasn't so ruddy wet . . . Sometimes I've seen chaps from work talking to their wives, then I've thought of you. Shrimp, did I call you? You're like a volcano waiting to erupt, like an earthquake that shakes my whole world. Those poor devils with their humdrum women — they can't know — '

'Oh, yes, they can. Love has nothing to do with volcanoes or earthquakes. They'd see me as a shrimp; I couldn't be a volcano or an earthquake or even a summer storm with anyone else.' She moved her mouth on his.

'You don't know what you're doing to me.'

'Oh, but I do. I want the same as you do. Let's be married soon, Alex.'

'Of course we will. I wish Miss Halliwell would take herself off again to see that old mother of hers. But, Tammy, I mean to make James Proctor see he's backing the right horse with me. There's so much I want to learn. But he's keen to help me. One of these days I shall be his equal, you see if I'm not. I have a key to the works now. See.' He dug in his pocket and brought it out to show her — as if she didn't know what a key looked like! 'I can work as late as I like. Of course, sometimes he's there, too.

150

But not always. Some evenings you could be there with me; we'd have the place to ourselves.'

Of course she was pleased at the prospect; of course she was proud of his promotion, and never doubted that James Proctor's confidence in him was merited; of course she was excited at the outlook of success that lay ahead of him. She wouldn't let him guess that her happiness would have been complete if he'd told her he'd find them rooms, somewhere where they could start a proper life together. That was being small-minded. He was right in wanting to put his career first. She must do the same and when Charles Hardcastle told her he had no more need of her — as he must do very soon — she would find something else. She'd had a year's experience; she was much more employable than she had been when he'd taken a chance with her. If they both worked and saved . . . her thought trailed off. Working and saving might be prudent, but what she wanted, she wanted *now*.

'Listen, Tammy. That's only part of what I have to tell you. There are flying displays planned for various places along the south coast. James Proctor is taking part, flying our Farley Moth and he is taking me with him — taking part, I mean. Between now and the end of the month when we go, he's going to spend as much time as he can in giving me instruction, but I don't expect I'll get a chance to actually fly the plane during the display. Just think, though, Tammy: going with him, being able to take an aeroplane up. It's the way forward. You wait ten years and you'll see flying won't be looked on as something that only interests a few men who people look on as some sort of cranks. Each year, there'll be more — and each year they'll fly faster, and higher too. We're working on an alteration in the wingspan — but I can't try and explain. You wouldn't understand.'

★   ★   ★

It was the last week in April. With no more typing to do, she was putting the books in order on the shelves in the workroom, when Barnes brought the message down that Charles wanted to see her.

She found him in the armchair by his bedside, supported by cushions and with the finished typescript on a small table in front of him.

'Well, my dear,' he spoke with unusual kindness, 'that about ties up the job you've done for me. Perhaps I've not always shown it, but I've been pleased with the effort you put into what you did. Couldn't have been easy for you, especially on that typing machine. But you had spunk, I'll say that for you.'

Tamsin smiled, the sort of broad smile that showed her dimple. Her reaction made his task easier; perhaps it meant that she already had another position in mind.

'I made a lot of bloomers — not *your* sort of bloomers,' she laughed. 'You were more patient than a lot of employers would have been,' she conceded.

'Look around for something else. But as long as I know you're looking, I shan't put you out on the street. Not with things as they are in your family.' Not the most tactful way of offering her a roof, but through the year she'd come to know him too well to be offended by it.

'I shan't be looking for another post, Mr Hardcastle,' she told him. 'You see, Alex and I are going to be married. I'm not sure of the exact date, but it will be very soon. Probably towards the end of May.'

'Well, I'm damned! Lucinda was here only a few days ago; she didn't give a hint.'

'That's because she didn't know. I mean, she knows we are going to be married, but she doesn't know just when. Alex is going away tomorrow. He and Mr Proctor are taking their flying machine to perform in various displays.' What pride in her young voice. For one moment, the life-hardened Charles felt frightened for her, tying herself up to a young man who risked his neck like Alex Murray seemed intent on doing. 'I'm seeing him this evening and, after that, we shall have a date fixed.'

'Can't think what all the secrecy is about, why the lad couldn't have told his plans to his own mother. Just like his father, that's what she says. I hope you know what you're taking on.'

Again that smile as she nodded. Oh, yes, she knew exactly. She'd been a little more certain each day for the past three weeks but, as her periods had never come with clockwork regularity, she had decided to wait until she missed the second one before she told Alex. It seemed to her like fate that Charles should have given her notice the very day before Alex was

153

due to go away for a fortnight. Tonight, she'd tell him; they'd make their plans then, while he was away, she'd go and see the vicar so that he could start calling the banns and she could look around for somewhere for them to rent. Perhaps fate would be kind again; perhaps there would be an empty cottage. But even a bedsitting room would do while they looked for something better. Tamsin wouldn't give space in her mind for even a hint of a cloud.

*　*　*

'Try and see it from my point of view. Everything is just falling into place for me. This is the worst possible time to start thinking about a family.'

'It wasn't the worst possible time to think of going to bed together!'

She couldn't believe it was happening. She'd cycled to the airfield as soon as she'd known the hooter would have sounded, just as she'd arranged with Alex. Except for his bicycle, the shed had been empty; everyone had gone home. There was no sign of James Proctor's motor car.

'Tammy, don't sound like that. Of course I want us to be married, but it's just not possible. A baby! Oh, dammit, why was I such a fool? Listen, I may be able to find a way out.'

'What do you mean? A way out?'

'Before I went to live at Lambton, I was boarding with a couple who had two grown-up children, a daughter who was married and a son a couple of years older than me. When they found the wife was pregnant, they were in a real

154

stew — the son told me. He was sent to the chemist to buy some concoction. I don't know what it was, but it did the trick. I hate to think of you like it — this stuff made her really ill — but it did the trick and she was prepared to put up with all the . . . well, stomach upsets, you know what I mean, just to get shot of it.'

'I don't believe it! It's a child you're talking about. Our child.'

'Don't look at me like that. Tammy, if it, were, say, next year, then it would be different. We would have something behind us. We can't start marriage like this, rushed into it before we're ready, living in some poky room, probably with a baby yelling. And just when I'm starting to get somewhere here.' He took her shoulders in his hands and drew her towards him, genuinely surprised at the way she pulled away. 'Try and understand, Tammy. Be rational. I'll go and see Bert Lee, this chap I told you about. I'll get the stuff. If I go tonight, I'll have to make some excuse to James Proctor, tell him there's something I have to attend to before we leave tomorrow. I hate to think you'll be so ill while I'm away — because Mrs Lee was really rough, I remember, but she took it in her stride, just thankful that it worked. Think of when I get home, though; it'll all be over. Everything will be right again. And old Hardcastle will just think you've got a stomach upset. No one need know. You've not told my mother, have you?'

'It's *you* I shouldn't have told. I don't want your filthy stuff. Don't touch me!'

'That's not fair. Tamsin, one day we'll be ready

to be married and have a family. You'll be glad we've got rid of this one. Think of that weekend. All right, we were silly: we shouldn't have let it happen. But it *had* to happen, you know that as well as I do. And when we're married — another year or so — we'll start afresh; it will always be like that.'

'Oh, no, it won't. Don't touch me! I told you, don't touch me!' She pulled her ring off her finger and threw it onto the desk he was so proud of.

'But what are you going to do? You're all on your own — '

'No, I'm not. You may be on your own, but I have the baby. *My* baby. And I don't need your help in deciding what I do.'

More hurt than she'd ever known possible, more angry than she'd ever been, she turned and left him, slamming the door behind her.

Had she been more rational, she might have noticed as she took her bicycle from where she'd propped it that she'd been mistaken in thinking James's car wasn't there; in fact, it was parked behind the works building.

156

6

He couldn't have meant it! Or was it all those other things he'd said to her that he hadn't meant? Her mind was numb with misery. She couldn't think coherently as she pedalled back towards the village.

'I thought I heard you come in.' Kitty appeared from the stairs leading to the kitchen quarters. 'We wasn't expecting you, Miss. I'll tell Mrs Jenkins you'll be wanting your dinner, shall I?' Then, imagining the mood it would put 'the old tartar' (as she silently called her) in for the rest of the evening, she asked hopefully, 'Or would you have had something to eat wherever you've been off to?'

Tamsin didn't want food; she just wanted to crawl away, to sleep and then wake up to find it had all been a horrible dream. But her fighting spirit was returning and with it her reason: if she didn't eat properly, she wouldn't be able to plan — and, even more important, whatever she decided she needed the strength to carry out.

'No Kitty, I've not eaten. What about Mr Hardcastle and Barnes? Have you taken theirs up?'

'That Mrs Murray's turned up again. Barnes, he's been given his marching orders from the master's room; he's along with us in the kitchen. She's up there, see.'

'I'll just have mine on a tray in the workroom.

157

I've a lot of things I want to see to.'

But it wasn't true, she thought, as she went into the room that had become so familiar to her through the past year. She had nothing to do . . . nothing. The future had no shape. She had to go from Oakleigh. She couldn't look for another post, not with a baby coming: but she must. She had to earn enough money to live on. Who would employ her when it began to show that she was pregnant, and what sort of work could she do when she had a baby to care for?

Out of the past came the echo of Alex's voice, words she'd not thought of from the day she'd first seen him on the airfield until now: 'S'truth, the shrimp a working woman! What are you doing, a children's nursemaid?' Perhaps she'd find a place where they'd take her with a baby of her own. Oh, but what woman would do that? What woman with a husband, a comfortable home and enough money to employ staff would take a single girl with an illegitimate child into her home? Tamsin's eyes stung with hot tears she wouldn't shed. If society looked down on her, she didn't care; but her baby mustn't suffer their slings and arrows. It wasn't the baby's fault. A little boy, perhaps, a little boy with red curls — 'a sign that the Devil has marked him out' came another echo, one that brought alive so many memories.

'There you are, Miss. The best of it had been doled out, but I brought you plenty of veg and a big helping of Mrs Jenkins's rhubarb flan. She makes a lovely flan, does Mrs Jenkins. Some days she can be in a mood fit to frighten old Nick

158

himself, yet her pastry comes out like fairy food, light as a feather.'

'Thank you, Kitty. I shall miss you when I leave.'

'You're not leaving, Miss?'

'I only came to do the typing for Mr Hardcastle's book. It's finished now, as far as my part goes.'

'You got another place? Not my business, but I've liked having you in the house, sort of someone my own age, like. Not that I'm educated, and all that, but we been what I call comfy together.'

Tamsin smiled warmly at poor, frightened Kitty. 'I've one or two things in mind. But I haven't made any decision, yet.'

Kitty giggled nervously. 'I been expecting to hear you and that handsome Mr Murray would be making a match of it. He's full of it, charm and all that. You'll be taking a place near Oakleigh, Miss? I know I would; I'd not lose tags on him.' Then, her face colouring at the sound of her own impertinence, she added 'Well, I must be getting back downstairs or it'll be me looking for somewhere else — and without a reference from the old tartar, too.'

Left alone, Tamsin attacked her food, surprised to find how much a plate of beef stew, without much meat but backed up with plenty of potatoes and carrots, could bolster her determination and clear her mind. She'd go to bed early; she'd put an end to the day. A new day would be a new beginning. Tomorrow, Alex would be flying south to somewhere on the coast. She would see the machine go overhead — no, don't think of Alex, don't let yourself remember. Go to bed, draw a line under everything, good and bad alike.

But it wasn't as easy as that. Lying in the dark, one bed was much the same as another: hers the same as his where she'd lain in his arms, where surely, surely, everything had been as wonderful and as *right* for him as it had for her. She pulled her mind away from him and tried to steer it forward. A little boy with red curls . . . but, almost immediately, he was pushed out by another image, this time of a girl. Small, so fair her hair had hardly any colour . . . half asleep and half awake, she and the child became as one. Not surprisingly, for the image was herself, moments that had lain dormant and forgotten. Feeling as proud as a queen, she had sat by her grandfather's side as they rode to Ringwood Market, their wagon loaded up with fruit and vegetables and, large in her young mind, with eggs from her very own bantams. She knew again the wonder of that early summer day when she'd been four, she could hear her mother's voice telling her that she must remember to keep her hat on because of the sun. And the feel of the pennies she earned from selling the eggs as she jiggled them between her fingers in her pinafore pocket.

'Was I a help, Grandpa?'

'My word, but you were, my duckie; see how fast we got cleared up.' The journey home was lost to her, all except the feeling of snuggling close to him, tired and satisfied.

More asleep than awake Tamsin may have been, but she frowned as memory carried her forward. Dressed in her best frock and hat, she was in the village hall further up the lane beyond Gorsemoor; the hall set out with rows of chairs and already crowded when she and her mother had arrived. It hadn't entered her young head to wonder how it was that two seats had been kept for them at the front. From the platform, Arthur Hillbright had talked for what had seemed like hours. That evening was the first time she'd seen him, but she'd felt uneasy about him; there was something in the way her mother had spoken to him and looked at him that made her uncomfortable. Then there was the one silver coin she'd brought home amongst her coppers, a Joey. She remembered how she'd rubbed it with a duster to make it shine. Her mother had said that it would be wicked to keep all her money for herself when there were so many children who had no parents and lived in the orphanage the preacher had talked about. Dropping the Joey and her few coppers in the plate had been the hardest thing she'd ever done, but she'd known that if she'd said she didn't want to part with her treasures, her mother would have been disappointed in her.

She didn't want to think about that evening. It led to all the other times the preacher had come to the house; it led to the utter misery she'd known when her grandfather was ill and nothing was the same any more; it led to the yard being empty of animals —

The yard, Snowy the sow, the chicken, her

161

own bantams — and the field, think about the field and the warm, secure, feeling of working there, following Grandpa, trying to do what he did, so sure of his, 'That's the way, my duckie,' or 'Where's my little helper, then? Are you coming to give me a hand today?'

Her pillow was wet with tears she could no longer hold back. If only he were still there; if only she could go back to Gorsemoor. He would understand that she was having a baby because she had loved with all her heart; he would say, 'That's the way, my duckie, you come home to your old grandpa . . . ' She stuffed the corner of the pillow into her mouth and clenched her teeth to stifle the sobs that welled up in her.

★ ★ ★

'Come to my room. I want to talk to you.'

Alex turned from the window where he'd been watching Tamsin ride away. James had startled him, partly because he hadn't known he was in the building and partly by the unfamiliar anger in his voice.

'Yes, of course. I'll come now.'

He followed James into the adjoining room, trying to pull his thoughts away from Tamsin and on to tomorrow's trip. Why couldn't she have seen the sense of what he'd suggested? Another year, and he'd be in a better position to take a wife. Wife . . . Tammy, his wife. He'd wanted that as much as she had. Those things she'd said, the way she'd pushed him away: she couldn't really feel like that. More than anything, he wanted

162

always to be with her — but not living in some poky room with a baby, never having enough money to buy the things they needed, seeing Tammy getting tired and worried. That's why it was he'd wanted her to take that stuff Bert Lee had collected for his mother. Why couldn't she be reasonable, put herself in his place? He hadn't worked and studied with James Proctor to throw it all away, just when everything was going so well.

'These walls are thin, so whether you consider it my business or not is immaterial.' James's blue eyes were cold as steel.

'You mean, you heard? But what else could I say to her? I can't afford to make a home for a wife and child.'

'You sicken me.'

It took all Alex's courage to look squarely at James, to read contempt where in the past there had always been encouragement. He swallowed an Adam's apple that was suddenly too large for the space allotted to it. In James's expression, he saw the shattering of all his own hopes and ambitions. If only he and Tamsin had met somewhere else, this evening. Too late for regrets; too late for recriminations; too late for hope . . .

'So you tell me how I can afford to get married?' It was disappointment and fear that made him aggressive, his voice raised.

'And how do you think Tamsin will afford to make a home for a child — *your* child?'

'It wasn't the way I meant it to be. She ought to have done as I said — '

'Have you no conception of what you were asking? Some filthy potion to poison the child she carries: perhaps to get rid of it, perhaps to bring it into the world malformed? How do you know — or me, either? None of us knows the effect of an illegal concoction some back-street apothecary might be persuaded to mix to get you out of a hole.' James sat in the seat behind his desk, looking up at Alex standing uncomfortably before it. 'Has Tamsin any family, other than a stepfather overseas?'

'Don't think so,' Alex mumbled. 'No one in Brackleford, anyway. They came from Hampshire; she told me about a place called Gorsemoor, somewhere near Ringwood. There may be family down there, but she never mentioned them.'

'Get a chair and sit down. We can't leave things like this.'

'I was a fool — but what happened wasn't just my doing. I didn't force her. Didn't even have to persuade — '

'I don't want to hear!'

Alex felt that everything he said drove another nail in the coffin of that golden future he'd been so sure of.

'I shall go alone tomor — ' James started.

'But — '

'You've more important things to do here. I can't force you to marry her. In fact, after the way you're prepared to treat her, I wonder if she wouldn't be better off without you. But her child will need a father.' He paused, but Alex knew better than to interrupt; he was sure there was more to follow, but suspected it could be nothing to improve his situation. 'That cottage beyond the airfield belongs to me. When I bought this land to have the works built, the cottage was part of the freehold. It's not been lived in since before the turn of the century; I've not looked inside it for years, but I'm sure there's a lot needing to be done before it's a suitable home to take her to.'

'You mean, you'd rent it to me? You've got enough faith in me to do that? I promise you won't regret it.' Such an offer was hardly in keeping with James's unsmiling countenance, but what else could it mean?

'I'm not making the suggestion on your account, Murray. I'm thinking of Tamsin — and the child.' He took a key from the drawer of his desk. 'Get your cap. We'll go across and look at it before it's too dark.'

'Right.' Then, with a grin that was sure evidence that his confidence was returning, 'She pitched my ring back at me. I'll collect that, too. In the morning I'll go and get her, bring her over to see the cottage. I say, this is jolly good of you. What sort of rent will you be asking?'

'Five shillings a week. Your wage will be increased by ten shillings. More than you're worth, at the moment, but I mean to see you earn it.'

Alex's mouth dropped open in sheer amazement. 'I say — I don't know what to say — how to thank you. You don't know what a weight you've taken off my mind.'

With his brows raised, James looked at him. 'Your mind? I should have thought the mind

165

weighed down with worry would be Tamsin's. On one thing I want your word: none of what's passed between us this evening is to go beyond the two of us. And, most importantly, she's not to suspect that I heard the way you treated her. Now, that said, let's get across the field and look at the cottage.'

Alex felt like a small boy who'd been let off with a caution lighter than his misdeed deserved. That did his pride no good at all; especially as he couldn't be sure whether James's action was out of interest in his career or Tamsin's future.

★   ★   ★

The house was silent. Packing her bag without breaking that silence made it a slow job. Tamsin was grateful that the heavy winter curtains hadn't been replaced yet, so at least if anyone chanced to look out into the night from another window no light would show from her candle.

Everything done and a note to Charles Hardcastle written, she snuffed out the light and groped her way to her door. Then, with a case in one hand and a large straw basket in the other, she crept down the familiar flight of stairs. In the hall, she put her note on the table, then tiptoed along the passage to the side door — this was the quietest to close — where she stopped to put on the shoes she'd carried in the top of her basket. Next, she had to collect her bicycle.

She was out, alone in the night, alone in the world. No, not alone. Another human being would be her responsibility: hers to love, hers to

166

share her life with. Just keep thinking of that. And Alex? No. All that was over; he hadn't loved her enough to trust their future together. He's a coward, frightened to take responsibility. I'm going to be better off without him — I *am* better off without him.

She had a long walk ahead of her, it was seven miles to Brackleford. Beyond that, she couldn't see through the haze. There would be plenty of time to think, though; seven miles pushing a bicycle with a case balanced on the saddle and one hand managing the straw bag and the grip on the handlebar would take her beyond first light.

Help me, please help me see what I have to do. I've not spent much money since I've been with Mr Hardcastle; as long as I can find somewhere to live, I can manage until I find another post. And then what? Then what? Help me, please. Are You punishing me for being selfish, like Mum thought? But you understood. You helped me get the place with Mr Hardcastle. But that was nothing of a hurdle like the one I've got now. I could probably get work in Brackleford, but I'm not going to try. Too many people know Father. I'm not ashamed, but I'm not going to have him hear about the baby and say the wicked, hateful things I'm sure he would. There are trains from Brackleford; I could go to Reading — or London. You can get lost in a big city, no one would know me. No one. Please, help me: help me find the right place to go.

* * *

167

''Scuse me, sir — m'um — ' It was about half past nine when Kitty made her timid appearance in Charles's bedroom doorway. 'Mr Murray has come looking for Miss Yelland. He looks in a pother — I didn't like to tell him she'd gone off. What had I better do with him, m'um?' After all, Mrs Murray was his mother; it was up to her to smooth his feathers.

'Bring him up here,' Charles ordered as Lucinda rose from the bedside chair as if she meant to follow Kitty down. 'I mean to get to the bottom of it.'

'She's a free agent, Charles. You know what I believe is behind her flitting. I'm only surprised she hadn't the courage to face you and say goodbye properly. That disappointed me.'

Ushered in, Alex closed the door purposefully behind him — to Kitty's disappointment. These thick doors made it almost impossible to follow what was going on inside.

'Well, young sir, and what have you got to say for yourself? Humph?'

There was nothing unusual in Charles's welcome being less than hospitable, but this morning Alex was only interested in finding Tamsin as soon as possible, putting the ring back on her finger and taking her to see the cottage. He could picture the scene, her look of adoring gratitude when he told her, 'I went to Mr Proctor and told him this was no time for me to be at flying displays: we were to be married at the end of May and my most urgent need was to find somewhere to rent. And you know what? That cottage beyond the airfield belongs to him.

168

He says we can rent it and, because he doesn't want me to leave the village and look somewhere else, he is prepared to give me a handsome rise in wages. He knows he won't regret it. Didn't he say that night, when we all had dinner at Lambton, that when he thought well of an employee he meant to keep him?' With a slight variation of the words but none of their implication, he had imagined the scene as he'd pedalled to Westwood House. Now Charles Hardcastle, looking about as cantankerous as he knew how, wanted him to waste time chattering in the bedroom.

'Good morning, sir. Hello, Mother; I didn't know you were here.'

'Don't ignore me, young man! I asked you a question. What can you tell us about this? Humph?' He thrust a single sheet of paper at Alex.

'Tammy's writing . . . What's she done?' He stared at the note, transparent fear on his face, fear that in that first instant made his arms ache and his mouth feel dry. The previous evening, he had faced the humiliation of James's anger; but that was nothing compared with the paralysing horror of this.

'Here, here, take it when I say. Read it for yourself.' Charles thrust it into his hand.

Dear Mr Hardcastle,
    Please don't think me ungrateful, leaving you so suddenly and without saying goodbye. I told you I was going to be married, but everything is different now. I need to find

another post and want it to be away from Oakleigh. There is more work in a bigger place. I ought to have told you myself. But it happened suddenly, and I don't want to talk about it. Please forgive me. And thank you for putting up with me when I made so many mistakes. I shall miss you. When you see Mrs Murray, please tell her that, even though I shall never be her daughter, I shall always admire what she does.

Yours truly, Tamsin

'You don't understand . . . ' Alex looked from one to the other, the surge of relief giving him back his confidence and optimism. 'We quarrelled. That's all it was. She threw the ring back at me. See, it's here.' It was like standing before an inquisition, two pairs of eyes accusing him. 'I might as well tell you. Mr Proctor has recently taken me off the workshop floor: you know, Mother, how he has always seen my potential. So he gave me a better salary. I shall have to work for it, though; he isn't a philanthropist. Yesterday evening, Tamsin came over. She found me in my office — that's where I work now, except when I'm with Mr Proctor or having flying lessons — she said that she didn't mean to find another job, she wanted us to be married when she left here. Of course, I refused. What else could I do? I may be on a reasonable wage, but I told her I'll have to put work before everything else. That way, one day I'll give her a good life. But not yet. You must see, I thought I was doing right. I never expected her to turn on me like she did; I thought she'd understand.'

'She may not have seen it, last night,' Lucinda gave her opinion, 'but she'll soon see that you've actually saved her from making a mistake. Tamsin is an intelligent girl; she has spirit. But she's at an age when it's all too easy to think herself in love. Free of all that, she will make something useful of her life. Good luck to her, that's what I say.'

'But things are different, now. After she'd gone, I thought of that old cottage beyond the airfield — you probably know it, sir. It belongs to the firm, you see: it was on the parcel of land Mr Proctor originally bought. So I saw him; he and I talked the situation over. Well, anyway, the upshot is that I can rent the cottage — and, what's more, he has upped my money so that I can afford to pay the rent and keep a wife. You recall what he said, how he believes in making sure he doesn't lose staff he sees as worth keeping.' By this time, Alex had talked himself into seeing the story the way he told it. 'So now, all I have to do is find where Tammy has run off to. And I will. By the time I've got the cottage ready for her, she'll be back.' Then, with the smile that never failed him, 'Here and now, I invite both of you to our wedding. Now I must get myself to Brackleford; that's where she'll be, you may be sure.'

The story was plausible enough. Charles didn't doubt his word, for Naomi had told him just how highly James thought of his protégé. Nevertheless, he was puzzled.

'I understood from Tamsin that you were

171

accompanying your employer to various flying displays. I thought you planned to set off today. By the time you come back, what makes you think she will still be in Brackleford? From what little she has ever talked of her time there, I'd not imagined it held happy memories for her.'

'First things first, sir,' Alex told him, still full of confidence. 'Mr Proctor understands that this next week or so I want to be wielding a whitewash brush. Of course, he expected that Tammy would be there holding the steps for me — and I hope she will be. If you'll excuse me, I don't want to hang about. I'll ride straight to Brackleford; I'll make some enquiries. Her family were well known; someone will be sure to have seen her.'

Charles nodded approvingly. Lucinda looked at her son speculatively through narrowed eyes. He'd always been an enigma to her.

* * *

The wheels rattled rhythmically over the sleepers as the train gathered speed, leaving billows of smoke in its wake.

Reason told Tamsin she ought to be travelling in the other direction; in a few minutes, she could have been in Reading. To look for work there? Or to buy a ticket on the Great Western line and lose herself in the crowds of London? In the dark, her long walk had seemed endless as she'd tried to sort out some sort of plan. Yet, by the time she'd arrived at Brackleford Station, both heels blistered and one already bleeding, she'd been as confused as when she'd set out. She'd tried to see herself in imaginary situations, but whatever place she conjured up, there was always one other that pushed to the front of her mind. Then, as if Fate had been pointing the way, the early morning train was already signalled.

She was alone in the Ladies Only compartment, being gently rocked with the motion of the train. Unbuckling her shoes, she took them off and turned to put her feet on one long seat while her case and basket were opposite on the other. Overhead was the hammock-like luggage rack; that's where she ought to have put her things. 'Shrimp,' she seemed to hear Alex's mocking chuckle. But she wouldn't think of him; she wouldn't let her thoughts stray back just twenty-four hours to the certainty she'd felt in their future. This morning, he would be flying with James. He'd told her the first demonstrations were to be somewhere near Dover — and she'd imagined the pride she'd feel when she saw the flying machine go over Oakleigh on its way. Again, she pulled her thoughts under control.

Every muscle ached, but her heels felt better without her shoes. Already half asleep she leant to get her straw basket; it wasn't ideal, but it was better than nothing as a pillow.

*   *   *

'What's all this?' She woke with a start, to find she was no longer alone. A large lady of indeterminate age was standing over her. 'People

173

have to sit on these seats; get your feet off them, child. I don't know what you young people are coming to! And what's all this luggage doing here? Not big enough to lift it aloft, is that it?'

'No. Of course I'm tall enough. I've been travelling all night; I suppose I was tired.'

'Humph.' Her new companion apparently didn't look on tiredness as an excuse. But, with one easy movement, she lifted Tamsin's case onto the rack. 'Travelling all night? Where are you from?'

Tamsin wasn't fully awake, certainly not awake enough to reason that to have travelled all night she might be expected to name some place at the other end of the country.

'Oakleigh, a village near — '

'I know well enough where Oakleigh is.'

What a pale little creature she was. Was she running away from home?

'Close your eyes and catch up on some sleep. I won't chatter. Tell me how far you're going and I'll see to it that you're awake in time. For myself, I'm being met in Brockenhurst. And you?'

'Ringwood. I was told to change at Brockenhurst. I've got my bicycle in the guard's van.'

'You'll be visiting friends, or is Ringwood where your home is?' Already the promise not to chatter was forgotten.

Tamsin swung her feet to the ground and put her toes back into her unbuckled shoes.

'I used to come from that area, but that was when I was a child. Since I've been grown up, I've been working in Oakleigh, but the job has

174

come to an end. I'd not meant to come back down to the New Forest, but the more I thought about it, the more I wanted to.'

It was a relief to talk to someone, especially someone she was never likely to see again. Her companion had settled herself in the opposite seat with her stout legs spread wide and her hands on her knees, sitting with more interest in comfort than elegance. Closer inspection showed her to be on the far side of middle age, a woman whose attire hadn't moved with the times and somehow helped Tamsin's illusion that she was stepping back down the years. The voluminous black dress reached to her laced leather boots, while her three-quarter-length black coat and bonnet had probably been kept for best a quarter of a century or so ago. Everything about her was in keeping with Tamsin's nostalgia for Gorsemoor and the love and security she'd known.

'Well, no one can blame you for that, child. You'll find nowhere more beautiful than the country around our forest. So you'll be visiting family, is that it? Or friends?'

Tamsin's predicament hit her like a blow. She shook her head, anything rather than hear herself say aloud that she had no one. Under her new friend's brusque manner lurked an unsuspected sensitivity.

'Well, if we're to be travelling companions,' the woman changed the subject, 'it's best we can give each other a name. Can't call you 'child' all the way to Brockenhurst. Mrs Braddock, that's who I am, Jane Braddock. And you?'

'Tamsin Yelland. And I'm older than you think. I'm nineteen.'

'You'd got me fooled there. I put you down a deal younger. So, if you're not visiting and don't live there, what brings you down my way? Another job? You seem to have enough clobber with you.'

'I have to find another post. But I don't know what I can hope to find down there. I just wanted to come back, see where it was I used to live . . .' And what could she hope to find there? A ghost of those far-off halcyon days: the ghost of the grandfather who was little more in her mind that the warmth and security left behind on waking from a lovely dream.

'And what sort of work would you be looking for? Not very robust, are you? And, unless I'm much mistaken, those hands haven't been used to grafting.'

'Oh, they've grafted well enough,' Tamsin chuckled, her dimple appearing. She liked Mrs Braddock more with each turn of the wheels. 'I've been typing the text of a book, but it's done now. That's why my job ended.'

'But not why it took you all night to get from Oakleigh to Brackleford. That must be where you caught the train. Walked it, did you? No wonder you want to keep your feet out of your shoes. Just look at that heel of yours.'

Tamsin nodded. Kindness could so easily have been her undoing.

'Got turned out?' Mrs Braddock wanted to know. 'What had you been up to? I dare say you think I'm a nosy old woman, but best we have an honest base between us. Why did you get turned out at night?'

'It wasn't like that.' What a relief it would be to tell this outspoken woman the whole truth. But of course she couldn't.

'So? If it wasn't like that, what was it like? There must have been some good reason for you to walk through the night with all that baggage. What happened? Did you work for some man who came the old soldier with you? The thought of a bit of young flesh, and some of them can't keep their hands to themselves. My George has never been like that, and I thank God for it. Is that why you ran off?'

'I told you, my job was over.' Then, before she could put a brake on herself, 'I was leaving in a week or two because I was getting married.' She held out her left hard, bare now of the opal ring. 'Yesterday evening, we quarrelled — I don't want to talk about it, don't ask me about that — the wedding is off. I just didn't want to have to tell everyone about it. It was cowardly, I know but I packed my things and crept away. Just left a note. No wonder you thought I was a thief or a cheat or whatever you imagined. It was just a disagreement — I'm putting it behind me. I'm going to start a new life.'

'Humph. Going backwards looking for your past doesn't lead you forward to a new life. You won't find Ringwood, or wherever it was you lived, the same as it was when you were small.' Jane Braddock sized up the situation, unexpectedly moved by the sight of the girl facing her. Nineteen she might be, and probably quite

177

capable of holding down a job, but you'd never think so from the sight of her thin, slight form. All alone in the world, by the sound of it. A practical woman, not given to fancy, but never one to shirk responsibility, Jane felt the stirring of compassion.

'If you mean to look for work in my neck of the wood — perhaps Christchurch, there might be something for a girl who can use a typewriter in Christchurch — you'll need a roof over your head. What do you mean to do when you get to journey's end? Humph?'

'Find a room. Just while I look round. If I can't get anything fairly quickly, I must go to a bigger town . . . ' It sounded lame; she wished she'd made better plans and been able to sound more impressive.

'George is meeting me at the railway station, I told you. That's Mr Braddock, you understand. We don't live in town — better for me to get out there than go on to Christchurch. Same as you'd have to get out if you're crossing to Ringwood. But it seems to me you'd be more likely to get work in Christchurch, a bit more flourishing you might say. Now, if you come along home along with George and me, we'd give you a bed for a few nights while you sniff out the chances. How would that be?'

Tamsin couldn't help it, the hot tears sprang into her eyes and spilt as she tried to blink them away.

'Now, we won't be having any of that. It's only a staging post for you. But if helping each other when we have the need isn't what we're put on

178

this earth for, then I'd like someone to tell me what is!'

What a moment for that image of Arthur to push into Tamsin's mind.

'I'm so grateful. Thank you sounds like nothing. You know — ' she wiped the palms of her hands across her face and smiled at her portly rescuer — 'I was sure it was Fate made me catch this train.'

'Stuff and nonsense.' But was it? Jane had been visiting her sister in Basingstoke; she'd stood out resolutely against sending a telegram to George to say she was staying an extra day. Was Fate what had put her on this train, made her open the door of this compartment?

At Brockenhurst, they found George Braddock waiting. He was probably not much older than his robust wife, but the years appeared to have shrivelled him; his shoulders stooped, and his cheeks were sunken in his thin face. There was no doubt of his pleasure when Jane swooped to plant a smacking kiss on his cheek. Into Tamsin's mind sprang the old nursery rhyme: 'Jack Sprat could eat no fat, His wife could eat no lean . . . '

'Go off and get your cycle,' Jane told her, without introducing them, 'while George and I get the bags out to the trap.' No wonder poor George looked mystified, but he must have been used to obeying orders without question, for he turned to the station exit with Tamsin's case in one hand and his wife's in the other.

Two minutes later, still with no more than a nod of acknowledgement passing between her

179

and the man who was about to take her into his home, Tamsin hopped onto her bicycle and set off following the trap.

Over the next few hours, despite the Braddocks's unquestioning acceptance of her in their home, she felt her life was in limbo. Her memories of Gorsemoor were of the sights and sounds, of smells, of the feeling of the sun (could it always have been sunny?) as she'd followed behind her grandfather and they worked in the field. All that, and perhaps most of all, of emotions. 'When we lived in the New Forest . . . ' her mother used to say and, foolishly, Tamsin had imagined that to return to the forest would be to glimpse the past. But it is a region with many facets; the treed area where the Braddocks lived near Boldre bore little resemblance to her memories. But Jane was right: it was beautiful, and the easy way she was accepted into their home was salve to her wounded spirit. For the remaining hours of that Tuesday, she looked no further.

The next day, she set out to ride to Christchurch. Suppose someone was prepared to engage her, was she being fair? How long before they realised she was going to have a baby? They'd soon get rid of her when they knew. If she found rooms in town, the same thing would apply. Society had no compassion for a woman with a child and no husband.

Whichever way I look at it, I can't see the way. But I had to say what I did to Alex. Our baby . . . and he wanted me to kill it before it's even been born. If he'd really loved me like he said he did (perhaps even believed it was true), being poor for a while, having a struggle, none of that would have mattered. So he didn't love me. I was like all those other sweethearts who were waiting for him at the snap of his fingers . . . like them, yet more stupid. He'd never made love to any of them. Had he suggested it and they'd said no? But me, I was just a stupid fool. I believed everything. I thought everything would go on being perfect. Now, what can I do? There's no one I can talk to. The Braddocks are kind — but that's because they don't know. Won't You listen to me? (Not the sort of prayer Arthur would have thundered to his congregation, but never had a cry for help been more heartfelt.) I'm not looking for things being made soft, honestly I'm not: just so long as the baby is all right. If only You'd show me what I have to do, give me some sign so that I know whether I've done right in coming here. Tomorrow, I'll ride out beyond Ringwood; I'll look for Gorsemoor. Perhaps, when I get there, everything will be clear.

Round and round in her mind went the thoughts as she pedalled towards Christchurch. She bought the local paper and scanned it for a vacant post; but there was nothing. The day was bright, even though there was a chill wind blowing off the sea. Despite everything, it was impossible not to be excited at the thought of being by the coast. So she bought two currant buns and took them to the beach at Mudeford, where she sat on the sand in solitary splendour to eat them.

Going back to Boldre, she kept to the bumpy

181

road that ran parallel with the coast until she came to the outskirts of Lymington. There she stopped to read some notices pinned to a board outside a General Store. Someone had baby rabbits for sale; someone else wanted to get rid of a phonograph and purchase a sewing machine; another had a tricycle for sale; and another was looking for a kind home for a tabby cat. But no one was searching for a young girl desperate to find work and willing to consider anything — well, almost anything, she added silently. Never mind. Tomorrow she would find Gorsemoor; tomorrow she would see the sign and know which road she had to take for the future Fate meant for her.

Hopping back on her bicycle, she set off down the High Street. And it was then that she saw the notice. Her immediate future was clear: tomorrow Gorsemoor and the next day . . . He'd not know she was there, it wouldn't even enter his head that she might be in the area. Surely it couldn't hurt just to watch him from a distance, so see how proud he'd be when he climbed into the machine to sit behind James Proctor? She'd known there were displays along the south coast, starting near Dover — probably this very minute, while I'm reading about Friday's display, he's up there swooping like a giant bird over the Kent coast — and finishing in South Devon at the end of the following week. But as she'd headed towards the New Forest, she'd been reaching towards her past; it hadn't entered her head that past and present could come together in the skies over Christchurch.

182

'No luck with a job?' George Braddock asked.

'Nothing in the paper and I asked in shops. Tomorrow, I shall go to Ringwood. I want to find the place where I used to live.'

'Doesn't always do, my dear. Sometimes it's happier just to hang on to your memories. No one's satisfied to leave things alone. You must be prepared to find the old place changed; that way, you won't get hurt.'

She remembered his warning the next day as she jolted and jogged over the ruts of the lane that led to Gorsemoor. Before her skipped the ghost of a little girl, jumping over her skipping rope as she ran home from school. Yes, there it was: the gate was just the same. Dropping her bicycle unceremoniously on the grass verge, she walked the last fifty yards. Grandpa, do you know I've come? Oh, you *must* do. Mr Braddock said it might be all changed, but the house looks the same . . . At the gate she stopped, feeling her first stab of disappointment. There had never been neat lace curtains over the windows. The house seemed to shout at her that it belonged to someone else. The sheds were the same — but her bantam run had gone. It used to be at the far end of the yard where now a motor car was parked.

'You wanting someone?' A woman came out of the back door.

'No. I was just looking. I haven't been around this way for ages. The field — that field over there — it used to be fruit — and just beyond there were peas, beans — '

'We had all that out. The old man who used to

own it never made the most of the place. We've taken the fields beyond, too: farm it properly, these days.'

'It was just the way we wanted it. It belonged to my grandfather — I lived here.'

The woman looked at her with more interest, but as for it being just the way anyone could have wanted it, she'd never heard such rubbish! It probably hadn't changed for centuries until she and Ernie took over.

'Fancy you knowing the old place. Come and see what we've done to it, if you like. Inside, we've got it quite nice, even though I do say it myself. Only last week the decorator finished in the side bedroom, the one that looks down on the yard. Pretty paper, I chose, with bunches of rosebuds all over it. Then that's the last of the old stuff gone. We've had it done bit by bit as we could afford; we don't use that room so it had to wait. You'd like to see how we cheered it up, I expect.'

Tamsin shook her head. Grandpa's room with bunches of rosebuds on the paper . . . his field ploughed up . . . everything changed, just as if he'd never lived.

'No. I like it the way it was.'

She turned away without a backward glance, glad of her rudeness.

'Bunches of rosebuds,' she muttered as she turned her bicycle to head back to Boldre. She was hurt and angry at the desecration of her memories. 'The old man . . . never made the most of the place . . . last of the old stuff gone. Stupid, stupid woman! As if wallpaper with flowers on and those beastly curtains shutting out the light can make a place better. It didn't help me one bit going to look at it. I thought I'd find *something* — but it was worse than nothing.' Head down, she pedalled. She tried to believe that it was anger that made her eyes burn with tears, but as the first overspilt to run down her cheek, she knew there was no way of hiding from her misery. 'Nothing,' she said aloud, the words catching on a sob, 'got nothing now. Not even Gorsemoor.'

'Come on, now, my duckie. Tears never mended anything.' Almost as if he were here, she knew the sound of his voice. 'You gotta be a brave soldier . . . ' How often he'd said that to her when she'd tumbled, waiting while she swallowed her tears before they came.

She back-pedalled to stop her bike, climbed off and proceeded to wipe away the evidence of her lapse. She so seldom cried that, when she did, her eyelids burnt and refused to let her forget. But this time was different. That moment of dreadful isolation had lifted. Looking up at the scudding clouds, she even smiled — not a deep enough smile to bring her dimple, but a smile for all that.

★　★　★

The voice carried by the loudhailer wasn't easy to fathom; she was too near the back of the airfield. Combining hearing with imagination, she thought the commentator told the waiting crowd: ' . . . Mr James Proctor . . . take to the air . . . Farley Moth . . . bi-plane of his own design . . . in his workshops in Berkshire. Flying alone . . . two-seater machine — '

She wasn't even listening. Alone. He'd failed Alex. After all he'd promised, he'd come on his own.

Alex's treatment of her was pushed right out of her mind by the anger she felt as she watched James climb into the cockpit. Alex made a hero of him, but he had feet of clay! Then she looked around her, for one frantic moment expecting he must be in the crowd watching, perhaps here as an engineer. He'd said himself that he hadn't the experience to take the controls at a display. He'd never notice her — he wasn't expecting her — but she couldn't bear to think he must be so close without her seeing him.

James taxied down the field, then, as he turned into the wind, the plane was airborne. At any other time, she would have watched, spellbound. But two things stood between her and the thrill she usually found in watching James fly: one, paramount in her mind, was Alex; and the other, which grew stronger with every second that she became more certain he wasn't there, was disillusionment with James Proctor.

Anger built on anger. By the time James climbed down from the cockpit, she had pushed her way to the edge of the landing strip in her quest to catch a glimpse of Alex. Even so, there were plenty of people standing between her and the plane as he lowered himself to the ground and into a circle of admirers.

In that moment of congratulation, perhaps it was the scorn in her eyes that made him turn in her direction. She'd not meant to be noticed, but it was too late. All she could do was slip back into the jostle of people.

7

'Funny old world it is.' Jane Braddock gave what she called a 'stir for luck' to the teapot before starting to pour. 'You tell me it was just chance you met up with each other, and there the girl's been out each day looking for a job of work, while all the time Fate must have been laughing up its sleeve. Sugar?'

'No, thank you, just as it is. As you say, it was sheer chance. I had no reason to expect her to be in the region at all; I hadn't even heard she'd left Oakleigh,' said James.

'Lovers' tiff, best I can make out. So you're not who was breaking her heart? No, of course you wouldn't be. You're old enough to have learnt better. Trouble with being young: pride won't let you be the one to climb down. Wicked thing, is pride. Not that there's any wickedness in young Tamsin. Only been here three days, but me and George'll be sorry to see her go off home. But there, that's me being selfish. I can't be doing with a permanent lodger, but I fancied having her popping in and out. No children of our own, that's been our trouble. Here, let me cut you a piece of my fruit cake.'

James liked the honest countrywoman. If Fate had made him catch sight of Tamsin melting into the crowd on the airfield, it most certainly must have had a hand in throwing her into Mrs Braddock's path. Now she was upstairs

188

repacking her case and pushing the overflow into her straw basket, while outside the horse impatiently pawed the ground and the cabby sucked contentedly at his pipe. The train was due to leave Brockenhurst in thirty-five minutes and if she was to get back to Oakleigh in daylight, she must be on it.

'You've been very good to her. She told me on the way here how you befriended her.'

'Ah, well, some folk touch a spring in you and some don't, I dare say. Took to the child the moment I set eyes on her, with her poor bleeding heels but her chin still high. Can't be doing with grizzlers: never could. And what about you? If you're not her sweetheart, where do you fit into the picture? His older brother, is that what you are?'

'No, we're not related. He lodges with an old family friend.'

'Married man, are you? Here, let me give you a refill.'

'No. I won't have any more tea, thanks. She should be down in a second.'

'You didn't tell me.' Jane never missed out for the sake of asking. 'You've a wife back in Oakleigh?'

James Proctor was a private person; he carried his heart safely in his chest and never on his sleeve. So there must have been something about Jane's rough and ready kindness that 'touched the spring' in him, as she'd described it.

'I lost my wife ten years ago. We'd been married just a year — she was expecting a child when she went down with pneumonia.'

189

'You lost the pair of them? Oh, dear. Oh Lawks, and you just a poor young man, as you must have been. We were speaking of Fate — giving it credit for sorting things out the way they should go. But where's the sense in a thing like that? Poor dear girl. You're sure you won't let me give you another cup?' Food and drink was her way of giving comfort.

'I'm positive, thanks. And here comes Tamsin.'

They bundled out to the waiting cab, Jane's eyes lighting with pleasure as she saw what awaited her on the road.

'Must get my shovel and pail when you've moved off. My George will be pleased with that little load to put round the roses. Pity he's not here; he'll be that put down when he hears you've gone, Tamsin.'

Of necessity, farewells were hasty. Tamsin was taken into Jane's bearlike hug; James was given a hand that had been well wiped on her pinafore.

'Thank you for feeding me, and for all you've done.' There was no doubting he meant what he said as he gripped her hand. 'I've enjoyed our talk.'

Tamsin settled onto the benchlike seat, her case safely stowed and her straw basket on her knee. She wanted to start her journey back, to find Alex and to tell him how wrong she'd been to doubt him. But, keen though she was to be on her way, she was conscious of a feeling of safety, of trust in James. How far from the truth she'd been in thinking he had changed his mind about bringing Alex; the real reason for coming alone was very different. No wonder a smile tugged at the corner of her mouth as she thought of what he'd told her, a smile that broadened and became an affectionate chuckle as she turned to wave goodbye to Jane and saw her already putting her pail and shovel to good use.

At Brockenhurst, James waved her purse away as he asked for her ticket.

'Look, I have money,' she protested. 'And I know how much my fare is because I bought a ticket coming.'

'Humour me,' he smiled. 'I like to feel that I've done all I can to see you safely home.'

Home. But where was home? Until that moment, she'd looked no further than that she was going back to Alex. James saw the sudden unease in her pale, strange-coloured eyes and guessed where her thoughts had carried her. Fortunately, he'd already planned ahead.

'When you get to Brackleford,' he told her, 'I don't want you pushing your bike all the way to Oakleigh. I want you to take this — ' he dropped a sovereign into her chain purse before she had time to snap it closed ' — and to promise me you won't attempt to make your own way alone. Take a cab from Brackleford Station and go straight to Lambton.'

'But I can't do that! Miss Halliwell isn't expecting me. Perhaps Mr Hardcastle will let me use my — '

'By the time you arrive, Naomi will be expecting you and will have a room ready. Don't look like that, Tamsin. I know her better than you do. I shall send a telegram to her as soon as you leave.'

'You've been so kind.' It was hardly more than a whisper, for she was suddenly frightened to trust her voice. 'If you knew about me — '

Never a man for outward signs of affection, he was as surprised as she was when his hand reached to caress her cheek.

'I know all I need to about you, Tamsin — and I know Alexander Murray is a lucky young man.'

'Tell me again: you say he came to talk to you on Monday evening. He was upset, you say . . . ?' Oh, why couldn't she have trusted him? Hadn't he been like a god to her, even when she was little; and ever since then, though she'd gone years without seeing him, hadn't he always been there deep in her heart and mind? 'I know it's silly, but tell me once more . . . ?'

'Yes, he was upset. He said you'd given him his ring back. He blamed himself because he wasn't able to give you a proper home, keep you in Oakleigh once your work was finished for Mr Hardcastle. If you found another post, it might be miles away — '

'That's not the whole truth. I wanted us to get married as soon as he came home from the displays. You see — '

'Hark, is that the train? Yes, I see the smoke.'

'Mr Proctor — '

'I call you Tamsin; couldn't you try and call me James?'

'You won't want me to, not when you know — '

He put his hand gently but firmly on her mouth.

'You can't tell me anything that would change

192

my opinion.' His blue eyes met and held hers. 'I thought we were friends, humph?'

She nodded. Then, as the train drew level with the platform and with a shudder and a hiss came to a standstill, she reached up to kiss his cheek.

He waited until the train had snaked its way out of the station, heading north, then went back to the waiting carriage. The next day James was to fly westward, but first he was to spend a night in Christchurch.

'How well do you know the area? I want to send a telegram. Can you take me to the nearest Post Office?'

'Have you there in no time, guv'nor,' came the obliging answer.

In fact, James wrote two.

To Naomi: 'Am sending Tamsin to you. Arriving tonight. Accommodation and your unfailing kindness please. James.'

To Alex: 'Tamsin at display. Returning to you. Meet her at Brackleford at 7.58 p.m. Told her only that you refused display to prepare cottage for her. James Proctor.'

★ ★ ★

Alex stood back and admired his handiwork. On the wooden gate of the previously nameless cottage, he had screwed his hand-painted sign: *Brambles*. What could be better suited to their home? The wild blackberry bushes had encroached during the years the property had been empty, until he had had to take a scythe to them to clear a wide enough path to the door so

193

that the spreading branches didn't tear anyone's clothes. During the three weeks between being given the key and moving in, the garden was the last of his considerations. There wasn't an inch of wall or ceiling that hadn't to be whitewashed, nor an inch of woodwork that hadn't to be painted.

'You do the skirting, Shrimp; I'll do the ceilings. I say, but this is going to be quite good, by the time we've done with it.' He looked around, his face breaking into that smile she loved. 'It'll do us well, for the time being. But not for always. James Proctor didn't bring *his* wife to a little hovel, and it wasn't what I wanted for us.'

'Don't you call this a hovel, Alex Murray! Just because you've got used to being waited on at Lambton. Just think what luck it was that Mr Proctor mentioned the cottage to you when he did. If we'd not believed in Fate before, we would after this.'

'Yes, but I wanted to do better for you. And I could have, too, now that I've had this promotion, if only we hadn't had to rush into the first thing we heard of. We could have looked around, found the sort of place I want to take you to — '

'But we couldn't wait.' Her lips teased his and he knew she wasn't talking about the baby.

Whitewash forgotten, he pulled her close. 'You know what I meant: what I mean now, this very minute. I want you just for myself. We haven't even started to live, yet. Tammy, don't let having a baby change you — not yet, not for ages.'

'Nothing will change me. Alex, our baby's only there because I love you so much.'

He bit back his spontaneous answer. It would have been easy to remind her that if she loved him so completely, she would have listened to his reasoning and agreed to take the mixture he'd told her about. But, had she done that, they wouldn't have been there in the cottage, somewhere of their own. The truth was, he couldn't bear the thought of her slight body being weighed down in the coming months with the child she was carrying. He wanted her always as she'd been during that weekend: slender, supple, just as he'd imagined she would be — and his, *just his*.

He couldn't bear the thought of the developing child possessing her; he couldn't bear the thought of her becoming like the wives of men at the works, careworn with chores, motherhood and housekeeping taking precedence over their being wives and lovers. He wanted her always to be free to run up Hinds Hill with him, to race him as they cycled, with the wind blowing through their hair. He wanted her always to have time to laugh, to be ready for the fun they shared. He wanted her to stay straight and slim, her lithe body never to change as she arched and strained in his arms, a volcano about to erupt. There was no place in their lives for a demanding baby.

'Come on, woman, don't tease me — or you'll get more than you bargained for!'

'On this stone floor?' She chuckled.

'Tammy . . . the things I said, about the baby

and everything . . . I know it sounded selfish. But it was for your sake, too. You're so tiny. If anything happened to you, I couldn't bear it.'

She didn't answer, just leant against him. She felt she was overflowing with joy. 'I've nearly finished the skirting.' She drew away, making an effort to sound matter-of-fact. 'When it's done, I'll hold the steps so you don't fall.'

That's what they were doing when James found them. It wasn't the first time he'd walked across to see their progress.

'Am I disturbing you?'

'No, of course not,' Alex welcomed him. 'Are you wanting me at the works?' He asked it with something like hope. Not that he wanted to leave the ceiling before it was finished, and he was glad of the time off James had given him to work on the cottage; but he half hoped that he was needed. It would be good to have Tamsin hear him being sent for.

'On the contrary. I've come to offer my services, if you have a job you can give me. Painting, whitewashing, cutting back the brambles? I'm multi-talented.'

★ ★ ★

James was tall, the bedroom ceiling was low, so he needed nothing to stand on to reach to whiten the ceiling that was yellowed with the years. What was he doing here? he asked himself as he dipped the wide brush in his bucket and worked with steady rhythmic strokes. From when he'd first taken Alex onto the staff, he had

196

looked on him as his protégé, but that didn't extend to helping him paint the home he was preparing for his bride.

Alex's bride . . . Now he was nearer the reason for his sudden urge to help. He'd found a way to bring this marriage about and yet, in his heart, he wasn't happy about it. She was hardly more than a child: just imagine her downstairs holding the steps and watching Alex with her heart in her eyes. She looked like a skinny child playing at being grown up, swamped by a too-large overall, her light hair tied in a scarf. At nineteen years old, many girls were married; many girls already had babies. But Tamsin was different.

It wasn't that her life had been cosseted and easy: rather it was because there was about her the sort of purity that most girls had lost at her age. Purity? Not everyone would say that about a girl starting married life already pregnant. Bending to dip his brush in the pail of whitewash, James let his mind stray. What she had done seemed to him to be evidence of her need to love and be loved — and again he went back to that word purity. Did Alexander Murray take her for granted, or was he capable of that same wholehearted emotion?

Pulling his thoughts back in line, James started another row of brushstrokes, concentrating on the ceiling of the small room.

In those days leading up to the wedding, he often came across the airfield, spending an hour or two wielding a brush — or a hammer, as he mended the gate. During that time, his relationship with the young couple moved

197

forward. He'd already told Tamsin to use his Christian name, but soon with natural ease it became James, Tamsin and Alex.

Brambles had two rooms and a tiny kitchen downstairs, and two rooms upstairs. Alex thought with longing of the bathroom at Lambton with hot water on tap from the kitchen range; it was a far cry from the tub covered with a wooden tabletop in the kitchen at the cottage, where water would have to be heated in buckets on the range.

Naomi looked around Lambton for pieces of simple furniture she didn't need; James bought the young couple a small oak sideboard, table and chairs for their wedding present; and men from the works called at their door with little packages — one came with a teapot, another a butter dish, someone else a mirror. However small their gift, their good wishes were genuine, for Alex was popular among the men, where he had a reputation for good humour and pleasure in a joke. He had a reputation, too, for being 'one for the ladies', but that didn't lose him face amongst the workforce.

'Well, I suppose I'd better do my motherly duty,' Lucinda said, as she came downstairs from her tour of inspection. 'You need things in the bedroom, they'd better be my contribution. I'll go into Merlin's in Brackleford and arrange for them to deliver a bedstead with the usual washstand and dressing table. I shan't order a wardrobe; the room is so small, you'll be better to use the built-in-cupboard.'

Tamsin wished the offer had been made with

better grace, and she wished that Lucinda's gift could have been for general use downstairs. But that was silly: that was childish, she told herself.

★　★　★

They were married just three weeks and one day after the calling of the banns, a Monday morning towards the end of May 1913. It was a wedding unlike anything Tamsin could have expected when Alex had first put that opal ring on her finger. Or was it so different? Subconsciously, she might have imagined herself standing at Alex's side, dressed all in white, the organ playing, bells ringing. But there could have been no logic in the dreamlike image and it had soon faded, leaving no scar of regret. Wearing her best dress — the same one that she had worn to that first dinner party at Lambton — surely no bride had ever been happier. Except for the front row, the pews were empty. Naomi and Lucinda sat on the right-hand side of the aisle, traditional for family and friends of the groom; only James on the left, even though he had known Alex for nearly three years, Tamsin less well and for only one. There was no walking up the aisle, no music, no father of the bride to give her away; the ring was safely in Alex's waistcoat pocket. So, as they waited for the vicar, Alex (also in his best suit) sat with his mother and Naomi and, just feet away, Tamsin with James.

'Here he is.' Alex's stage whisper announced across the aisle as the surpliced figure of the vicar came through the vestry door. 'Ready?'

How different he was from the evening he'd been told about the baby. Now he was brimming with confidence; already he saw himself in the role of husband and provider. And father? No need to rush. That would fall into place when the time came.

Tamsin's hand was gripped hard in James's; her fingers responded as she bestowed on him an expression of undisguised rapture that tugged uncomfortably at his heartstrings. His gaze moved to Alex. Kill that trust and joy and I'll not forgive you. All that she is is yours, her whole heart. Do you realise it, do you appreciate it? Do you even start to understand the responsibility of that sort of love? But he was being unfair, he tried to tell himself, as the young couple made their vows, both of them so clear and certain. Hadn't he known Alex's potential right from the start and put his own faith in him? He was letting his imagination run away with him, something he seldom did. They were no different from any other young couple pledging to bind their lives together . . . His mind slipped back more than ten years.

★   ★   ★

They'd been married about a month when the sound of a motor car stopping at the gate told Tamsin that she had a visitor. She looked out of the window, more than half expecting it would be James. Instead, waiting for Barnes to get out and open the door for her, it was Lucinda who alighted. Her immediate reaction was pleasure for, despite moments of irritation, the torch she carried for her mother-in-law still burned bright.

'Lovely surprise!' She had the door open before Lucinda had walked up the path. 'Aren't you bringing Barnes in?'

'No. Leave him where he is. I don't want him listening to everything we say. In any case, he's like a child with a new toy in that auto; nothing pleases him better than sitting behind the steering wheel.'

'He'd been trying to persuade Mr Hardcastle to buy one for ages. What made him change his mind?'

'Who — not what.' The brown velvet voice didn't enlarge; there was no need.

'You?'

Lucinda pulled off her doeskin gloves, easing each closely fitting finger separately as if the task took all her concentration.

'I get down from London very frequently. Indeed, except for organised marches or rallies, I can do our cause as much good in one part of the country as another. But I was saying, I come frequently and always have to get that horse-drawn cab from Brackleford. It makes the journey so trying. In fact, if my visits hadn't become so important to poor Charles, I often wouldn't bother. He could see I found it irksome.' She smiled, a secret, satisfied smile.

'If only he could be brought downstairs, perhaps he could be lifted into the seat of the auto. Imagine how he'd enjoy a change of scene! It must be so miserable for him, always in that one room — '

'My dear, you're behind the times. I have reorganised Westwood House — transformed it, over these last few weeks. Charles's bedroom is now where you used to work. I've had the table taken out: in fact, everything is gone except his bookshelves. He wanted those to stay. His bedroom furniture has been brought downstairs; it looks very well in there. Barnes lifts him into a wheelchair and pushes him outside to the garden.'

'That's wonderful. I've hated to think of him always indoors. Even before he fell, he was dreadfully restricted — that's why he was often so cantankerous.'

Ignoring the interruption, Lucinda went on: 'The master bedroom, the one that used to be his, is the best room in the house. He has no visitors except me. So he left me to sort out what I wanted put in there and now it's my own.'

Remembering how impossible it had always been to persuade Charles into anything that didn't fit his own plans, Tamsin assumed the idea must have been his. She ought to have been prepared for Lucinda's next announcement.

'Tamsin, I had a reason for coming here today. I wanted to tell you what I've decided. As I've already said, Charles has become very dependent on my visits. So far, I haven't given him my answer, but my decision is made. I shall agree to marry him. Westwood House needs a mistress.'

'Marry . . . ? But what about your husband — Alex's father? I thought he was alive still?' But why should she have thought so? Alex had no contact with him and, indeed, no more than hazy

202

memories. She knew, though, from the chance remarks he'd made about his father, that as a young boy he'd felt an affinity with the only other male in the household.

'Alive or dead, I have no idea. My life was disrupted by his chasing rainbows of his own making — '

'Mrs — Alex did tell me — I forget what he called her.'

'Amelia Sherbourne was the one he ran off with. I heard later that she was back in her own nest; she'd been replaced. Where he is now — or how many others there have been through the years — I neither know nor care.'

'But, Mother, you can't risk a bigamous marriage. And what about all the work you do: the rallies, the talks?'

'Charles is sympathetic to our cause. If he weren't, do you think I would have let a friendship develop? There is no need for me to spend as much time in London as I do. Every woman in the country should be made aware of the fight we have on our hands. I've worked in this region before and shall continue. Of course, for organised events, I shall travel up to town. The first time I married, I gave up my freedom — something I shall never do again. Charles knows that. He and I hold each other in respect, a necessary ingredient for a successful partnership — more important than the so-called love you young people waste yourselves on.'

Tamsin's emotions were an ill-assorted combination of anger and pity. 'But if anyone finds out you have a husband?'

'Tamsin, I am not a complete fool: nor yet some inexperienced girl thinking there is nothing in life but a wedding ring on her finger and a man in her bed.' This time, the inference was clear and there was no pity mixed with Tamsin's anger.

'How do you know what other people think? It's that sort of arrogance that does your cause more harm than good!'

'It was impertinent of me, I'm sorry.' The softly spoken apology was so unexpected that, even though Tamsin's feathers were still ruffled, she could think of no suitable reply. 'I have given a good deal of thought to my situation. The first thing I shall do is go to a solicitor,' Lucinda went on, the brief exchange already out of her mind. 'I shall tell him the position and no doubt he will arrange that a notice is put in the *Times* and anywhere else he considers necessary. If Rupert — Alexander's father — responds, then I shall tell him I am agreeable to give him grounds for divorce; if nothing is heard, I shall follow whatever course is open to me without actually breaking the law. Perhaps it will be proved that I'm a widow but, if Rupert can't be traced, then I shall change my name by deed poll and, as far as the busybodies of the district are concerned, I shall be Mrs Hardcastle.'

Tamsin frowned. She was faced with something she found hard to accept.

'I got very fond of Mr Hardcastle.' Then, fearful that her normally pale cheeks might give away her embarrassment, but knowing it was important to say it, she continued, 'And you've

204

always meant such a lot to me. When I was a child, I dreamt of growing up to be just like you: courageous, not caring what people thought of you, speaking your mind — '

'Dreams like that, Tamsin — yet what do you do with your life? Marry when you're too young to know anything of the world, throw your future away just for a man's gratification. I don't care if he is my own son: it's what will happen.'

'We're not like that.' And she believed she spoke the truth. 'Oh, I stay at home and look after things, of course I do. And — Mother — ' the word was spoken carefully, it still didn't roll naturally off her tongue ' — Alex said we needn't say anything for a month or two, but I want to tell you.'

'No! Not that! Stupid boy! And you — why couldn't you have seen to it that he was careful? It's as I said, you are both too young. Do you even know anything about birth control? Well, too late, now. Or is it? How overdue are you? Have you tried anything?'

Tamsin wouldn't let her mother-in-law guess at her hurt. Anger was her armour. 'I shouldn't have told you!' Standing very straight, she clasped her hands tightly behind her back, feeling her nails cutting into her palms. 'I suppose you're going to tell me of some witch's brew that will get rid of my baby. Well, even if I were only one day late, I wouldn't do it.' She heard the croak in her voice and ought to have stopped there. But she was on a roller coaster. 'I want my baby. Can't you understand?' She knew she was making a fool of herself, but she was beyond stemming the flood of tears; Lucinda's reaction was so exactly like Alex's that it opened the wound she'd believed was healing. 'Go away and leave me alone. Don't know why I ever thought you were so wonderful: you've got no heart. No wonder he went off and left you.'

'Pull yourself together. That you can behave like it shows I'm right — you're too young for parenthood.'

'Well, you were a rotten mother — ' What was she saying? This was Alex's mother; for the rest of her life Lucinda would be her mother, too. This was the woman who had been her childhood ideal. She ought to apologise, to say she hadn't meant it. But she couldn't. Alex hadn't understood why it was she couldn't try and get rid of the baby; but Alex was a man. He couldn't know the protective feeling that made her weak with love for the unborn child. 'Don't you remember?' She gulped. 'Don't you remember how you felt when you knew about Alex?'

Lucinda looked at her, her expression worried. She ignored the question. 'What does Alex think of the prospect?'

'He's pleased, of course he is. Just like I am.'

'Yes, I dare say he is. I seem to remember Rupert was, too. Not that having a child ever clipped his wings. Well, my dear, my own news seems to be overshadowed. What's done is done, but if you're wise you'll see he takes care what he's doing. You can't be very late: perhaps this is a false alarm. There's no point in running unnecessary risks.' Carefully she pulled on her

206

gloves, pushing down each finger separately until they fitted like a second skin. 'And don't upset yourself over all this. Some women get over emotional in the first weeks; it won't last. Don't apologise.' Then, as she turned to the front door that opened from the little dining room directly onto the front garden, she smiled serenely, as if the scene had never happened. 'Cycle over and see Charles some time, won't you? Tell him you're pleased about us.'

Tamsin didn't walk to the gate with her. She didn't want Barnes to see her blotchy tear-stained face. Hearing the front door close, she sat down on one of the dining chairs James had given them, her elbows on the table and her chin in her hands. Why should she feel so alone? It wasn't as if it mattered that Lucinda hadn't been pleased.

Driving back to Westwood House, Lucinda relived the scene, unable to overcome her disappointment and her alarm for their future. Then her thoughts were back on herself and the answer she would give Charles. She smiled, imagining his pleasure. Dear Charles. She'd grown surprisingly fond of him, an emotion no doubt heightened by his dependence on her. Her smile deepened as she imagined her solitary occupation of the room that had been his. Even his being so incapacitated had its advantages.

★   ★   ★

Tamsin had spent the morning cycling to Westwood House. Back home, she went upstairs to change out of her cycling suit, thinking back to her talk with Charles, well pleased at how she'd handled him.

I must be getting cunning, she chuckled silently, putting ideas in his head and letting him think they were all his own. I don't know anything about solicitors and even less about private detectives, but if he's so keen to find Alex's father, then that must be the way he has to go. A divorce would be difficult: what sort of grounds could Mother give the man she called Rupert? She's not lived with him for years and it never bothered him, so he's not likely to go to the trouble of divorcing her for it now. Mr Hardcastle is right to want everything above board. They can't start off living a lie. A sad marriage, though: not a proper marriage at all. But I suppose that doesn't matter, at their ages. For, to her nineteen-year-old mind, Lucinda's forty-six years and Charles's fifty-eight wouldn't expect anything more than friendship in their new relationship. Lucinda had more or less said so, herself.

Tamsin took off her beret and threw it on the bed, then spiked a hairpin through the end of her coiled plait that threatened to fall loose. It must be sad to be marrying when you're so old, she and the girl in the long mirror on the clothes cupboard door agreed. Being with Alex got better every day, every night, every hour.

Lucinda and Charles were forgotten. Standing alone in the low-ceilinged bedroom that James had decorated, Tamsin gave her thoughts full rein. She meant to change from her cycling

208

clothes into her old calico gardening dress — in fact she started to undress automatically as her imagination ran ahead of her. Remember how he'd watched her as he'd got ready for bed last night. 'My shrimp.' Even thinking of the way he'd said it gave her a yearning ache. How he'd stood close behind her, looking at that naked girl in the mirror just as she was looking at her now (Naked? What was she doing, taking her clothes off in the middle of the day, here in the cottage, alone?), how he'd put his arms around her, his hands feeling the new and unfamiliar weight of her breasts — just as hers did now. Her eyes closed, as if that would bring him closer. Desire tingled in her veins. Clenching her teeth, she jerked her hands down to her sides, opening her eyes.

What's the matter with you Tamsin Yell — Tamsin Murray? It's the middle of the day; the sun's shining. Get dressed and go out in the garden. Yes, I will. But not to run away from how I feel. I'm so happy that it scares me. Has anyone the right for everything to be so wonderful? Not just the loving part of it, but everything. Every day is like an adventure, a discovery of something else new and wonderful. And the baby . . . Alex can't mind about it, now. Don't change, that's what he told me. And of course I shall change; already I'm getting proper woman's breasts instead of those little bumps I used to have. But he knows that if my body changes, nothing can take me away from him. Catching her lip between her teeth, she smiled.

Then she reached for her underwear and

started to dress. As she threw a quick glance in the direction of the airstrip, visible from the bedroom window, her expression might easily have been seen as one of guilt. Five minutes later, garbed in her well-worn calico dress and old boots, her head tied up with a scarf, she flailed her scythe, collecting brambles to add to the pile that was already sending a spiral of smoke into the still summer air.

★ ★ ★

So the weeks went by. The patch of ground belonging to the cottage began to resemble a garden and there was no shadow on the horizon to threaten the pleasure Tamsin and Alex found in each other and in being together.

By September, the personal detective engaged by Charles's solicitor had picked up the threads of Rupert Murray's whereabouts in the early years after he left Lucinda. With something to work on, he proceeded through a series of female connections, one leading on to the next, until his final paramour was able to confirm that he had died sometime during the summer of 1912. A trip to the Records Office at Somerset House, and Lucinda had proof of her widowhood.

Autumn was giving way to winter when Lucinda brought the news to Brambles.

'When he walked out on me — leaving me with a child to care for without so much as a penny's help — he was very comfortably off. Not money of his own making: no, Rupert was always better at spending than earning. It seems that he ended in rooms in Pimlico, everything he'd had he'd squandered. Not that *I* wanted to gain from anything he left behind; had the situation arisen I should have refused to accept it. But, it seems, neither will Alex. Everything gone! Stupid man. The world is full of them, Tamsin.'

Tamsin laughed. These days, it would take more than Lucinda's moods of bitter anger to prick her bubble of contentment.

'And women too, Mother — some of them. But they can't all be like thee and me.'

Lucinda made no attempt to hide her quick look of irritation. 'And you don't care that there is no inheritance for Alex?'

'I'd never given it a thought that there might be. Neither of us had. But, more important, now that you know you are free, you and Mr Hardcastle can go ahead with your plans.'

'I would have gone ahead months ago. But Charles is a stickler for doing things what he calls correctly. We shall be married in Brackleford. A civil contract, drawn up for us at the Town Hall. There is an office at the hall licensed for the registration of marriages.'

'Why not in the church, here in Oakleigh?'

'Seeing that we never go there, it would be complete hypocrisy, something I can't tolerate. A civil contract is all that is required. And why should we want to give the village free entertainment?'

Tamsin looked at her defiant mother-in-law, always so determined to go against the grain.

'Why should you? I suppose, because people in the village are jolly proud to have Charles

Hardcastle as one of them. They look on him as quite a celebrity.'

'So they'd all come and have a good stare at him in his wheelchair, then all go home whispering smutty remarks. Is that what you want for us?'

How touchy Lucinda was.

'They're nice people, Mother. When they hear about the wedding, they'll all be wishing him well — wishing you both well.'

'That's enough about it, anyway. We've made our plans — and, as far as I'm concerned I can do without their blessing. Charles and I have a good working arrangement: and that's our own business. I must go. I told Barnes I'd only be five minutes. He's taking me straight to the station; I have a meeting in town this evening. You won't forget to tell Alex about his father?'

Alex never mentioned his runaway parent, but Tamsin recalled the day he'd told her how it was he and his mother found themselves in the humble villa in Tannery Lane. Even as a young child, she'd been conscious of his pride in his own maleness, his feeling of empathy with the man who'd forsaken them.

'How well do you remember him?' she asked, when Alex had digested the news in thoughtful silence.

'Mostly I remember that it was always fun being with him. I expect Mother's right; he was probably a rascal. But a rascal is one heck of a lot more fun to be with than someone ready to fight the world for some stupid cause.'

'Suffrage isn't stupid,' she defended. 'If it's

right for men to have a say in who runs things, then it's right for women.'

'You'll be telling me next that women ought to be driving railway engines, bringing coal out of the pits — taking flying machines into the air — '

Her face broke into the smile broad enough to bring the dimple into evidence. 'Flying an aeroplane — now that's an ambition worth fighting for.'

He couldn't resist her and, anyway, he didn't want to get involved in some serious discussion probably set in motion by thoughts planted during his mother's visit.

'If Father went off with — who was it? Mrs Sherbourne, I think her name was — then half the blame must have been my mother's.'

'For having a mind of her own? What arrogant nonsense!'

He bent down and kissed the tip of her nose. 'Oh, but she's pretty when she's roused,' he teased. Then, more seriously, 'Mother never laughed, you know. I ought not to criticise her. She must have had a hard time bringing me up on her own. But she never laughed. Not like he did.' Tamsin heard the note of regret in his voice. 'Having fun is what you remember best, isn't it?'

'Then we'll have to see that this baby has plenty of it.' She snuggled her face into his neck. 'And that we — you and me — we go on having it. Even when you're rich and successful: even when we're old and grey.'

In that moment, she believed that's how it would always be.

James knew he was always welcome at Brambles. Alex was glad to have him there, for surely his interest could only mean one thing: certainty of progress up the ladder that would lead to responsibility and perhaps ultimately a partnership at Proctor's. Tamsin liked him coming, partly because she knew his visits were important to Alex, but mostly because he was such easy company.

Their cottage had once been the home of a pig farmer; the land that had become the airfield had once been where his animals had rootled. The nearest house was further down the lane beyond the engineering works, and it was into that that a young couple moved at the end of the summer. They were the Rileys: Tom Riley, who worked for the blacksmith near the green, and his wife Maureen.

Setting off to call on the newcomers, Tamsin's thoughts turned to her mother, who was always ready to welcome new parishioners. Honesty made her admit that she would have been less keen (in fact, honesty prodded her again, she probably wouldn't have bothered) had it not been evident on the one occasion she'd seen Maureen Riley that she too was expecting a child. At Brackleford, Mavis had even sometimes helped bring babies into the world but, with all the prudishness of her era, she had kept any talk of such affairs strictly from her daughter's ears. Tamsin was learning as she went along, and was grateful that there had been nothing to throw her usual good health off course.

'When's your baby due?' she asked Maureen, even now her mother's ghost reprimanding her and reminding her that the polite thing was to pretend she hadn't noticed.

'November. And I tell you, I'm not doing a thing that's going to risk it this time. I lost my first one.'

'How awful. How old was it?'

'Before I had it, I mean. So, this time, I'm taking care. About ten weeks more to wait.'

'I have to wait until the end of January.' How good it was to say it aloud, to hear herself talking about it to someone who would understand.

'You? But you're so tiny. January, you say? You must be halfway and look at you! Me — my Tom says it's once round me and twice round the gasometer!'

'I've always been skinny; I'm big compared with normal. I've had to alter the buttons on my skirts.' For Alex, she wanted to stay as she'd always been; yet, talking to Maureen who sat cradling her stomach and with her feet planted firmly apart for comfort, she felt inferior. Shrimp!

They spent the rest of her visit on baby talk, neither sure what was ahead of them. By the time Tamsin walked briskly back to Brambles, she knew she had a friend in the rosy-faced girl with a ready smile and a wide gap between her front teeth, one of which was chipped.

The friendship held and strengthened. When Maureen went into labour, Tamsin was on hand to help Mrs White, the Oakleigh midwife.

215

'I can do with a bit of help, but I don't want you getting upset if you've not seen a baby born before.' Elsie White looked at her uncertainly; she might be more trouble than she was worth. A slip of a girl: just look at her thin wrists and ankles. Before long, she'd be on the receiving end of the battle Maureen Riley was huffing and puffing her way into, although all she'd got to show for it was a bump no bigger than a puddin' basin. Look at her back view and you might think she'd be more at home in the schoolroom. 'You sure you're up to it? Not a pretty sight — and I can't be doing with you passing out on me.'

Tamsin was sure. Whatever lay ahead, she wanted to know. So, when a daughter was born to Maureen, except for Mrs White, Tamsin was the first to hold her. Her hours by her friend's bedside had taught her not to expect an easy passage, but what was a few hours of pain compared with having her baby?

*   *   *

It was the first day of the New Year, 1914. Armed with her faithful straw basket, Tamsin set out for the village. Usually when she'd finished her shopping she'd call at Westwood House and that's what she intended on this particular morning. The tone of Charles's reception was still as unpredictable as she'd come to take for granted, and she was never certain Lucinda would be in Oakleigh. It would have been easier to cut across the green without passing the door,

216

but that was something she wouldn't let herself do. Lucinda and Charles (she managed 'Mother', but Charles was still Mr Hardcastle) were Alex's family, so they were hers too — and her baby's.

It was bitterly cold. Puddles from the previous evening's rain were minature skating rinks and the road was white with frost, except where it had melted under the wheels of traps or bicycles.

She passed the boundary hedge of the airfield, casting a glance as she always did, in case there was a sign of Alex. This morning, the big doors were closed against the wintry day. She'd never slipped on the ice before; it didn't occur to her that she might. Instead, she stepped out firmly, humming under her breath, enjoying the crisp air that made her cheeks tingle.

'You ought not to be walking with roads like this. Suppose you slip.' James's voice surprised her as he drew up alongside.

'Nonsense. I've never slipped on the ice in my life. It's a glorious morning.'

'May I give you a lift?' Already, he was leaning across to open the door on the passenger side. 'I'm on my way to Brackleford. I could drop you in the village as I go through. Or, better still, why don't you come into the town with me to do your shopping? I have an appointment with my accountant, but we could arrange a time and place to meet and drive home together. How about that? Does it appeal?'

'What a lovely start to a new year. You don't know how much I've missed getting about on my bicycle these last weeks. I'm sure I could still ride it, but Alex says I shouldn't.'

'And quite right, too.'

She settled by his side, prepared to enjoy the treat of her wintry ride.

'There's nothing wrong with me, you know. I'm as fit as anything.' She frowned, allowing herself a sideways glance in his direction. Would he think she was stupid, if she said what was in her mind? Something must have prompted her to take the chance. 'I'm glad I've been so well, but sometimes I get scared.'

Still looking ahead as he drove, he took his left hand off the steering wheel and covered hers with it. If only there were some way he could lift her fears, reassure her.

'It'll soon be over, Tamsin. You'll look back and know it was worth everything, even the fear.'

'The baby, you mean? Oh, it's not that that scares me. I know that will hurt, but that's just something everyone has to put up with. No, it's not having a baby that frightens me: it's just that everything is so — so right. Is anyone entitled to so much happiness? How long can it last? Do we have a sort of quota and, when it's used up, there's no more?'

His mind went back to when he and Myrtle had been waiting for their baby, both of them so certain of their future. His hand tightened on Tamsin's.

'Perhaps the danger comes when we take what we have for granted,' he tried to reassure her.

'Oh, but I don't do that. I just never knew that happiness was like it is. I don't mean I was ever unhappy: it's just that I never knew there was

218

anything other than the day-to-day living I was used to.'

'Alex is a lucky young man.' And I hope he appreciates it, he added silently.

'We both are. You know James, ever since I was small — about five or six, I must have been — when I first knew him, he was — sounds silly, but it's true — he was the centre of my universe. For years we didn't even see each other, not until we were grown up, but he was always there in my mind. He called me Shrimp, when we were little. Did you know that? And the day we met again, he still teased me with the old name. We'd both remembered. It was as if, even though we hadn't seen each other for so long, we belonged together.' She shivered. 'I know it's silly to be frightened, but sometimes I can't see ahead. I'm scared to try, in case it's tempting Fate. Taking good fortune for granted: isn't that what you said we shouldn't do?'

'Your future should be good. Alex is doing well, you know. He's become my right-hand man.'

'He's been flying quite a lot lately, hasn't he? I watch from the window.'

'He's become quite competent. You mustn't worry about him.'

She laughed, the dimple digging deep into her cheek. 'I'm not worrying when I watch him. I'm envying. I remember seeing you test fly the Farley Moth — that was the first time I came to the airfield, the day I met Alex again.'

'You mean you want to go up?'

'Could I?' The thought of it lit lamps behind

her eyes as she sat forward in her seat and turned to look at him. 'Would you take me up in the Farley Moth?'

'We'll strike a bargain, Tamsin. For the next few weeks, having a baby — that, and getting used to looking after it — is going to take your time. But as soon as you're ready, you tell me. I shall take you myself. Selfish, perhaps, but I want to be the one to share that moment when you leave the ground and rise up over the trees.' He smiled at her, wondering whether she remembered that those were the very words she'd used when she'd talked about watching him on the test flight.

In Brackleford, he put her down at the junction of Station Approach and George Street, arranging to meet at the same place at half past eleven. She was surprised at her pleasure in being among the bustle of town once more; the few shops on the green at Oakleigh served a day-to-day purpose. She bought coloured candles to put on their table, she bought quails' eggs — which seemed to her the height of luxury, even though she wasn't at all sure how she would serve them — she bought celeriac and she bought three yards of narrow white ribbon and a yard of lace. By then, it was after eleven and she still had the necessary groceries to get.

Another twenty minutes, her straw bag weighed down with the items she'd had on her list when she'd left home, she started towards her meeting place with James. Dear James: he would never break a promise and he'd promised to take her up in the Farley Moth. As her imagination leapt away with her, she stepped out briskly.

The guttering of Hambleton's Ironmongery in George Street had been blocked with leaves for weeks; every time it had rained, Bruce Hambleton had promised himself that he would see to it, as soon as the weather cleared. Had Tamsin's mind not already been high above the airfield, had she not in her mind's eye been looking down on Brambles and the lane to the village, then she would have noticed how everyone who passed the ironmonger's stepped off the pavement that shone with ice and walked in the road. But not Tamsin.

★ ★ ★

'Alex!' James shouted as he opened the back door of the works. 'Alex, leave what you're doing.'

Alex knew nothing about Tamsin's trip to Brackleford; he had no idea that James had seen her. But it was to Tamsin that his mind sprang when he heard that call and one glance at James's face was all it needed to tell him something was wrong.

8

'Can't you go faster?' Alex sat on the edge of his seat as if that would will the automobile forward. 'How long did you take to get from Brackleford? How long has she been there?' Then, without waiting for any answers: 'James, supposing she's done some damage, suppose she'd not all ri — ' He couldn't bear to hear it said.

'Alex, she's been very well, right through. Her fall has started her in labour, but she was almost at full time. She's normal, she's healthy: that's what you've got to keep telling yourself.'

'All very fine to talk like that! Slipping on the ice wasn't normal and healthy. She must have been so bloody frightened.' As if it had a life of its own, his clenched right fist hammered a rhythmic tattoo on his knee.

'Tamsin doesn't frighten easily, we both know that.' James remembered the moment he'd drawn up at the junction of Station Approach and George Street to find no Tamsin waiting for him and his premonition of disaster when he'd seen the cluster of people outside the ironmongery. Turning the motor car down the street, even before he'd reached them, he'd known what he would find.

His mind had leapt ahead; again he saw Bruce Hambleton on one side of her and Horace Dunne from The Old Rose opposite, helping her to her feet.

'James . . . ' He'd heard her relief at the sight of him.

He swallowed the Adam's apple that seemed to fill his throat as in his mind's eye he recalled her look of thankfulness that he was there. With her safely back in the passenger seat, they had started for home, but had hardly got to the edge of town before her sudden strangled gasps had told him all wasn't well.

'James — must be — ' her breath caught in another shuddering moan ' — must be baby.' She'd bent forward, her hands tight against her groin: 'Something's happening — James . . . James . . . '

Her always pale face held the pallor of death: beads of perspiration and the way her teeth clamped on her bottom lip made his hand move spontaneously to cover hers. He turned towards the hospital, his foot pressed hard on the accelerator. Once there, he hadn't attempted to leave her while he went for help. Instead he had gathered her into his arms and carried her inside.

'How long will we be?' Alex's voice cut across his thoughts. 'Will it be over — I mean, will it be born? Christ! Why couldn't she have done as I said? She shouldn't have to go through this. She's so small — what'll happen to her?'

'She's in good hands. Alex, you've got to pull yourself together. She needs your strength.'

'Easy for you!' Alex almost spat the words at him. 'You don't know what it's like.'

In truth, James knew only too well what it was like. The morning had brought alive the helplessness and despair that had overwhelmed him as his own Myrtle had slipped away from him. It took all his willpower to push the tide of emotion to the back of his mind, where he had trained himself to keep it in place. He never talked of his past — and this was no time to tell poor young Alex that indeed he knew exactly what it was like. Anyway — he set his mind back on course — Tamsin wasn't going to die.

Then another echo whispered to him. This time the voice was Tamsin's, her own fear that such perfect happiness couldn't last. Don't change things for her, he prayed silently. Keep her well; give her a healthy baby; make her eyes always shine with trust. And, just as he had to her, he covered Alex's clenched fist with his own hand.

'It's my fault,' Alex croaked. Older and more experienced, he might have been able to keep his fear hidden. But in that moment, he was just a boy, shaken by an emotion that terrified him in its intensity.

'Having babies is natural. You'll see: she'll be home and herself in no time,' James tried to bolster him.

'If she dies . . . ' He turned his face away.

'Don't say it,' James spoke quietly, as he pulled the car to a halt in the hospital forecourt. 'Don't even think it.'

★ ★ ★

In a hurry to come into the world, Tamsin's daughter had already announced her arrival with a lusty yell by the time Alex arrived.

'Just take a seat on the bench there,' a bustling nurse told him, her crisply starched apron seeming to him to crackle as she moved. 'As soon as the infant is bathed, you shall see her.'

'And Tamsin — my wife.'

'By and by, you'll be taken in. It'll only be a quick visit, mind. I don't want her to get excited. Peace and quiet is what she'll need, when the doctor is done with her. Never seen a baby more impatient to get itself born. Now, you and your friend sit and wait, while I see if baby has been tidied up ready for you to see.'

'And my wife? How long will she be?'

'There's more to having a baby than just having a baby.' It took years off the angular and officious nurse when her face broke into a smile. 'Husbands always find that hard to accept. As I say, the child was in a rush; there's internal stitching as well. Just bide your time a while. I'll fetch you as soon as the doctor's finished attending to her.'

Obediently, they sat on the hard bench, their backs to the tiled wall of the corridor.

'This place stinks of antiseptic,' Alex mumbled, the back of his hand to his mouth. 'Must find the WC.'

'Down the corridor, I noticed it. Are you all right?'

Without waiting to answer, Alex sped down the corridor. When he emerged, a few minutes later, his face was almost as white as Tamsin's had been on the way to the hospital.

'Be strong for her,' he muttered, as he flopped

back onto the bench. 'That's what you told me: be strong for her. I'm bloody useless. Been sick as a dog.' With his eyes closed, he leant his head back against the wall.

Watching him, James felt a great sense of relief. It was as if a weight had been lifted. Through the months since their marriage, he had never been able to dispel his doubts. Now, looking at Alex, his fears melted.

'Baby's ready. Here she is.' The nurse was approaching, this time with a bundle in her arms. 'Now, Papa, hold her carefully.' Alex held his arms so that the bundle could be passed to him. 'Just two minutes and I shall be back for her.' The nurse turned on her heel and left them just as rapidly as she'd come.

A small, pink and wrinkled face was all that was exposed; the baby bore little resemblance to a human being. Alex held her stiffly in front of him, unprepared for the emotion that such a tiny creature could evoke. Hardly knowing he did it, he bent his arms so that he held her closer.

He was ashamed; he couldn't stop shaking, any more than he could hold back the rasping sobs that shook him. It was all over. Tammy was going to be well.

⋆　⋆　⋆

From the bedroom window of the cottage, Tamsin saw them coming along the lane, Lucinda pushing Charles in his wheelchair. There was nothing delicate about her handling of the chair; rather, she strode along as if she

226

were pushing a barrow. No wonder Tamsin smiled as she watched. But, as they came closer, she could see that their conversation never faltered; it looked to be as brisk as their pace. This was a very different Charles from the all-too-often morose man she had worked for.

When they were almost at the cottage, he glimpsed something in the hedgerow that took his interest.

'Typical,' Tamsin chuckled, watching as, with disregard for her polished shoes, Lucinda squelched her way over the sodden grass verge and clambered across the dividing ditch to reach what it was he wanted. Then, while she bent over him, they examined the specimen. He was apparently explaining something to her; she was listening intently, nodding, questioning. Tamsin thought of the hours spent poring over his books, and knew that most of what she'd learnt had already been forgotten. He would find a more satisfactory student in Lucinda.

By the time they came up the garden path, the front door was open in welcome.

'What's happened to Barnes and the motor car?'

'He's polishing it,' Lucinda laughed. 'What do we want with a motor car, on a day when the sun has at last decided to shine? So, how do you like being home? And did you get any sleep with a new baby to look after?'

'She was very good,' Tamsin lied. Or was it a lie? The trouble had probably come from herself, not wanting Alex's night to be disturbed, uncertain whether Kate was unsettled because she was hungry or because she was overfed.

'You look tired,' Charles told her, with more honesty than tact. 'Pasty. A slip of a girl like you are, you've got to watch yourself.'

'You'd look washed out, too, if you'd gone through what she has.' Lucinda was quick to defend. 'I hope Alex isn't expecting you to wait on him, Tamsin? You see that he does his share; most women are resting with a baby only two weeks old.'

'Of course he'll help me, if I need it. But I'm fit as anything.'

Lucinda took out her cigarette case and holder. From the way she arranged herself in the armchair, Tamsin could tell she was about to launch herself on her favourite topic.

'We have an added responsibility now, Tamsin. You and me, too. Little Kate. It's her future we have to think of. Incidentally, what made you call her Kate?'

'We liked it.'

'Oh, well, what's in a name? I was saying — it's Kate and all those others who are growing up today: for their sake we must strive for what we know is just and right. Don't let yourself become one of those dreadful women who harm our cause.'

'Women harm it? By not joining in the fight you mean?'

'Worse even than that.' Lucinda drew slowly on her cigarette holder, then exhaled and watched a perfect smoke-ring rise towards the ceiling. 'By being contented to accept, by seeing themselves as there to keep the wheels of home

228

oiled. This is the dangerous time for you: happy in your domesticity, busy with the piffling chores of each day, never reading the newspaper, not thinking or caring what goes on in the world beyond your own — '

'That's not true! There are so many ways of caring and showing that you care. Mum used to work endlessly for other people. You could say she did more to help women than you and your lot do.' She hated arguing with Lucinda, but she wasn't going to stand by quietly and be dictated to as to how she should think.

'And why did she do it?'

'Because she cared — ' Tamsin started, but was cut short, as if she hadn't spoken.

'She did it to please her husband, of course. And she was one among millions. Sometimes I despair of them; I wonder why I waste my energy. They give more attention to preparing their man's favourite meal than they do to reading what's going on in the world. And why do they do it? Because they haven't the wit to realise that God has given them brains to use. Or has he? With some of them, I wonder.'

'You denigrate women.' Tamsin might look drained and pasty, but she still had plenty of spirit. 'The men may be the breadwinners, but the women have a job that is every bit as responsible. At least, she does if there are children. They need more than the food that's put in their stomachs and the clothes on their backs. Who is it gives them their moral code? Who shows them the difference between right and wrong? Who gives them the confidence not

229

to be frightened when things go wrong? Gracious, Mother, do you think Alex learnt all those things at school? Of course he didn't: you gave him his principles.'

'So you are going to turn into one of those women who busies herself in her little house, never looks beyond the end of her own nose? God, give me patience. What sort of a model will that be for Kate?'

Charles gave an unexpected guffaw.

'With you for a grandmother, my dear, she'll be left in no doubt of her responsibility to get justice for her sex. And she's only fifteen days old!'

'By the time she is old enough to understand, the battle will be fought and won. It has to be. Year after year, we give all that we are. Equality. That's all we ask.'

Tamsin felt that old tug of affection for her. 'I want it, too, Mother. I want to see the working man — I don't mean just *men*, I mean mankind — given the dignity of his labours. I want to see a fair wage for a fair day's work. It doesn't start and end in parliament. In Brackleford, there are houses where outworkers for the clothes trade stitch, hour after hour, straining their eyes by lamplight during the winter — and for a pittance. Those are the wrongs I want to see righted. Things near at home, things under our own noses.'

'Then get the vote for women. You can't put things right at home until the laws are changed.'

'Hark!' Charles held up a hand. 'As if two female voices aren't enough, there's a third.'

Lucinda was on her feet, the unsmoked half of her cigarette in the fire.

'I'll get her.' Then, with a laugh that made Tamsin suspect she was ashamed of her outburst, 'I want a word in her young ear.'

* * *

Spring came early that year. Tamsin could almost believe it was for her benefit that there was so much warmth in the March sun. The previous year, she had planted bulbs, so daffodils danced in the breeze, soon followed by tulips. The garden at the Manse had been her salvation. At Brambles, it was sheer pleasure to plant vegetables for their own table, to know Kate was lying close by in her perambulator, delighting in the examination of her own hands and ready with a beam of pleasure if her mother leant over to speak to her.

Life was good. Before Kate had been born, Tamsin had been frightened that her happiness was too intense to last. Now, she knew she'd been wrong. What she'd thought of as perfection had been but a preliminary; each day, she became more confident.

'Are you too busy for an interruption?'

At the sound of James's voice, she looked up from the row of shallots she was planting.

'Nothing wrong, is there?' Perhaps she wasn't as confident as she imagined, for even now her alarm bells rang at the slightest provocation.

'The contrary,' he reassured her. 'I've come to see my god-daughter. Alex has just asked me.'

231

'And you've agreed? James, I'm so glad. I hope she'll always have Alex and me to teach her, but — oh, well, no one can be sure. It's quite a responsibility. You don't mind?'

'I hope she always has you, too, Tamsin. But, as to minding, even if I'm not needed as a spiritual guide, I hope she'll see me as an honorary uncle.'

'More than that. I didn't know till Alex told me last night — you held her even before I did. Have you time if I make a jug of coffee? I've already ground it and the kettle will be boiling. I'll just scrub the shalloty smell off my hands.'

'If I hadn't, I'd make time.'

'Go and tell Kate you're to be her special uncle while I go in and see to it.'

If she'd been aware of his expression as he watched her hurry up the path to the cottage, she might have been less at ease with him, less open-handed in her friendship. But, by the time she'd poured the boiling water onto the coffee and glanced out through the kitchen window, he was bending over the pram, communing with ten-week-old Kate.

'You remember what I promised you?' he said as he joined her a minute later. 'Tell me when you're ready for your flight.'

That lit the lamps behind her eyes; it dented her pale cheek with the dimple he always looked for.

'You really meant it? You haven't forgotten? Any time. Just so long as I can leave Kate with Alex. I expect he'd like to be the one to take me — but I'll feel happier to know Kate is with him.'

232

If her answer took something from the pleasure he'd taken in his offer, he didn't let her guess it.

'Then, this afternoon. You'll need to wrap up very warm. Borrow his flying kit; it's cold up there.'

'Imagine . . . ' Words failed her. Instead, just as she had on Brockenhurst Station, she reached up and lightly kissed his cheek. So might she have acted had he been her 'special uncle', as well as Kate's.

★   ★   ★

That afternoon she knew that however long she lived, whatever life had in store for her, that forty minutes she sat behind James in the Farley Moth made an impression that nothing could ever erase. Her hands were lost in the sleeves of Alex's leather coat; his leather helmet framed a face almost hidden behind the goggles that had been fastened on their tightest notch.

From where she lay in her perambulator by the open door of the assembly shop, Kate sensed there was something unusual going on. Instinct rather than familiarity made her recognise the strangely clad creature as her mother — just as instinct made her yell when she was left behind and the people who comprised her world turned away and left her. Tamsin didn't look back to her; this afternoon, the baby was to be Alex's responsibility. Another minute, sitting strapped into the rear seat of the open cockpit, and a thousand butterflies of

233

excitement fluttered inside her.

'Take care of her,' she heard Alex say as James climbed to sit at the controls. He didn't hide his disappointment that he wasn't the one to take her up. He might not have had James's experience, but one thing he never lacked was confidence.

Then, the propeller was spun, the engine burst into life and the machine started forward. James had made up his mind that he would be the one to see her dream fulfilled yet, when the time came, he was the one who saw none of it, not even her irrepressible beam as they taxied forward. Up, up, up they climbed. Peering over the side, she looked down on the pattern of fields, to her left she could see the silver gleam of a river. The Loddon? Yes, it must be, far away she could see where it joined the Thames. The world was spread out beneath her: Oakleigh Green, Farley Woods.

'Wonderful!' she yelled, not knowing whether James could hear her above the roar of the engine. 'I wish I could do it.' The words were shouted, an idle dream — and yet, once spoken, one that she would never forget.

⋆   ⋆   ⋆

James came often to the cottage: sometimes when Alex was there, sometimes when he wasn't. As far as Tamsin was concerned, he was a friend she was always at ease with — her friend; Alex's, despite being his employer; and Kate's, too. It was Kate who gave him a never-failing excuse to walk across the airfield and through the garden gate. By the time she was six months old, supported by cushions to protect her if she slipped, she would be sitting up in the perambulator and screeching with excitement at the sight of him.

Around that time, Alex often worked far into the evening; in fact, the assembly shop was active from early morning until last light. Tamsin had known that the flying performance James had carried out a month or so previously had been for the benefit of a delegation from the Defence Ministry. She had felt a personal pride as she'd watched the machine, spiralling high, swooping low then soaring again, zigzagging across the sky. Soon after that, Alex had told her of the order they'd received: flying machines built to the specification of the Farley Moth but with a difference, for these were to be fitted with rifles that could be swivelled as they were aimed. The pilot would sit in front, the gunner behind. The original Farley Moth had been the epitome of freedom; the Farley Moth mark II sent a chilly shiver down her spine.

'But people don't want war. Who do you ever speak to who wants war?' she said, one evening at the end of July. 'I was talking to Maureen, this afternoon. She's really frightened that it will happen. Her eldest brother was killed in South Africa. No one could be so silly as to send our soldiers to fight in some foreign land again. Could they?'

'Once countries start making pacts with each other — dividing into blocs, opposing sides

— then it will never die away. They pile up armaments which, sooner or later, will be used. Look how busy we've been these last weeks and you may be sure it's the same everywhere. Whether it's their side, Germany, Italy and Austria or ours, us, France and Russia; pound to a penny, all of them are piling up munitions. And as for the Balkans, that's been a bubbling cauldron for two years or more. James was interviewing staff today, more for the assembly line.'

She didn't attempt to hide her pride that Alex was so knowledgeable. She wished, though, that Maureen hadn't said what she had about firms that grew rich making killing machines.

'It's not ordinary people. It's politicians.' She frowned, resenting that ordinary peace-loving people — not just at home but the world over — had to be swept along with the tide of events.

Alex grinned; one look at him was enough to sweep away her temporary anger.

'Politicians,' he teased, 'and all of them *men*!' With one arm around her shoulder, he hugged her. For both of them, the subject was closed. 'Here, pass me that scuttle. I'll go out to the shed and fill it for tomorrow.' For, even at the tail end of July and in the midst of a heat wave, one of the essentials for living at Brambles was a fire in the kitchen range. They were coming up to the August Bank Holiday weekend and neither of them meant to let the threat of a European war cast a shadow on it.

When a note came from Westwood House, asking them to come for lunch on the holiday

236

Monday, they both clutched at the first excuse that came to head while Barnes waited for their reply.

'I'd promised Maureen I'd be on hand. She and Tom want me to look after Trudie for a while.' That from Tamsin.

'The works are shut, but James will be in. I've asked him to come here to eat with us.' That from Alex.

So he scribbled a note explaining they were sorry not to be free. As Barnes wound the starting handle and got back into the driver's seat, they avoided each other's eye.

'It's only a slim chance that Maureen might ask — '

'I'm sure James will be there, but I haven't actually asked him yet.'

Then, looking directly at each other, they laughed.

'This is a Bank Holiday. We can do without Mother's tirade on the follies of men,' Alex said.

'Even though she's right.' Loyalty brought Tamsin to Lucinda's defence, but she smiled all the same. The day lay ahead of them, no cloud in the sky, and they were determined no thoughts of faraway troubles in Europe would spoil their fun. Unfortunately lies have a way of catching up with the culprit, so they couldn't go and join the merrymaking at the fair on Oakleigh Green. Instead, they gardened in the morning with Kate sitting watching them and getting more than her fair share of attention. Neither of them suggested that she was being kept awake through the morning in the certain hope that she would sleep in the afternoon.

Once she was safely in her Moses basket in the cool dining room, the two of them crept like thieves up the narrow stairs. There was excitement in their stolen hour. The sun streamed through the uncurtained window, caressing their naked bodies as they lay on the bed. It was a long time since they'd made love in the heat of the day.

'Like Mothering Sunday,' he whispered, his face buried in her fine hair.

'Better. A thousand times better. I want it never to stop: to be like this forever.'

He wanted it too. Pale and thin as she was, when her passion was unleashed, she was untamed. They wanted it to last forever, but they drove frantically on, and all too soon they were lying still and breathless in each other's arms.

'Better. Each time,' she panted, running her fingers through his auburn curls, 'new miracle.'

'Tammy, never change.'

They heard the click of the garden gate; they recognised the footsteps on the brick path.

'James,' she whispered unnecessarily.

'Sh. Don't move.' Alex spoke in a whisper, even though there was no chance of their being overheard, holding her tight lest she had any wild intention of peeping out of the window. 'I locked the door. He'll think we're out.' They heard the loud knock. 'Hell! Don't let him wake her.' He spoke through clenched teeth, as if forcing the little house to stay silent.

'If Kate cries, he'll know we're in. Sh . . . Listen, he's going. Feel awfully mean,' she muttered against his shoulder as they heard the footsteps retreat.

'Do you? Do you?' His hands caressed her warm body. 'This afternoon is our own. It's not over yet. Don't let her wake: not yet, not yet. Tammy, I love you.' Even though the click of the gate told them James had gone, even though Kate obligingly still slept, yet still they whispered. This was stolen time, magic time: nothing must break the spell. Those things rekindled their passion. Each time was a new miracle, she'd said. Lovemaking was a journey of adventure; they held nothing back. With hands, mouths, tongues, they gloried in the joy of the wild surge of passion they shared, until the ultimate union that bound them together body and soul.

$$\star \quad \star \quad \star$$

In the evening, James came back. This time when they saw him approaching up the path Alex opened the door, their welcome was warm.

'I came earlier, but you were out,' he told them.

He didn't notice the quick glance that passed between the couple; he did notice the way Alex's hand moved to touch the nape of Tamsin's slender neck.

'I was on my way into Brackleford — that's where I heard. It's happening: there can be no other way, however long the government here hesitates. Yesterday, Germany declared war on France, demanded free passage for its army through Belgium. It was refused, of course. Belgium is a neutral country. But a treaty of neutrality isn't going to stop the Huns invading. Belgium is small and helpless.'

'So what will happen?' Even as she asked it, Tamsin knew what the answer must be. No country stockpiled munitions for nothing: wasn't that what Alex had said?

'It's gone beyond all chance of anyone pulling back.'

The echo of Maureen's voice filled Tamsin's mind, the scathing sneer about men who were ready to line their own pockets by making weapons of war. But *somebody* had to make sure the country was defended.

'We're an island race, that's what Maureen says. Surely if ever a country should sign a neutrality treaty, it's us.'

James shook his head. 'We are the mother nation of a great Empire. We can't stand by and see treaties broken, small nations overpowered by strong neighbours.'

They all knew he was right.

'I'm going into town late this evening,' James told Alex. 'Yesterday Germany was threatening to invade Belgium. According to the report pinned outside the Town Hall, in the early hours of today they crossed the border. They have until tonight to withdraw; the alternative is that we, like France, declare war. They won't withdraw. To do that, at this stage, would be synonymous with accepting defeat. You know and I know, they've been building towards this. The trouble in Serbia has been no more than

240

the final excuse to pull the trigger.'

'You say the notice is on the Town Hall. So why are you going in again? Are they expecting to hear anything else today?' Alex had moved away from Tamsin. Watching them, she felt herself to be pushed to one side. But if there was war, it was her war as much as theirs

'They have until midnight. As soon as word is telephoned through, the Town Clerk is to make an announcement. Do you want to drive in with me later on, be there to hear it?'

'Rather!' Alex agreed with enthusiasm. 'Pity you can't come too, Tammy. But we couldn't take Kate, so of course you can't.'

Looking from one to the other of them, Tamsin's mind sprang to Lucinda and her fight for equality. Men! Just look at the mess the world was in!

*　*　*

War . . . was it really going to happen? She must have lived through the Boer War but she couldn't remember anyone at Gorsemoor ever talking about it. It would have been different for Maureen: she'd had a brother in the army. Was there anyone in Oakleigh with anything to do with the army? The Rector's son was in the navy: would there be battles at sea? How must the Rector and his wife feel tonight? Would faith help him to be sure his son would be safe? Then there was someone whose name she didn't know, a woman who lived by the Green: she'd been talking in the butcher's the other day about her

241

son who was serving 'with the regiment'. Burrowing her head into the pillow, Tamsin was ashamed of her own peace of mind, her own thankfulness that Alex was a civilian.

★ ★ ★

'I wish you could have been there, Tammy,' Alex whispered as he climbed into bed at her side, talking quietly for fear of disturbing Kate, who snorted on the verge of waking in the other bedroom, with both doors open between them. 'The atmosphere was like nothing I could have dreamt. Honestly, you could almost feel the silence when the Town Clerk came onto the steps. We're at war. This is it: it's actually happening. Can you believe it? Even though we knew it was pointing to it, that's not the same as knowing it's started. Tammy? Say something.'

'I've been thinking of the Rector's son — he's in the navy. How must all those families be feeling tonight, people with sons and brothers — even husbands — in the army?'

'I expect a lot of them were at the Town Hall to hear. Tammy, I wish I could explain it better. That silence: every word the Town Clerk spoke was clear, even though there was such a crowd listening. Then, when he finished speaking, it was as if a spring was released. Someone shouted 'Three cheers for the King, hip, hip', and you should have heard the roar! Then a man started to sing the National Anthem, there wasn't one who didn't join in. A woman next to me was crying, but she sang just the same.' He held her tightly against him. 'I don't think any of us wanted to go home. It was as if we were all part of one whole. Does that sound silly? If you'd been there, you would understand what I'm trying to say. The mother nation of a great Empire, wasn't that what James called us? And you could feel it. Just ordinary people, strangers to each other: yet we belonged. And that's the way it always has to be, Tammy.'

'Was the Boer War like that? Can you remember how it felt?'

'South Africa is far away. You know, in that moment when we all stood together, I bet there wasn't one person who wouldn't have gone out to slay the dragon for St George.'

Involuntarily, she shivered.

'You can't be cold?' His warm hand moved down her body.

'No. Just a goose walked over my grave. Alex, nothing is going to change, is it? War is for other people, soldiers, sailors — not that I don't care about them, but I'm so thankful we're who we are.'

He remembered that moment when he'd raised his voice as loudly as any; he remembered, too, James's words as they'd come towards home.

'This war won't just be on land and sea. This time, there will be fighting in the air — no one is more aware of that than we are,' he'd said, their minds on the hours of overtime the men had worked and the guns that had been fitted to the machines that came off the assembly line.

There was urgency in Alex's caresses. Sleep

was a million miles away; every nerve in his body was alive and driving him towards a future that had no sure shape. Only the present was real; only the present could still his racing thoughts. How different it was from the sensual pleasures they'd shared in the afternoon. Now, when he moved onto Tamsin, she drew him close; she found comfort and reassurance in the belief that, with his emotions heightened by the night's experience, it was her he needed, it was only she who could bring him the peace and sweet content that led to sleep.

★   ★   ★

In those first few days it seemed that once the declaration of war was accepted, life was to settle back into its pattern. For some people, perhaps, the illusion would last: but not for Tamsin, nor for Maureen. Even in a small community like Oakleigh, unrest stirred among the young men. Word passed that a Recruiting Office had been opened in Brackleford.

'It's not fair. It's not right.' Maureen sat on the small patch of grass, watching Tamsin dig a root of potatoes ready for supper. 'There are plenty of fellows without wives and babies. Let them rush off, if they must.'

'I never expected so many ordinary men would go. Mother said, when she came down from London yesterday, there was a band playing outside Brackleford station, and quite thirty young men were being seen off.'

'That's what happens. One goes, then the next

244

feels he's less of a man if he stays behind. The Royal Berks Regiment: that's where they're off to, to the barracks in Reading, I suppose. But where after that? It makes my stomach turn right over to think of it. It's easy for you. Alex is busy making flying machines; he can stay at home and not feel that people are looking at him and thinking he's got a yellow streak.'

'There's talk that those who have motor cars will go back to pony and trap, that's what I was reading in the newspaper. So a blacksmith's job will be a kind of war work, too.'

'And how many extra horses would there be around here if the few motor cars were taken off the road? Horses are being sent to France: dozens of them, hundreds of them. That's what Tom says. And wherever there are horses, there must be men who can keep them shod.' She lifted Trudie out of her perambulator and put her to crawl on the grass. 'Can I lift Kate? She feels left out of things.' Not waiting for an answer, she fetched Kate, then sat back on the grass, jiggling her on her knee, occasionally moving her knees apart and catching the baby as she fell. It was a favourite game, one that guaranteed to bring peals of excited laughter from both tiny girls.

'It's not fair.' Maureen returned to the subject that was at the forefront of her mind. 'You're so lucky — I don't grudge you, it's not that. People like Mr Proctor and all the men there, they'll have to work extra hard, I know that. But think of the money Alex will bring home in his pay packet. You know what they get when they join the army? A shilling a day. A shilling a day and the chance to get themselves shot.'

With her root stripped of potatoes, Tamsin came to sit by her friend.

'I know I'm lucky. Never a day goes by that I forget to be thankful. But, standing back and looking at things, Alex is probably going to do more towards winning the war than a lot of the young men who are queuing up to enlist. I'm not saying more than Tom: he is trained, he has a skill.'

'Stupid damn war.' Maureen buried her face in Kate's silky red curls. 'Who wanted it, anyway? Nobody, except a bunch of arrogant leaders. And I don't care whether they're British, French or even German, they're all the same, the lot of them.'

Two days later, her eyes bloodshot with weeping, Maureen brought the news that Tom had enlisted; in a few days, he would get his instructions.

Afterwards, Tamsin wondered whether Tom's action had an influence on Alex. The work he did was useful and necessary; it honestly hadn't occurred to her that he would leave Proctor's.

'The Flying Corps? But, Alex, you are helping the war with the work you do. Think of all you've learnt. Why, you know so much more than the men who are taught to fly the machines you build.' She heard herself say it; she knew the truth of the argument — but even more surely, she knew that in his mind, Alex was already in khaki. She felt shut out from his thoughts, helpless to hold him. 'Does James know?'

'I told him this morning. Of course, he tried to dissuade me, just the same as you are. I don't expect *you* to understand. You're a woman, your place is here at home. Men have always gone to battle. I think I've known — no, not think, I know I've known — right from that night at the beginning of the month, when I stood in that crowd outside the Town Hall. Tammy, I can't stay at home and watch other men go, lads from our own village and with nothing to offer but to march with a rifle and bayonet. But me? I'm streets ahead of most of the chaps going into the Flying Corps. How many of them have ever flown an aeroplane? You ask James what he thinks of my flying! He'd even talked of letting me take over some of the test flights.'

'There you are, then!' She forced herself to sound positive, even though her heart felt like a lump of lead in her chest. 'And you think that what you're doing isn't helping win the war. If you go, you'll be letting James down. There's no one else trained to fly.'

'He'll manage. At his age, I suppose he doesn't feel the same as I do . . . ' His words melted into silence, but the echo of his enthusiasm for the venture hung between them.

'Even if he wanted to, how could he? Proctor's depends on him — and he's more use to the Flying Corps there than he would be up in the air.' She felt she was hitting below the belt, wanting to hurt him for his eagerness to make a hero of himself.

He'd known that, as a fully trained pilot, there

247

would be no delay in taking him: but things moved with speed beyond anything he'd imagined. He signed the papers offering his services; within days he was called for duty.

My darling Shrimp,

Hold your head high, Tammy, you have a husband who is a fine specimen and passed his medical examination A1. They couldn't find a single thing about me that wasn't perfect!

The accommodation here is Spartan, but the lads are a great bunch. Things are moving fast; they won't hang about long deciding I am ready to hold the King's Commission. What a difference it makes that I am already a skilled pilot. Just you wait till I come striding up the garden path a fully fledged Second Lieutenant.

I think a lot about you and hope you are managing without me — not too easily, of course: I want to be missed. I love to think of you happy, laughing and showing that funny dimple that's just the right size for my little finger; but I hope you are pining at least a little bit. It's harder for you than it is for me, I suppose, for at home everything is just the same as usual — except that I'm not there — while here new things are happening all the time. Added to which, of course, I know I am here for a purpose. Next stop, France. But before that, I shall have a few days' leave.

I miss you very much. I miss everything about you — even in the busy hours of the day, my thoughts keep finding their way back

248

to you. And lying in the loneliness of my hard bed . . . I'll say no more, in case this gets censored! Anyway, I'm a man of action, not words.

I hope James is keeping an eye on you and Kate; he promised me he would. And I hope Kate is being good. Is she missing me?

Always, your Alex.

Tamsin read it through once, unable to prevent her feeling of isolation. Of course he was missing her: didn't he say so? But the overriding tone of his letter was one of exhilaration, eagerness to be getting on with whatever lay ahead. Then she read it again, this time a smile tugging at the corners of her mouth. He sounded so cocky, like a little boy given a new drum to beat. 'Fine specimen', 'skilled pilot', 'great bunch of lads', 'striding up the garden path': she seemed to hear the laugh in his voice as he talked. Her own smile deepened. She knew she was being childish and fanciful, but that didn't stop her closing her eyes and raising her hand to her left cheek, twisting her finger in 'that funny dimple' just as he so often did.

* * *

When he came on that promised leave, there could have been no prouder pilot in the Royal Flying Corps than Second Lieutenant Alexander Murray: it could be seen in the set of his straight shoulders, and heard in the sound of his firm footsteps. On his chest he wore the flyers' emblem, the pair of wings embossed with the letters RFC. For seven days he was home and, despite their not going further afield than one cycle ride to Brackleford while they left Kate with Maureen, they were days lived with intensity. The nutty, smoky scents of autumn had never been more poignant; the sight of the smoke rising from their chimney into the still air had never been more symbolic of home.

Most days, Alex walked across to the works, where he knew he was sure of a warm welcome — a hero's welcome, despite not yet having been given a chance for heroics. No one else had rushed to volunteer, and why should they? They were helping the war effort where they were — and, he added silently, aware of his 'wings', none of them could fly.

'Tammy tells me you often drop in on Kate and her. You don't mind keeping an eye on them, do you?' he said to James on his last morning.

'I've always liked going to Brambles, you know that. Tamsin knows I am here if she needs anything. And, as for my going there, I promise you I look forward to it. Even so, the sooner you get home, the better. What she needs is a husband, and Kate a father. I'm no more than a helping hand if the tap needs a new washer or the logs need chopping.'

'It's jolly good of you. Well, I suppose this is goodbye. I told her I'd not be many minutes.'

Alex held out his hand and felt it taken in James's firm grasp.

'God's speed. Everywhere, there is confidence you'll soon see the Boche back where he

250

belongs.' There was so much James would like to have been able to say to this confident young man he'd shaped since he was little more than a boy. But he wasn't a man who could speak his heart easily, so he contented himself with putting a friendly arm around Alex's shoulder and telling him, 'The business can ill spare you, so finish the job out there quickly and get back to us all.'

'Jerry'll wonder what's hit him,' Alex answered, with a cocksure laugh.

Walking back through the assembly shop, he was assailed by shouts of good wishes, handshakes, thumps on the back. He revelled in every second of it. But then he was out of the door, skirting along the edge of the airfield to the garden gate of the cottage. This was it! Already, he felt removed from what he'd left behind. The curtain had fallen on an important part of his life. How long before he was back at Proctor's? Even if the war didn't last long, would he be able to slip back into the gap his leaving had made and find he fitted?

That's when he felt his first real pangs of fear. It wasn't the thought of going to France that frightened him: he was confidant he was the equal of any pilot the enemy could put into the sky. Fear came from a sense of finality, the knowledge that every experience would take him further from all he'd known, all he'd been. Away from Proctor's, away from James — who had been his hero through adolescence — away from Tammy, away from Kate . . . No, whatever the future had in store, nothing could alter for Tammy and him. But Kate? She was a baby;

251

each day, her dawning intelligence developed. He'd been away only a few weeks but, when he'd arrived home, he might have been a stranger. Now, after one week, he was part of her life again.

The perambulator was in the garden where she'd been put for her morning sleep. Instead of going straight in to Tamsin, he went across and looked down at her, giving her just the excuse she wanted. In a second, she struggled to sit up, her arms held out to him.

'You'll get me hung,' he laughed softly, unbuckling her straps and lifting her to be rewarded by a beaming smile showing four front milk teeth. 'Katie, I don't want to leave you. Or Tammy. I can tell you my secrets can't I, humph? I'm not scared, not of what's out there. Just scared of being without her. And you. You little monster, you're all wet!'

Delighted with her own cleverness, Kate threw back her head and laughed, jigging up and down in his arms. He took off her bonnet and rubbed his cheek against her auburn curls, turning his back on the cottage as if he expected it would know he saw it through a mist of tears he was quick to blink away.

9

Darling Tammy,

So far, I have seen nothing of war, not if you think of war as being a series of battles. You'd have been proud of me on the crossing. We got tossed about like a cork: never seen so many heads hanging over the side! But mine wasn't one of them. When we disembarked, I was still fighting fit and ready to do justice to a breakfast of bacon. Had more than my share, for the sight of bacon was more than some of the lads could take. Then for the overland journey. Every town and village we stopped at, our welcome was the same. Flowers were thrown at us — and girls, plain and pretty alike, showered us with kisses. And that's before we've even had a chance to get at the enemy! Imagine what the Victory Parade will be! They kept shouting what sounded like 'Long live and tear'; wherever we went we heard it. Didn't understand what they were trying to say; but, by the time we've been here a bit longer, they'll have learnt better English.

We have now arrived at the aerodrome (I'm not allowed to tell you where) and I've met up with my machine. Imagine how proud I was to see what I am to fly — a Farley Moth mark II. Tell James.

I have a couple of engineers, trained to keep her in the sky. I wouldn't mind betting I'm the only man on the aerodrome with the knowledge I have of the *Farley* — that and the ability to take her up.

It all seems a long, long way from Oakleigh and Brambles, so you can imagine how important your letters are to me. I know you can't have much news to tell me, when the highlight of your days won't go beyond pushing Kate to the shops on the Green or perhaps calling at Westwood House. But write all the same, Tammy, write and tell me you're missing me.

Tell James that my rigger is fitting wooden racks in the cockpit so that the gunner can also carry hand grenades. Suggest that if that were done at Proctor's, it would save time here. Tell James, too, just for interest, that each gunner is issued with steel darts — *flechettes* is what the French call them — to drop on the enemy. I don't see that they can be much use, unless they land bang on top of a chap who's forgotten to put on his tin hat.

You know, Tammy — and don't misunderstand my meaning — in a way, I'm glad things worked out the way they did. I hate being away from you, but on the other hand I know that I am here to fight for you people at home, for you and for Kate, and it makes me feel good to think of you safely untouched by the sort of upheaval you can tell people are already suffering over here. It's up to every man to fight for the ones they love.

Take care of yourself, Tammy darling, and of Kate. The nights are getting cold and, without me there to keep you warm, I hope James is keeping his promise and seeing you have plenty of wood etc. I picture you by our fire — I picture you in so many ways. Go into Brackleford when you get the chance and have your photograph taken. Some of the chaps have pictures by the side of their beds. That's cold comfort for having the real you, but beggars are grateful for crumbs.

Always, your Alex.

There was no doubt that Alex was enjoying his new life. Just as his letters always did, the first reading made Tamsin feel cut off from his life. Then she turned back to the beginning. Her second reaction was relief: he hadn't been made ill by a rough crossing, he was safe, he was enjoying the comradeship, he was in an environment that suited him. Her third was that familiar tolerance for his boastfulness, and the fourth the recognition of his underlying loneliness for her and her own for him. This time, though, his description of the highlight of her days had ignited another emotion in her. Ignited? No: she faced the truth. It had already been smouldering, waiting for something to fan the flames.

Other letters followed, usually two or three at a time and then a gap. He'd been in France a month or more when he wrote

. . . Remember when I first came out here, I told you we were welcomed with shouts of 'Live long and tear'. Since then, I've started to understand much more. Some of the chaps I'm with learnt a lot of French at school; I wish I had. Anyway, they're a good crowd — and they can see I'm keen to learn. *Vive l'Angleterre* is what the locals were shouting at us. Makes you feel jolly good, Tammy. I can't think how any man worth calling a man can stay comfortable at home and not want to do his part . . .

Tamsin dug into her mind, trying to recall the smattering of French she'd acquired at Miss Searl's school and was well satisfied that Alex and his 'good crowd of chaps' had fallen among friends.

⋆ ⋆ ⋆

'Six weeks today since Tom went off to France,' Maureen told her as they pushed their wide-awake daughters the three-quarters of a mile to the village shops. There was something in the way she said it that made Tamsin turn to look at her before she answered. So often she'd heard Maureen angry and resentful, but that 'six weeks' had sounded neither.

'And less than four to go before Christmas.' An answer and yet no answer.

'I've waited long enough now to be sure. I was due ten days after he went, but nothing's happened. I was scared to say anything — to you or even when I've written to Tom — in case it was tempting Fate.'

'You're pleased? Well, I can see you are.' For it

256

was evident in the tilt of Maureen's head, her purposeful walk.

'Pleased? Of course I'm pleased. By the time it gets born, perhaps he'll be home. Oh, but of course he will: that's months away. Having a baby on the way gives me a sort of purpose.' With her wide-apart front teeth, she bit her bottom lip, as if that would help her find the right way to express what she felt. Words never came easily to Maureen.

Looking at her, Tamsin realised just how fond she'd grown of her down-to-earth friend.

'You must feel the same as I have, since Tom went. Our days don't get us anywhere: it's as if we're just marking time until life gets going again when they get home. You know what I mean?' Tamsin nodded. All too well, she knew. 'But now, with this new baby to think about, I've got a purpose. It's like something of how things used to be for Tom and me.' Then, quickly, as if she was afraid Fate might have heard and found a chink in her defences, she added, 'Used to be and will be again. But until then, I've got a purpose, something I shall be doing for Tom — for us as a family.' Her face flushed with embarrassment; she'd never spoken so freely.

'I know just what you mean. I've been thinking about it, Maureen; in fact, I was planning to talk to you. But promise you'll give me a straight answer . . . '

★ ★ ★

257

'Is there any reason why some of the assembly work can't be done by women?' There was nothing in Tamsin's question to hint that she had a personal reason for asking.

'No reason at all,' James answered. 'There's talk that women will be called in to work at many levels while the war lasts.'

'And so we should. You should hear Mother on the subject! It gives the movement a trump card. If women are good enough to work alongside men during the war, then they're good enough to vote alongside men afterwards! All her prickles are showing.' She laughed, thinking affectionately of Lucinda with her prickles showing. Then, looking at James seriously, she continued, 'But she's right, of course.'

'In fact I have taken an advertisement to the *Brackleford Standard*, asking for assemblers — men or women. It will be in this week's paper. Not that anyone is likely to travel out to Oakleigh from the town; if they want war work, Fulford's are taking on staff making munitions. But there may be people — more particularly women — within cycling distance, perhaps even here in the village.'

'But they won't know anything about the work; even the men won't. There's no one around here except you who builds flying machines.'

'They will be trained for their immediate responsibility. For the present we aren't looking to develop anything beyond the *Mark II*. The work will be routine, once they've had initial training. I shall just have to wait for the weekend to see what response I get, whether I can be selective or whether I have to be grateful to get an applicant at all. That's one of the disadvantages of being in a rural area. Shall I put another log on the fire, or is it too late?'

'I never go to bed early.' The nights were the hardest time without Alex. It was then that the ghosts lay in wait for her, taunting her with images of air battles; or bringing her out of a half-remembered nightmare in a sweat of terror, her mouth dry with fear, not knowing if it had been her voice she'd heard trying to shout — or his.

James was watching her, guessing at some of her thoughts. This was how so many of their evenings had been spent as autumn had given way to that first winter of war. Did she want him here so often? Sometimes he was firm with himself. Once home and having eaten the food his housekeeper had prepared, he made himself concentrate on reading the newspaper, or working in his study. But at the back of his mind was always the thought of the cottage, the shadows from the flickering flames of the fire dancing on the ceiling.

'Tamsin,' his voice cut across her wandering thoughts, 'I ought not to come here so often. I know Alex asked me to keep an eye on you, but you'll be thinking of me as a warder.'

Immediately, he wished he hadn't said it. Just for an instant, her pale face bore a startled expression he couldn't bear to see. But only for an instant. He and Tamsin had one thing in common: neither of them let the world read their hearts. Her smile was so quick, he could almost believe he'd imagined that look of hurt.

'You mustn't worry about me, James. I can manage very well. I'm never a person who craves company. It's been terribly kind of you to bother; I know how busy you are. And, honestly, I understand if you haven't the time to spare.'

'It's not been kind at all. More likely it's been selfish. It's like a miracle seeing Kate's grasp of understanding; every day she is more sure of herself.' Better to hide behind his natural godfather's interest in the baby. The bad moment passed. Kate was the bond that held them.

'James — promise me you won't do me any favours. I couldn't bear that — promise before I say any more.'

'Of course I promise. I told you, I come here out of selfishness, not to do you favours.'

'It's not about that. It's about work. I've talked to Maureen: she is prepared to have Kate every day — '

'Is that what you want? Bringing up a child is a privilege — '

'I don't want privileges just because I'm a woman. There's a war to be won — every one of us has to do *something*. If you don't think I can be any use in your workshops, then I'll look somewhere else. Mr Rampton at Hangersley Farm is supposed to be taking on women to work in the fields. I could do that.'

James looked at her slight form, her almost childlike earnestness.

260

'Do you honestly want to hand Kate over each day?'

Her expression didn't change, yet he could feel her bristle.

'No, don't be so stupid, of course I don't. But did Alex want to go off to France?' She stamped down a thought she wouldn't acknowledge and, on safer ground, 'Did Tom Riley want to go and shoe horses for the army? I'm not some delicate flower who isn't capable of anything except keeping the home fires burning for when the heroes come home. Most women aren't. You'll see, now that they are being given a chance. But about Hangersley Farm: you know I like growing things. I used to help Grandpa when I was small. It's just that if I had something to do with constructing the Farley Moth, it would be like doing it for Alex. Perhaps I'd work on an aeroplane that would go to France and he'd be the one to fly it.' Her voice trailed into silence. Both of them knew Alex was already flying a Farley Moth; there could be only one reason for him to need a replacement.

'There's no doubt I can use you, Tamsin.' James kept his voice matter-of-fact. 'And that's not a favour, it's a fact. We'll have to talk about wages.'

'You must know what you intend to pay, otherwise how could you be interviewing?'

'That's people with no knowledge of our work. You know more about the Farley than those other women who'll apply — always assuming some do. You understand something of the structure, the thinking behind it — '

261

'James, I told you. No favours. All I ask is fair treatment, for me and for any other person who will be doing the same job. If men's work is different, then I suppose you pay them at a different rate. Perhaps you expect women to do something simple.' She was ready to stand her ground.

'In the construction of an aeroplane, there is no such thing as one assembly job being of less importance than another. Men's lives depend on our work. But while we're on the subject of wages, Tamsin: in paying you, I want to bear in mind the work Alex has done — and will do again when he gets home.'

'I want the same as anyone else who answers your advertisement. Otherwise, I shall go and see Mr Rampton. James, if you believe in fairness, then you won't offer a lower rate to an applicant because she'll be coming to the workshops in a skirt! Pay in accordance with how much work each one gets done in a day — that's a difference that's fair; but one rate for a man and one for a woman is — is — *wicked*!'

Her eyes shone in the golden light of the flaming log fire; he noticed the rare patches of pink on her cheeks. Turning away so that she didn't see the smile he couldn't hide, he went to where his heavy overcoat was hanging on a peg by the doorway, then felt in an inside pocket.

'Here.' He passed her a folded sheet of paper. 'This is what I intend.' Then, unable to repress his smile any longer, he asked, 'Do you approve?'

She read the scale of pay, the same for either

sex. One rate for three months under supervision, then a set and equal wage.

'James, I was rude. I'm sorry. I ought to have known you better.'

★ ★ ★

The following Monday, she delivered Kate, complete with perambulator, her favourite wooden push-along train and a pile of nappies, along the lane to spend the day with her friend Trudie under Maureen's caring eye.

'What does your Alex think of your being here?' asked her instructor, the man she'd come to know to be Ken Hodge, the brother of the baker on Oakleigh Green. 'Well, of course, he must have agreed, or you wouldn't have offered yourself.'

She laughed. 'He doesn't know yet. I wanted to make sure I didn't get drummed out on my first day before I told him.'

'Fancy that. You ladies are keen to make your mark. When the letters came through the box this morning, you know who delivered them? That Mrs Birchell, the one whose man looks after cutting the grass in the graveyard. One thing war does, it stands life on its head, and no mistake. Now then, what you've got to do here is take your measure to these wires . . .'

When the hooter went at midday, she ate her sandwiches with the others, sitting on upturned packing cases near the coal-burning stove at the far end of the workshop. During the morning, she had toyed with the thought of going to make

263

sure Kate had settled, but she trod down the temptation. She and Maureen had agreed that a flying visit might only serve to upset her.

'The guv'nor's quiet, today: haven't heard a peep out of him,' someone she only knew by sight observed as he crammed the last corner of a doorstep sandwich into his mouth.

'Most likely got more newcomers to talk to,' Ken said, his eye on Tamsin, as though she were a specimen of things to come.

Tamsin suspected James's main reason for keeping out of the workshop was much the same as hers for not paying a fleeting visit to Kate. To talk to her as he would at home would put a barrier between her and her new workmates; to give her no more than a casual nod would put an uncomfortable barrier between her and him. So did that mean he would no longer drop in casually at Brambles? She almost wished she had left the situation as it was, only now realising how much she looked forward to his comfortable presence in the evenings. But she wouldn't let the thought quite take shape: there was a war to be fought and, when victory was won, she wasn't going to be left feeling she'd played no part.

★ ★ ★

Reading her letter, Alex frowned. He'd worked hard, studied hard, modelled himself on James and been rewarded by leaving the workshop floor. Now Tamsin, his little Shrimp, his wife and with a baby to care for, was there in that crowd of men, her life dictated by a hooter, her small hands getting roughened. He was touched that, in working at Proctor's she felt she was helping him: but, dammit, why couldn't she be content to be at home? She was as bad as his mother. And look at what she'd written about the wage James was paying: the same for women as for men. He felt his manhood denigrated.

Pushing the letter in the top pocket of his tunic, he pulled on his leather flying jacket and helmet and went off to lead his first patrol of the day. These expeditions were fraught with danger; they reconnoitred beyond the enemy lines and were invariably intercepted by enemy planes and a skirmish. Flying at the head of his patrol, he tried to focus all his concentration on the events of the moment. Yet the image of Tamsin, her pale hair tied up in a scarf, her small hands attempting what had always been assumed to be man's work, her friendly laugh as she talked to her workmates on the assembly shop floor: these things repeatedly pushed to the fore of his mind.

A bunch of *Albatros* scouts appeared from out of the sun, one flying just higher than his Farley Moth but straight across his bow. Immediately his mind was clear of all else, both he and the gunner behind him raised their mounted guns and fired. They were close enough to see the way the young German pilot clutched at his wounded shoulder, and to see the look of naked terror on his face as the *Albatros* began to dive like a falling dart towards the ground. He looked no more than a boy: someone's son, someone's brother . . . It happened in a second, the division between life and death, a second that stamped an indelible mark on Alex's memory. Inside his leather gloves, his felt his hands wet with sweat; his arms ached as if all the power had gone from them. This wasn't the first plane he'd shot down — but it was the first time he'd seen that look of helpless terror and thought of his victim as other than a number to be notched up.

For a split second, he lost his iron control, a sure recipe for disaster.

'Christ!' Was it he who shouted, or was it his gunner? Neither was sure. The Fokker's attack was unexpected; in that brief loss of concentration Alex had failed to see it.

'Bloody hell,' he swore, more at himself than at the Fokker. There was a thud; the Farley Moth shuddered as a bullet shattered the propeller. If a drowning man sees his life flash before him, Alex — and the young gunner behind him, too — found it was the same for a man hit from out of the sky. His immediate reaction was to switch off the engine. He had to get the plane back across the line; his one object was to prevent it from nose-diving as it gathered speed in its fall. It vibrated as though any moment it must disintegrate and, all the time, despite his grip on the joystick, they were losing height, even though he managed to hold it out of a nose dive. At about 2000 feet, the pilot of the Fokker must have been satisfied that they were mortally wounded; he would report them as a 'kill' when he returned to base.

They were back over the line, ahead of them were green fields. Mustering all his skill, he brought them safely down.

'Well done, sir. Well done. Bugger gave us a close shave ... well done ... thought our number was up.' The young gunner hardly knew what he was saying; he was jabbering for the comfort of hearing his own voice as they climbed onto friendly soil.

'I'm going to phone the base. Stay with the machine.' Alex's confidence had returned: he'd diced with death and won. No wonder he strode off towards a nearby battery, more than willing to put the incident behind him. Two months before, newly arrived in France, he wouldn't have been able to pull out of that initial shock so soon. He smiled to himself, well satisfied with what he thought of as his 'war worthiness'.

A telephone call to the base brought a truck carrying a newly trained mechanic and a replacement propeller. Watching the lad set to work on the Farley, Alex's self-esteem was given a further boost for, unlike most pilots, he wasn't dependent on someone else's skill. Anxious to get the job done and fly back to base, he put himself in charge of the repair, earning the respect of the mechanic and the gunner too.

As far as Alex was concerned, that was the end of the incident. The job done, he flew on back to his home aerodrome and made his debriefing report to the C.O. The war was young and Alex had been in France less than two months, but his morning's work was noted: a promising young flyer, a man of courage and ingenuity.

* * *

Tamsin need have had no fear that her relationship with James would be changed once she worked for him. During the day, she saw very little of him; in the evening he came to Brambles, just as he had before. As the winter went on, production was stepped up at Proctor's. The staff worked every possible hour, Tamsin the same as everyone else. For her, though, every possible hour still meant that she had to leave by half past six to collect a fed and watered Kate. Each Friday, she shared her wages with Maureen.

'But she's good as gold, and having her here keeps Trudie happy. I'm not going to take anything extra just because you've got a bit more in your pay packet now. It's you who's been trained and has more responsible work to do. Me? All I get is the pleasure of seeing the two of them together.'

'It was our agreement, Maureen. I'm not leaving her here if we don't go halves with the money.'

By that time Tamsin had completed her three months' training, Maureen was halfway through her waiting time, but the likelihood of the war ending seemed ever more remote.

'This is our war work,' Tamsin insisted earnestly. 'Yours and mine, too. That's the way we planned it and if you don't take half, I shall feel I'm being done a favour.' Perhaps it was because she had always been small for her age that she so resented favours. 'Let Tamsin stand to the front or she won't see' if there was a procession, or 'give Tamsin a two strides start' in the races at school. Then, putting an end to the

268

argument, 'I left before Edie Birchell got round with the post. Did you get anything today?'

War work or not, the mail was still the high point of their days.

★ ★ ★

Kate was a small child, just as Tamsin had been. But there all resemblance ended. Her hair was the same red that Alex's had been before it had toned down to auburn in adolescence, and her eyes were the same gingery brown as his. Whether personality was inherited or whether it developed according to environment, who could say? Either way, she was a happy child, an eye always ready to see the first hint of adventure.

'I hope she's not getting too much of a handful for Maureen,' Tamsin said to James as she lifted the giggling, wriggling little tornado out of the sink, where she'd been given her pre-bed wash.

'Oo — ' Kate strained in James's direction ' — me Unc Jame.'

James laughed and took the towel to envelop her in.

Kate had come into his life like a miracle. Never before had he been close to a young child, losing his own before it was born. The innocent love of the precious little bundle he carried across to the wooden rocking chair in front of the kitchen range did more to heal the grief he'd tried to overcome by work than he would have believed possible.

'If Maureen says she likes having her, then

why not believe her?'

'Imagine two like this.' Tamsin pointed at naked Kate, lying on her back on James's knee with her legs kicking towards the ceiling, as if she were running a race. 'That and little Matt, too. Honestly, working in the assembly shop is a piece of cake by comparison. Come on, young lady: time you got your nightie on. Is she dry?'

'You'd better check. I'm a novice at this game.'

But when Tamsin picked her up, Kate made her feelings known.

'Me Unc Jame . . . ' And, arms out towards James, 'Oo, oo do Tate. Game.' 'Game' was a word recently added to her growing vocabulary, and quite her favourite.

'Nightie on first, then just one game.' He smiled at her as he said it: he didn't sound at all cross, yet even at just two years old, Kate knew he meant what he said. So she let herself be pinned into her bedtime napkin and helped put her arms into the sleeves of her flannelette nightgown. Then, wriggling to stand, she tottered towards him.

'Game. Ooo said game.'

More often than not, this was her nightly ritual, for more often than not James spent an hour or so at Brambles. He told himself he did it because he felt responsible for Tamsin and the baby: after all, hadn't it been *he* who had made it possible for them to live at the cottage? What if he hadn't chanced upon her at Christchurch and sent her back to Alex: where would she and Kate be now? But there was no 'if'. He had been behind the marriage; he had taken solemn vows for Kate's guidance. As he lifted the small, warm child onto his knee, to be rewarded by a wet kiss on his cheek, he watched Tamsin letting the water out of the sink to flow into the waiting zinc bucket outside, and he knew a moment's mindless panic.

'Any letters this week?' he asked, bringing his thoughts back under control.

'Yes. I wasn't going to say anything — in case it doesn't come off — but he has been recommended for another promotion.'

'Another? Captain. He's done well. But then, it's what I should have expected of him, you know that. When this war's over and he comes back, I see a good future for us together. Flying is no longer seen as a dangerous pastime for cranks. Those young men who have learnt to fly in the war won't be content with life on the ground. It's the vanguard of the future.' Then, hoisting Kate — who was getting impatient and tugging at his tie with requests for 'dat game' — he stood up and carried her to examine the framed paintings that decorated the wall, just as they did in every house. Not exactly a game, but such was her trust in her 'Unc Jame' that she was well content and seemed prepared to absorb all he told her about them.

When Tamsin came downstairs from tucking Kate into her cot, James was outside, emptying the bath water into the ditch. She knew from experience that, on the way in, he would fill the coal scuttle. Her days would be so different without him. Even if he was only with her for an hour or so, then went back to work, it was an hour that helped her through the other twenty-three.

She wrote to Alex:

James dug a deeper trench for the waste water. You should have seen Kate: she was out there in her waterproof coat, desperately keen to do her bit.

Or another time,

James has been a wonderful friend to all of us. I know he promised you he would see Kate and I were managing, but hardly an evening goes by that he doesn't come to see us. Remember when we asked him to be her godfather, he said he'd be a special uncle? He certainly is. Unc Jame, she calls him.

Her life was so routine; his was so full of action. She dug in her mind in the hope of finding something, *anything*. She wanted to pour out to him how much she yearned for him to be with her, but how could she make being with her sound exciting to a man who wrote of his exploits as if the meaning of his existence was excitement and action?

Perhaps it was the sound of the wind howling in the chimney on that January evening, the acrid smell of the smoke blowing back and hanging in a haze across the room, that made her lonely for Alex. James had only stayed a few minutes so, with Kate in bed, Tamsin was alone.

James still gets an allowance of petrol, although he cycles if he's only coming to the works. He had to collect a box from Brackleford Station, last Saturday, so Kate and I went with him. It's ages since I'd been so far. It was a cold clear day: frost hung on the trees in Farley Wood, even though it was afternoon. Looking at the bare branches, I prayed really hard — and crossed my fingers, too, in case that helped — that you would be home in time to pick primroses. Could you be? You don't know just how lonely I am for you. Even a leave, just something. Sometimes I'm frightened that none of the past was real, that what we have now is all there is. I know I'm luckier than so many. I have Kate — and James is a wonderful friend to us. But surely you ought to get some leave soon?

In fact, it was July by the time he came, arriving in the station taxi a day before she was expecting him.

He'd imagined his homecoming: it had been a secret dream always there at the back of his mind. But when it happened, he found the little cottage empty. The door was unlocked, but why not? No one thought of locking a door.

'Tammy.' He knew there was no point in calling, but he shouted up the stairs all the same, then went up, two steps stairs at a time, suddenly glad that he was alone. He'd not expected to feel like this, his heart hammering, his hands reaching out to feel the silk of her washed and newly pressed summer dressing gown hanging on the bedroom door. He smiled; he rubbed the soft material against his cheek. Tammy . . . On the table by the bed was the photograph they'd had taken at the studio in Brackleford, a week or so after their wedding. She must look at it every night of her life; she must think of them as being unchanged from that young couple . . . Sitting on the edge of the bed he held the picture, not looking at Tamsin but at himself. Could that have been *him*? So young, so untried. Still carrying the obviously posed portrait, he went to the mirror on the dressing table. Where was the difference? In more than three years, of course he looked older. But it was more than appearance. To look at the boy in the picture was like looking at a stranger.

The small, low-ceiling bedroom seemed to close in on him. This was where he and Tamsin had been exhilarated by the joy of their union. Putting the picture down, he lay full length on the bed, staring unseeingly at the ceiling. Nothing must have changed for us, he vowed. Nothing could ever change . . . even before Kate was born, Tammy was always there for me: never a duty, never a favour. Only hours away, and it will be like that again, — make it be like that again. Every inch of her was clear in his mind, so clear that every other thought was driven out. Get up, get up, don't lie here. Look at the state just thinking about her gets you in. He rolled on his side, breathing hard, fighting for the control he was on the verge of losing.

That's when he heard the front door slam shut; that's when he heard her voice.

'I've undone the buttons; now you take your coat off,' he heard.

Then a child's voice. 'All off. Now shoes.' Kate! All this time he'd carried an image of her, a baby sitting in her perambulator, a baby not even standing — even though Tamsin had boasted of each new thing she'd learnt to do. His throat felt tight; his heart was pounding. Sitting on the edge of the bed, he felt like an intruder in his own home. There was nothing now to hint at where, only seconds before, his uncontrollable thoughts had been carrying him.

'Listen!' Again it was Tamsin she must have heard him moving in the room above her. 'James! Is that you? Are you screwing that curtain rail?'

'No, it's not James. It's me.'

He'd been expected the next day. Tamsin had been planning to wear her new skirt she'd saved especially. But suddenly none of that mattered. Alex was home. She could hear his footsteps on the stairs and, when he reached the bottom, she was in his arms.

'Don't oo do that!' He felt Kate's small fists punching his leg. 'Don't oo 'queeze my mum.'

'Hey, hey, hey,' he laughed, drawing back from the onslaught. 'Get her off me!'

'This is your daddy. Stand up tall and let him see how big you've grown.'

Instead, Kate's sandy eyebrows puckered in a scowl and, when Alex stooped to her level, in truth as uncertain as she was herself, her trembling bottom lip stuck out, expressing her feelings in a way her vocabulary wouldn't allow.

'She'll come round when she gets used to

you.' Perhaps it was Kate's uncertainty that put a barrier between them, for it hadn't been there in those first seconds as they had clung to each other. Now, they each thought of something to say that would rekindle the way things used to be.

'The curtain rail? In our room? I didn't notice anything wrong.'

'Then he must have been in and done it. It fell down. I couldn't find the screw to put it back up. James said leave it to him.' Short, disjointed sentences.

'I couldn't let you know I was arriving earlier — or you could have left it for me to see it.'

Then, saved by the confident swagger that never deserted him for long, Alex stood further back from her, his shoulders squared, the cocky smile she remembered so well on his face.

'Well?' He challenged her. 'What do you think?' She knew what he meant: not what did she think of *him*, what changes in the twenty-one months since she'd seen him. No, what he was waiting for was the pride he wanted to see when she looked at the ribbon he wore over his breast pocket. 'Captain Alexander Murray, DSO. How about that?'

Her eyes shone with pleasure, just as he'd dreamt, yet there was something that held her back.

'You know what I think,' she told him. 'The same as *they* must do, or they wouldn't have given it to you.' She instilled just the right enthusiasm into her tone. But why wasn't her answer spontaneous? She had been so proud when he'd written to her with the news: she had gone straight to Westwood House to tell Lucinda.

Then, the following day, before collecting Kate she'd cycled to Lambton. There had been no doubt of Naomi's delight, even though Tamsin had arrived when she was entertaining a room full of local women all busily rolling bandages. 'No more than he deserves, you may be sure of that,' had been Naomi's reaction. 'You may be sure the DSO isn't given lightly. He's a brave young man.'

The scene came back to Tamsin as she stood a few feet from Alex, admiring his decoration. Yes, he was a brave young man: he was a hero. But that very heroism seemed to set him apart from her.

'Unca Jame come!' Jumping with excitement Kate stared at the door, waiting.

'She knows his step — knows it even better than I do,' Tamsin laughed, wanting to be alone with Alex, and yet at the same time glad of the interruption. With James here, she'd forget this feeling of disappointment, a disappointment that had no reason. Of course Alex must have altered. How else could he have survived his sort of war? It never occurred to her that she was any different from the girl he'd left behind.

'Surprise,' she called as James opened the back door — for, as was his custom, he'd cut across the airfield and through the gate at the end of the garden. 'See who's here!'

'Unca Jame. Me heard oo — didn't I, Mum?' Kate held her arms up to him. It was the usual

277

ritual. 'Fly me, like airp'ane.'

It was part of the almost daily pattern. Today, though, James came straight to Alex, gripping his hand.

'But it's good to see you! He looks well, Tamsin. When did you get here?'

'An hour or so ago. I forgot Tammy wouldn't be here. How are things going at the works?'

'Busy. Tamsin will tell you. But, of course, you'll be coming over to see everyone.'

Alex grinned, looking towards Tamsin, little realising how it lifted her heart to see that teasing expression. 'Sheds full of women now, I suppose, like this one? Will there be any of the chaps still with you?'

'I think they're all still there — plus a lot of women. And very good at their job they are, too.' James too smiled as he looked towards Tamsin.

Watching them together she was struck by how different they were from each other. Alex, bounding with energy, brave, full of fun — in her mind, she thought of a terrier, a wire-haired terrier, good at catching rats, frightened of nothing; James, reliable, unchanging, thoughtful, gentle — he was like a labrador.

'You mean none of the chaps from the works has volunteered for active service? No wonder the government is bringing in conscription.' Alex spoke with such scorn that Tamsin turned away from them; she didn't want to see the look on his face and, particularly, she didn't want to see it fixed on James.

''m on, Unca Jame. Give me fly in air'pane.'

'You've made a rod for your own back,'

278

Tamsin laughed, in an attempt to relieve the tension that she knew was mostly in her own mind. Then to Alex: 'This is a routine flight, once round the room.'

'You ask your daddy,' James stooped down and rumpled Kate's curls. 'Your daddy flies real aeroplanes.'

Kate looked uncertainly at the stranger, who made no move towards her.

'You . . . p'ease,' she insisted to James.

'I have to go, Katie. You ask your daddy. I just looked in, Tamsin, to say I'd fixed your rail.' Then, taking Kate by surprise, he swooped her into the air, twirled her round and dumped her down again.

As flights went, it was a short one, but she knew it was all she'd get and coming when she had given up hope cheered her up enormously. Her face was wreathed in smiles as she planted her normal smacking kiss on his cheek.

'You're to start your leave tomorrow, Tamsin, now that Alex has arrived. I'll tell them in the workshop.' Then, his last word to Alex as he opened the back door to leave the way he'd come: 'Look in when you can, won't you.'

'He seems very at home here,' was Alex's comment as they listened to the retreating footsteps.

'Of course he does. We always made him feel at home. Visiting us then, though,' she chuckled, 'he didn't have to get in the coal and chop the wood. He'll have a fortnight off, now you're here to do the honours.' Surely that would put them onto a comfortable footing, help build a bridge across the void of their time apart?

They both made an effort. Kate had never known an evening like this; the changing seasons made no difference to her bedtime as a rule. But now that this new man had come, nothing was at all what she was used to. Instead of being sat in the sink and splashed with warm water, she was helped into her 'garden boots' and they all went outside to play. That was a promising beginning, but she had an unfamiliar feeling in her tummy; it had something to do with the way the man she was told she should call Daddy kept looking at Mum. She tried to pretend he would soon be saying goodbye and going home — but, even at two and a half, she knew in her heart that he wouldn't be going. There was a picture by the side of her mother's bed. She'd been told often enough that, 'That's your daddy and me together before he went away. One day he'll come back; you'll have a real daddy, not just a picture.'

It had all sounded very muddly. She didn't know about daddies. Trudie didn't have one either, but it had seemed to make Mum happy to talk about the picture, so she had listened obligingly. Now, he was idly kicking a ball in her direction so that she could run after it and try to kick it back. Her legs were aching. He hardly had to move and she had to run all over the place. Nearly two hours after her bedtime, what had started out as a treat had turned sour. When she fell over, she didn't want to be told to be a brave soldier, she didn't feel brave. She was miserable; she wanted to be cuddled; she wanted all her mother's attention. And, mostly, she wanted the stranger gone, so that everything was the same as it used to be.

★ ★ ★

'Maureen would have her. Anyway, she probably misses having that other one — what's her name? — to play with.'

'Trudie: you remember Trudie.'

Kate knew they were talking about her; she felt uneasy, not understanding what was being arranged. But she recognized her friend's name and perked up hopefully.

'Trudie? Me going to play wiv Trudie?' These last few days hadn't been nearly as much fun as she was used to. She'd been pushed in her perambulator, just as if she were still a baby, and gone to see Nanny and Grandad Charles. She never felt very comfortable with Nanny: she was always talking without a laugh in her voice. Grandad Charles didn't say a lot, but she felt that he and she understood each other. They both knew what it was like to be wheeled about and have to sit where they were put! Just sometimes, without saying anything at all, he would give her a funny, secret sort of smile. Yes, she liked Grandad Charles. But she'd much rather spend her time with Trudie so, at the sound of the name, she looked hopefully from Tamsin to Alex.

'It's not fair to expect it when I'm not working.'

'I'll go and see her. I'll pay something on top of — '

'No! Alex, don't suggest that: she'd be dreadfully hurt. I'll go and ask her. Leave it to me.'

From one to the other, Kate watched, eager to get her coat and be off.

By that time, it was Alex's second week. They had walked to the village; they had visited Westwood House; alone, he had spent a few hours with James, taking special pleasure in the impression his visit made on the men — and perhaps more especially the women — in the workshop. But a fortnight couldn't be spent solely in Oakleigh. He wanted them to have a day in Brackleford. A day on their bicycles, with no Kate to turn them from the carefree young couple they used to be into parents of a child who impeded what they did, yet couldn't be left out. It was what Alex was sure they both needed.

Maureen agreed to have Kate for the day and, pedalling along the road through Farley Wood, they could almost believe nothing had ever separated them. These moments were precious: Tamsin knew Alex had been right to insist they should get out by themselves. She hadn't been blind to the difficulties and yet, without putting the clock back two years, how could it be different? They were no different from any other couple who'd lived separate lives: surely none of them could be unchanged by those last two years? One night, James had come to supper with them; another day, they'd taken Kate with them to have tea with Naomi; then there had been the visit to Westwood House where, as Alex said afterwards, Lucinda spent the time riding

282

her hobby horse, this time confident that the vote would come with the armistice. Whether or not it would didn't concern him and, on that occasion, even Tamsin's interest couldn't be rallied.

So the days passed, good moments and difficult ones. But one thing could wipe the difficult ones from their minds: in love-making, all the magic, all the glory they'd known, was still there for them. Everything else was forgotten except their need of each other, the voyage into eroticism that each time was new and wonderful. Eagerly, when the night was young, half waking in the depths of night, aroused by the dawn chorus, time had no meaning for them; each knew every road to lead the other, and nothing was forbidden as they climbed towards their ultimate peak where their world held nothing but themselves.

★   ★   ★

As the days went by, Kate became less guarded with Alex. One day, Tamsin purposely left them alone while she cycled to the shops by the Green — taking the precaution of slipping out while Kate wasn't watching, which wasn't easy, as it was drizzling with rain, so there was no easy escape while the little girl was in the garden.

'Let's play with your train, shall we?' Alex suggested as he heard Tamsin quietly shut the back door behind her.

'Me get.'

A promising start. He hoped Tamsin wouldn't

283

be too long — and yet, was that the whole truth? This was his daughter, his baby . . . into his mind came the memory of that day before he went to France. He remembered the warmth of her as he'd picked her up from her pram, he remembered the feeling of her baby-soft curls.

'Why you ook at me? Daddy?'

That Adam's apple threatened to choke him. He held his hand towards her, not speaking, not even knowing what it was he wanted to say. They were kneeling side by side, the train pushed away and temporarily forgotten as, for a second, she looked at him and seemed to be as much at a loss as he was. Then, taking his hand in hers, she bounced up and down on her bottom, throwing back her head and laughing uproariously without having the slightest idea why. When he pulled her towards him and hugged her, she didn't know why that was, either. But it all seemed glorious fun. For a moment, she hesitated, then she planted a loud and rather wet kiss on his cheek.

The next day, he went back to France.

10

Both Tamsin and Alex had looked forward to his leave, somehow expecting that, as if by magic, all the pain of separation would vanish for the time they were together. But every experience must leave its mark. So those days together showed them clearly that both of them were changed by the circumstances of their lives. Naturally enough, Alex had become war-hardened; in a life of 'kill or be killed', he'd learnt to be quick to attack and even quicker to avoid being its victim.

And Tamsin? He'd liked to imagine her safely at home, 'keeping the home fires burning', her work at Proctor's making no impact; after all, whoever heard of a woman being interested in aeroplanes? The fact that she did some routine job in the assembly line had been no more than a confirmation that she wanted in some way to feel she was helping him. In the beginning, that had certainly been behind her choice of war work, but that was long ago.

Silently, they had had to accept that nothing could ever be as it had been in those halcyon days of peace — or were even their memories tinged with more nostalgia than truth? They might have been changed, they might have left something of themselves behind for ever, but of one thing there was no doubt: if there was a barrier between them, then they must always find a way to destroy it. Without each other, there would be nothing. To be near each other heightened their senses, sight, touch, sound; sensually and emotionally, they were drawn to each other.

The work Tamsin did at Proctor's was no different from that of the other women, but her interest went far deeper. It had roots that went back to when James had taken her for her promised flight — or perhaps even further. More likely, the first seeds had been sown when she'd sat on the gate and seen the Farley Moth wheeled out of the shed and watched spellbound as James had put it through its test flight. That must have been the beginning, just as it had been the day that had changed the course of her life. With the shortages of war, there was no petrol for joyriding, but every plane that came off the line had to be rigorously tested. For this, James always flew alone. Only when he was satisfied did he deliver it to the airbase.

'Shouldn't you have two people on the test flight?' she suggested to him, one evening, when they were in the garden making the most of the last hour before dusk. 'You go up, swooping and twisting all over the place, but would it be the same with a second man behind you?'

He was watching her speculatively, an indulgent smile in his eyes. 'And you'd like to be that man?'

'I didn't say that. But of course I would.'

'I wouldn't take you, Tamsin: not on a test flight. I never anticipate trouble, but the possibility is always there — why else would the flight be necessary? But the transit to the airbase, that's a different thing. Not much more than ten miles: only a few minutes in the air. In future, I shall take you with me. You shall sit behind me in the gunner's seat.'

To see her face in that first second, he might have been giving her the Crown Jewels. But common sense soon caught up with her.

'What about the others, the men who've been with you for ages? Are you sure you don't want to take a man?'

'You or no one. If only we had enough fuel for pleasure flying, I would have taught you before this.'

Silently they looked at each other, neither trying to read the other's thoughts, both too engrossed in their own.

'Yes,' he was the first to speak and even then he might have been doing no more than voicing his thoughts aloud, 'that's how we'll start. You shall come with me, to watch, to learn: and, when you're ready, to take the controls while I watch.' His face broke into a sudden smile and, quite spontaneously, she grabbed both his hands.

'Yes, oh, yes, yes! It's what I've wanted since that first day I watched you. You remember, I told you. Let's not tell Alex: not yet, not till you pass me as proficient.' She had no fear. Looking up at the pale evening sky, she seemed to hear the hum of a Farley Moth; she seemed to see herself alone in the cockpit.

That's how she had her first lessons. In the workshop, no one commented or hinted in so many words that she was the boss's favourite — at any rate, not within her hearing. Yet she was aware that she wasn't looked on in quite the same way as she had been. She assumed the change in their manner was because of the time she spent away from the workshops and in the air. No petrol for pleasure flying, James had said. It wasn't Tamsin's suggestion that, once she became proficient, she could ferry the new machines to their base: at least, it wasn't her suggestion in so many words. But surely it was she who put the thought in his head. The truth was, she had a natural aptitude: he recognised it from the first day she took the controls.

So, if she sensed a coolness in the attitude of her workmates, she supposed it was no more than natural jealousy that she'd been chosen to be taught to fly. If she could have overheard some of the remarks when she and James were out of earshot, her own eyes might have been opened sooner.

'Off she goes each night at sixish to fetch the child. Then what?' Said in a voice that spoke volumes: a female voice, for the women were keen to condemn. Although none of them admitted as much, they saw Tamsin as already having more than her share of good fortune, without having the boss fawning around her. Their husbands were in the Royal Berks, out there in the thick of it and at best with a stripe on their sleeve; hers was a Captain, no less, and full of his own importance. They worked to add something to the miserable few shillings the government allowed each week: not like she'd get as the wife of a Captain — and a flying man, at that! So why did she spend her days at

Proctor's, while someone else looked after her child? The answer was obvious.

'She can't go gallivanting in the evening, not with that little ginger-top to see to.' That from Ken Hodge who, like the other men who'd known her since she used to go off with Alex to eat their midday sandwiches, had always had a soft spot for her. To them, she was a 'pretty little slip of a thing, but brave as a lion the way she goes off in that aeroplane'.

But even the men began to take note of James's comings and goings while they were working overtime in the evenings. The only difference was that while the women shared what they saw or heard, the men kept their own counsel.

★   ★   ★

During that summer of 1916, life had become progressively more difficult for Charles. He was in a vicious circle, one on a declining spiral. Once he'd got over the shock of his fall, and spurred on by the uplift in his spirits brought about by the advent of Lucinda, he had tried to propel himself around the house on his crutches. He had even managed on one or two occasions to be eased — and not without excruciating pain — into the motor car she had persuaded him to acquire. But all that had changed. With the coming of war, the motor car experience had been short-lived; with no petrol, it stood idle in the old coach house. Lucinda spent a good deal of time with her friends (fighters for her cause);

immobility was the opportunity his arthritis needed to tighten its grip. He grew progressively more depressed and despondent, and movement grew more painful; all of which served to drive Lucinda away ever more frequently.

Working full time and with her own mind full of her own affairs, Tamsin gave no thought to Westwood House. Since her visit during Alex's leave, she hadn't been there: and, to be honest, neither had she thought about them. Afterwards, she was filled with guilt for, despite the many days when he had been unbearable, she had grown very fond of Charles. But not fond enough, her conscience prodded, not caring enough to realise what it must be like to sit day after day alone and a prisoner of pain.

★ ★ ★

James was waiting for her as she brought the plane down after her first solo flight.

'Well? How did I do?' she asked even before her feet touched the ground, her eyes shining in anticipation of the praise she was sure she would hear.

'I was called away,' he told her. 'Tamsin — '

'Oh, no . . . ' Alex! There must have been news of Alex! Please, not that. Please, not that . . .

'Lucinda came. I've sent her over to the cottage to wait for you.'

'Lucinda?' His mother — ?

Only then did James follow her thoughts. 'My dear, no. Thank God, not that. It's Charles. He's dead: his body has been taken to the Brackleford

Hospital for autopsy. Go and see her; she needs to talk. It's hit her hard.'

'Autopsy?' But Charles had been ill for years. Couldn't they even give him dignity in death?

Without taking off her leather flying clothes, she ran across the airfield and through the garden gate of the cottage. In her mind she saw Charles — not the disagreeable man with a grudge against life, but the one who on his better days had shown glimpses of what he must once have been; and Lucinda, brave, ready to take on the world, and yet ready to give up so much for Charles. An autopsy? But why? And how dreadful now for Lucinda to know that, in death, he wasn't to be left in peace.

'Mother?' She burst in through the back door, even the exhilaration of her flight forgotten.

'What's this?' Lucinda looked at her in amazement. 'James said you were out — I supposed you'd had to go and see that woman who looks after Kate.'

'He's taught me to fly. We'll talk about that later.'

'Well done! So you're not turning out to be such a mouse after all!' Said with a smile that surely held as much triumph as pleasure.

'What happened?'

'I was in London. I knew nothing about it until I arrived back in Oakleigh, just before midday. Barnes says that Charles sent him off to the post office, told him he'd sit by the window for a change of scene. He said he seemed very calm — almost happy was what he actually said. The table where his medicines are kept, that's in the window. When Barnes got back, he found Charles half conscious, and he saw the bottle empty and all the tablets gone. You never call there: you don't know how depressed he's been lately.'

'Suicide . . . to be so miserable . . . '

'The fight had gone out of him. I knew it. Barnes knew it.'

'But, Mother, he was so much better: he was interested in things again.'

'Men make bad invalids. I suppose they haven't the staying power of women. More physical strength: but if they lose that, they go downhill, feel sorry for themselves.'

Her pedestal rocked, then finally collapsed under her.

'What difference does it make if it's a man or a woman?' Even then, Tamsin wanted to hang on to the hero worship of her childhood, wanted to believe that Lucinda's attitude was only a cover for her hurt. 'We neither of us know what it must feel like to be so wholly dependent.'

'No one need be, not if they have half a brain. And Charles wasn't a stupid man. No: he let himself be swamped by self-pity.'

'So would any of us if we didn't feel loved, needed.' It was hitting below the belt. She knew it and was glad.

'We know very well what the result of the autopsy will be but, of course, having it will delay the arrangements for the interment. I'll let you know.'

Tamsin nodded. 'All his knowledge . . . And his books, his papers . . . '

'I'll offer his things to the college. As to his knowledge, I agree. A waste, a wicked, irresponsible waste. He still had so much to give.' Pulling on her light, summer-weight gloves, she eyed Tamsin's flying attire. 'What does Alexander make of your learning to fly?'

Tamsin was ashamed for her that she could so easily be diverted. 'He doesn't know.' She had no power to stop her mouth twitching into a smile. 'We — that's James and I — we agreed not to say anything, until I can write and tell him that I had been given the job of delivering each new machine to the airbase. James does the test flights: he insists on that. But he says I have natural aptitude.'

'And why not? We know the same can be said of Alex, and why should you be different? Because you're female? Is that what you think?'

Tamsin turned away. What a bore her mother-in-law could be! In the last ten minutes, she had almost persuaded herself that she'd been worshipping a false prophet all these years. It was Lucinda's parting words that made her reach out, relief and affection making her grasp the gloved hand.

'I was very fond of him, you know. Even now that I'm so angry at his foolishness, despite myself I am fond of him. I saw him as a fighter — now this.' Then, without another word, she set off for home.

But how long would it be her home? Her interests weren't in Oakleigh.

* * *

293

Hurt mixed with anger as, for the second time, Alex read Tamsin's letter. How long had she been learning to fly, keeping it a secret from him, sharing her triumph with James? If anyone taught her, it ought to have been him. He was the real flyer, the one with the experience. What could James do? Take a plane into an empty sky, make sure the controls all worked. Yes, that was about all.

As he sat on the edge of his bunk, his glance travelled to the two photographs standing side by side on the small deal chest. One, Tamsin had sent him more than two years ago. Wearing her best dress, standing with her hands clasped like a well-behaved child told to be seen and not heard: rather than bring her closer to him the picture made a stranger of her. It always had. And the second, the one that had arrived in the previous batch of mail, removed her even further — her and Kate, too. Tamsin was sitting on an upright chair, the white wall of the photographer's studio behind her and the tall pedestal with its aspidistra to the side — not only was she wearing what was clearly her best dress, but one that he'd never seen. By her side stood Kate. When he'd gone home on leave, he'd had to get to know her all over again. But that was a year ago; there was nothing of a baby about the child who gazed at him out of the picture frame. His wife . . . his daughter . . .

The sound of the klaxon pulled his thoughts up sharply. Enemy planes approaching. Automatically he pulled on his leather coat and helmet, running towards the airstrip where his patrol of Farley Moths waited.

For the next hour, neither Tamsin nor Kate found a space in his thoughts. Only when he was in the makeshift mess where the officers assembled did he remember the news she'd sent him.

'It seems I'm not the only flyer in the Murray family.' There was a swagger in his voice; to boast had always been the way he'd kept his spirits high.

'A brother coming to join us?'

'I've no brothers. No, it's my wife, Tamsin. She wanted to wait until she knew she was going to manage; that's why she didn't tell me she was learning. She is delivering the Farleys from Proctor's works to the airbase, flying them solo.' The admiration of his fellows was salve to his hurt. At least, it was for the time being. But, by the time his lamp was out and he was alone in his none too comfortable camp bed, he couldn't control the way his thoughts took him.

'James and I,' ... 'James and I decided' ... Damn James! Back there in the safety of Oakleigh — looked on as a bloody god by his workers — looked on as a bloody god by Tamsin — no, she couldn't ... bloody Unca Jame. Christ! If only I could get home. I could teach her what flying is all about. What does he think he knows? What does he know about kill or be killed? Bugger all! In speech, Alex seldom — if ever — swore but on that night, he needed to whip up his anger and aim it at James, his one-time hero, just as accurately as in a few hours he would be aiming his rifle at some enemy he'd never met.

What was it Tamsin had told him? James had a petrol allowance but he never used it just going to the works. In the darkness, Alex felt his face contorted into a sneer. Poor dear James: fancy having to travel by bicycle! God, it made him sick. Men who were fit and able, staying at home, willing to let others do their fighting for them.

His conscience prodded, telling him that what James did at home was more important that anything he could have been doing in France. But on that night, Alex wouldn't listen. There might have been a swagger in his voice as he'd talked to his colleagues, but now it was silent.

His opening words never varied.

Darling Tamsin,

What news you've sent me! Well done. I know how much you've always wanted to fly. In fact, I had been promising myself that, when I come home, I would teach you. It seems James has got ahead of me and, I'm sure, for as much as is required of you — or of him — that is sufficient. He wouldn't let you go solo unless he was confident. But there is more to mastering the air than flying from A to B — or, in James's case, soaring, banking and so forth to test the controls. One day I'll teach you: I'll give you the mastery of the sky I have learnt. If I hadn't, I wouldn't still be here to write this letter.

She heard the old bragging tone, but that time it brought no indulgent smile to her face. She'd so

296

wanted him to be proud of her. He'd said 'well done': what more did she expect? There was an underlying criticism in his letter; yet, reading it the second time, there was nothing she could point to.

'Mum?' She looked down to see Kate tugging at her skirt, her face puckered anxiously. 'Will I play a game with you?' In her young mind, a game was a sure way of chasing away the blues.

Tamsin swept her into her arms. 'I need a squeeze, that's what I need. Have you got one for me?' she mumbled, burrowing her face into Kate's sweet-smelling curls.

'Huge one,' Kate chortled, throwing back her head with pleasure. 'Ready for it. Here it comes.'

The blues were banished, Alex's letter put away in the drawer of the kitchen table to be answered later.

'Come on, Kate. Let's go and start cutting the hedge; then you'll get lovely and dirty, ready for your wash. I'll cut and you sweep. How's that?'

'That's good game.' And that's the good game they were still playing when James joined them.

None of it went unnoticed by the prying eyes from the workshops where on the summer evening the doors were still wide open. Whispered comments recorded that when Tamsin took the little girl indoors, James still went on clipping the hedge. It made overtime worth while to view proceedings and there wasn't one there who couldn't add two and two and make four.

'Little one will be ready for bed by now. The boss has gone inside.'

'It's not right. She ought to be ashamed of herself.'

'Sometimes, I wonder if we might not be misjudging them,' Ken Hodge put in, for he didn't enjoy thinking badly of Tamsin. 'Remember how young Alex was always a favourite of the boss. It could well be he's no more than keeping an eye on things for Alex.'

'Long as it's just his eye!'

'Well, that's my belief,' Ken defended stoutly. 'Anyway, if it's young Alex Murray you're concerned about, the best thing is to keep your thoughts to yourselves. The last thing a man out there in France wants is rumours — ah, malicious rumours at that — about his wife.'

'Reckon you're right,' Lilly Crabbe, whose husband was at the front, agreed. 'Well, girls and boys, it's coming up to nine o'clock. I'm knocking it on the head for one night. Anyone else coming my way?'

Five minutes later, the place was locked up for the night. But they couldn't help noticing that, although James hadn't returned, his bicycle was still propped up against the back wall.

★ ★ ★

Daylight faded earlier; the kitchen range became a comfort as well as a necessity. There were a few occasions when Tamsin's transport flights were postponed because the autumn fog lingered right through the day; autumn melancholy was all too ready to tighten its grip on a country that had grown war-weary. What news there was brought little cheer and, since the inception of conscription the previous year, it touched so many homes. But not those where the menfolk worked at Proctor's: the making of aeroplanes of war was counted as a reserved occupation.

It was a morning in November; the fog hung damp and cold, giving an aura of mystery about even a walk as short as from Brambles to the villa where Maureen lived. Tamsin and Kate went straight in without knocking, just as they always did.

'Tamsin, I feel dreadful letting you down, but I can't have her today. It's Trudie, you see: she's ever so poorly.'

'What's wrong? Will it help if I take Matt back with us for the day?' For if Maureen couldn't look after Kate, Tamsin knew it would be impossible for her to go to work. She'd have to call in and explain on the way home.

'No, Mum looked in yesterday evening. She could see how things were. She took Matt home with her for the night. Trudie was that grizzly yesterday, not a bit herself: didn't Kate tell you? Poor Kate couldn't do a thing right for her. She wouldn't eat her food properly, hardly a thing all day long. But she's been sick as sick all night long. You feel all right, do you, Katie?'

Kate looked at her without answering. No one had ever talked about feeling all right before . . . was there some way of feeling different?

'Oh, that's one blessing.' Motherly Maureen understood a nonanswer was as good as an affirmative. 'I was worried I'd fed them with something that had done the damage.'

299

Trudie appeared at the head of the stairs. 'Mum.' It was more of a moan than a call. She was a pathetic sight, standing there, rubbing her fists across her eyes.

'I'm coming, lovey. Pop back into your room.' Then, to Tamsin: 'I've left the curtains pulled in there. The light seems to worry her. And there are spots on her back. Oh, I do hope it's not measles. If it is, the others are sure to get it. I feel awful having to let you down, but they ought not to be together.'

Tamsin and Kate went back along the lane to Proctor's.

'Why did Trudie cry, Mum? Why couldn't I stay and make her feel better?'

'You'll have to put up with me instead today,' Tamsin told her cheerfully, suddenly pleased at the thought of a day free of the assembly line. 'By tomorrow, I expect Trudie will be quite well again.'

Kate started to skip happily at her side, delighted that they were turning in at the gate of Proctor's.

'We going to see Unca Jame?' Things were getting better by the second.

* * *

The day started well for them. Back in the warmth of their own kitchen, Tamsin raked the fire that she'd banked up to burn slowly all day, then opened the damper to make it draw.

'That'll soon be bright. Now, Kate, there's just you and me. We'll have to have a girlie day. It's a treat for us.' It surprised her how much the prospect appealed to her. Given the routine of a similar treat every day, she was honest enough to admit to herself that the thrill of 'girlie days' would pall. But on that November morning, both of them could feel the companionship almost as a tangible thing. Tamsin made an apple pie for supper (James could share it with her; she'd suggest it to him when he looked in during the day, as she was sure he would). Kate had a piece of pastry to be rolled and squeezed in the time-honoured way until it became an unappetising grey before she gave it to her mother to be put into the oven. Then, in an equally time-honoured way, Tamsin surreptitiously replaced it with a clean piece, unpummelled by small hands.

When it was that things started going downhill, she wasn't sure. Perhaps Kate was tired: perhaps that was why she wouldn't eat her dinner. By mid-afternoon, she was rubbing her eyes and getting irritable.

'Sleepy? That's our busy morning,' Tamsin laughed, hoping to rally her.

'Mum . . . head hurts.'

'Oh, poor love. Let's have a cuddle.' She sat in the fireside rocking-chair and took the little girl on her knee. From out of the mists of the past came the memory of her grandfather. 'Shall I tell you about when I was about your size?' she suggested. The movement of Kate's head against her chest indicated the offer had been accepted. 'I lived with my mum and my grandpa — '

'Like Grandpa Charles?' Kate thought of the

301

elderly man in his chair.

'Older than him. I think I loved my grandpa more than anyone in all the world.'

Kate sat up straight, her own troubles temporarily forgotten. 'Not more than your mum?'

Had she? Loyalty to her mother made her evade the question. 'Oh, well, mums are different.'

'Umph.' Kate settled back, seemingly satisfied. 'Go on. Tell me 'bout things.'

As she talked the world of Gorsemoor came alive in Tamsin's mind . . . the smell of Snowy the pig, the feeling of responsibility as she'd collected up the eggs from the yard, the companionable love that had been part of helping her grandfather. She realised her audience had gone to sleep, but she went on telling the story, simply for the comfort she found in it.

About an hour later, something changed. Kate woke with a start and struggled as if she were fighting. 'Head hurts . . . Mum, I hurt . . . ' With a violent convulsive movement, she retched. With no time to spare, Tamsin got her to the sink.

Measles. That's what Maureen had said. After all, if one of them had it, it was more than likely so would the other. Certainly, she had a fever; her forehead felt like fire. Tamsin turned the lamp low. It seemed that the light hurt Kate's eyes and didn't people say that measles could damage the sight? If only James would come.

Then she pulled herself together. What would James know about children's ailments? But what did *she* know about them?

Usually he arrived at about half past six or even later. Perhaps on that day, telepathy played a part: he felt Tamsin's need of him — or, more likely, he was tempted by the thought of a cosy teatime with the two of them.

'Unca Jame.' Kate's feverishly red face broke into a smile, then it crumpled as she started to cry.

'Hey, hey, that won't do.' He picked her up but, this evening, he didn't attempt to fly her like an aeroplane; neither did she suggest it.

'I's got hurts.'

'Poor old lady. Sit on my knee and tell me where you hurt.'

Tamsin watched them, suddenly afraid of her own feelings. Why had Alex had to go to war and prove himself? Why couldn't he have stayed here, like the other men at Proctor's? She asked the silent question and heard the silent answer. He'd gone because he wanted to make a hero of himself.

'What was wrong with Trudie?' James asked.

'Maureen thought it might be measles. James, if that's what it is with Kate too, I shall have to stay at — '

'Of course you'll stay at home. Has she any sign of a rash?'

'She's been sick, very sick. She says her eyes hurt: that's why I've kept the lamp so low. I don't think there's any rash.'

But by the time Kate was stood in a large bowl in front of the range while her nightie warmed on the tall fireguard, they could both see the red

303

blotches on her skin.

'I've seen measles before; I don't think these are measles spots,' James said. He and Tamsin were kneeling one either side of where the little girl stood forlornly in the bowl. 'Get her dry and keep her warm, Tamsin. I'll cycle home and get the car. As soon as I can, I'll have the doctor here.'

'Tonight? Perhaps she'll be better in the morning. Yes, of course she will.'

'Perhaps she will. But humour me, Tamsin. Remember, I promised Alex I'd look after you both.' Their eyes met and Tamsin knew his anxiety went far beyond anything he had promised Alex.

By the time he returned with Dr Boothby, Kate was thrashing restlessly on Tamsin's knee, the sound of her whimpering more like a sick animal than a child.

'Her friend was sick all night, hot and feverish.' Tamsin heard the note of hope in her voice, as if that would prevent the doctor telling her something she was frightened to hear. Something? But what? Her experience of measles was non-existent; she knew she'd had it when she'd been small, but it had left no memory. 'Do you think it's measles?'

By now, those small red blisters were evident on Kate's hot face.

'Her friend? Who is her friend? Is she in the village?'

'Maureen Riley's daughter; Kate goes there every day while I work.'

'Victoria Villas: yes, I know the Rileys. But I

haven't been sent for. Measles, you say? No, this is definitely not measles, my dear. Keep her wrapped up. She must be got to the hospital. A blessing you have a vehicle, Proctor. Quicker to take her yourselves than wait here while I send for the ambulance. Perhaps you could drop me off on the way, so that I can telephone the hospital and tell them to be prepared for her.'

It was like living a nightmare. Only hours ago, Kate had been skipping happily by her mother's side on the way home for a 'girlie day' together. Neither Tamsin nor James had any idea of what the doctor suspected to be the trouble, but she wouldn't have been rushed to hospital for any of the usual children's complaints. No one talked as they drove towards the doctor's house. Perhaps he'd been over-cautious; perhaps in the morning they'd be bringing her home again. Over and over, these were the things Tamsin silently repeated.

Hope was dashed by the doctor's parting remark.

'I'll alert the hospital straight away. Then I must go to see this child of the Riley's. In cases like this, it's no use her putting off calling for a doctor.' Then he rested his hand for a second on Tamsin's shoulder. 'Bear up, my dear. She'll be in good hands.'

★   ★   ★

Tamsin hadn't been inside Brackleford Hospital since James had taken her there when Kate was born. What cruel irony that now again it was

James who took her. There is joy in a child coming into the world, but only fear beyond words in clutching the bundle dressed in her nightgown and wrapped in blankets.

On they went, James staring steadily ahead of him, driving slowly, hardly seeing beyond the front of the bonnet as the fog enveloped them. Only going through Farley Wood did it clear enough for them to see twenty yards before them.

'She's asleep, I think,' Tamsin whispered.

So, too, did James. 'I daren't go faster, not in this.'

At last they stopped at the foot of the hospital steps. Getting out of the car, James came to unlatch her door so that she could climb out without disturbing the sick child, and took off his coat as he did so.

'Pass her to me: that's easier.' He bent forward, the coat making a cradle in his arms. Kate didn't stir as she was wrapped in it and carried in. Only when they were inside the building, in the hard glare of electric light, did they see that her eyes were open. She was breathing — breathing unnaturally fast, yet it was as if she had slipped away from them. No use speaking to her, no use touching her. Kate . . . Kate . . . please, God, please hear me. She's only little: she's never done bad things. Don't let her suffer. It's not fair.

Then Tamsin's mind leapt to something she hadn't thought of for years: a picture that used to hang on the stairs at Gorsemoor. A picture of tiny children with wings (angels, that's what her grandfather had told her, but she'd liked to pretend they were fairies) and a man with a beard wearing a nightgown and holding out his hands towards them (Jesus, that's who she'd been told it was, and she hadn't liked to say that she didn't much care for the look of him). She'd been told that the words under the picture were 'Suffer little children to come unto Me.'

Cold fear gripped her as she watched Kate being laid on a stretcher and carried away. Suffer little children to come . . . no, not that, not Kate . . . she'd done no wrong . . . what sort of a God would take away an innocent life before a child had had a chance to live?

And me? If Kate goes — no, no I won't think it, I *mustn't* think it — fear turned to guilt, as if for that brief second she had lost faith and allowed doubt to find a way in. Please, don't let her be ill, not *really* ill. But who was she pleading to? That God of vengeance Arthur had set such store in? 'Suffer little children . . . ' Who was there? Where could she turn?

She felt James's arm around her shoulder and let him lead her to sit on the hard hospital bench while they waited.

They were still there when the ambulance arrived.

'Oh, God.' James gripped her hand. 'It's Maureen Riley. They've brought Trudie in.'

That's when the last glimmer of hope died. It had to be faced that whatever ailed the two little girls was serious. Now there was nothing to cling to but the doctor's assurance that in hospital they were in good hands.

307

Soon, instead of two of them sitting on the bench in the corridor, there were three. And when they were finally called to hear what the doctor had to tell them, the three went into his room together. Meningitis, a word they'd heard but knew nothing of.

'Are they together? Could they have beds next to each other? You'll let us see them to say goodnight?' Maureen appeared to collect her wits more quickly than Tamsin. After the day she had had, frightened of the expense of calling a doctor unnecessarily, and in any case unable to leave Trudie to go to fetch him, clutching at hope every now and again that Trudie seemed brighter, her feeling of relief when Dr Boothby had arrived at her door had been overwhelming. Now, the two little girls were together in hospital; neither of them would be too unhappy, and soon they'd be better.

'Together? Oh, no: separation is essential. They are isolated. You may see them briefly, but through the screen of course. Physical contact is out of the question.'

They drove home in silence. Just once, as they left the town behind them and moved into the thick layer of fog that hung over the open countryside, James took Tamsin's cold hand in his. It was a brief contact; she made no response. And on the back seat, alone in her misery, was Maureen.

'Thank you for the ride,' she said as they pulled up outside her gate. They'd already moved away by the time she went inside and closed the door behind her. Only then, alone and in the darkness, did her courage fail. 'Tom, Tom why aren't you here? Damn, bloody war,' she sobbed. 'That's what it is ... *Damn* ... *cursed* ... *bloody*. She's only a baby. Tom ... What am I going to do?'

★ ★ ★

Next morning, uncaring of the shortage of petrol, James took them both back to the hospital. Just as they had the night before, he and Tamsin looked at Kate through a glass screen. But she didn't know they were there. Staring unseeingly out of fever-glazed eyes, she knew nothing. They waited, sometimes keeping a silent vigil over her, sometimes turned out to sit on the hard bench while she was with doctor or nurse. It was evening by the time they left the hospital, again taking Maureen with them.

The previous night, they'd travelled home in frightened silence. The whole scene had changed since then. In the back of the car, Maureen cried; in the front, Tamsin sat, numb with misery too deep to be borne. And James? Never a man to let the world know his heart, and neither Tamsin nor Maureen gave him a thought.

This time, Maureen didn't so much as offer her thanks as she climbed out; all she did was drop a kiss on the back of Tamsin's head. Once indoors, relief, misery, grief, pity for her friend — all these things welled up in her as she dropped to sit on the bottom stair in the dark. 'Tom, Kate's gone. That little baby, little ginger-top, gone. Is that what's going to happen to our Trudie? No, no, please, God: no. They said she's holding her own; they sounded cheerful. Was that just to be kind? Dead. That's what can happen with meningitis. Please, God, help Tamsin. Bring Alex home to help her. What's happened to everything? What's gone wrong? But they say she's not as bad as Kate . . . they say . . . ' Practical, loving, motherly Maureen turned to lie against the cold lino covering of the stairs and cry.

Instead of stopping at Brambles, James drove straight on to his own home. In the morning before he'd left, he had told Mrs Huntley, his housekeeper, to have a room ready for Tamsin. He'd known she ought not to be alone, but he hadn't anticipated the day would end as it had.

'You mustn't worry about me,' she told him, but the toneless way she said it did nothing to reassure him.

'Tomorrow you can go home. Tonight, just humour me.'

She shrugged. His house, hers: where was the difference?

'Tamsin, I have seen to it that Alex is sent for. He won't know . . . ' 'That she is dead', but he couldn't say it.

She nodded. Kate . . . Kate gone. 'Fly me, Unca Jame' . . . Her childish, merry voice seemed everywhere. Don't think . . . don't think at all.

Did she eat the supper Mrs Huntley put in front of her? Probably. Like a zombie, she did as she was told: there was only one thing she was sure of and that was that she mustn't let herself

310

think. Like that same zombie she undressed, keeping on just her chemise and knickers, then climbed into the bed that had been warmed with no less than three hot bricks.

James went back out into the foggy night. At Brambles, the fire had to be banked up and, even more important, evidence of yesterday removed — could it be only yesterday? In the shadowy lamp light, he could see Kate's wooden train on the floor; at the sight of it he felt his eyes burn with the sting of tears. Grateful to be alone, he knelt to reach it, unashamedly letting tears spill to roll down his contorted face as he bit hard on the corners of his mouth. 'Me play wiv oo,' he heard her baby lisp.

Kate, if only you could, dear, sweet Kate. Tears were a relief. No one here to be brave for, no one to know how much it had meant to him when she had jumped in excitement at the sight of him. His grief was his own: he was no more than a godfather, a special uncle. Tomorrow, or the day after, Alex would be home. Together he and Kate would share their loss. And him? He would be there for them. He would spare Tamsin the ordeal of seeing the undertaker; he would go to the church and arrange the burial with the sexton.

When last had he wept? Many years ago, back in his childhood. He'd lost a wife; he'd lost their child before it had been born. But tears? Perhaps the wound had been too deep; his only protection had come from shying away from grief, from immersing himself in work, building Proctor's Aeronautics into a successful company.

Running the little train backwards and forwards on the floor as he knelt, he found relief in the outlet of tears, in the unfamiliar sound of his own sobbing. Kate seemed very close, the baby who'd turned into a fun-loving toddler, who was growing into an intelligent, affectionate child. Tamsin's little girl.

He stood up, then bent to put the train in the toy cupboard, checking to make sure there were no other treasures left in view. Tamsin's little girl. But that wasn't the only reason he'd loved her. Tamsin's and Alex's. Alex, the boy he had treated almost like his own son. Going into the kitchen, he turned on the tap and rinsed his face in the cold water, then rubbed it hard in the roller towel that hung on the door of the larder. He'd come to Brambles for a purpose: he must pull himself together. Tomorrow, she would come home. There would be ghosts enough waiting for her. He could do no more than see that when she arrived, the fire was still burning and the room tidy, traces of those last hours erased. He plumped the cushions on the rocking chair so that they didn't hold the shape of where she had sat nursing the little girl; he emptied the bowl that was still on the hearthrug in front of the range where they had stood her to be washed. Then, just as he had on so many nights, he went into the garden to empty the outside tub into the ditch, then to the shed to fill the coal scuttle.

Such humdrum chores in this little home where he and Tamsin had spent so many evenings: but they were the only way he had of serving her.

* ★ ★

Tamsin knew he was expected; she recognised the sharp military click of his heels as he walked up the short path to the front door as the station taxi drove away. She wanted to rush to him. Yet she seemed rooted to the spot. Alex had come home.

'Tammy!' he called as he opened the unlocked door. 'Thank goodness you're here. I nearly went straight to the hospital, but I didn't know which days visitors were allowed. Tammy?'

She shook her head helplessly. What was she telling him? Always pale, but he'd never seen her like this, her face ashen, dark shadows of sleeplessness under her eyes.

'What do they say is wrong with her?' Still the whole room divided them: neither seemed capable of making the movement towards the other.

'Nothing.'

'What? But James sent for me, I got special — '

'Nothing now.' Again that helpless shake of her head 'Gone. Meningitis.'

'Christ!'

'You mean 'suffer little children'?' Her words rasped: he'd never heard her speak like it. All her hurt and bitterness were in those words.

'Can't be dead — just a baby — '

Not quite looking at him, she moved towards him and raised her face to kiss him. His hands rested on her shoulders; he wanted to shake her, to bring some sort of emotion — any sort of

313

emotion — into her expression.

'James will be in soon. He's in Brackleford,' she told him, her voice small and composed. 'Things to arrange. He wouldn't let me.'

'James! It should have been *me*.' Everyone has their own way of hiding from emotion they can't face. Alex hid behind a barrier of anger.

'Yes. I suppose it should.' She shrugged. She hardly appeared interested.

'Have you seen Mother?'

'Yes, I think she was here.'

Think! You *think* she was here? he wanted to scream at her. Perhaps he would have, but at that moment the back door opened and James came in.

11

'You've got here,' James said unnecessarily. 'I saw the station cab going back. It passed me on my way here.'

'Just arrived.' Words, empty words. Anything to fill the silence.

'I've been to the vicarage to make the arrangements, then I saw the sexton. Come over to the works, when you're ready; I'll tell you about it.'

Tamsin seemed to be watching them from some far distance, seeing, hearing and yet removed. The sexton . . . The place where they'd arranged for her grave to be dug . . . Kate, alone in the churchyard . . . Kate, *her* Kate. Suffer little children . . . 'She's *mine*. I can't bear it.'

But she said nothing; the power of speech seemed to have deserted her. Kate wasn't hers, she wasn't theirs; like the pure golden flame of a candle, she'd been snuffed out. Remember how she laughed . . . Listen, can you hear her? Yes, and listen, listen harder, do you hear? She's running up the path. 'Mum, come see what I seen. A froggy, him hopping.' That's what she'd said — last week? — last month? Now? Listen, you can hear her laugh: shut your eyes, you'll see her there by the back door, jumping with excitement at what she'd found.

'I'll walk across with you now,' Alex was saying. 'That's all right, Tammy? James can explain to me.' Was he trying to spare Tamsin the misery of the telling, or would he find it easier to hear from James?

She wanted them both gone. She wanted to listen again. Perhaps Kate was trying to call out to her, like she did sometimes in the night. 'Mum, Mum, don't like it: it's all dark.' Let it be light for her. Don't let her be frightened. Suffer little children . . . but little children wanted to be where they'd always known. Paradise . . . Paradise was where you were with the people you loved, and where you knew they loved you. Paradise . . . Alex, we found paradise. We were two halves of one person — two halves, with baby Katie seeming like a living proof. Remember her in her pram, the way her face used to beam with pleasure if we bent over her? Years ago, when you were home, when the three of us added up to one whole.

Only minutes ago, surely Kate's spirit must have been close: her voice, her footsteps, all of it had been real. Now it was gone. Kneeling down, half afraid of what she did, Tamsin opened the door of the cupboard where Kate's train, a teddy bear that James had given her, a golliwog she'd had for Christmas from Lucinda, a spinning top and her favourite book of nursery rhymes were kept: all her childish treasures. Tamsin was drawn there in the unconscious hope that she would hear that happy voice again.

Kate's last job of each day, before she had been undressed (been undressed? Once the buttons were undone, she had undressed herself, and how proud she'd been) for her nightly dip in the kitchen sink, had been to put her things in the cupboard. But this wasn't Kate's handiwork. There was nothing to rekindle that moment of closeness in the sight of the neat pile. James . . . he must have put her things away. Sitting back on her heels, Tamsin stared at the worn and much used treasures; her face was void of expression.

When Alex came back, he told her where the grave was being dug, on the far side of the churchyard. She wanted to say something anything. But there was nothing. In mute misery, they looked at each other.

She prepared a meal; they ate it. She even talked, much as she would have made an effort to talk to a guest.

'How's the flying? I told them in the Mess what you were doing. They were impressed.'

'It's only delivering new machines. Nothing brilliant.'

'Still, well done, all the same.'

'And you? Are you still with the same crowd?' Did she really care?

'Those of them who are still left.' He wished he hadn't said it: it took them onto the quicksand of misery. So, before they had a chance to sink, he grabbed at the first thing that came into his mind. 'Not much change in the staff at Proctor's, not amongst those I remember. Plenty of women, of course — and a few strangers amongst the young chaps. I was surprised to see so many still there from my day, especially now conscription has been about for so long.'

'They're reserved. You would have been.'

'Reserved! Staying at home and doing jobs that a woman can do. Some of them are getting on, I suppose: in their forties, at any rate. There are plenty of men at our base quite as old as James, though: older, some of them. I wonder he's content to hang about in Oakleigh.'

'You're talking nonsense. James has a business to run. Do you want cheese?'

'Cheese? No, I've had plenty, thanks. I suppose I ought to go and see Mother. How is she getting on?' Now Charles is gone, he'd been going to say.

'She's not there a lot, I don't think.'

'But, now?'

'Yes, she's there now. She called here yesterday. She said she would be in Oakleigh until after . . . ' After Kate's funeral. It hung between them: unsaid, unsayable.

That night, without being asked, Alex emptied the tub into the ditch, banked up the fire and fetched in the coal. Tamsin watched him, feeling nothing.

In bed, a thousand memories crowded in on her. But there was nothing new in that. It had been those ghosts that had brought him near to her as, night after night, she had lain alone, starved for the love they'd shared and, willingly, eagerly, followed the instinct of her body as her mind reached out to him. But that had been when Kate had been asleep in the room across the passage. Then, pretending they were his hands caressing her body, pretending it was he who brought her rising passion to its ultimate

318

release, she had known she was doing what she did willingly, partly to satisfy her own needs and partly to bring his presence into their home where she and Kate waited.

Now, he was here. She lay flat on her back, staring at the dark ceiling, seeing the emptiness of the room across the corridor.

She felt his hand on her breast; as if he'd hit her she drew away.

'Let me,' he whispered. 'Let's be together. Tammy, let me.' He guided her hand, as if she didn't understand the urgency of his need.

'No, Alex. Please, no.'

For a minute, he was silent. Then, the distance was back between them. 'I'm sorry. It's not just you, you know. I've lost her, too.'

'Yes. I'm sorry.'

It was hopeless.

★　★　★

'Man that is born of woman hath but a short time to live, and is full of misery,' the rector's powerful voice boomed, filling the still November air. But this was Kate he was talking about. Full of misery? She'd been full of joy.

'Deliver us not unto the pains of eternal death.' The small white coffin was being lowered, down, down into the cold earth. Kate. Your little hands . . . I was going to cut your toenails at bedtime, remember? Kate . . . An arm came round Tamsin's shoulder, holding her back as she stared down into the deep hole.

'Forasmuch as it hath pleased Almighty God

319

of his great mercy to take unto himself the soul of our sister Katherine here departed . . . '

Our sister Katherine — Kate, my baby . . .

Only one thing had the power to pierce Tamsin's misery and make her see anything beyond: Lucinda, her face contorted as she tried to fight down her tears.

* * *

Alex had been given seven days' compassionate leave. They were the most difficult days he'd ever lived through. He felt an outsider at Brambles. Yet was it his fault that he had sacrificed his homelife in defence of his country, in defence of those who lived safely and, as he thought bitterly, untouched by the daily tragedy he saw in France? He felt like a guest in his own home, treated with courtesy but never with warmth. Yet he was as powerless as Tamsin to cross the abyss that divided them.

Twenty-four hours hence, and he would be on the other side of the channel. He and Tamsin couldn't part like this. She had already gone upstairs to bed, the fire was banked for the night and the damper closed. Their only fire was in the range. Saving fuel, that's what Tamsin had told him: but in truth it was because it was easier to be occupied in the kitchen. Neither of them was capable of relaxing; they had to keep working. He'd spent hours digging the garden; she'd cleaned windows until they shone like diamonds; she'd cooked and they'd made pretence of being hungry. It was a charade, just a way of filling time, preventing the need to talk. They couldn't talk about Kate; they couldn't talk about anything else.

Sitting in the rocking chair, he pictured Tamsin. What happened when women lost babies? Didn't they cry? If only she'd cry; if only she'd turn to him for comfort. He ran his fingers through his dark auburn curls. We got married because of Kate; now Kate's gone. Is that what Tammy feels, that Kate was the only reason we were together? No, she can't think that: it was wonderful, perfect, for her as well as for me. She can't bear me to touch her. She's wrong. She needs me as much as I do her.

Gently rocking the chair, he leant back with his eyes closed. Emotion must find an outlet. Tomorrow, he'd be gone; there would be nothing for them but separation. Didn't she care? Think of the nights they used to spend together: surely they'd meant as much to her as they had to him. A volcano about to erupt . . .

'Come up quietly, in case I'm already asleep,' she'd told him.

In front of the fire he undressed; then, turning out the lamp, crept up the lino-covered stairs, carrying his clothes. There was a full moon; the foggy spell had given way to a clear days and starlit nights, so that when he opened the curtains, the bedroom was flooded with silvery light. Even if Tamsin had been asleep, that would have disturbed her; he knew from the way she lay so still with her eyes closed that this was part of the charade.

'Don't pretend,' he whispered getting into the

bed. 'Tammy, it's no good going on like this. Tomorrow, I shall be gone. Darling, we can make things good again between us; we can't part like we've been these last days.'

She couldn't answer him. Make things good, he said. She could tell from his voice that he was tense; she could tell from the way he touched her, the way he breathed, just how much he needed the physical release of lovemaking. Love? Was that love?

Tonight, there was no foreplay; they shared no magical mystery tour of eroticism. She didn't push him away when he moved onto her; as if she were a stone statue, she lay beneath him, her hands at her sides and her eyes wide open. How could he do this: how could he bear to? Make things good — as if she'd not mattered, as if for them nothing had altered.

For days, her brain had been numb; but as he lowered himself onto her, one fact penetrated that numbness. Naked he entered her, flesh moving against flesh, just as he used to before Kate was born. Did he think he could give her another child, replace Kate? Was that what he thought she needed? Or was he thinking of nothing except the goal he was rushing towards?

'Tammy, move: don't lie there like that. Move, darling. Come with me — together, Tammy.'

She heard the urgency of his whispering. She couldn't move; she couldn't climb with him to that pinnacle they'd reached so often. How could she when, a mile away in the cold moonlit churchyard, Kate lay alone?

As he reached his climax, she believed she

322

hated him; she wanted to hate him. Hate is an easier emotion to live with than misery.

Long after he slept, she lay awake. Supposing, just supposing, she had conceived another baby. She felt sick at the thought. The weekend Kate had been conceived had been filled with wonder; she'd brought love into the world with her.

⋆   ⋆   ⋆

Next morning, Tamsin woke to find Alex already up, and in the same instant she was hit by the memory of the night. Running away from it, she swung her feet to the ground and stood out of bed, dimly catching sight of her reflection by first light. Moving near to the long glass on the cupboard door, she stared at her reflection as if she were seeing it afresh. Last night, Alex had made love to her and she had felt nothing. It was at that second that something else pushed to the front of her mind.

'Thank goodness.' She dropped to her knees. 'Thank goodness.' There was no doubting the sensation: her period had started. She wanted the blood to gush from her; in some crazy way, she felt that would cleanse her of hate.

⋆   ⋆   ⋆

Back in France, Alex was as keen as she to wipe out the memory. He had raped his own wife: for what else had it been but rape? He felt Tamsin was as lost to him as Kate. If they'd quarrelled, even fought, at least there would have been emotion. But she had treated him like some distant relative, someone to feed and be polite to, but someone who possessed no key to her inner self.

Always courageous, but now there was a difference in his flying. He went out of his way to chase trouble, revelling in the rush of adrenalin as he conquered it. During the months of winter, with short hours of daylight, he spent long — and always convivial — evenings in the Mess. The aerodrome was some way out of the nearest town, but give Alex the companionship of a Mess and no one would suspect there could be loneliness hidden behind that ready laugh.

This was his fourth winter in France, but it was the first he'd had to face feeling isolated from Tamsin and resentful of men who were still comfortably at home. It would take only one letter from her, a letter opening her heart to him, sharing her grief, and he would be able to write freely to her again. Instead, with every passing week, they grew further apart.

There had been a time when never a mail came through without a letter — or more — from her, telling him things of no real importance, but making him feel that he was still part of her life: she had planted the peas; the first roses were in flower; the wind was from the east, and he would surely remember what that meant — a kitchen filled with smoke that blew back down the chimney; Kate had taken three steps; Kate could manage the flight of stairs; Kate had made a whole sentence; Kate was a chatterbox; James had been to tea; Mother had pushed

Grandpa Charles (neither of them felt comfortable calling him Charles, and his mother's husband could hardly be Mr Hardcastle) to see them, adding that she was still riding her hobby horse! And always, shining through the lines of daily happenings, had been the sure brightness of her love for him, her dreams of the day he'd come home.

Now he saw her weekly letters as a duty. No mention of Kate, yet he knew thoughts of her must be always in Tamsin's mind. But those thoughts excluded him, she'd shown that clearly when he'd been home.

An old friend of yours has come to work on the assembly line, at least that's what she tells me. Edith, the rector's daughter.

He'd almost forgotten Edith, one of the many girls he'd amused himself with in the days when he'd had 'one for each day of the week'. Tamsin must have been desperate to find something of interest to tell him.

Then, in the first week of January,

Maureen went to the hospital today to bring Trudie home.

She seems to have grown taller and thinner.

Two stark sentences, making him feel more shut out from her hurt than if she'd told him nothing. He replied, in the same vein, 'Tell Maureen how glad I am Trudie is home.'

In February, she had a card from him with a

picture of the Eiffel Tower.

A 72-hour leave, so here I am. Imagine the contrast of the gaiety!
Shall need a rest to recover! Beautiful city. Alex.

Paris! Alex in Paris — 'shall need a rest' — what was he telling her? Into her mind, uninvited and from seemingly nowhere, sprang a conversation they'd had a lifetime ago. It had stemmed from the excitement of their lovemaking; he'd said something about the dull wives of the men on the shopfloor. Dull, that's what she felt now: dull, dull, dull, all her spirit crushed out of her. Yet there was no running away from the pain his letter gave her. How could she blame him if he looked elsewhere and took his fun? She knew there was none in the few prosaic lines she penned him each week.

Usually, hers was his only mail, so he was surprised when his batman handed him three letters. The usual thin envelope from Tamsin, a rare (and equally thin one) from his mother and the third typewritten. That was the one he opened first.

Hardly a letter, no 'Dear . . . ', no signature. Simply one typewritten sheet.

Someone has to tell you. When I watched you in November, I felt I ought to say something, but you had sadness enough. I've known for ages and you have to be told. You deserve a wife who is loyal and faithful. But night after night, he is there with her. She must be the talk of the village — and him, too. 'No man wastes his evenings just poking the fire', that's what I overheard said about them. I don't care what people say about her — or him — but I'm not going to keep silent while you're made the butt of jokes behind their backs.

You must have wondered about them yourself; perhaps you would rather not face the truth. To treat a man on active service like she has shows she is not good. Perhaps she got her just deserts — but it wasn't right that you had to lose your daughter just to punish her immoral living.

This is written in friendship.

He couldn't believe it! Couldn't? Wouldn't? But why is it so impossible? Because of how we were together, because when we were together life was — was what? Happy. More, much more . . . joyous. Remember when we married, it wasn't how I wanted: a small rented cottage, not much money. I thought those things mattered; Tammy knew they didn't. Joyous . . . a wonderful word, full of youth and hope. Is this true? James . . . Of course it must be James. Christ, when I think how I used to admire that man. And he waits till I was out of the way and fawns around my wife. 'I'll look after her,' that's what he'd promised. Stole Kate from me, stole Tammy . . . too cowardly to risk his neck out here like the rest of us. Growing rich with his bloody aeroplanes, just like the munition makers. James taught her to fly. James this — James that

— I ought to have seen.

Well, I did see. When I was home, who was it made the arrangements for Kate? Doesn't spend the evening poking the fire. She turned me away, didn't she? Till I forced her. I ought to have known. Write and ask her, ask her openly.

At that point, his mind seemed to have ceased to function. Holding the single sheet of typing he stared at it, not reading it, simply staring as if it were beyond comprehension.

Those days in Paris: had he been running away from what he'd been too cowardly to face? A wild weekend. But sex was different for a man: he could have sex without love. Living the way the chaps did out here, poor devils in the trenches, or us going up each day never knowing if it'll be the last — sex is an escape. Clears every thought from your mind — like a dam bursting — like a volcano — Tammy, Tammy, you can't love James. You can't share all that you and I had together with James. It's disgusting: I can't bear it.

Without realising it, he'd screwed the letter up. Now, seeing what he'd done, carefully and with unnatural calm, he opened it on top of the cabinet, pushing Tammy's pictures out of the way so that he could smooth out the creases. Tammy didn't love him, was that what the letter was telling him? Until those last nightmare days, she had wanted their lovemaking. Oh, yes: if only he'd been at home and they'd still had that, then she wouldn't have needed James Proctor or any other man.

His confidence had taken a blow. Setting his

jaw, he determinedly slit Tamsin's envelope, schooling himself to be prepared for whatever she might tell him. The few paragraphs about the daffodils being through the soil, and a visit from a man from the Ministry to Proctor's might have been sent to anyone.

> You'd hardly know me — I've had my hair cut off. It's really short, and so much easier under my leather helmet.

He didn't expect anything of interest from his mother, and today's missive started very much to pattern. Only the last paragraph caught and held his attention.

> I suppose there is no chance of your getting leave. Tamsin has been through a good deal of late. She is living with a constant reminder of what she's lost. No wonder she looks so wan. To be honest, I worry about her.

He knew his mother almost as well as he knew himself: her maddening tunnel vision about the things she believed in, her bigoted views, her honesty, her trust and her truthfulness. And he knew, too, that whatever she suspected might be going on between Kate and James, under no circumstances would she stoop to malicious gossip. Again he read what she'd written, seeing it as confirmation of the seeds of doubt planted by some meddling busybody.

This time, he tore the anonymous letter into shreds, then opened his writing pad on the cabinet top, the only flat surface. He wrote the date, looked around as if the right words would suddenly appear before him — and was interrupted by the klaxon.

That next hours must surely have had some effect on his emotions when, the sortie and debriefing over, he returned to the privacy of his cell-like quarters. Jeremy Downs, Harry Burnett and he had been together for more than two years; the sorties they made weren't always in the air! They were affectionately nicknamed by their patrols as the Three Musketeers. That day, the raid over the enemy lines was intensive. They'd flown into the gates of hell and, of the three, only Alex had limped back to base.

He'd lost friends before; in his own patrol, he'd known young inexperienced men fresh out from England who'd been shot out of the sky on their first raid. But to lose Harry and Jeremy was like losing something of himself; anger and misery was a physical pain. On his camp bed was the screwed-up pile of torn paper, in the cabinet drawer the other two letters that had come that morning. Home, Merrie England, where even in wartime Tamsin had written to him about cricket on the airfield at Proctor's. And for that, men like Harry and Jeremy lost their lives.

For the second time, he took up his fountain pen.

*   *   *

'I've come to tell you that I'm leaving Oakleigh, at least for the present. There's plenty of work to

330

be done in London,' Lucinda announced, explaining the reason for making one of her infrequent visits.

'What's the use of rallies and marches? Nothing will be done. The war is the only thing that matters at the moment.' Talking to her mother-in-law always put the mettle in Tamsin.

'I didn't say I should be working for the cause. Although indirectly I shall, whatever else I may be doing. Women are relied on for so much. No, I am taking on the running of a soup kitchen.'

'You? But you've never done anything like that.'

'You'd never flown an aeroplane before, either. It's only a question of applying oneself. And I must say, Tamsin, you have come up to all my hopes in the work you do.'

'Thank you.' She wished she could say it graciously, but she felt uncomfortable; she wasn't used to praise from Lucinda.

'However, I haven't come to pay you compliments nor yet to talk about myself. Tell me what I'm going to say is none of my business — you don't have to *tell* me, I know it isn't. But you may be too blind to see the obvious.'

Tamsin drew back as if she'd been hit. The obvious. But how could Lucinda possibly have seen how far apart they had grown, how impossible it was to let her heart dictate words to spill onto the paper like they used to? If what she heard came as a shock, it was nothing compared with what followed.

'Do you realise James Proctor is in love with you?'

331

Tamsin's reaction was relief. So it was nothing to do with Alex and her: it was just some impossible notion Lucinda had got into her head.

'That's the craziest thing. Because he comes here, you think *that*? James has been our friend for so long — why, it's laughable.' As if to prove it, she laughed.

Lucinda sat elegantly, one slim leg crossed over the other, concentrating on fixing her cigarette into its holder while she decided whether to leave the subject there or drive home her point. The decision made, she eyed Tamsin speculatively. The craziest idea, the girl had said — and clearly she believed that to be the truth. For a moment, Lucinda was tempted to believe her: after all, what could a man like James Proctor find to attract him in such a scrawny, pasty little creature? Look at those legs visible below the hemline of her skirt like two sticks; as for her wrists and hands, it was hard to imagine that they could master the controls of a Farley Moth. Yet she probably had a good many more flying hours behind her than the poor young pilots who were being sent to France. Look at her — and then think of James. Twice her age, successful, talented, well-heeled: logic told her the situation was impossible — but what has logic to do with emotion?

'If it's laughable, then it's probably amusing the village hugely. Dear, kind James — is that really all you see him as? Alex's friend, Kate's godfather — '

'What are you accusing me of? Are you saying I encourage him here for any other reason than because he's a friend? It's ridiculous! You insult him — and me, too.'

'Then, my dear, I've carried out my mission badly. I don't know and I don't want to know what is between you and James, whether it's anything or nothing. I'm merely telling you there is gossip. It probably stems from the works and in a village like this, it spreads like a heath fire. I dare say the men watch you and let their smutty little minds wander where they will, and it's likely some of the women might be jealous that the boss has such a favourite amongst his staff. You look angry. Tamsin, I haven't come here pleading for an absent son — '

'I should hope not!' Lucinda couldn't miss the anger in Tamsin's quiet voice. 'I'm surprised — shocked, not surprised, shocked — that you of all people could stoop to listening to tittle-tattle. Not just listening, but spreading it. It's lies, just cruel lies. James is my dearest friend; he's cared for me and for Kate, and he's helped me a thousand times. So when you hear the cruel innuendoes, you can say that that's all they are.'

'That's precisely what I do say, what I said to Naomi, even — and she's no idle gossiper. You know her better than to think she is. You're such an innocent: had it never entered your head? But open your eyes; be on your guard. Your dear, kind James is the same as any other man. Friend of Alex or no, his feelings for you are not for Alex's wife.'

'I wish you hadn't said all this. Don't talk about it any more.'

Tamsin stood very upright, fiercely defying Lucinda. She might look colourless and feeble but Lucinda wasn't fooled. Beneath that pale exterior, there was the naturalness of a young animal; she'd watched Alex and her together, been aware of the girl's unconscious sensuality. Was Alex being good to her? Or was he his father all over again? Either way, it couldn't make a lot of difference to them at the moment; they were too far apart for broken hearts.

'Sit down, and I'll tell you about my soup kitchen . . . '

*   *   *

Lucinda had come on a Sunday, believing that the surest time to find Tamsin at home and alone. Sunday or not, she'd not been gone more than a few minutes when James arrived. He was the same as usual: easy to be with, talking about the business, helping with the second turning of the soil ready for her spring sowing, fetching in the coal while she filled the lamp. Yet Tamsin found herself seeing him with new eyes. Despite her vehement denial to Lucinda, it was impossible to put the suggestion out of her mind.

*   *   *

Alex's letter was waiting for her when she came home from work the following Saturday

334

afternoon. She read it, every word clear, the meaning plain. She felt nothing, neither shock nor pain.

. . . Fifteen months of marriage and three and a half years of separation . . . friends who have died . . . but thank God they knew how to live, to snatch at life while they could . . . Who knows if there will be a tomorrow? The white feather brigade at home would condemn men like me, expect us to live like celibate monks and die like heroes. They don't even start to understand. Sex is as essential to man as food — not the same for women. Although I always did have a dastardly charm! None of you at home could start to understand. After years apart, who can wonder if we are like strangers? Not write more now, better to wait until I hear how you feel.

She put the letter back in his brown envelope with the Field Post Office postmark and sat gazing at it much as a monkey examines part of its anatomy as if it's something totally unconnected with itself. Until I hear how you feel, he'd written. Clamouring at the back of her mind was a voice she was frightened to listen to, for, if she let herself go down that road, it would uncover too much pain that lay buried. Buried, deep in the ground, alone in the dark . . . No! It was a physical movement as she shied away, picking up the poker and raking the fire, not caring what she did but knowing she had to be doing something.
    'Tamsin, thank goodness. I was frightened

you'd be working late.' Without knocking, Maureen burst into the room, dragging Trudie by the hand and carrying Matt for quickness.

'Pu'me down,' he demanded wriggling in her arms.

'What's happened?' The sight of Maureen's face was answer enough and threatened to puncture her own hard-fought-for calm.

'I had this. It just came by the teatime post.' She thrust the envelope at Tamsin and, without giving her time to read it, asked 'Can I leave them with you? I'm going to get Mum. She'll pick them up from you. Can you lend me your bike? She'll come and get them — just that I must get off quickly. I'll leave your bike at the station.'

Listening to her while she read the short note, it appeared that Tom had been wounded and brought back to England. The letter was written by a nurse; he was in a military wing of the Royal Berkshire Hospital in Reading.

'Of course you can. He'll be all right, Mo; he'll be home with you in no time.' She felt a rush of affection for her friend: the first warmth to find a way through her defences.

'It's just . . . I'm frightened. Frightened even to say what I think, in case it tempts Fate.' Clamping her bottom lip between her far apart teeth she looked helplessly at Tamsin. 'Trudie's well again . . . '

'And so will Tom be. Leave them here and go and see your mother. If she can't have them, just get going; I'll keep them here for the night.'

'Hark! You've got a visitor.' Maureen panicked. 'You won't want children if you have a visitor.'

'It'll only be James.'

Unlike the writer of Alex's letter, Maureen was kept occupied with her young family; she had no time for gossip. James had been with them when the girls had been taken to hospital; he was almost family. So when, as soon as he came into the room, Tamsin passed him the letter, she felt a surge of relief.

'My car is at the works. I'll get it. We'll stop at your mother's as we pass, then I'll take you on to Brackleford for the train. You'll look after the children, Tamsin?'

For a moment, their eyes met. This would be her ordeal of fire. She nodded, then her thin, pale face creased into a smile as she turned to usher Maureen on her way.

'Don't worry about them. You know what I said.'

'I'll be back as soon as I can.'

As they'd arranged it, it all sounded easy. But children aren't inanimate objects and neither of them understood why they were being dumped so unceremoniously. Then there was something else they found unsettling. Trudie had been told that Kate had gone to live in heaven (in fact she'd been told 'in heaven, like great-grandma Riley', which had done nothing to cheer her. Great-grandma Riley hadn't known anything about having fun); but although Matt had heard what was said, he'd somehow expected that now they'd come to Kate's home, she would be there to play with them.

'Where's Gate?' he demanded. Ks didn't come easily to Matt.

'Sh, you know where she is,' his big sister told him in a loud whisper. 'You're just showing off.'

'Not,' he pouted. He was already unsettled by the events of the last few hours, so tears weren't far below the surface.

This is it: this is the challenge, Tamsin told herself. Did the children know how hard it was to keep smiling?

'Let's see what we can find for you in the cupboard.'

'Train. That's Gate's train!' His plump little hands grasped it.

Kate's toys on the floor . . . No Kate, no Alex . . . Alex taking other women just as he had her: as essential as food. Was that why he'd taken her to Naomi's house, in the first place? He'd married her because of Kate. Now there was no Kate, no Alex . . .

★ ★ ★

'They've gone?' James asked unnecessarily, finding her alone.

She nodded. 'Maureen's mother collected them.' Then, involuntarily clenching her teeth, she opened the cupboard door to show him the empty shelf. 'Gate's train, that's what Matt called it: he always had coveted it. All her things — Trudie and Matt were her friends.'

He took her hands in his firm grasp. 'She'll be pleased.' She will, not she would. He spoke softly; she couldn't lower her gaze from his.

'Tamsin, I want to talk to you.' His tone had changed. She suspected he wanted to put them on easier ground.

She smiled. 'Come in the kitchen and talk while I get our supper.'

'I want you to finish in the workshop.'

'You mean — ' But he couldn't be getting rid of her! How much else was to be stripped from her?

'I mean that I want you to learn more about running the business. I can recruit for the assembly line; even young lads are keen to train, knowing they'll be saved from serving in the army. There's more to running a successful business than the building of the machines.'

'But James, I've never learnt maths — proper maths, like Alex used to talk about when you were training him.'

'And neither need you. You know about people; you know the sort Proctor's needs; you know just how much is wanted of them before they start to be taught their job.'

This time, her smile almost lit the lamp behind her eyes. 'Not much, if I was anything to go on.'

There was no doubt of the warmth in his as he watched her. 'I knew you had the ability to learn — and the will, too. Tamsin, my time is spent more and more on things I would like to be able to hand to you. Don't look alarmed: I'll always be close by if you need me, and I won't throw you in without teaching you. Then, think of the love affair you had with that typewriter at Westwood House; you could

339

even refresh your skills.'

'But why me, James? You could engage someone who has had experience in business.'

'Why you . . . ' He was weighing up the question. 'The war won't last for ever, Tamsin. Alex will come home. You know I always had plans for him; secretly, I hoped that one day he would become a partner.'

She turned away, the unexpectedness of what he said threatening to destroy her armour. In her imagination, she saw them so young, so sure, Alex and herself, confident of their future.

'I doubt it, James,' she heard herself telling him. 'Things are uncertain between Alex and me. Married for fifteen months, apart for three and a half years — and who knows how much more?' She'd said it. Now it was real. Alex gone, Kate gone . . .

James's hands were firm on her shoulders as he came close behind her. He was her anchor, her dearest friend. Was he more? Was what Lucinda had said so impossible? She leant back against him, thankfulness for his presence surging through her. Then the reality of the situation caught up with her.

'So you see, James, there's no point in giving me that sort of responsibility if — '

He swung her round to face him, raising her chin so that there was nowhere for her to look except into his eyes.

'There's every point, Tamsin. Have you any idea how dear you are to me?'

'You've been so good to me. Just like you promised Alex.'

'Three and a half years ago, isn't that what you said? Have you welcomed me here all that time because it was what Alex wanted? No. We have more than that.'

'You know I've wanted you for yourself.'

'I've tried not to let you guess how I felt about you. I've tried to make myself think of you simply as Alex's wife. Tamsin, you're dearer to me than I know how to say — dearer than life itself.' When he drew her close, she leant against him; she tried to close her mind to everything but the relief she found in his words. Dear, true, honest, kind James. He'd shared her pride in each of Kate's achievements: Unca Jame. In that moment, she recognised how deep his own grief must have been — a dangerous recognition, one that threatened to melt her protection of ice.

'Don't say anything, Tamsin. I don't expect you to feel the same as I do. I don't want to hear you say it.'

'Don't know how I feel. James, I've become frightened to feel at all. But I do love you: I don't think I could have got through these last years — last months — without you.'

Tenderly, he kissed her forehead. 'All this talk of love gives a man an appetite.' He laughed softly. 'Something smells good.'

Before she could close her mind to it, Alex's letter pushed to the front of her mind. Man's appetite . . . sex. A hunger for carnal lust. But James wasn't like Alex. Don't think about Alex: don't let yourself remember.

★ ★ ★

It was an evening like no other had been. Between them there was a new awareness: or, for him, had it always been there? Even when they talked about the new part she was to play at Proctor's, there was an intimacy, a closeness. Yet, except for that one embrace, there had been no physical contact.

'I ought to go,' he said, when it was half an hour or so beyond his usual time. Outside, the tub hadn't yet been emptied; the coal hadn't been collected. He looked at her; her small fists clenched. There was something in her tenseness that touched him, heightened his own knowledge that this moment mattered for both of them.

'No!' There was nothing gentle in the unfamiliar rasp of her voice.

Standing up, he pulled her to her feet.

'No? What are you saying? Tamsin, don't play with me. I want you too much, love you too much.'

'Don't go, James. Stay with me. I want us to be together. Now. Tonight.' Women don't understand men's needs: Alex's letter haunted her. Oh, but no man — not Alex, not anyone — could be driven by a need greater than this. For weeks, months, alone in the cottage, she had held every natural urge in check. Like a wine that has been bottled too soon, it was forcing the cork. Her face raised to his, she sought James's mouth; her lips parted. Memories . . . memories . . . No, this is *now*; this is tomorrow; this is the future.

★ ★ ★

In James's tenderness, she felt ashamed of the animal craving that drove her. Naked, they stood before each other; she ached for him to touch her, and drew his hand to caress her small breast. When he dropped to his knees, a wild thankfulness filled her. She was unprepared for the way he laid his lips gently on her flat stomach. She could scarely hear the words he whispered.

'My blessed, beloved Tamsin. Whatever I am is because of you; whatever I am is yours.' It was as if he knelt at a shrine.

She touched his fine, straight brown hair. Don't think of the feeling of those coarse, springing curls. Don't think of anything: just live the moment. It's going to happen. He loves me.

Getting to his feet, he drew her towards the bed then lifted her to lie on it. She guided his hand to her. She felt she could hardly breathe: she was on the edge of a precipice. She knew her body was wide open to receive him, starving, greedy to devour. No, don't think. Don't think. Just take it, with every thrust get nearer to reaching the miracle. Like a wild thing, she arched and strained, pulling him closer, driving on, harder, faster. It was as if something outside herself possessed her: she was with Alex, she was moving towards . . . towards . . . Then it happened. In the first second of attainment, the dream held; it was Alex who wreathed in trembling triumph as, in that same instant, his climax came.

But the illusion was gone so soon; even as James still pressed hard against her, muttering her name over and over, reality hit her at a moment when she had no power to hold it at bay. In all these months, she'd not cried, she'd been too numb for tears.

Half wail, half sob, the sound filled the room, filled her head and her heart. As if she rejoiced in the freedom of at last finding an outlet for her pent-up misery, she could no more have held back her tears than she could have contained her passion, only minutes before.

'It's all right, sweetheart.' James held her just as he might have held Kate. 'Don't cry like that. I shouldn't have — '

'Not that. I wanted us to. James, she was only a baby. If there's a God, why did he do it to her, why did he take her away before she'd had time to know about living? Can't stop crying,' she snorted. 'Ashamed. Sorry.'

'I've cried, too,' he whispered, his face against her short, silky hair. 'I hadn't cried since I was a child, but I cried when we lost Kate.'

She noticed the 'we' and tried to move closer in his tight grasp.

'Talk about heaven.' She tried to talk, but it was hard when she couldn't stop crying. 'Talk about heaven: that's where everything is supposed to be happy. But she's all by herself. Doesn't know anyone.' It was a silly thing to say, she knew it was: childish and stupid. And she was glad — she wanted to sink low, to drown in her misery.

'You don't have to be with a person to know you're loved. It's fifteen years since I lost Myrtle. Do you think she hasn't known all this time that

I love her, just as I know she loves me?'

His words came as a shock to Tamsin. Hadn't he said it was *her* he loved? She pulled away so that she could look at him, with eyes that were nearly closed from weeping. He understood what was in her mind. 'I loved her when I was a young man; the man that I was will always be hers. I think — no, I'm sure — nothing would have changed for either of us. The pain of losing her was — well, you know without my telling you. But life goes on: it has to. What has been, has been. Nothing can change it.'

'But she was a woman. She knew about proper love. Kate was just a baby; her world went no further than us and Trudie's place. She hardly even knew Alex.'

'Perhaps she knows him better now, darling. There are no earthly barriers for her any more. If he thinks of her and opens his heart, she'll find a way in. You've lost people you've loved before Kate. Your mother, for one. Was her dying the end of your knowing her, speaking to her with your heart and mind? Kate's spirit lives in your heart — in mine, too — and Trudie's — in everyone's who knew her and loved her.'

'Matt's, too, tonight.' She forced a laugh through tears that still flowed, although the frantic sobbing had died away. 'Bet he took her train to bed with him.'

James kissed the top of her head; she felt it was a tribute to the effort she'd made.

'And I bet she knows and is glad. Not glad in a staid grown-up way, but as if she shares his pleasure.'

For a minute, she was silent, then she asked, 'All those things you said — were you being kind or do you honestly believe them? Father used to talk about heaven; he used to stand in the pulpit ranting and raving about heaven or hellfire. He never talked about spirits who knew they were loved, who still had a place with the people they'd left behind. I believe he would think all that was rather wicked — suffer little children and God's will be done.' She ended on a hiccup that showed she was well on the way to finding her self-control. 'Do you honestly believe? You're not a religious person. Or are you?'

'Fly an aeroplane — sail a ship — climb a mountain — anyone who does those things must know there is something beyond our day-to-day existence. Something beyond our understanding.'

Through her childhood, she'd been preached at, but Arthur's God of vengeance had been distant and that was the way she had tried to keep him. Then, with Alex, there had been the sort of happiness that doesn't need a helping hand from anyone, not even God. Lying close to James, she was calmed by the comfort of his gentle voice, of the sincerity of his trust.

'I miss her so much,' she mumbled.

'I know, darling. You always will. Let her into your heart: talk about her, remember the things she said and did. Then she'll know she still has you with her.'

They lay still a long time, the night ahead of them. There was tenderness but no passion in the way he held her. She had never felt so loved.

12

On that Sunday, the day after James first stayed with her, they came downstairs in the morning to find that the fire, neglected the previous evening, was little more than hot ash. Not even practical James had remembered the nightly chores. So on their first morning, before they could make breakfast, life had to be stirred back into the dying embers. For the moment, they were left in limbo.

'Tamsin, why stay here?' he urged her as they watched the slivers of wood burst into flame. 'Why not make your decision, close the cottage? I hate the thought of your name being dragged through the divorce court. But it has to be Alex who petitions. So why live here alone? He will cite me as co-respondent, so let's be open about it, let the world know. Can you even start to know how proud I'd be? Then, as soon as you're free, we can be married. You must love me: wasn't last night proof?'

How could she tell him of the fantasies that had filled her head as she'd strained to hold him closer, to be one with him? One in body, one in soul . . . had they ever been, she and Alex? A proper marriage would stand up against separation: think of Maureen and Tom.

'I can't run away from Brambles, not until I've told Alex — not until I offer him the means of getting his freedom.'

He looked at her thoughtfully. She felt he saw into her heart and knew her confusion.

'Of course, you're right,' he said. 'Casualties of war are far more than the wounded sent home from France. I'm grateful for every hour I have with you. But I want more. I want you to share my whole life — the business, the home.'

'And I will, James. We'll be happy.' Then, with a chuckle that sounded like the Tamsin she used to be, she said, 'By the time you've tried to teach me my new job, you may feel like changing your mind about the business part. Look, the kettle is starting to sing. Time I fried the bacon.'

Later on, after he'd left her, she sat alone at the kitchen table, a blank sheet of paper in front of her. For months, it had been impossible to write anything other than banalities; this morning she wanted her pen to race across the page. She wanted to remind him of all the things that had made up their life. It was as if last night had given her release. Kate . . . she wanted to tell him they had to learn not to shy away from thinking about her, not to be frightened to talk about her. She wanted to tell him that they couldn't hide from grief; that way they'd lose her.

'Dearest Alex.' But how could she call him that? Dearest, darling . . . He wouldn't want to read it. It would make him feel wretched that she could think of him as that. The top sheet of the pad was torn off and a fresh start made.

Dear Alex,
    Your letter came yesterday. Yes, I was sad: of course I was, and you must be too. It wasn't

348

the way we thought things would turn out for us. Casualties of the war, I suppose that's what we are — like lots of other couples, we couldn't stand up to separation. I understand how you feel; we were neither of us cut out to be alone. You see, I haven't been faithful. James is my lover. If you want to get in touch with a solicitor, there will be no trouble in getting grounds to divorce me. Alex — this is so hard to say, but I must say it — please remember the things that were good: don't let it all be soured. Perhaps that's selfish of me, but it's important for both of us. And most important — think often of Kate. She needs you and she needs me. I can't explain how it is I'm so sure, but I know it's true. It's no good running away from sadness. Keep her in your heart. Keep safe, Alex. Tammy.

P.S. Tom is to be sent home when he comes out of hospital.

The head wound has taken his sight. A different sort of casualty of war.

In the spring sunshine, she walked up the road to the post box set in the wall at the end of the row of villas where the Rileys lived. She heard the envelope drop. Then silence, the silence of Sunday morning. On the Sabbath, no children were allowed outside their doors to skip; no women shook their mops out of their windows; no neighbourly gossipers hung over their gates.

Turning back to Brambles, she was surrounded by ghosts: Alex and her together, hand in hand running down Hinds Hill; heads down, pedalling home through the rain, she saw the teasing triumph in his expression as he looked behind him and laughed to see the way she forced the pedals in an attempt to keep up with him; then together they were cutting back the brambles; together they were leaning over the pram; she could see his pride as gently he touched Kate's baby-fine gingery hair — pride not just in Kate but in the replica of his own genes. Everywhere there was the sound of laughter, laughter that had had no doubts.

Somewhere along the way, as she'd let her mind take her where it would, she must have stopped walking. As suddenly as they'd come, so the images vanished, there was nothing but Sunday-morning silence. The finality of her reply to Alex had drawn a line under the past. And the future would be good: she would make it good. Loving, faithful James, her dearest friend: James, who had truly loved Kate — no, she corrected herself silently, not had loved, but did love.

If there was any outward sign of her determination to look to the future, it was her firm step as she walked home.

★   ★   ★

'He's coming home! Tamsin, they told me this afternoon. Tom's coming home! Oh, I'm sorry, bursting in on you like that. I didn't stop to think.' Maureen stood in the doorway, embarrassed and yet not being sure why she should be. Often enough, she'd walked in on Tamsin without knocking, just as Tamsin had on her.

350

Often enough, James called at Brambles. Yet there was something in the atmosphere that was unfamiliar.

'You're not barging in,' Tamsin laughed. 'Since when have we knocked? Mo, that's wonderful news. When's he coming? Will you manage?'

'I'm fetching him tomorrow. Mum's coming to be with Trudie and Matt. Manage? With Tom? What a question! Wouldn't you manage, if it was Alex? Nothing wrong with *my* eyes: they'll just have to do for the both of us.'

Tamsin felt James watching her. She'd never been more aware of her own failure, but there was nothing in her face to show it.

'And they will, Mo. I wasn't thinking of that: I was thinking that Tom won't be able to go back to his smithying.'

'Oh, money. He'll get a bit from the government and, yes, we'll have to draw our horns in, I know. Once he gets used to being at home, I'll try and find a few hours' work to bring in a bit extra. I don't care what sort of jobs I do. But none of that matters. He'll be home, safe. Another one of our lads gone, Tam — Ossy Binns had a telegram today. Mum told me. You know Ossy, the sexton at the church. His boy has been killed. Not missing: not even a shred of hope. Killed. Tom's coming home and I'm just so thankful. He'll be fine, you'll see. Tom won't let things get on top of him.' She looked around the little sitting room, again sensing something different in the atmosphere. Perhaps it was in the fact that she'd grown used to finding Tamsin in the kitchen, the room permanently warmed by

351

the fire in the range.

'Nice to see you using this room. Once in a while, you have to spare the coal, don't you, otherwise the house gets so cold and damp.' Her news told, Maureen clutched at some way of making conversation, trying to dispel her feeling of unease.

'Mo, about Alex and me.' Go on, don't stop. It has to be said. 'I don't expect he'll come back to Proctor's — '

'I've been reading in the newspapers: big changes to the Flying Corps. Not going to be part of the Army any longer. What is it to be called? Royal Air Force, I think that's what I read. But why should that make any difference to Alex, once they all start coming home? After all, call it what you like, he'll be out of it once this war's done.'

'No, Mo, that's not what I'm meaning. He won't come back to Proctor's because he isn't coming back to me.'

Maureen folded into an upright chair as if her knees had given way under her. She had arrived with her rosy face radiant with joy; now she looked at Tamsin helplessly.

'It's this war. That's what it is. Let things ride along, Tamsin, love; try not to worry about it and, when things get sane again, you'll find you both pick up the pieces. Men live on their nerves, — well, it's natural. They must do, with lives like they have to lead. Not like us, sure from one day to the next. Word's got back to you that he's been kicking over the traces, I suppose that's it? Don't you think it may be his way of forgetting? We can't know what it must be like for him — for all of them. Must be a living hell for the poor souls.'

Tamsin had never felt fonder of her friend.

Carefully, exaggeratedly carefully, James was pushing tobacco into the bowl of his pipe before he took a spill from the jar on the mantelpiece. Tamsin was grateful to him for not watching her.

'It's more than that, Mo.' Go on, say it. You've gone this far; don't stop now. 'I've written to him, asking him to divorce me.' She held out her hand to James, aware of the comfort as he put his arm around her shoulder.

'You two . . . ? You'd do that to him while he's away there, helpless in France? Why, it's — it's — rotten! What's the matter with you, Tam, all the troubles you've had, the both of you? Kate's mum and dad . . . Don't know what to say. Best if I go.' She stood up, prim and condemning. 'I knew I shouldn't have come barging in on you. Well, I won't again — '

'Mo — '

'It's an awful thing to do to a man. And you two? Do you truly believe behaving like that can lead you to happiness? If there's a God in heaven, you'll get your deserts.'

If there was a God in heaven, Kate would still be here. 'Fly me, Unca Jame.' Tamsin felt James's arm tighten around her, drawing her to him. She heard the door shut and knew Maureen had gone. For a minute, she hid her face against his shoulder. A village of gossipers had no power to hurt her; a few words from Maureen and every bruise and wound was laid bare. Courage. Nothing but courage can give the future a shape.

'James, do you still want me to shut the cottage?'

His answer was clear for her to read as he raised her face towards his. Her decision made, she wanted to act on it now, that very day, before she had time to give doubt an opportunity.

'Can I come with you tonight? I needn't pack everything. But, James, I want to do it now. What's the point of waiting until I hear from a solicitor?'

'No point, Tamsin. You know how I feel.'

She nodded. Yes, she knew. James's feelings were as sure as the stages of the moon. He'd told her he wanted her to share every part of his life, to be in his home and in his business. So she would. Silently, she vowed she would never fail him.

'Put your things together, darling. I'll ride home and fetch the car, so don't worry if you can't pack properly.'

It was final: there was no turning back. She'd drive away, leaving Brambles empty and deserted, the fire dying down until it was nothing but cold ashes. Don't think about Brambles: look ahead. You'll be a proper partner to him; you'll be everything he wants.

'What about your housekeeper — Mrs Huntley, don't you call her? Does she know about me?'

He didn't give her a direct answer; he simply said, 'She will love you when she knows you.' Then, with a smile that etched deep lines at the corners of his eyes, 'Mrs Huntley is a sensible woman.'

★ ★ ★

Had James been less fond of Mrs Huntley, he would have found it easier to tell her his plans.

'Bringing her tonight? Mrs Murray — that's the lady flyer you've got working for you isn't it?' She was pleased with her knowledge. 'Quite a stir that caused in the village, you know, a young woman learning to take up a flying machine. Lost her digs, has she? The bedding's all aired, of course: the hot water tank sees to that. But it's years since that mattress had anyone on it. I'll put coals in the warming pan — '

'Mrs. Huntley, I haven't explained properly. Tamsin — Mrs Murray — won't be using a spare room. She is coming here to live with me.'

All expression was wiped from the housekeeper's plump, homely face. When she'd heard there was a lady flyer at Proctor's she'd built a picture in her mind of someone mannish. What would he want with a woman like that in his bed?

'Oh, my dear Lord . . . '

'I'm sorry it has to be this way. Please try and understand. Mrs Huntley, you've known me a long time: can't you trust me in this? As soon as she is free, we shall be married. In the meantime, her husband will be naming me — '

And again, 'Oh, my dear Lord.'

'You're thinking of Myrtle.'

'And how else can you expect me to think? What would she make of it . . . Oh, my dear

Lord.' There in the drawing room, Martha made the out-of-character move of sitting down uninvited on a straight-backed beaded chair. Any second, she would realise what she'd done; so, to put her at her ease, James sat down, too.

'I think of her, too, you know. And I believe, I honestly believe, that she doesn't want me to spend the rest of my life alone.'

'That's very likely. But a married woman . . . '

'It won't be easy for Tamsin, either, coming here and knowing all the things you must be thinking — having to face the gossip there inevitably will be. I don't know what sort of a person you're imagining her to be, but I'm sure of one thing: once you come to know her, you will love her. And, Mrs Huntley, this evening, when I bring her, whatever your feelings — I beg you, greet her kindly.'

'If it's your decision, then, sir, it's not my business.' She moved to stand up. But there was much she didn't understand. 'What about her own family? How must they feel about what she means to do?'

'She has no family. She has no one.'

'Oh, my dear Lord.' But her tone had softened.

★ ★ ★

Lindley, as James' house was called, was typical of many built around the turn of the century. From the outside, Tamsin knew it, but it was on that evening, arriving to make it her home, she saw it afresh. As if he were a third in the car with

356

them, she could feel Alex's spirit. She had loved preparing the cottage together: castle or cottage, it had mattered not a jot. Alex had seen it differently, though. It hadn't been the sort of house he'd wanted to take her to; and she'd known even then that he was comparing it with the home James had made for his bride. If he could have looked ahead, seen her as Lindley's mistress . . . She forced herself to keep her blinkered view just on the future. But it wasn't easy when memories lurked to pounce on her when she least expected.

A red-brick house, standing four-square behind a neatly clipped privet hedge, Lindley was about half a mile beyond Hinds Hill, and very near Lambton. On the ground floor was a neatly curtained bay window on either side of the front door and, above, a neatly curtained bay window in each of the two front bedrooms, with a long sash window above the front door which let daylight on to the landing and stairs. On the second floor were two more rooms, both used by Mrs Huntley. Except that there were sash windows instead of bay, the back of the house was similar to the front, one ground floor room being a kitchen and one what James called his workroom. Remembering Westwood House, Tamsin expected it to be a book-lined study. Up to a point, she was right, but it was also an insight into a James she hadn't suspected.

'Woodwork?' She looked at him enquiringly.

'Wood-carving. It may not be wonderful, but it's a satisfying occupation. Working with my hands, making things that are purely ornamental . . . ' Hearing what he'd said, he laughed. 'Neither pure nor ornamental, but therapeutic.' On the shelf was an array of his handiwork: fish, some sort of monster that surely had no earthly equivalent, an aeroplane, a squirrel. 'My first attempts, like this chap — ' he picked up the monster — 'they were so bad that I wonder I didn't burn them. But I didn't. And later, as I improved — at least a bit — I was glad I still had them. Something like Robert the Bruce watching the spider, you know. Feel the wood.' He passed the squirrel to her. 'Smooth . . . beautiful.' Then, suddenly self-conscious, he took it back and replaced it with its fellows. 'Mrs Huntley never comes in here. If it needs cleaning, I do it myself.'

Taking his hand, she raised it to her face, nuzzling against it. This was his secret place and he'd let her in.

* * *

At Proctor's, there had already been raised eyebrows when she had been taken off the assembly line. Probably someone saw her arrive with James the morning after she'd moved in to Lindley: probably a knowing look, a whispered hint had been all it took for word to spread.

Of all Alex's one-for-each-day-of-the-week romantic liaisons, only Edith, the rector's daughter, had opted to do her war work at Proctor's. And, when it had been noted that for two mornings Tamsin had arrived with James,

358

she decided it was time to get at the truth. She owed Alex more than hints and innuendoes.

'How's Alex?' Showing an array of large, white teeth, she bore down on Tamsin, who had been collecting the weekly timesheets.

'He's very well.' Find something to say that doesn't let her guess you're on your guard. Why should she suddenly show such interest? 'Our Farleys take good care of him.'

'What does he think about the cottage being closed? Are you going to stay with Mr Proctor until the war finishes?' Edith's bright blue eyes were fixed on her in mocking triumph.

'If you want to know what Alex thinks, then why don't you write and ask him? We haven't decided yet about the cottage. He and I are being divorced.' But were they? Only Alex knew the answer.

Her honesty silenced her inquisitor. Watching her walk away, Edith was filled with a confusion of emotions. In her own mind, she had been only one stage from Alex's proposal when that skinny little creature had queered her pitch; but their marriage hadn't worked. So triumph was paramount of those emotions. Her life had been narrow; most young men worth a thought had marched away. Dreams of what might have been combined with hope. Of the other emotions, jealousy, dislike and malice all jostled for place. She went back into the workshops, eager to spread the word that their suspicions were correct: Tamsin had been having a confidential chat with her.

With her tunnel vision fixed on the future,

although Tamsin was neither blind nor deaf to the sly glances and remarks among the staff, particularly amongst the women, she schooled herself to pretend they didn't exist.

But it wasn't so easy to forget the way she and Maureen had parted. They had shared too much for her to be able to brush aside her friend's change of heart towards her. They had never quarrelled before; being at odds with Maureen seemed to cast a cloud over so much else.

She made her decision and put away the accounts she was checking. She didn't look forward to raking over the ashes with Maureen, but it was important to see her straight away. By the next day, Tom would be home.

Yet, less than half an hour later, as she closed the wooden gate of the terrace house behind her, she knew the rift was too wide to bridge.

Maureen saw nothing beyond the fact that Tom was coming home and that, no matter what his injuries, nothing had made so much as a dent in the bond that made them one. The Tamsin she'd always looked on as her friend ought to have been capable of that sort of faith and trust. Instead, she had been encouraging James Proctor into her home. And what was she asking? Did she expect that what she'd done — and intended to continue to do — would be accepted with no thought to her selfishness?

Maureen had always been outspoken.

Their friendship went back little more than five years in time, but in depth it went deep into their hearts. Watching Tamsin walk away, even the thankfulness in Maureen's own life was forgotten. Although memories of Kate prevented her voicing the thought that Tamsin had put her own petty ambitions at Proctor's (and what's to say she hadn't been chasing after James Proctor all the time she'd been there?) before looking after her own child.

Tamsin turned back towards the airfield, knowing that yet another memory had been tainted. James would know, even though she wouldn't tell him the things Maureen had said. It was impossible to hide her feelings from him. Before she went back to the works, she would call at the cottage. Perhaps this morning the letter would have come; perhaps already Alex had written to a solicitor. There was no going back — and nothing to go back to, she added — so she wanted to move on quickly.

On the mat were two letters, neither of them from a solicitor. First she read the one from Lucinda, brief as always. Alex had written telling her their marriage had broken down. She was sorry. But marriage wasn't the only thing in life; it was up to women like Tamsin to set an example, 'As, my dear, I know you will. Indeed, you already do.'

Then, their marital breakdown disposed of, the other piece of news was that she had put Westwood House on the market and intended to buy something smaller and nearer London.

With a sense of real loss, Tamsin folded it and put it back in its envelope, a line drawn neatly under yet another chapter of her life.

Next came Alex's.

Your letter came as no surprise. And I don't expect you are alone in finding comfort from a man prepared to stay at home while someone else fights his battles for him. You suggest I write to a solicitor. I suppose that would make life easier for him. At the moment, I see no point. Who knows, you may find yourself free of me without the degradation of the Divorce Court. You tell me to remember the good times. Just at the moment, I would rather not remember any of it — except Kate. Do you ever wonder whether there may, after all, be some glorious pattern? She was taken from us before we failed her. We didn't deserve her. One of these days, you may get a letter from a solicitor. Alex.

Spring became summer. Hope began to stir in Europe, where the Americans had joined the battle. Unlike the war-weary British and French, they arrived full of confidence, well equipped and in their thousands.

Under James's instruction, Tamsin learnt to drive the car, even though he only had petrol for essential use. It became yet another stage in the sharing of Proctor's: any journey that necessitated using the car was a chance for her instruction; if he had a business meeting she was there — to listen and learn and soon to become involved. As for driving: the roads were relatively empty, so handling a motor car proved easy to master. Their common interests, their natural companionship and her very real affection for him, all helped to point to their years ahead.

It wasn't in Naomi Halliwell's nature to stand in judgement, but she was saddened by what had happened. She'd known James all his life; he'd never fallen short of her high expectations. Then, like a breath of fresh air, Alex had come to Lambton. She was a typical spinster of her era, and Alex had been like the son she knew she'd never have. From France, his spasmodic letters meant a lot to her and, close as she and Lucinda had become, she secretly considered her friend a most unnatural mother.

By chance, Naomi the scarecrow was clipping her hedge as Tamsin approached on her bicycle. So they were brought face to face.

'Hah! Well, we had to meet some time.' The scarecrow put down her shears. 'I dare say I ought to have called before this. James must have wondered . . . '

'I'd wondered too, Miss Halliwell. I hope we shall still be friends.'

'Not for me to make the rules you see fit to play by. James is a good man — '

'I don't need you to tell me that,' Tamsin was quick to take offence. 'What are you suggesting? Why do you think I've done what I have?' Inches shorter than Naomi — and it was hard to feel dignified, standing balancing a bicycle, the chain case and pedals between her legs — she held her chin high. Was she being accused of moving in with James for the sake of a comfortable life?

Naomi missed the point of her anger.

'Why? I don't know, Tamsin. James is a good man, but so is Alex. A good man, and a brave man. Do you think by running away from him, you're running away from your troubles? My dear, tragedy can't be escaped that way.'

'You don't understand.'

'No. I don't.' But she said it kindly enough. 'Sometimes I'm thankful no man ever thought me worth taking off the shelf; as I am, I have no one to upset the applecart. And that's what you've done, you know, the three of you. Upset it properly.'

'If you're thinking of the gossip, I don't care about it and I'm sure James doesn't. As for Alex — he'd laugh at such a pathetic suggestion.' But there was no laughter in the way Tamsin said it.

'That he would,' Naomi agreed. 'I can hear him now.' She wiped her hands vigorously on her skirt, a sure sign that she wasn't as much at ease as she liked to pretend. 'Good news about his decoration, what?'

'Yes, but that was ages ago.'

'My dear, you haven't heard? He's been awarded the Military Cross.' She spoke in a hallowed voice. The young engineer who had come to lodge at Lambton had risen to heights beyond anything she had known. 'I just pray he's not being foolhardy, risking his neck unnecessarily.'

'He wouldn't.' Oh, but he mustn't: if he's doing wild and dangerous things let it be because he loves the challenge. Let it just be that. And keep him safe: please, please keep him safe. 'Alex isn't stupid.'

Naomi's plain face lit in a beaming smile.

'And there we have something we agree on. Well, my dear, as long as what you're up to isn't

364

destroying anything in Alex and as long as you make my dear James happy — goodness knows, he deserves it, but why he couldn't have found it with someone who was free, I don't know — then I wish you well. Lucinda thinks a great deal of you, you know. She always has — and still does. Not much of a mother. You'd think she'd be ready to champion her own son — right or wrong. And I dare say there was as much wrong on one side as the other. But he's a dear boy; James did me a great service when he asked me to take him in.'

'I wish you'd come and see us Miss Halliwell, James and me.'

Since Tamsin had been at Lindley, Naomi's silence had gone unremarked, but she was sure James had been as aware of it as she had.

'Now we've had this talk, I'll do that. I'll just drop in; it's the way I always have with James. And Tamsin, if you're to end up as his wife, don't you think it's time you tried to think of me as Naomi?'

Tamsin smiled, a smile deep enough for her left cheek to find its dimple. 'Come soon, Naomi.'

★ ★ ★

Had there been nothing in the past, no memories to beckon and taunt, that summer of 1918 would have been a cloudless one for Tamsin. She learnt all that James taught her about running the business; in fact, she enjoyed the day-to-day challenges it presented. Had she been a little more worldly, she might have realised that filling a contract for the government in wartime bore little resemblance to filling luxury orders from the public in peacetime.

James was looking ahead. The war couldn't last for ever and, when it was over, there would be a surfeit of trained pilots. He'd never doubted the future of air travel and, while production went ahead on the Farley Moth, he was working on its replacement. This wasn't to be a two-seater plane fitted with guns, built for manoeuvrability. What was on his drawing board was designed for the future, a bi-plane to carry passengers. At that stage, it was no more than a dream in his head, equations in his neat figures on sheaves of paper and drawings on the board on his desk. During that summer, every man's time had to be given to the government contract; there was no easing of the production of the tested and tried Farley Moth.

* * *

It was about midway through September that the letter arrived. Written by Mr Bloom of Bloom, Wilkes and Bloom, solicitors in Brackleford, it advised Mrs Murray that her husband, Wing Commander A. Murray D.S.O., M.C. was petitioning for divorce and citing Mr James Proctor as co-respondent. By the same post came James's letter telling him exactly the same.

'No regrets, darling?' James looked at her across the breakfast table where they'd opened their post.

'I want us to have a proper married life, children.' For both of them, the memory of Kate was there. Don't be afraid of it. When there are other children, there will always be Kate. 'Everyone has regrets, though. Especially when they've failed like Alex and I did. But I've no doubts, if that's what you mean.'

'September now.' He was thinking aloud. 'Perhaps by Easter it will be finished.'

Nothing else was said about the letters, but they were there at the back of their minds as they left the house together and the day fell into its usual pattern.

From the assembly workshop came the familiar sound as work on the latest Farley finally completed. It always seemed to Tamsin that the men talked that bit louder, whistled with more abandon, were freer with a saucy remark or two to the women, laughed with more gusto, when the moment came to push the result of their work out onto the airfield. It had been the same when she had been in the workshop: shut her eyes and she would know from their voices that they were satisfied with a job well done. Just before midday, James climbed into the cockpit for the test flight. He waved as someone swung the propeller. Tamsin waved back with her fingers crossed; it was all part of the ritual. Then in the afternoon came her part, the short hop to the airbase.

So much of that was familiar and routine. Yet she felt it must be obvious to the world that for James and her, nothing was the same as it had been twenty-four hours before. The wheels of divorce were in motion; the knot that had joined her to Alex was already loosened and would soon be untied.

In making love, just as in every other way, James was gentle, tender and thoughtful. So thoughtful, that through the months she'd been with him he had never let passion come before prudence. Now there was nothing to hold up the divorce proceedings, so even allowing for the six months before a decree nisi being made absolute, they would be married before the birth of any child she might conceive. Even to herself, she wouldn't acknowledge she felt any lack in their lovemaking; she wasn't even sure that it would have been the truth. She wanted nothing about James to be different. And yet there were times when her body was driven as if with a will of its own. Those were the occasions when, afterwards, she would feel empty, drained of all hope. And why? She turned away from the silent question even before it formed in her mind, for that was too like a criticism and she loved him far too dearly for that.

Now he knew that, within months, they would be married. If only when he moved towards her she could have felt his new lack of caution came from that wild passion she longed for! She drew him to her, every nerve in her alive to his touch, screaming at him to — to — to what? This was James, her own dear James, taking her because she was who she was, because he loved her. Lust, love . . . oh, but surely the two could merge into one, blotting out everything but the moment. Let it be good, let it be good. Whoever it was she silently cried out to must have been listening. Minutes later, lying close in his arms, she heard his whispered, 'I love you so,' and her, 'And me, I love you', and she seemed to be enveloped in peace.

That was in September. Looking back, a month or so later, she never doubted that that must have been the night she conceived.

At the end of the first week in November, they went together to the county court for the divorce to be heard. It was straight-forward: Wing Commander Alexander Murray D.C.O., M.C. (and from the way the judge pronounced both rank and decorations, and from the way he looked at Tamsin over the top of his half-moon glasses, it was plain for all to see exactly the category he put her under) was the petitioner, citing Mr James Proctor (and again the emphasis on 'Mr' was a clear expression of this contempt for a civilian who broke one of the country's heros' marriage) as co-respondent. Had the said Tamsin Murray anything to say in her defence?

'No, sir. I have left my husband's home and am living with Mr Proctor as his wife.'

A wave of sound hung over the public gallery.

'Silence.' Then, his voice as thin and unsmiling as his face, 'You may stand down. Bring Mr Proctor to the stand.'

'I am given to understand that the petitioner was at one time your employee, until at the onset of hosilities he enlisted to serve his King and Country?'

'That is correct.'

'In his absence, you ingratiated yourself into

his wife's affections. Is that also correct?'

'Put that way, it is.'

'I see from the papers before me that the petitioner makes no claim on you for damages.' His stony stare was designed to cut both James and Tamsin to size and beyond. 'I have no choice but to agree his request and issue a decree nisi. But let me say for you and for the whole court to hear, that my opinion of those of us who cannot keep faith with those who offer their lives in service of this country is low beyond words.' He rose, his bearing giving the impression that he had come to the end of his endurance. 'The case is closed. This court will reassemble at half past two this afternoon.'

On their way back to the car — for today's proceedings were important business and a case for using petrol — Tamsin was quiet. James glanced down at her, dressed so soberly in her dark green suit, her felt hat hiding her cropped light hair, her pale face giving nothing away.

'It was wretched for you. I'm sorry.' He took her arm as they crossed the road towards where the car was waiting. 'He had no right to speak to you like he did.'

'Yes, he had. What he said was right. I'm not proud of what I've done.'

He stopped walking. 'What are you saying?'

'Of course I'm not proud. Do you think Maureen would have done what I did? No: she would have held on, waited, hoped that one day she could find something of what she'd lost. I hate half measures. If a thing is lost, it can never be the same again.'

He took her for lunch at the Great Western Hotel; he even surprised the dull and plodding waiter (and Tamsin, too) by ordering a bottle of champagne. It was as hard to come by as gold dust, but they managed to produce it for him.

It was her first champagne. The pale gold, the unending bubbles that rose in the glass, the clear dry taste: all these things added to the sensation of unreality in the events of the day. To have a meal in a hotel was almost unheard of for her, so when the waiter brought James the bill, curiosity made her lean forward to look at it. But that was wicked! They were spending more on one meal for two people than Maureen would get from Tom's pension — and she had to keep the family for a week!

'You drive,' James told her when they got back to the car. 'A bit further than usual, but it'll be good for you.' For, today, they had had to be in Reading for the hearing.

He watched her affectionately as they set off through the town, seeing the concentration on her face and supposing it was put there by the thought of the longer drive. In fact, he was wrong: driving never worried her. On the corner of Queen Victoria Street, she saw a young man with a notice round his neck: 'Blinded at Ypres.' In his hands he held a tray with boxes of matches. In Broad Street, a young man was singing, holding his cap to passers-by in one hand while the other sleeve hung empty. 'Please help. Wounded at Ypres.' Two of them, young: perhaps friends who'd gone off together like the boys from Brackleford had, keen to join the

Royal Berkshires at the first call. Further on, as they came towards the junction by the cemetery and took the Wokingham Road there were a group of them together; one with an accordion, one with a fiddle, one with no more than a comb and paper. As she crossed the junction, her mind was back in that summer more than four years ago: Alex so keen and eager, Tom rushing off to shoe horses at the front. Now the papers told them the Germans were broken, it was almost over. And for what? Casualties of war, wherever you looked. Whoever you spoke to, somewhere in their lives was sadness and loss.

She couldn't forget how much they had spent on their lunch. And what had those men eaten? What would they eat tomorrow? Next week? Next year? The newspapers told them the war would soon be won: the German forces were in chaos, the German navy in revolt. She couldn't forget the young men she'd seen, men who had probably rushed to the first call just as Alex had — and Tom. Thousand upon thousand were under the fields of France, homes that would never be the same without them. And those who came home broken, hopeless . . . Was there nothing better for them than taking their begging bowls to the people they'd fought for? Tom Riley, as blind as that poor fellow on the corner of Queen Victoria Street: what was Tom's future? Or Maureen's?

'We've got to do more for them. They answered a call to duty for us; we've got to see

372

we have a duty to them,' she said, following her own thoughts.

'We must,' he agreed and, not for the first time, she marvelled at how in tune were their thoughts. 'No one can replace the limbs nature gave them, nor give back sight, but they must have the chance of training: they must be allowed to know they're useful. No pension — and I believe what they do get is meagre beyond belief — but no pension can take the place of a man's earnings.'

It was her turn to take her hand off the steering wheel and reach for his.

'James Proctor,' she turned her head to smile at him, 'I really do love you.' It was spoken from her heart.

★ ★ ★

A west wind carried the clamour of the church bells; the men and women from Proctor's gathered outside to listen in silent rejoicing. It was over: no more killing, no more maiming. In the early part of the war, so many families had been untouched, seeing the first eager batches of youths volunteer, youths who had belonged to homes other than theirs. But two years on conscription had brought war closer. Of the workers at Proctor's, there wasn't one who hadn't had someone serving: perhaps a husband, perhaps a son or brother, even a cousin. Oakleigh was proud of its bells; not every church could boast a peal of eight. From that distance the separate tones weren't clear; all combined to reverberate, reaching out to the heavens in thankfulness.

Yet an end to fighting could never be a return to the life they'd once known.

Standing behind Tamsin, the window of his room thrown wide open to the crisp November morning, James rested his hands on her shoulders. He knew where her thoughts were; how could they not be?

'We're different people, aren't we,' she said: a statement not a question.

'Everyone,' he agreed. 'Even for those who come back unscathed, nothing will ever be as it was.'

Both of them were thinking of Alex; both of them knew it. Yet, for reasons they couldn't explain, neither could speak of him.

Further along the lane, just on the village side of the airfield, Maureen and Tom stood outside their open front door.

'Hark!' Matt pushed between them. 'Why they playing bells?'

'Because the war's over,' Tom told him.

'Humph,' the little boy grunted, meaning the sound to convey an intelligent understanding. But if the war was over, like they said, then what was going to happen? What did it mean for the war to be gone? He wasn't even sure what there being a war meant.

'It means that the men who went over the sea to fight will come home again.' It was Maureen who guessed at his puzzlement. 'Like Daddy.'

'Won't they be able to see, not any of them?'

'Stupid.' Trudie cut him down to size. 'Stop

showing off.' She slipped a hand into Tom's. 'I don't see what we had to have a stupid war for, anyway.'

'Amen to that,' Maureen agreed. 'Come along, indoors, all of you. This evening we will all go to church, to the Thanksgiving Service. Oh, Tom, poor Rector: just the one son and him lost.'

★ ★ ★

It took many months for the troops to be demobilised. It took less for the staff at Proctor's to be cut and, with the exception of a few men, for those taken on during the war to be dismissed. The contract with the Ministry finished with the signing of the Armistice and, although James meant to keep production of the Farley Moth going until those being worked on were fitted with their engines and ready to fly, he saw no market for them in the foreseeable future. He was anxious for work to start on the prototype of the new passenger plane; his mind was moving ahead at a pace. Before the war, flying had been seen as a hobby — and most of the men who'd flown had been looked on as cranks. Four years of war had changed the public's perception. Probably it would only be the wealthy, or the very adventurous, who would venture up as a means of travel: but gradual acceptance would come. And James meant Proctor's to be at the forefront of development.

★ ★ ★

When Tamsin had been pregnant with Kate, the lying-in nurse had thought she looked like a child with a pudding basin under her skirt; this time was different. By the time she was seven months, she was disproportionately large for her slight frame. It seemed impossible to believe she still had eight weeks to wait.

'I hear Tamsin Murray was at the works again,' from a wife of one of the men to another, and another, word and disapproval snowballing on its round. 'If you want to know what I think, I think it's nothing short of indecent, living in sin, flaunting herself in front of a workshop of men in that condition. When I had mine, I stayed decently indoors. But not her, little minx. I've heard say that her father is a minister. No wonder no one in Oakleigh sees hair or hide of him: ashamed, I should think.'

Tamsin remembered those months at Brambles, a passion that had seemed heightened, hers and Alex's too. For her, so it was this time. Perhaps James was extra careful because of past experience. Almost from the time they were sure about the baby, frightened that he might hurt her, he wouldn't let them make love. Driven by desire, haunted by memories, she used every wile to bring him to her. Even in the secrecy of her soul, she wouldn't let herself consider that what she was doing was calling out to a past that was lost to her; better to try to believe that what she felt was no more than carnal lust, heightened by the movement of the child in her.

'It can't hurt.' She wanted to sound reassuring, but she heard her voice as begging.

'It's not right.' But was he weakening. 'We might hurt you; we might hurt the child.'

'We wouldn't.' Memories urged her on. Her voice was soft, enticing. With warm hands, with soft lips, she wooed him, her heart racing. The child strained and kicked, one with her. Time and again it happened during those months, but James had a will of steel. Often, long after he slept, she would lie with her hands cradling the restive child, believing herself to be wide awake. Somewhere, she must have drifted through the barrier dividing waking from sleeping, for thoughts became dreams, the child moving in her was Kate . . . And Alex . . . Alex . . .

'What is it darling? You must have been dreaming.' Gently James drew her towards him. There was no passion in his action. Her dear, blessed James: she buried her face against him.

Lucinda is with me for a few days. Shall be delighted if you can both join us for *supper*. Don't dress — very informal. She so wants to see you. Naomi.

'My dear, you look wearied to death,' Lucinda greeted Tamsin. 'Men have no idea.'

'I'm really not,' Tamsin laughed, relieved how easy it was to be with Lucinda again. 'I always was pasty; you know that. If you ask me, men miss out on quite a lot.'

'Is this baby going to impede you? You mustn't give up flying — or the business, for that matter. You know, this war hasn't been over for six months yet, and the women are being pushed back into what is still looked on as 'their place'.

'But Mother — ' the name that at one time had been difficult to say, now slipped out all too readily ' — you're getting the vote.'

'I am. I'm over the magic age of thirty and I'm a homeowner. But how many women fall into that category? How many women who worked in the factories making the munitions? How many of the women who worked at Proctor's? Precious few.'

'More important to my mind is that every man over twenty-one will be able to vote.'

'More important? What a lot of rubbish!'

'Yes, I believe it's more important. It's a huge step. Those boys from France — boys when they went, but not when they came home — those of them who did come home — they've earned the right to shape the way things go. You watch who they vote for. It'll be a government who will pay the wounded a pension they can live on; it'll be a government who does something about homes for everyone.'

Lucinda's serious expression suddenly vanished, her face lit in a smile.

'Oh, but this girl's wasted! She needs a cause! You wait a few weeks, my dear. Get this baby job over and I'll recruit you yet.'

It was a comfortable quartet. Three women and one man, but all equally interested in the changing times. Conversation flowed easily.

'You know Alex has been given the chance to retain his commission in the Air Force?' Lucinda said, although there was no reason to suppose Tamsin should have known.

'Not coming home?' Home? Where was his home? Their furniture was still in Brambles; the clothes he'd wore in that other life, the life before the war, were still hanging in the bedroom cupboard.

'Flying is his life. I haven't actually seen him. When do you get your absolute?'

'May the third.' That was in ten days' time.

★ ★ ★

The prototype was ready for its first flight. Tamsin knew about flying a plane, she was beginning to know about running a business, but aerodynamics were still a mystery to her. Even with only six weeks to wait before the baby was due, seldom a day went by when she didn't spend a few hours at the works. She felt no embarrassment at what most of the local women referred to as 'flaunting herself in *that* condition'. Clumsy she might be, but ill she certainly wasn't so she had no intention of hiding herself indoors as if having a baby were something to be ashamed of. The third of May was less than a week away, and James had already made arrangements for them to be married by Brackleford's Registrar, at the Town Hall, just as Lucinda and Charles had.

James was taking the Farley Falcon on its test flight at midday.

'It's designed for passengers' — Tamsin brought out what she hoped might be her trump card — 'and James, this isn't like the Moth. I wasn't with you when you designed the Moth.

This is *our* plane: at least, that's how I think of it. It's come out of our being together.' Then, with a huge smile, 'I was going to say 'like our baby has', but you know what I mean. We've watched it together every step of the way. Can't you see how right it would be for us to go up together?'

'I know what you're saying. But, no, Tamsin. I promise you that you will be my first passenger, once today is over. How's that?'

She sighed. There were times when it was no use arguing with James.

Together, they watched the machine being wheeled out of the shed.

'What a big bird it is,' she said admiringly. 'Doesn't it look grand? Aren't you proud, James? I am.'

'I'm looking forward to seeing what it can do.' Which was the nearest he would admit to pride.

'Look at the wingspan, look at the width of the wings.' She was horribly aware of her lack of understanding. Thrust, drag, brake-horsepower, shaft-horsepower: expressions that were familiar to her, but only half understood. When she'd been with James to Scott Parmenter, the makers of the engine, she had listened attentively; every now and then she had almost been able to believe that the pieces of the jigsaw were falling into place. But that day, as so often, a single sentence was all that was needed for her tenuous understanding to evaporate.

She was resolved to learn. She had determination enough and James would be unfailingly patient; but she had no illusions. Her knowledge of mathematics went no further than the ability to tot up a column of figures or to work out the men's wages. Conscious of James's look of pride as they watched the plane wheeled to the end of the landing strip, she sighed.

'I know when I'm beaten,' she said, but the way her eyes shone with merriment told him she had known all the time what his answer would be. 'Stand still and let me pin this heather on your coat.' It was part of the ritual. At the far end of the garden of Brambles was a patch of heather and, ever since she'd first gone to live there, each time he'd taken a plane on its test flight, she had picked a sprig for him to wear on his coat for good luck.

'I always feel guilty doing this,' she laughed. 'Pagan superstition, that's what my mother would have called it. And as for him, Father, he would have thumped the pulpit and threatened hellfire for following devil practices. There!' She stood back to admire her handiwork. 'But me? I believe in belt and braces.' She laughed when she said it; she mustn't let him guess at the way her heart was racing. Heather, prayer, knocking on wood, crossing her fingers: every time he went up in a plane that had never flown before her stomach was home to a thousand butterflies. But the Farley Moth was an old friend, tested and tried.

As always, there was no hiding anything from James. Drawing her towards him, he raised her face. Smiles were gone; the moment mattered for both of them.

'Try not to worry,' he said softly.

'Why should we worry? It's a fine plane. The pride of Proctor's.' She swallowed the lump in her throat. 'Take care, James.'

'That I promise.'

They went out through the workshops. Men called, 'Good luck, Guv,' 'She's a beauty, sir, best ever came out of the shed.' And Tamsin, pagan superstitions forgotten, whispered so low that he could hardly hear her, 'God bless you.'

As the propeller was swung, he raised his hand. Tamsin held up both of hers, fingers tightly crossed. Please, please take care of him. The tone of the engine was deep and unfamiliar as the machine started forward, rose above the hedge, up, up, above the trees then banked steeply as it turned towards Hinds Hill. Two or three times it circuited; then, rising higher, left Oakleigh behind.

'Reckon he'll be giving that one full marks,' one man said.

And another, 'Be plenty of work for us at Proctor's, be sure of that.'

Tamsin had to get away from the group gathered by the shed door. It was crazy to feel like this. The plane was doing everything he asked of it. So why did she have this dreadful ache in the pit of her stomach. Why was her mouth so dry and her hands clammy? In half an hour — less — he'd be back on the ground. Blindly, she kept walking, following the track across the field to the garden gate of Brambles. She was scarcely conscious of where she was going, any more than she was that she was speaking her thoughts aloud. 'Please, take care of

him. Feel sick. Can't be. I'm never sick. Mustn't be . . . not here . . . mustn't be . . . hurry . . . '
Panting for breath, moving faster than her ungainly figure found comfortable, already retching, she blundered through the garden gate of Brambles, making straight for the ditch where each night they'd emptied their waste. She got there just in time.

Minutes later, weak and trembling, she leant against the side of the cottage. She heard the plane approaching.

Thank you. It's all right: he's almost home. Whatever happened to me? I've never felt like that before. Must have been because I felt so sick that I was frightened — or was I sick because I was so frightened? I mustn't tell him; it'll worry him. Feel better, now. I'll walk back round the field, be there for him when he lands.

Two or three deep breaths, then she smoothed her hair and brushed her hands over the front of her skirt, somehow drawing a metaphorical line under what she preferred not to remember. Going back through the gate onto the field, she could see the Farley Falcon just beyond Hinds Hill, already losing height, ready to land.

The sound of the explosion rent the air.

13

While Lucinda was indoors composing a letter to send to *The Times*, Naomi was on hands and knees in the garden, neatening the edges of the lawn. She had become very fond of her friend and she respected her views; but spending one's life rowing against the current could lead to nothing but frustration. Just feel the sun on the back of your neck, listen to the birds, see the leafbuds forming on the hedges. Those are the things that life is all about: man or woman, those are the things that are there for all of them. Who could be an atheist in a springtime garden?

So went Naomi's thoughts as she methodically clipped her way along the edge of the border. Not that anyone seeing her would have guessed that her mind was on anything other than the knife-edge perfection she was leaving in her wake; no-nonsense Naomi the scarecrow was in the garden to work, not to dream.

'I'm just going to walk to the post box,' Lucinda told her. 'Why don't you come?'

'Give me two minutes to scrub my hands and put something decent on my feet.' She took her shears and the piece of sacking she'd used as a kneeling mat to the shed, then disappeared through the side door of the house. Never one to waste time, she was back before Lucinda had mentally gone through the letter she had ready to post to the newspaper. But would they print it? Or would it go the way of so many more she'd sent to the press, both national and local?

'Look, see the plane.' Who but Naomi could bring about such a swift transformation? A handsome worsted coat covered her gardening dress, her lace-up boots had been replaced by buckled court shoes and her battered felt hat with one quite twenty years younger. 'That's James. A passenger machine. He passed overhead two or three times while you were indoors, then he went off somewhere further away. He didn't get up to the antics he does with those little Moths they used out in France, but look at the size of this. Coming over quite low, isn't he — I expect that's so that we can see him.' Perhaps it was, perhaps it wasn't, but she waved anyway. Her arm was still raised when it happened, the blast rattling the windows of the house.

'Oh, dear God. James . . . James.' In panic, she looked at Lucinda. 'Will he have a chance? Oh, dear God.'

'Just a fireball. He couldn't have had time to know.' But what solace could that be?

'It's coming down between here and the hill. Come on.' And Naomi started to run, something she hadn't done for years.

'It's no use, Naomi. We saw what happened. Charred wreckage, bits of plane scattered everywhere: that's all there will be.' Tall and slender, Lucinda kept pace with less effort than her less agile friend.

★   ★   ★

385

Some came on bicycles, some on foot — and managing a better speed than poor, breathless Naomi. By the time Tamsin had stumbled back across the field to the workshops, everyone had gone. Over and over, she said his name, as she climbed into the car and started the engine. Don't let him be burnt, don't let him be hurt. But how could he not be hurt? Perhaps when the plane exploded, he could have been thrown clear; perhaps his fall was broken by the trees on Hinds Hill; perhaps he'd have nothing worse than a broken leg, a broken arm. Perhaps . . . perhaps . . . please . . .

The child squirmed and turned. Our baby, James . . . James . . . please — James. It was as if all the love he'd given her, all the comfortable companionship they'd shared, all the gentle trust crowded in on her. Unca Jame, his unchanging devotion to her and to Kate; James, understanding and compassionate; James the lover — there was no space in her memories for her own frustrations. All she knew as she sped towards the pall of black smoke was the words that seemed to come almost involuntarily from him as he lay close to her, passion spent, 'I love you so.' Please, make him be safe . . .

The clanging of the fire bell warned her that the fire tender was on its way. She pulled into a field gateway to let it pass, then saw a group on bicycles coming into view, following it as they always did. Even from the village, the explosion must have been heard. They wouldn't have known how the debris had been scattered, but they would have seen what was left of the

386

fuselage plunging to the ground in flames. An ambulance. She ought to have waited and telephoned the hospital. An ambulance for James.

She followed the fire tender, seeing it through a haze of burning tears. Please . . . but what was she asking? She knew in her heart they wouldn't be waiting for an ambulance. Please take care of him: if you've taken him, then please give him peace — peace that passeth all understanding. Simply words she'd known as long as she could remember. Until that moment, that's all they'd been.

★　★　★

'I've cooked you your meal. But food! Feel as if it would stick in my throat.' Mrs Huntley said, when she heard Tamsin come in. 'I went along, of course — well, not a soul who didn't, I should think. Oh, my dear Lord.'

'I don't want supper — '

'Oh yes, you do, young Miss.' There was a new tone in her voice: a brusque kindness but none of the respect she'd known James insisted on. 'Anyway, want it or not, you'll just see to it that you eat it. You've got the master's child to nourish and as long as you and me are still here, I'll see to it that you don't let him down over that. Oh, my dear Lord. Right as ninepence this morning — now he's gone. I never thought I'd see the day he'd be struck down like that. Never known him suffer so much as a cold, then one of those dratted machines takes him.' She peered at

387

Tamsin, feeling a touch of pity for the girl despite herself. No better than she ought to be, of course, married to one man and living with another — but, my word, she does look a poor washed-out thing. Wouldn't be surprised she never came through having this child. And, even if she does, what's to become of her — them? What's to become of any of us?

'I think I'll just go upstairs. Really, I'm not hungry — '

'Up or down, you'll eat what I've cooked for you. What do you think the master would say, if he could see you neglecting your duty? Sometime, we'll have to have a talk, you and me. But another day'll be soon enough. Now then, up in your room or down at the table: where do you want this food?'

'I'll stay downstairs, the same as usual, Mrs Huntley. But please, not too much.'

'That's the way. Same as usual. That's what he'd want, if you ask my opinion.' But how long can anything go on the same as usual? Oh, my dear Lord, what's to become of us, me and her too? Fate, that's what folk might say. Fate be damned! Another month and that young minx would have been his wife. Now she's naught but his paramour, and that poor child will come into the world a bastard. The master's child — and folk will be shunning him as if the little madam had picked him up from dear Lord knows where.

Tamsin put her food into her mouth. She chewed, she swallowed, her actions mechanical. She heard the loud clang of the front door bell.

'Mrs Huntley, I don't want — ' she started, as

388

she heard the housekeeper cross the hall.

'Want or no, you'll not turn this one away. I know the shape through the glass.' Then, to the caller, 'Just told her, I recognised you through the glass. Come in, Miss Halliwell. What a business!'

'Never lived through a sadder day,' Naomi answered. 'How is she, poor child?'

'Frightened, I wouldn't wonder.'

Naomi made no answer as she and Lucinda were ushered into the room.

★ ★ ★

It was Lucinda who took both Tamsin's hands in a firm grasp, as if that way she could pass some of her own strength into her. But it was Naomi who had come with practical help.

'There are things that have to be done. The Coroner will conduct an inquest, but what nonsense. We all know what happened. And there is little enough of the plane for anyone to know why it failed. All that is out of our hands. Do you know James's solicitor?'

'I can find out.' She mustn't fail him; she must do all that had to be done.

'He used Rutbridge and Clampton, the same as I do. Mr Edgar Clampton sees to his affairs. Will you contact him, or shall I? Perhaps it's easier if I do; I've known him many years. And the vicar?'

'I'll do that, and Dawkins.' Dawkins and Sons was the firm of undertakers. 'James did it all for me — for Katie. I'll do that.'

'Good girl.'

'Another month, and you would have been his wife. He would have seen to it you were taken care of.' This from Lucinda. 'Naomi tells me his only relative is a sister living in South Africa. What will she want with a house in Oakleigh? And the business? A year ago, it was thriving, working full out on planes of war. But what now? I suppose she'll hope for a buyer — and, for the sake of the staff, we can but hope she finds one. Not that any of that is our main concern. It's you, Tamsin, you and this child.'

'Look, my dear, that's another purpose of my visit. James was as dear to me as any family; he was like a young brother.' Naomi's never-beautiful face was battling to hold itself steady. 'There's room for you at Lambton. As for James's child — one day, all I have would have come to James, so of course his child would have a home at Lambton.'

Not once had Tamsin let herself cry. Now, faced with the gallantry of Naomi's effort for control, that and her honest love for James and for the baby who for hours hadn't been still a moment, she turned her back on her visitors and felt the hot tears course down her face. Lucinda's arm was strong; her soft, deep voice reached back through all Tamsin's years and helped her face what lay ahead.

* * *

It was getting dark. The visitors had gone.

'If you've done with me, I'll get to bed,' Mrs

390

Huntley told her. It was what Naomi had said that made Tamsin aware of the change in her manner. Twenty-four hours ago they had been mistress and housekeeper ('Mistress — oh she'd been that all right, *his* mistress. But she'd had to be accepted; in a few weeks, she would have been the master's wife so I just had to keep my opinions to myself.') Now, they were two people soon to find themselves without a home. 'Best thing you can do is follow suit. Everything's locked up. What a day! You get on to bed, why don't you? No good being frightened of ghosts.'

'Ghosts of James? How could I be frightened? I'll come up soon.' In the fading light, she hoped Mrs Huntley couldn't see her swollen eyelids.

It wasn't fear of his ghost that kept her downstairs so much as an overwhelming sense of isolation. She reminded herself of the kindness and support she'd been given by Naomi and Lucinda, but it made no difference. She didn't light the lamp; she didn't consciously think of anything. There was nothing elegant in the way she lolled in the large armchair, half awake and half asleep as dusk faded.

'There's always a reason, Tamsie, sweetling.' Almost as if her mother were in the room, she heard it. 'We don't know what's right for us.'

'Can you still say that?' she cried silently. 'You died, too, just like James. You must have expected years of life ahead of you, just like he did. There's always a reason? What reason? If there's a God, if there's anything, *anything* except what we make for ourselves, why should he punish James? And me? This loving God, he took Kate,

391

he saw to it that Alex didn't love me, now he's taken James. If there's a reason, is it to punish me he did it? No, I don't believe it. I don't believe there's a God at all.'

'Tamsie, sweetling, don't! I can't bear it when you talk like that!' With her own eyes tightly closed, she could see her mother's lovely face, those deep blue eyes swimming with tears.

Somewhere, she must have crossed the threshold of sleep. One dream pushed another from her mind, this one the fire bell as the tender sped towards a wall of black smoke. She woke with a start, the bell still jangling. The front door!

Mrs Huntley heard it, too. Now what sort of a person would come calling at this hour of the night? Barefoot, her hair in two thin pigtails, she came down the attic stairs, pulling on her dressing gown as she came. It was when she reached the first floor landing that she realised Tamsin was still up and pulling back the bolt to open the door. With the house in darkness, no one with a scrap of feeling would come visiting — more likely, some rascal who'd heard there were just two helpless women in the house. Light or dark, she knew exactly where to reach to pick up a heavy brass candlestick. Yes, and she'd use it, too. With the master gone, it had to be up to her.

'I couldn't come before. I had to wait till the children were asleep before I left Tom.'

'Mo — Mo, you came. Missed you . . . '

* * *

392

If Mrs Huntley's opinion of Tamsin had been that she looked 'pasty and washed-out', the long hours of night did nothing to help. Tamsin hated self-pity, and through those hours she fought to hold it at bay. Her greatest comfort came from thinking of James. She ached with sadness that he was gone, his life snuffed out, but her memories of him held no regrets. She would have their baby, bring it up with only one parent: but one that must have the strength of two. She would see to it that the baby 'knew' James, and was proud, no matter how society might spurn a child born out of wedlock.

That hour with Maureen had helped her more than she realised. Maureen, living on a pension so small she must have had a struggle to pay the rent and put food on the table, yet she wouldn't change places with a living soul. One decision Tamsin made as she lay gazing at the dark ceiling: Naomi had offered her a home and she was grateful, but she couldn't spend her life accepting charity. Perhaps she'd go back to Brambles. No: Brambles, like everything else, would be sold as part of James's estate. She'd find work. She could go away where no one knew her; she could pretend she and James had been married. One idea chased another across her brain: she could do *this*, she could do *that*. The only thing she couldn't do was sleep.

★   ★   ★

The next morning, Naomi called for Tamsin in her car and they were driven to Brackleford, stopping at the rectory on the way.

'Shall I come in with you?' Secretly, Naomi thought that being accompanied by someone who was accepted in Reverend Thompson's social circle might make him receive Tamsin more graciously.

'No. I must do this by myself. But I'll not be long.'

'Don't worry, my dear. Take as long as you want.' But she was sure that Clifford Thompson wouldn't waste time with the young woman whose morals had become the talk of the small community.

She was right. In less than five minutes, Tamsin was getting back into the car.

'The service won't be until Wednesday next week. He says there has to be extra time because of the autopsy.' There was a matter-of-fact note in her small voice. It was as if all this was happening to someone else. 'I've asked him to open up Myrtle's plot. It's right they should be together.' Then, turning to Naomi in a moment's uncertainty. 'It is right, isn't it?'

'I think, my dear, it is. One of these days, not for very many years I hope, you will be laid to rest with Kate.'

Tamsin slipped her hand into Naomi's and felt the pressure of her fingers. Afterwards, looking back on that part of her life, it was those moments in the car she remembered as if they had been a turning point.

It was with sadness that I learnt of the tragic death of my client, Mr James Proctor. In this respect I shall be glad if you will call at my office.

Not a word wasted in Edgar Clampton's brief note. Would Mrs Huntley have had something along the same lines? For there was no doubt what he had to tell them: the house was to be put up for auction, the house and all its contents, and they must find somewhere else to go. Perhaps, because Naomi had been to see him, out of respect for her, he thought he ought to tell Tamsin face to face rather than put it in a letter. For the first time, she felt she had no right in James's home. No one was to have his wood carvings; they would be hers. What was it he'd said about keeping his early efforts? They were, to him, like Robert the Bruce's spider's web. So they would be to her. Each time she had doubts, each time she felt defeated, she'd look at them and have the courage to try again.

Opening his bureau she took a sheet of paper, dipped her nib in the silver-topped inkwell and started to write, carefully and in her best writing.

I acknowledge your letter received this morning. As I shall be in Brackleford in the afternoon of Tuesday of next week, May the third, I propose calling on you then. I hope three o'clock will be convenient.

No need to tell him that she would only be passing through Brackleford on her way back from the court house in Reading.

When Tuesday came, the leaden sky hung low;

even the temperature had dipped. She'd battled with any show of her misery in the days since the accident, but it took every ounce of her courage to face the day that waited for her. Most mornings, she woke to the familiar feeling of movement from her unborn child, a comforting feeling as if it were reassuring her that she wasn't alone. On that morning, even when she rested her hands on her naked body, it didn't stir. Her backed ached; no matter how she lay she found no relief.

There was no sound yet from Mrs Huntley, but already the room was light enough to see. Nearly six o'clock. Usually, it was far lighter by that time. But on that Tuesday morning, the clouds looked solid, the air was damp with something between mist and rain. She ought to get up. Today she was determined to look her best and that was a miracle that would take time. Out of bed, she took off her nightgown and stood before the long mirror, her childlike hands pressing against the small of her back. Tiny shoulders, skinny arms, legs like beanpoles: the child was growing out of all proportion to the body that sustained it. She'd never looked like that with Kate, even at the end. Pulling her thoughts into line, she made herself stand tall (by her standards). Miserable weather and an aching back weren't going to defeat her.

'Is Miss Halliwell coming to fetch you?' the newly familiar Mrs Huntley asked.

'I'm driving myself.'

'Never! It was one thing driving when the master was with you, but whoever heard of a woman gallivanting round the country on her own — and in your state too? Why, it's not seemly: that's a fact, it isn't.'

'What old-fashioned nonsense. Women drove in France during the war, and no one thought that was unseemly.'

'They only had themselves to consider. I've a good mind to run along to Miss Halliwell and tell her what you're up to. Bumping all those miles: oh, my dear Lord, you could find yourself giving birth like some gyppo in the countryside and before it's even ready for the world. Not just your baby: you've got responsibility for the master's child. And time you remembered it.'

Rather than be annoyed, Tamsin looked at her accuser with something akin to affection. 'I promise you, I remember it.'

But, once through Brackleford, rattling on towards Reading, the warning came back to her. Kate had come into the world almost without warning: supposing this one did the same? Not yet, though; it wasn't due for more than two months. Perhaps it was all part of that pattern her mother used to talk about. This leaden feeling inside her and a back that felt as though it was breaking in two might have been sent to her to keep her mind away from the events of the day. Last time she and James had been to the court together, remember they'd had lunch at the Great Western Hotel: champagne, too. That was the day the knot that had bound her to Alex had been loosened. Today, the knot would be untied, the two ends thrown away. Shrimp . . . She bit the corners of her trembling mouth.

Not much of a shrimp, now! No more Alex, no more James: gone just as surely as little Kate.

Going though Reading, she saw the same three men that they'd seen before: one with a concertina, one with a fiddle and the third still with his comb and paper. Six months had passed for them, too; they were still in the same poverty trap, still just as disabled, still with no glimmer of hope on their horizon.

If Mavis were right in her belief that everything works for a pattern, that trio must have been brought into Tamsin's path for a purpose. Certainly, the sight of them haunted her. And certainly, too, the thought of them helped her stave off her enemy self-pity when the judge looked down on her with contempt and ruled that the decree granted to Wing Commander Alexander Murray D.S.O., M.C., be made absolute.

When at last she came out of the court, her papers safely in her handbag, it would have been much easier to drive straight back to Brackleford. But because it would have been easier, that's just what she wouldn't do. Just as they had last time, she went to the Great Western Hotel; she even ordered the same food. But no champagne. Then, more weary than she would admit, she drove back to Brackleford and at one minute to three o'clock presented herself in the outer office of Rutbridge and Clampton.

'Mrs Murray, I'm delighted to meet you.' It wasn't the greeting she'd expected from the balding little man who reached for a pair of gilt-framed spectacles and clipped them to his nose as they faced each other across his desk. 'An unbelievably sad occurrence: yes, unbelievably. I'd known my client for many years and had utmost respect for him: yes, utmost. A man who always showed forethought, as indeed he did on this occasion. A careful man, never one to leave business unfinished. But you know these things. You don't need me to explain him to you: no, indeed, no.'

She smiled at this unexpectedly kindly man. If he wasn't what she'd expected, the same could be said for her. He'd known the circumstances of the woman James Proctor meant shortly to marry, but he'd not expected a white-faced, fragile creature like this.

'James was the best person I've ever known,' she told him.

'Humph.' He cleared his throat. 'Yes, indeed yes. Now, Mrs Murray, I have here a will he instructed me to draw up: his last will and testament, overriding all previous bequests and dated — upon my soul, I'd not realised it until this moment — dated exactly one year ago today. I will read it to you in its entirety.' And he proceeded to do so.

'A year ago?' What she had heard seemed to have stripped her of all logical thought. 'But we couldn't be married until after my divorce.' She knew there was no sense in what she said, but she had to keep talking. 'A year ago, he wouldn't have known about the baby — well, of course not — a year ago, I hadn't even given up living in the cottage. Are you sure?'

This time, he forgot he'd thought her plain

and pasty; his smile was warm and genuine.

'Not only am I sure, but *he* most certainly was. He told me that he hoped one day — one day, mind you — he would make you his wife and, when he did, he would come back to me to amend your name *et cetera, et cetera*. A man of great forethought, my dear Mrs Murray. Could he also have been a man of premonition? Dear me, what a sorrowful business it is.' Then, taking off his clip-on spectacles, he seemed to square his shoulders. 'You are involved with the business, I believe. The things you ladies do today . . . Changing times: yes, changing times.'

It was as well there were so few motor cars on the road for, as she drove back to Oakleigh, Tamsin's concentration leapt from one decision to another, envisaging Proctor's without James's skill and knowledge, rushing off at a tangent in the hope of seeing a solution. Always she was conscious of her own limitations.

But James had had faith in her. Yes, but James hadn't expected not to be here. Then why had he drawn up a will that would have meant nothing, *nothing*, if the accident hadn't happened before they were married? So it was for this very contingency that he had arranged it.

James, dear dear James, I know so little. Working on the assembly line, learning something about how to run a business, flying a Farley Moth: what use will that be for the future? Proctor's, Aeronautical Engineers, mine; the livelihood of a staff that have been loyal, mine. I won't fail you, James. Remember what you told me about Kate — and about your Myrtle — they would know that they were remembered, they would know that they were loved. So, James, can you hear me? But even if you can, I can't hear you. Proctor's is a fine business. Look at the orders we've filled for the Ministry. If we still had that contract, I could have carried on.

But what now? I don't know what went wrong with the Farley Falcon. I can't follow that road. No, I have to build on what is tested and tried. But you said yourself that no one would want small, manoeuvrable flying machines: the future had to be for carrying passengers. Ought I to take someone else into the business? Is that what you want? You'd hoped that one day Alex would have been your partner. That can't be what you want: please, not that. I couldn't bear it.

Alex: today will have made a free man of him. Imagine him managing Proctor's, probably remarrying, living in Oakleigh.

Of course, it was a meaningless flight of fancy: Alex was retaining his commission. He'd never come back to Oakleigh. On the lonely road through Farley Wood, she heard herself whimper; she held her hand to her aching back. But there was no way of easing her aching heart.

★   ★   ★

The church was full for James's funeral. Not all the locals came out of affection or respect; there were those who were drawn there simply to see what was to be seen, whether his mistress would have the brazen face to flaunt herself at the graveside where he was to be laid to rest with his wife. But, apart from those, there were the men from the works, those still there and those who had escaped serving in the forces by being employed manufacturing Moths, and the women who had supplemented a soldier's married allowance by working on the assembly line. There were business acquaintances, some of whom had travelled distances; there were friends of long standing.

Tamsin stood, dry-eyed and isolated, among the crowd. All these people, friends of James: they were nothing to do with her. And she was neither blind nor insensitive to the way she was being ignored by them. They must have known about her — if they hadn't, they wouldn't have gone out of their way to disregard her. Their presence was evidence that James had severed himself from his one-time social life — and he'd done it for her.

By her side, she heard Naomi swallowing the sob that rose in her throat as the coffin was lowered. The Rector's voice recited the prayers of committal, so why didn't Tamsin listen? Instead, in her head echoed and re-echoed something she only half remembered: no more seen . . .

But you didn't see just with your eyes: wasn't that what James had helped her to understand? You saw with your heart and mind. Forcing her hands deep into the pockets of her new black coat, unseen by anyone, she rested them on the moving mound. Yesterday, the baby had been a dormant heavy weight; today it stretched and kicked, as if it wanted her to know she wasn't alone. She closed her eyes, unaware of the worried way Naomi watched her. She knew James was close; she knew he could hear her silent promise. You put all your trust in me. James, show me the way to go; point me to what I should do. I'm not frightened, I'm proud. I won't fail you.

★ ★ ★

It was less easy to believe she wasn't frightened as she lay awake, the night already half over. Mr Clampton had given her no more than a vague idea of James's estate, but two things she knew: the first, he had left her well provided for; the second, money brings with it responsibility. And it was that responsibility that caused the problem.

Local men had worked at Proctor's since James had first set up the company. It had been a thriving business because of James. Round and round in her head went the problem, like a dog chasing its tail and getting nowhere. Still worrying, and believing herself still wide awake, she must have hovered on the edge of sleep.

She was standing with James looking out over the airfield. But what were they watching? Farley Moths: not just a single machine with James on a test flight or her taking off to deliver it to the airbase (how could they, when they were standing on the grass, watching?), but Moths like children at play in the sky.

Suddenly, she was wide awake, catching the

403

dream before it vanished. Wriggling her increasingly cumbersome body, she sat bolt upright. James, I knew you'd help me. We have to go on producing the Moth. It wasn't what you intended — but what else could you be telling me? Guide me. Tomorrow, I'll write the order for the engines; I'll talk to the men.

By daylight, she wouldn't have believed there was logic in her decision. She might even have been tempted to think that feeling James's presence so strongly was no more than the dream of an overtired mind. But it wasn't daylight, it was night: silent, except for the distant hooting of an owl. Lying down, she tried to recapture that moment, to know he was still close to her. Even though the dream had gone beyond recall, her mind was clear and within minutes she slept.

★ ★ ★

'I'm surprised the gov'nor could have been so overkeen in her. What is she but a bit of a kid? He had vision, did James Proctor. Passenger travel, that's where he saw the future.'

'He might have put her name on his will but you know, and I know, he never expected things to work out like they did.'

It was the midday break; although one or two cycled home, most of the men brought sandwiches and, making the most of a sudden hint of warmth, were outside eating them, enjoying a smoke and a gossip. They all had their opinions and they all meant to air them.

404

'He's not the first man to keep his brains in his trousers. But wouldn't you think he would have had a bit written in — a coder — coder something — '

'Codicil?' put in one with superior knowledge.

'Ah, that's the word for it. Wouldn't you think he would have had one of those put in saying that, even if the place was ever hers, she had to see to it that someone was brought in with some idea of aeroplanes?'

But was that fair? Young Mrs Murray wasn't like most women. How many were there who could take a plane up in the air as neat as any man? No one actually said it, but the thought hung in the air.

'I'll tell you what I think if you like.' And they knew they'd hear it, whether they liked or not. 'You can't take a woman on face value. All you can be sure of is that, given a half pretty face, then the chaps don't stand a chance. Most of us were here when she and Alex Murray got married — and not a day too soon. Then pretty well as soon as he's off fighting for his country, what does she do? Gets the gov'nor in bed with her.'

'Steady on, there! She's a good enough lass. And I don't envy her, having the responsibility of this place landed on her plate.'

'Then she should get a man to run it. A flyer she may be, but when it comes to running a business, especially a business of this sort, it takes a man.'

'That's about it, time to get back inside.'

'And one thing we ought to be glad about.

Foolhardy or not, putting us back on Moths, it's a hell of a lot better than putting us out of a job.'

'So let's make the most of it. Like enough, that's what we shall be heading for.'

★　★　★

Tamsin, too, had her moments of doubt through those next few weeks. Naomi suggested she should find a suitable manager; Maureen tried to persuade her; reason told her they were right. She would listen to none of it. How could she when, time and again, that dream recurred: she and James standing on the airfield, overhead Moths like children at play?

A day didn't pass without her spending an hour or two in the office that had been James's.

'Time she stayed at home,' the men agreed. But even though they thought she was making a mistake — and risking losing the business and their jobs in the bargain — they had a sneaking respect for her total disregard of the narrow conventions.

'The way she rackets around in that motor car, it's enough to shake the little 'un into the world.'

And perhaps those bumpy roads had something to do with it.

★　★　★

It was midsummer's day, the morning sultry and overcast.

'You don't look fit for much this morning.' Carrying Tamsin's breakfast tray to the dining room, Mrs Huntley watched her coming down the stairs. 'Had a bad night; I can see that without asking.'

'Nonsense. I slept well. And you?'

'Me? Isn't me who's having this baby. Now, you listen to me — ' and, as an afterthought ' — ma'am — more than time you stopped chasing your tail for two minutes and calmed down. That firm will carry on well enough without you — well, very soon it'll have to for, like it or not you'll have more to think about than aeroplanes. If you don't soon ease up, you'll be heading for trouble. Slip of a thing like you are and carrying on as if you've got the strength of Colossus.'

Tamsin ignored the warning. Chasing her tail was easier than facing up to her uncertainties. So she ate her breakfast; then, despite the housekeeper's tut-tutting in disapproval, she reversed the motor car out of the coach house onto the rutted lane and set off for the works.

Within an hour, she was home. This time, there was no James to give her confidence; this time, she was alone.

★ ★ ★

One thing this new baby had in common with Kate: he was anxious to get into the world. By the afternoon of that same day, he'd demonstrated the power of his lungs, been given his first bath and was lying in Tamsin's arms.

'I nipped along to Miss Halliwell to tell her,' Mrs Huntley told her. 'The master's baby: she'll want to be the first to come calling. But she'd been driven in to Brackleford, gone to meet that Mrs Hardcastle. Always here, that woman. Seems to me she regrets getting rid of her own house. Her own, did I say? Easy pickings she had there: no time at all with the poor invalid gentleman — can't tell me she was ever a proper wife to him.'

'Mrs Huntley, that's not our business.' Even a quick birth takes its toll, but Tamsin's spirit rallied in Lucinda's defence. At the back of her mind was the uncomfortable knowledge that the housekeeper would never have talked as she did, had James still been here. 'I'm glad they'll both be coming. Thank you for thinking to send the message.' She said it so calmly, almost over-politely. No one must guess at the strange, frightening feeling that possessed her as she held her new son. 'Leave the baby with me. Take Mrs White down and see she has something to eat. She had nothing at midday.'

'Neither did you. Best I see to you first.'

'No, just do as I say. I'm not ready to eat.'

'That's all very well. Maybe that new wee man is ready. Can't go through life just thinking of yourself, you know. Not now you've got him depending on what bit of nourishment he can get from you.' And from her disparaging sniff as she said it, it was clear she didn't give a lot for his prospects.

'Thank you, Mrs Huntley. I'll leave you to look after Mrs White.' She wanted both of them gone; they mustn't guess the emotion that welled up in her.

'I'll be as quick as I can,' the midwife told her. Unlike Martha Huntley, she was more than pleased with Tamsin. It wasn't every patient who gave so little trouble. When the call had come that the baby was on its way, she had been ready for trouble. But not a bit of it. Not so much as a scream out of her: not like some of the women she'd had to care for. A nice baby, too — Mrs White took personal satisfaction in the thought as she plodded down the stairs behind Martha — sound in wind and limb. No wonder she was feeling a mite peckish. It was a responsibility seeing a new life into the world. Yes, she was ready to do justice to a good plate of food and no mistake.

Tamsin heard the door close behind them. With her eyes closed, she listened to the footsteps retreating down the stairs. Thankfully, she relaxed; every muscle seemed to sag as she leant back against her piled pillows. This baby . . . Kate . . . She held the tiny, warm bundle close against her. She was too tired to fight the tears that rolled down her face. Alex — no, don't think of Alex, just of James. James, this is our son. Poor little boy, with no father . . . And Kate, darling Kate: did Alex think of her? If he didn't, then it was as if she had no father, either. Don't let him forget her; please make him love her still . . .

She heard the hopeless sound of her own crying. Even if he doesn't think about me, even if he doesn't love me, make him always love Katie. I wish . . . I wish . . . no, don't think about it. Look at this little boy. He's yours. He depends on you: whatever you do will be for him. Loosening her hold on him enough that she could pull the sheet to her face, she wiped her tears.

That was her lowest moment; she resolved it *had* to be. With eyes still burning from her tears, she gazed at her son. The recurring dream still lay at the back of her mind, preventing her listening to reason that told her she ought to be engaging someone to do what James would have done — find the reason for the Falcon's crash and concentrate the firm on a future in making a passenger plane.

James, can you see him? Yes, of course you can. I'll call him James — not James Proctor, he'll be James Murray. But he'll know about you: he'll be proud of you. I'll make him proud of me, too.

As if he knew he was the subject of her attention, the baby opened his mouth in a wide yawn.

'Oh, you darling,' she whispered. 'Little James.'

So engrossed in her thoughts had she been that she hadn't heard the door bell, so the first she knew that she had visitors was when she heard them on the stairs.

'Here we are.' Naomi burst in, Lucinda following more sedately. 'Oh, my dear, I'm so thankful. Well done! He's beautiful. If only James could see — ' Realising her tactlessness, she bit back her words mid-sentence.

'He can, Naomi: I'm sure he can.'

'If I'm careful, may I hold him?' The scarecrow

410

was waiting to take over when she got back to Lambton; it was the duchess who had been driven to Brackleford. But there was nothing of a duchess in her humility as she took the bundle from Tamsin. 'I was allowed to hold James when he was first born, you know.' She might have been talking to herself. 'I was fourteen.' Fourteen, with all the hopes and dreams that only a fourteen-year-old can know.

They didn't stay long. A well-fed Mrs White made sure of that. Promising to call at the Rileys' and tell Maureen the baby had arrived, they stood up to leave.

'I had a letter from Alex, yesterday,' Lucinda said. 'That in itself was a rarity; neither of us are great correspondents. He has decided to leave the service, after all. He's risen too high too fast, I dare say. At his rank, he sees his future behind a desk instead of in the air. It seems he's been offered a job with a firm of aeroplane makers in America, a test pilot. Of course, he's taking it; after these last few years, he couldn't live with his feet always on the ground. But it's the same for all these young flyers. And most of them will have no choice. I'll see you again before I go back to town, my dear.' And, another rarity, she swooped on Tamsin and kissed her. 'Well done. The boy looks well made and healthy. You deserve something to go right for you.'

Mrs White took young James to get acquainted with his crib and Tamsin was thankful to lie down. She'd rest now, so that she'd be ready for Maureen later. Or so she planned. But how could she rest? Alex going away, much further away than a divorce could take him: a life that could never have a place for Kate and her. He'd fall in love with someone else, he'd marry, and his children would be Americans. What about Kate? Would he ever think of Kate? Or her? He'd be gone in body and spirit; he'd be further from her than James.

She must have been weaker than she wanted to accept; for the second time in an hour her eyes filled with tears.

She could understand that he couldn't face a deskbound job. She seemed still to hear Lucinda's words: ' — Couldn't live with his feet on the ground. It's the same for all these young flyers. But most of them will have no choice.'

Rubbing the back of her hand across her stinging eyes, she sat bolt upright. The reason for that recurring dream was suddenly clear. The mist was clearing from the way ahead.

14

There was only one person she could confide in during those first days — and that person was the baby. In fairness to the men at the works, she couldn't even talk to Maureen about her plans.

It was customary for a new mother to languish in bed for two or three weeks and then to be looked on as only one stage short of an invalid for another two or three. Tamsin was impatient to get on; lying in bed, she felt her life was in limbo. Once her plans started to take shape, every moment she idled was a moment wasted. Mrs White had been engaged to live at Lindley for a month, and that month had to be used wisely: for a tiny baby couldn't be bundled into a motor car and there were places she had to go, people she had to see.

When James was thirteen days old, she decided she couldn't let her plans be frustrated any longer.

'Here, here, here, what's all this, then? Mrs White said nothing about you getting up.' Mrs Huntley appeared in the hall when she heard her on the stairs.

'That's because she didn't know. James won't need me for nearly three hours. I'll make sure I'm home by then.'

'You think you're going out? That, you're not! Whatever can you be thinking of? Straight from your bed — '

'Mrs Huntley, I am not straight from my bed. I've been getting up and wandering about every day and I'm not wasting any more time. This morning, I shall only go as far as the works, but there are things I want to talk about to the men.'

'It's not right! Why, it's not even decent! What the master would say, I tremble to think.' Time and again she overstepped her position, treated Tamsin as though she were her daughter — or, more accurately, her granddaughter — than the mistress of the house. Perhaps it was because Tamsin had neither a mother nor a grandmother that she found a strange kind of comfort in the bossy manner.

'He would be delighted.' She smiled, her dimple coming into play. 'He'd tell me I am doing exactly the right thing.' For one brief moment, she was almost tempted to say, 'He *is* delighted: it was he who put the idea in my head.' But she wasn't certain how far Mrs Huntley's spirituality would stretch, so she let well alone. She couldn't resist standing in front of the hall mirror, slowly turning right round with her arms held out to her sides. 'See? I wore this last summer! The bodice is a bit tight, but see the skirt.'

'Humph. Nothing of you — never was.'

Tamsin laughed. 'Now there's something you couldn't have said a fortnight ago! Tell Mrs White I'll not keep him waiting. By the time he's hungry I'll be home.' Then, adjusting her hat and giving her reflection one last look of satisfaction, she was off.

Parking at the back of the works building, she

414

felt as if she'd stepped back in time. She could almost expect that, when she went in, James would call a greeting. For a moment, her confidence flagged. Then, squaring her shoulders, she walked round to the other side of the building and through the open door of the workshop.

She had been able to accept Mrs Huntley's criticism of her coming out so soon, probably because it had been voiced so openly. The men greeted her cordially, but she was conscious of their disapproval: disapproval that bordered on embarrassment. She knew that they too considered she shouldn't be here. Most of them were married men, most of them with families, most of them with wives who would have followed the accepted practice of staying 'respectably' indoors until the bleeding had stopped and they'd arranged with the Rector for him to lead them in prayers of thanksgiving.

Standing in front of the men who had once been her colleagues on the assembly line, a picture of Arthur forced itself into her mind for a moment. She remembered something of the words of the prayer of that thanksgiving: 'Children . . . fruit of the womb . . . like as arrows in the hand of a giant . . . happy is the man that has his quiver full of them . . . ' Well, she wasn't like those wives. She did say thank you — she said it in the silence of her soul to the mystical spirit James had such faith in. In the bat of an eyelid, all those thoughts swamped her and were gone.

'I want you all to stop work and listen to what

I have to tell you. As you know, I am responsible for what we do here now — and I am not an aeronautical engineer. But there is nothing new to us in building the Farley Moth and I mean us to finish those on the assembly line. That will be the end of aircraft production at Proctor's, and this is the one thing that does honestly sadden me — not for Proctor's sake, but because it will mean that I can't keep all of you on the staff. At the most I shall need three and I think the fairest is to say that will be the three who have worked here longest. I'm giving you warning now, although it will be some time before all the work is done. But if you want to find something else, it's fairer to know what the situation is.'

For a moment, they looked at her in disbelief. Had giving birth turned her brain? If she'd got orders for the planes that had been shelved when the Ministry contract finished, surely that was good news, not grounds for getting rid of most of the workforce? If she'd got an order for those planes, who's to say there wouldn't be more? And if there was no more work coming in, what did she want with three men left on the payroll to kick their heels? No matter which way their thoughts went, there was one thing on which they were all agreed: if she couldn't run the place, then she ought to sell out to someone who could.

'What's the plan, then? If we've got an order for these five planes — that's a good order — perhaps we were all wrong. Perhaps there's a future for our Moths still.'

'Oh, but there is,' she told them. 'You ask

416

anyone who's flown them in the Air Force.'

'So . . . ?' Still it made no sense. She talked about the Air Force; did that mean that now the guv'nor had gone, she'd got Alex Murray back in her pocket again?

That's when she told them what she meant to do. And before she went home to a two-week-old baby who sucked furiously on his knuckles, telling the world he was neglected, she wrote the order for the five engines they'd be needing.

*   *   *

Next morning's trip took her further. James was given his ten o'clock feed early and Mrs White was left to wind him. By ten past ten, Mrs Huntley watched as 'that young minx' was off again. This time, she didn't stop at the works, nor yet in the village. She went straight on to Brackleford. There were three firms of builders in the town and she called on each of them. She had to be sure no one was given the chance to take advantage of her lack of experience.

*   *   *

The third day, she went to see Maureen.

'You mean you're starting it on your own? I know you've learnt a lot of business ways but, Tam, this is something different. Taking orders to make planes; that's one thing; but spending out of your own money, making them and keeping them . . . Supposing when you're all ready to open, no one comes along? All that money gone.

417

And you have little James to think of. What do you think, Tom? Do you think she's doing right.'

Tom Riley was totally blind, but there was little he missed. As they'd talked, his head had turned towards first one, then the other, his sightless eyes hidden behind their dark glasses.

'Do you think I'm being silly, Tom?' She hoped he didn't for, whatever anyone said, her mind was made up. To have a change of heart now would be like breaking faith with James: but even to Maureen and Tom, she couldn't bring herself to talk about the dream that haunted her, or her trust that that had been James's way of guiding her.

'I reckon you're brave more than silly, Tam. That's not to say I don't wish you had someone partnering you. Sorry, that wasn't a clever thing to say, was it? The way you've made an effort these last weeks, well, I reckon there's not many would have coped like it.'

'Coping is a lot easier if you have a goal,' she told him. 'I could have looked for a buyer for Proctor's. James has left enough that little James and I could have lived without my having to earn. But life's empty if it doesn't give a challenge.'

'Challenge, yes. But Mo's right: you're risking an awful lot of your capital. You say the fellows who have been flyers won't be content to keep their feet on the ground. And very likely they won't be content. But money dictates, when it comes down to it, and how many of them will have the cash to belong to a flying club? That really is something new, isn't it, eh? Flying Club.'

He chuckled to himself. 'I know the Liberal Club, the Conservative Club — ah, and the boys who used to cycle to Brackleford to play billiards on a Thursday evening — I'm going back to the days before the war — they used to say they were off to the Billiard Club. But a Flying Club . . . '

'Once you've flown, it's something you can't just put behind you.'

'Can't, you say,' Maureen was worried for her friend. 'Depends on the hand life deals you. There are some things you have to put behind you, like it or not.'

'Some things we have to learn to live without, but Mo, we don't put them behind us. Kate, James: they're never put behind me. Nor Alex. And Tom, you've had to live without being able to see — but in your mind's eye, everything is as clear as it ever was. Isn't it?'

'Just as bright.' Then, with a smile directed somewhere in Maureen's direction. 'To me she'll always be just as pretty as she was at twenty-one.'

'Oh, Tom.' Maureen's rosy face grew even pinker. While he still half smiled at the effect of his words, he couldn't see the way she was biting on her quivering bottom lip.

'It'll be a long time before the Club opens. We shall need bigger hangars, and a club house for the members. I say 'we': I hope you two will feel you're part of it. I expect I'm jumping ahead, but what's the good of a dream if it doesn't carry you forward? I can see that if we get members from some way away — and they can't all come from round Brackleford — then we shall need to serve food.'

She didn't put her suggestion into words, but Maureen saw the idea as a way out of their poverty trap. But what about poor Tom? What sort of work could there be for a sightless man among a lot of flyers?

★　★　★

As the weeks went on, Tamsin was to be seen each day pushing the perambulator along the lane past Hinds Hill on her way to Proctor's. One by one, the five planes were completed, and when each one was wheeled out to the grass it had to be she now who took them up to test them while Maureen looked after James.

The memory of James's last flight was always with her, even though the Moth was an old friend, tested and tried. Climbing into the cockpit, she would never fail to call silently to James: help me to do all the right things. Don't let anything be wrong with it. I know I can do it — yes, of course I can — but help me. Make sure I do all the things you always did, then bring it back safely.

Not exactly a prayer in the normal sense of the word, but each time it was a cry to James's spirit and, as she heard the familiar shout; 'Chocks away,' his presence never failed her.

Before the onset of winter, the builders were busy. The existing works were to be extended to give additional hangar space and, at one end, a workshop for repairs and maintenance. On the

420

opposite side of the airfield, a completely new building was rising, a club house divided into three sections. At one end would be a changing area, two hand-basins and a geyser to give hot water, plumbing that was attached to a septic tank. The main entrance led to a small vestibule behind which — out of bounds to club members — would be a kitchen. A dining room was to be to the right of the entrance and, beyond that, a room which Tamsin planned to furnish with the type of woven basketwork chairs which were beginning to make an appearance on the market. It would be a room where, even when the weather was against taking to the skies, men used to the communal life of the Air Force could meet and for a few hours forget their civilian work that kept their feet on the ground.

Tamsin was fully aware of the whispered criticism — in Mrs Huntley's case, it wasn't even whispered.

'Be more sense if you left aeroplanes to the menfolk. All very well while the master was here; I dare say he took pleasure in seeing the way you took to the business. But it's not the thing for a woman.' Or, on another occasion, 'In all weathers, you have that poor wee mite down in those sheds. No wonder you're the talk of the village.' And on yet another, 'If you'd been left with a living to earn to bring the boy up, then there would be some excuse. Although, even then, what a way for a woman to make a living. Make a living? More likely squander all the master worked for.'

'Mrs H., what a gloom you are!' Tamsin was in

no mood to let either local gossip or the housekeeper's forecast of ruin knock her off course. 'You just wait a year or two; you'll be singing another tune.'

No one — not Mrs Huntley, not even Maureen — was shown a hint of the moments when her confidence would evaporate and she would see what she was doing as foolhardy, a risk with little James's security. But the moments were never given the opportunity to take root. She would prove to all those fainthearts that they were wrong. By the time James was walking there would be planes flying over Oakleigh. Proctor's Flying Club would be more than a figment of her dreams.

The Air Force was already running a regular ferry service for passengers and mail to the continent, and those pilots who were part of it were the envy of thousands who, with demobilisation, had lost their opportunity to fly. Before the war, the vast population had accepted aviation as something for 'dreamers and cranks'. First the Royal Flying Corps, then latterly the Royal Air Force had dispelled that conception, but it still remained outside the orbit of the working man. Yet before the year of 1919 gave way to the start of a new decade, aeronautics had advanced. The Atlantic had been crossed by air non-stop; the Australian Government had paid prize money of ten thousand pounds to the first man to fly a British-built machine from England to Australia. Even those completely unconnected with the world of aviation felt a stirring of excitement; they were living on the brink of a new age.

Carefully, Tamsin penned her advertisement.

'Opening shortly — ' She made two or three attempts: stark facts, dates of opening. Each one was screwed up and thrown into the basket. A bald statement wasn't enough; this needed a different approach.

Calling All Qualified Aviators

If you've once known the ultimate freedom that's only to be found in the air, you will be interested to learn that Proctor's Flying Club is about to be opened in Oakleigh. You may be among those who flew the Proctor Farley Moth during your service, in which case you will know its capabilities.

Proctor's Flying Club is based at the home of the Farley Moth, and the machines used will be serviced and maintained by the men who originally built them. The newly erected club house provides changing facilities, a dining room and a room for relaxation and comradeship, a place to discuss your afternoon's flight or to re-live previous experiences with other pilots.

If you are interested in membership of the club, write to The Manager,

Proctor's Flying Club, Oakleigh, nr Brackleford.

Common sense told Tamsin it was better to refer to herself as the manager, not manageress and

423

not Mrs Murray; even so, she felt she was failing Lucinda! Unlike the usual two-inch notice in the local papers, she decided this was an occasion when she would have to be prepared to spend. She wanted a quarter of a page given to her notice, the whole thing printed within a bold edging, and she meant it to go in local papers as far distant as Oxford, Maidenhead, Basingstoke — then, throwing caution to the wind, as well as locals she sent it to the London offices of every national daily. It was pointless spending a fortune on setting the club up if the one-time pilots who pined to fly knew nothing of it.

She had pamphlets printed and application forms for membership. It was as if she were hurtling downhill with failing brakes. In the beginning, it had been she who had made the decisions, determined to turn a dream into reality. But with the buildings almost ready for use and the notices in the papers, she had lost control. With young James in his perambulator propped by supporting pillows, wide awake and taking an interest in the world, each morning she hurried along the lane past Hinds Hill.

'Do you think we'll get any post, Jamie? Humph, yes?' She took his beaming grin showing six tiny white teeth, two in the top and four in the bottom, as an affirmative. 'Nearly there. See — ' she pointed ' — that's the works. No, we mustn't call it that any more. We have to say 'That's the Club'.'

He threw back his head and laughed, rocking backwards and forwards, as if that would add to their speed.

* * *

Membership forms were returned with joining fees, cheques, postal orders, bank notes. It was soon apparent they would need to be able to put more than five machines in the air at one time. So she applied to the Aircraft Disposal Company for war surplus Farley Moths and, one by one, made the journey to collect them and ferry them back to Oakleigh. Long before James had taken her on her first flight, she had longed for the freedom of the skies; she knew as well as any wartime pilot that, once you have flown, nothing can take its place.

By the summer of 1920, the people of Oakleigh were very aware of the success of the new flying club. How could they fail when there was so often the buzz of aeroplanes overhead? A few might pretend to object and grumble that 'if men wanted to take the noisy dangerous machines into the air, they ought to do it somewhere else', but those were the few who enjoyed any cause for complaint. Then, out of earshot of their menfolk, there were those of the local women who thought it all wrong that a girl should be in charge, taking that illegitimate child of hers with her as often as not and spending her days with a lot of men. 'But what else would you expect? It's no secret that she's a fast one.'

Tamsin cared nothing for their opinion. In truth, she was too busy to hear it.

Before the club had been operating for many months, a new venture grew naturally from it. The members were experienced pilots; their aerobatics had been born of necessity as they'd learnt to avoid trouble in the skies over France. All of them were drawn partly for the camaraderie; particularly at weekends, there was always the sound of male voices, male laughter, in the lounge of the club house. They'd all paid their membership fee, but to take a plane into the air each time they came was beyond the means of some of them.

That's how Proctor's Flying Circus came into being: another advertisement was sent to the newspapers. They were booked to give displays at fêtes and festivals and, where there was adequate landing space, to take paying joyriders, all of which brought money into the coffers of the Club. From then, there was no turning back. The name spread, and engagements came in from as far afield as Dorset and Hertfordshire, Wiltshire and Surrey.

In the kitchen of the club house, Maureen prepared snacks, at the same time keeping an eye on Matt — and Trudie, too, when she wasn't at school.

'I think you'll have to look around for someone else,' she told Tamsin, and it was clear from her voice and from her worried expression that all wasn't well. 'The money's useful: I'd be a liar if I didn't admit that. But, Tam, there are more important things than that.'

'You're finding it too much? Could we get a girl in, one not started work yet? It wouldn't cost a lot. She could help you — '

'Not the work,' Maureen turned away, but not before Tamsin had seen the misery on her face.

426

'So hard on my Tom. I tell you, Tam, I'd rather we went without, than he was made to feel he couldn't keep his own family.'

'Mo, there must be something he could do here. We'll think of something — '

'No.' And by this time, Maureen had given up the battle. It was as if she'd been keeping her unhappiness tightly bottled until at last the cork had blown. 'No, he'd know. And I can't let you — can't let anyone — give him a chance to earn out of sympathy. He'd hate it. Hasn't he suffered enough in losing his sight? But, you see, me working and taking home the money, that doesn't even leave him his self-respect. Tam, it's awful to see him,' she wept. 'Sometimes, he doesn't know I'm there. I feel low, like a cheat, looking at him and he doesn't know. But his face — Tam, I can't bear him to be so miserable.'

'There ought to be training for the men who've been maimed. That's not charity. It's what all of us owe to them.'

'Council talked about it. Said they were going to do something. *Do!* What do that lot do? Sit on their behinds in that council chamber and think they're God Almighty! But *do?*' Her voice rose out of control, higher and louder. 'Bugger all: bugger, bugger, bugger all. That's what. Lot of old buffers, most of them living comfortably off their own businesses, shops and the like. They don't know what it's like. Your Lucinda Murray was right: what we want is some women running things. Oh, Tam, I'd give him my own eyes if only I could: that's God's truth.'

Tam put her arms around her friend. She felt

humbled. But humility doesn't get things done. Maureen's miserable outburst had sown two seeds in her mind: humility nurtured one, anger the other. There was no easy way of bringing the first to fruition, but the second was far easier. That same day she wrote to the Chairman of Brackleford Rural District Council, Councillor Horace Hoskins, elected to represent Oakleigh Ward.

We read much in the local press of the plans for the memorials which, quite rightly, are being erected in villages throughout the District. Certainly, we honour the dead; certainly we are resolved neither they nor their sacrifice will be forgotten.

When Oakleigh's memorial is unveiled on the Green, the council will be in evidence, the members well satisfied that they have done their duty by the local dead.

But we have another duty, a more pressing one, one which cannot so easily be carried out. Help is needed for those who have come home maimed, unable to pick up the threads of their old lives. Look around the whole area and you are confronted by evidence of our omissions. Men do not look for charity. Those who can no longer carry out the work they used to do should have an opportunity to train for something else. What of those who have returned with no hope of a home for their own families, still being housed in crowded conditions with relatives? Is that what they fought for? Is that all their local authority cares about them?

None of that can be as simple as ordering a stonemason to prepare a monument. But, as a community, we must resolve not to fail them.

When a reply came, it was even less satisfactory than she had expected:

I acknowledge receipt of your recent communication and note your views are in accordance with those of my council, that those who gave their lives must not be forgotten. The memorial will be unveiled on Oakleigh Green on the twenty-ninth of April and will be my last official engagement, as I shall not offer myself for re-election in May.

So Councillor Hoskins dismissed what he didn't want to know about. Reading his letter as she ate her breakfast, Tamsin's anger mounted. Every word that Maureen had said was right! The council was failing its returning men, able-bodied and disabled alike. And the government had been no better. What had they done in the early days after the armistice? Never mind how long a man had served, demobilisation had come first to those who were skilled in a trade. Plenty of work for them, after four years of war. If there hadn't been such an outcry, those unskilled lads who had marched off with such enthusiasm in the summer of 1914 would have been the last to be stood down. And, as it was, there wasn't work enough for them; many of them were on the scrap heap with the same disregard as the thousands of disabled all over the country, men who stood at street corners trying to sell matches; men who sang outside public houses.

'Mama? Up Jame, Mama.' The little boy held his arms towards her, uncomfortably aware of an expression he wasn't used to.

'Finish your breakfast first. Open wide, one more big bite.' He obliged, happier now that that funny look had gone off her face. 'Eat it all up. Then, before we go to the Club, we're going to call on Auntie Naomi.'

He might not have followed the whole of what she said but, at Naomi's name, he brightened considerably and opened extra wide in an effort to get breakfast over.

'Jame see Na'mi.'

★ ★ ★

'My dear, lovely surprise. There's nothing wrong is there?'

'Not with us personally. But there's lots wrong, Naomi — and it's no good writing letters. It's no good staying outside it all and grumbling — '

'Calm down, child,' Naomi laughed. 'Start at the beginning and tell me what's set you on your hobby horse.'

So Tamsin did. She even brought Councillor Hoskins' letter and, at Naomi's spontaneous, 'Stupid, arrogant man. Always was,' felt her face relax into a smile.

'I want you to be honest with me, Naomi. I don't want favours.'

'I hope no one can accuse me of less than honesty.'

'I know. But you mustn't be influenced just because we're friends. This election in May, I want to stand. It's time we had a woman on the council — and there's nothing to prevent it, except people's inbred belief that all women are fit for is to clean a house and bear children. It's not good enough! What are you laughing for?'

'You, my dear. I wish Lucinda could hear you.'

But Tamsin didn't laugh. She knew that in the weeks between then and election day in May, she would find little to laugh about.

'I need someone to nominate me, and someone to second the nomination,' she said. 'I know I only had that letter this morning but I'd been thinking of it for weeks. Then, hearing that there will have to be an election for this Ward, well, don't you see? This must be the right time.'

'They could do with someone with a bit of spirit, I'll give you that. I'll either nominate you or second it, whichever is most helpful. But that's the beginning of the struggle, not the end. If only James were here and prepared. There's no hiding from the truth: a man stands a much better chance than a woman.'

Tamsin laughed, suddenly looking forward to the battle. 'We'll see about that. Have you any idea who would go down well in the village for the seconder?'

Naomi sat down and took James on her knee, rubbing her chin against the top of his baby-fine, straight, light-brown hair.

'Leave it with me. If you're game for a battle,

then so am I. Give me a treat and leave James with me for the morning, too, if you like. I'll trundle him home at about one o'clock. By then, I'll have had time to think. Tell me, Tamsin, do you get word of Alex?'

'Does he write to me, you mean? No. I wouldn't expect him to. Why, is there news?' Could Naomi know what it did to her just to hear his name, have him part of their conversation — still a living part of their lives? All thought of the council evaporated. She held herself in an unnaturally controlled stillness, prepared to hear that he was going to marry again, an American girl, one who would set his roots firmly in her own land. Wasn't that what she'd always known would happen?

'He writes to me sometimes.' Naomi gave no hint that she'd noticed any change in Tamsin's manner. 'I had a letter yesterday. His heart isn't out there, Tamsin.' Pretending to be concentrating on James, Naomi gave her a quick glance to see how the news was received. 'He's living well, no doubt about that. Off the fat of the land, by our standards. I was always so fond of Alex: like a breath of fresh air in the house.'

'But he's flying, that's what means more to him than anything. What did you tell me the firm is he's working for?'

Now it was Naomi's turn to hide the way her thoughts swept her. With exaggerated casualness, she told Tamsin not only the name of Alex's employers but the address too. 'I was telling you, he seems very unsettled there.' How deep did she need to plant her seed of hope? 'To my way of

432

thinking, he'd be better to come home. There must be work for a flying man in England.'

'Perhaps it was just his mood when he wrote, Naomi. About the nomination form — '

'Leave all that with me, dear. And little James: leave him here all day if you like. I expect you've got his needs packed in the well of the perambulator?' Then, to James, 'Would you like Mummy to leave you here with me for a little while? You could help me pick some daffodils.'

'Me 'tay wiv 'ou.' He even held a more than willing face to Tamsin to be kissed goodbye.

Back at the Club, Tamsin donned her leather coat and helmet, and put on her goggles. On a mid-week March morning, there were no members there; she had to call someone from the workshop to swing the propeller. 'Chocks away,' came the familiar shout. And she taxied across the airstrip. Whatever her worries or problems — in her loneliest moments or her most joyous — to be alone, high in the air, unravelled the tangles and helped her to see her way ahead. And on that morning, she needed the solitude. She'd asked Naomi to nominate her for the Rural District Council; if they could find a seconder, then ahead of her was a struggle.

But flying, free as a bird, in the early spring sunshine, it wasn't the council she thought about. Alex, not settled in America. Alex: what does that mean? Is it England you pine for — or is it the same for you as it is for me?

Alone, with nothing between her and the clear blue springtime sky, there was comfort in hearing her own voice.

'Why did we let it happen, Alex, my Alex? I used to try to make myself believe that you'd *never* really loved me, that you'd only married me because of Kate. But my heart had known that couldn't have been the truth. Remember it, Alex, the joy of living, simply because we were together. Remember — all of it. Loving, all so beautiful, so perfect. Do you wake in the night, wanting me, like I do you? Even when I was with James, dear, dear James — truly I loved him. I always will love him; he was the *best* person I've ever known — better person than you, Alex, better person than me. We're like two halves of one whole. We are? We were? I know where you are, now. No good flying around up here like some brainless bird; if you want a thing, you have to fight for it. Please, please when he gets my letter, make him be glad. We could start again. We've learnt our lesson. Please make it be like that for him, too.'

The flight had cleared her mind and pointed her way forward. She brought the Moth back and made a perfect landing.

★ ★ ★

Naomi waited until evening before she paid her visit to Sheeplatch Farm to see Gerald Hoskins, cousin of the chairman of the council. She had known him and his wife Emily for years; she'd always got on well with them. In her opinion, the two Hoskins men were different as chalk and cheese, for Gerald was neither stupid nor arrogant. Self-opinionated Horace, owner of a large hardware shop in Brackleford, had always been bumptious, something that had become quite intolerable in the years he'd sat on the council. Gerald ran a successful farm, was prepared himself to do any job that he asked of his labourers and — most importantly, in Naomi's view — had a boyish sense of fun. But what she wanted of him on that evening was deadly serious.

'A woman? Will voters wear it? That girl from the flying club. There's been plenty of gossip about her, you know.'

'Gossip breeds in ignorance,' Naomi answered smartly. 'I've known her since she worked for Charles Hardcastle: not just as an acquaintance but as someone I'm proud to call my friend. Just tell me, how many people, men or women, would have the courage she has shown? I remember the first time she came to Lambton, before she married Alexander Murray, she talked then of social reform. It's what we need, Gerald, someone not frightened to speak out. Some of them on that council, what do we hear out of any of them?' She didn't put it as succinctly as Maureen had, but the sentiment was the same.

'Horace is standing down, you say? Stayed long enough to get his turn in the chair, I suppose. He'll be full of himself when they unveil the memorial, out there in his own patch, full of his own importance, with his chain of office. After that there's no way to go but down.' His jolly weather-beaten face broke into a laugh. 'Down or out — so he prefers out. All right, Naomi, my dear, I'll put my name to second

435

yours. Or — and don't take this amiss — what if I propose the lass, then you second her? It might not go down too well if, the first time a lady tries for the council, it's one of her own sex who puts her forward.'

'I think you're right,' Naomi agreed. 'A lot of nonsense, but people are slow to take to change.'

'Be a joke if we could pull it off, eh? I tell you what, she couldn't be worse than some of the dead wood they've got there.'

'So we all say. But how many of us has the gumption to do anything about it? Bless you, Gerald. I'll take a trip into the council office tomorrow and pick up the forms. This election is going to be an education to all of us. Not just you male ratepayers choosing for the rest of us. More than time the working man had a say. And those who went off to fight, they're home now — and, God help them, for some of them there's precious little for them to come home to. Every adult male will be putting a cross.'

'And you, Naomi, m'dear.'

'The suffragettes won't be satisfied with that, though — it's still no use to those under thirty, or those in rented accommodation. But it's a step in the right direction. Well, we shall see. If we end up with a lot of dead wood, as you call it, then we've no one to blame but ourselves.'

* * *

In the privacy of the air, Tamsin had spoken from her heart. An hour later, behind the closed door of her office, she held nothing back.

436

If you want to forget, then throw this letter away. But I have to write it.

If she heard nothing, then that would be her answer. But perhaps . . . She was frightened to give rein to her imagination, yet she had no power to stop it.

★   ★   ★

The notices were displayed through Oakleigh:

Candidate: Mrs Tamsin Murray of Oakleigh, Proprietor of Proctor's Flying Club. Proposed by: Gerald B. Hoskins, Farmer of Sheeplatch Farm, Oakleigh. Seconded by: Miss Naomi Halliwell, Gentlewoman, of Lambtons, Oakleigh.

There were two other candidates: one was a solicitor from Brackleford who lived in the village; the second was the blacksmith.

As long as she could remember, Tamsin had followed Lucinda's activities. She knew about the out-of-door rallies, she knew about the talks in local halls, the question and answer sessions — not to mention the demonstrations which, if she were honest, she had never completely upheld. But what she'd learnt from Lucinda had left its mark; now that she needed it, it was there to guide her. If anyone had suggested to her that Arthur, too, had left a lasting impression, she would have scoffed at the idea; yet, as she stood on her soap box on the Green, with a megaphone alerting people

437

from the neighbouring houses, it was impossible not to remember an evening when she'd stood with her mother in the market triangle in Ringwood while people gathered round hanging on his words. Or so, as a bored young child, she had assumed.

But, looking back, she realised that in his case most of the audience had been women, not so much listening to the handsome creature he'd been, as gazing. So she learnt something even from him. Before she set out for her evening meetings, leaving the always willing Naomi to listen for James, she was careful to make sure she did the very best she could with her appearance. Every man over twenty-one would have a vote; the only women with the franchise were those who were at least thirty years of age and either ratepayers in their own right, or married to a ratepayer. That cut the number of women voters in the Ward of Oakleigh to very few indeed. It would be the men who would decide who best to represent them. And Tamsin was worldly enough to use all the feminine attraction she could muster.

No meeting, whether out of doors on the Green, in the village hall, in the hangar at Proctor's or on people's doorsteps, went without mockery. Often there would be cat-calls; sometimes there would be abuse of a more personal nature. But Tamsin was learning to grow a thick skin, at least as far as her challenge for the council was concerned.

In the midst of an impassioned pledge to work for more housing, she was interrupted by a

438

leering habitué of the Jolly Fiddler, who lurched across the Green and pushed to the front of the small group.

'What you goin' to do about it then, missus? Make room for 'em in that home what your fancy man left you?'

'Steady on, Bert,' from someone else. 'Let the lady have her say.'

'Yes, shut up and listen, can't you?' And this from most of her audience.

'What am I going to do?' Tamsin addressed the man who stood swaying in front of her, his mouth open in a ill-humoured grin that showed stained and broken teeth. Her words fell into the sudden silence. The men gathered around her waited to see how she would cope; after all, she was only a slip of a woman. Would they be wise to put their cross beside her name? 'For a start, no, I am not offering my spare room. It's not charity men look for, it's independence. There is not a bottomless purse of money and we'd be deluding ourselves if we believed there was. What I mean to do is try to influence the spending of what is at the council's disposal. Flowers on the Green, repaving our pathways, all very fine — but luxuries. Three things most important as our country — our village, and villages like it everywhere — recover from the war — '

'War? War's been over this year and a half. How long are we going to be paying for the bloody war?' This from her yellow-toothed friend.

'Shut up, Bert, and listen.' And this from a

young man with one empty sleeve tucked into his jacket pocket.

'We have to be paying for the war until those who fought in it are paid the debt the rest of us owe them. Three things have to come before all else. One is local authority housing. How many are there even in Oakleigh who are trying to bring up their families, living with parents or in-laws? Too many. It's not fair on anyone. So housing should be number one on the council's list of priorities. Second is a better way to rehabilitate those who have been wounded. No matter what a man's physical disability, there isn't one who couldn't be trained to use the faculties he still has. Yes, the country owes every disabled man a pension; but even more it owes him a chance to work, to find his independence.'

'Fine words, missus. Ain't seen too much of it yet, though, have we?'

'And what's the third thing?'

Tamsin smiled, little realising that that dimple was doing her election chances no harm.

'The third thing I shan't have to do battle over, at least not for Oakleigh. It's education. We have cause to be proud of our school and both the teachers. If other villages are less fortunate, then I'll fight their corner. No matter what is proposed, I know there will always be those who see things differently, have other objectives. I've told you mine. None of it will be easy — but where's the satisfaction in a fight that's easy? If you put your faith in me, I give you my word I'll try to be your voice in the council.'

★ ★ ★

On the sixth of May, a policeman stood at the door of the village hall as the good folk of Oakleigh went to the poll. That evening, Maureen left Trudie and Matt in Tom's care and went to Lindley to take charge of James, while Tamsin drove herself, Naomi and Gerald Hoskins to Brackleford Town Hall, where the votes were counted. Her opponents were both confident of success: the blacksmith had been in Oakleigh for twenty years, and the solicitor felt himself by far the most able of the three candidates.

Tamsin was elected with an overall majority. She meant to work with all her power to effect the changes she believed in so strongly. She was elated by her success: of course she was. This must be her future: the Flying Club must go from strength to strength, and she would dedicate herself to the community work that had been entrusted to her. As long as she focused on those two things, those and the never-failing pleasure of little James, who delighted in being her shadow, then she gave no space in her thoughts to the letter she'd sent and the reply she looked for in vain as the months went by.

The local paper carried reports of Councillor Murray's work for the rehabilitation of the disabled. In fact, she found the hurdles less difficult than she'd feared. No member of the council dared to thwart her openly, for in every ward there were men who needed help with rehabilitation. If her fellow councillors thought

441

she was wasting her time, none of them would be the one to voice the opinion. So a training agency was set up and, ex *officio*, Tamsin was put in charge. With no more than a raised eyebrow or a knowing smirk, it was silently agreed that 'that should give her something to do and stop her meddling.' She had notices printed and pinned on every official notice board in the district, suggesting those unemployed through disability should contact the agency. She worked tirelessly, finding firms who would take part in the scheme, visiting employers herself before sending an applicant. The incentive was that the council would pay half the wage for three months of training.

'A man doesn't need two legs, or two arms either, to learn to keep the books.' She tried to sound completely businesslike but it was the earnest expression in her wide, strange-coloured eyes that often won the day. 'I have engaged someone who lost an arm at Ypres. Before the war, he worked for the dairy in Oakleigh, drove the milk cart. But he is bright, he is keen, and above all he is thankful not to be solely dependent on the state.' Then with that smile that held power she never suspected, 'Already, I wonder how we managed without him.' All of which was true, for the young man who had listened to her electioneering, and tried to keep the unsavoury Bert quiet, was relieving her of much of the day-to-day bookwork.

For the blind, it was more difficult. With Tom — and Maureen — in mind, Tamsin talked to Oswald Denby, who played the church organ.

'All they have is their hearing.' How could he turn her away, when she looked at him like that, even though choir practice was over and he wanted to get home to his supper? Not many young women with lives as successful as she'd made hers would have bothered about other people. And, too, he was flattered that it was him she looked to for help and advice.

'Too late for them to learn music,' he told her. 'Well, many of them have tried to teach themselves, of course, but only well enough to put their hat on the ground and wait for the pennies.'

'If you lose your sight, don't you think your hearing takes over? It has to. How much music would one have to know to be able to tune a piano?'

He gave her question his serious thought.

'What's needed for tuning is an ear: yes, an ear. That's something that can't be taught. If losing his sight gives a man better perception of hearing, does it do the same for the sense of touch, do you suppose? Because that's something else he would need; he'd have to become familiar with the keyboard and the relevant stringing of the piano, by feel to know where to apply the tuning fork. It would be no mean challenge.'

'For a man who's lost his sight, all of life is a challenge. Mr Denby, could you spare the time to talk about it to Tom Riley? Would you be able to tell if his ear would be accurate enough? I'm not asking you to give your time to teaching him: just to seeing if you think that

443

might be an answer.'

'Tom Riley . . . I remember when he worked at the smithy. I've seen him about. Breaks your heart to see some of our young men. Yes, my dear, I'll do what I can. But if he hasn't the natural gift, there's nothing I can do, you realise that?'

That was the beginning of Tom's long climb back.

* * *

Tamsin's days were full to overflowing. She gave herself to her council work just as wholeheartedly as she did to the Flying Club. As for James, except for meetings, when Naomi proudly took charge of him, he accompanied her everywhere. Official wheels turn slowly but, even so, by the beginning of December the foundations had been dug for a terrace of houses at the entrance to the village. Brackleford, like every other town, still had its match vendors; there were still plenty of unemployed who were looked on as unemployable. But for many in the rural district surrounding the town, 1921 had given new hope, no small thanks to Tamsin.

There was nothing masculine about Tamsin, there never had been. Of her own sex, the kindly would call her petite, dainty; the less charitable would say scrawny. Perhaps, without being aware of it, they realised that, completely unconsciously, she had far more appeal to the opposite sex than many a curvaceous temptress. Whatever the reason, apart from Naomi, Maureen and

Lucinda, who occasionally stayed at Lambton, Tamsin inhabited a male world. There was never anything bordering 'woman's talk' from Naomi or Lucinda — and although Naomi had cunningly mentioned how Alex could be contacted, she'd let the subject drop. As for Maureen, only to Tom would she let herself wonder how a couple as happy together as the Murrays had been could have let their unhappiness over Kate drive them apart.

They saw Tamsin as unfailingly energetic, never wasting a minute, dashing from one task to the next, untiring, unchanging. No one, not even little James, knew the depth of her hurt as the months went by and there was no word from Alex.

It was in November that Naomi said to her, 'I told you Alex was unsettled. I had another letter, today. He's not let the grass grow under his feet. Something like these displays your flyers give, I suppose. He has bought an ex-government machine. He gives what he calls 'barnstorming flying exhibitions', says it makes him a living and has given him the chance to see the country. Dreadfully hard for young men to settle.'

Tamsin tried to stamp on hope, before it had time to take shape, but it was too late. He was travelling around; perhaps he'd gone before her letter even reached him.

'How long ago did he give up his test pilot job?' She threw the question casually into the air.

'He doesn't say. But I wasn't surprised. Remember, I told you something was amiss.'

Perhaps it was hope that stubbornly refused to

be quashed that made sleep so impossible that night. Getting out of bed, Tamsin moved across the familiar, dark room to the window. Not a breath of wind stirred. The window pane was icy-cold against her forehead. Naomi had known something was amiss, he couldn't settle, moving from one place to another, no fixed address.

Then uncertain hope was crushed by certain reality. Naomi had always written to him, so he would have known about James's accident. He would have known that Proctor's was hers. Would that have prevented him writing? Or was he just so arrogant that he wouldn't let himself say to her as she had to him, from her heart, almost begging him . . . and he'd not come.

'Mama, Mama,' James screamed, a rare thing for him in the middle of the night.

'All right, Jamie, I'm here.' From his cot in the room next to hers, she lifted him into her arms, felt his arms tight around her neck. Small, frightened and utterly dependent: James or Kate, Kate or James. His little body was warm; his need of her was her salvation.

'Just two minutes' cuddle,' she whispered to him. She knew it was a bad habit, but tonight she needed him as much as he needed her. So until he was safely asleep, she drew comfort from his nearness. Only when he was back in his cot, leaving her still wide awake, did those familiar longings stir to haunt her.

There was no escaping them; she didn't even try. This was the bed where Jamie had been conceived . . . Think of James, dearest James who'd given her the sort of love she could never deserve. He was there at the front of her mind; it was his body, warm and tender, she imagined as her passion heightened. Then he was gone. There was only Alex, drawing her forward, nearer, nearer, her and Alex, just for a second they were as one. Then he was gone, she was alone and the physical joy still alive in every nerve no more than a taunting mockery.

★   ★   ★

New Year's Day 1922, the day Kate would have been eight years old. In the morning, Tamsin had to collect some papers from the council offices in Brackleford, but she wouldn't be there a minute. Then, before she came home, she would buy some flowers.

'We going to car?' James jumped up and down with pleasure as the pushchair was left behind and they made for the old coach house.

'Yes. We're going to Brackleford,' she answered. Although he couldn't always follow her conversation, he wasn't too young to appreciate being treated like a grown-up person. Some people talked silly talk to him. He didn't like that. 'You know what today is, Jamie?'

'Nice day,' he told her obligingly.

'Yes, it is. And it's more than just that. It's Kate's birthday.'

'We go see Kate?' He climbed onto the back seat and knelt to look out of the rear window in his usual position.

'On the way home,' she promised.

As they travelled the familiar route to

447

Brackleford, he amused himself watching the road grow long behind them, making occasional excited and not always intelligible comments. In town, she collected the papers she wanted then, choosing them carefully, they bought a bunch of greenhouse chrysanthemums. With James in tow, she couldn't dash about at her usual rate, so by the time they started on their homeward journey the morning was almost gone. Looking back over her shoulder, she saw that his busy morning had caught up with him. He was lying on the seat, thumb in mouth, first finger stroking the bridge of his nose just as Kate used to.

Tamsin let her mind wander. Kate's birthday. She must have been glad when Unca Jame had come to join her. Not lonely, as long as she was loved and remembered; wasn't that what James had been so certain about? Oh, but she was certainly that. They both were. Three years old, just a bit bigger than Jamie (no, not bigger: older perhaps, but not so tall). Tamsin let her own mind slip back as far as she could remember, recalling those far-off secure days at Gorsemoor. These last years, so busy had she been with her own life, she'd not listened for the voice of yesterday, yet always she'd known that her grandfather had been there for her. A smile tugged at the corner of her mouth as she opened her heart and listened. He'd never be forgotten. And as long as he was loved and remembered, he'd never be gone.

'What's this? You come to keep me company, then, duckie?' To her . . . to Kate? The road ahead of her was misted by tears, not of anguish but of acceptance. 'Grandpa, she must be loving you just like I did. You, Mum, her precious Unca Jame: take care of her, my little girl. Mine, Alex's . . . '

★ ★ ★

James woke as she brought the car to a standstill by the gate of the churchyard.

'Where's us?' he asked, rubbing his eyes and nose.

'We've come to bring Kate her flowers, remember?'

'Umph.' He wriggled off the seat and out of the door she held open for him. They often came to the church yard, he knew just where to find Kate's grave.

'You know where to find her. You can run on, if you like.' All part of the usual routine: he knew which path to take, a little way to the left then to the right, until he came to the little grave near the back hedge. Just as he always did, he shot off, leaving her to follow with the flowers. Where he turned right, he stopped, looking around him, suddenly uncertain.

'Go on. I'm coming,' Tamsin called.

'Man . . . man there.' He came back to her and slipped his hand into hers. It was all too easy to lose his developing confidence.

Man there! Oh, but she was a fool to let this sudden image spring to mind. Even so, with the flowers in one hand and James's warm little palm in the other, she started to run, with James stumbling and leaping in an effort to keep up.

The winter sun was glinting on his auburn hair as he stood by the graveside, one hand on the headstone.

'Alex!'

James gave up the battle. When she ran like that, he couldn't keep up.

'I came as soon as I got it.' Alex pulled her letter out of his pocket, the envelope covered with addresses as it had followed him.

'Didn't hear from you — I was so frightened — '

'Tammy . . . my little shrimp . . . ' It was happening: she was in his arms, held so close she could hardly breathe. The years between might never have been. 'Her birthday, Tammy. Our little girl. Eight today.'

Tamsin knew it was silly to cry. There was no sadness in her tears, only thankfulness almost too great to bear.

James was coming slowly nearer, even more uncertain in this new turn of events.

'And you, young man.' Alex held out his hand. 'You must be James?'

The boy looked at him with the same solemn expression Alex had so often seen on his father, then nodded.

'I's James.' He liked the look of the stranger; he liked the way his eyes looked as though he wanted to laugh. So, for good measure he added, 'I's James Murray.'

When the man rumpled his hair, he laughed, laughed uproariously loudly. Why was everyone suddenly so happy?

Other titles in the
Charnwood Library Series:

LOVE ME OR LEAVE ME

Josephine Cox

Beautiful Eva Bereton has only three friends in the world: Patsy, who she looks upon as a sister; Bill, her adopted cousin, and her mother, to whom she is devoted. With Eva's father increasingly angry about life as a cripple, she and her mother support each other, keeping their spirits high despite the abuse. So when a tragic accident robs Eva of both parents, Patsy, a loveable Irish rogue, is the only one left to support her. Tragedy strikes yet again when Eva's uncle comes to reclaim the farm that Eva had always believed belonged to her parents. Together with Patsy, Eva has no choice but to start a new life far away . . .

COLDITZ: THE GERMAN STORY

Reinhold Eggers

This is the story of the famous German prison camp Colditz — as the German guards saw it. It was a place where every man felt that in spite of the personal tragedy of imprisonment, it was his duty to overcome. The book vividly describes the constant battle of wits between guards and prisoners, the tunnelling, bribery, impersonations, forgery and trickery of all kinds by which brave men sought to return to the war.

THE POPPY PATH

T. R. Wilson

It's 1920 and, the years of wartime rationing over, the inhabitants of the seaside resort of Shipden are turning again to the good things of life. The hottest news is that a new doctor has arrived in town: a handsome young man who would sweep any one of Shipden's many hopeful females off their feet. So when James Blanchard decides to marry pretty Rose Jordan the community is both shocked and outraged. Like many of the 'war widows' around her, Rose is an attractive, highly intelligent, single mother. But the scandalous difference is that Alec Taverner — the father of her four-year-old daughter — is still very much alive.

STILL WATER

John Harvey

The naked body of a young woman is found floating in an inner-city canal. Not the first, nor the last. When another woman disappears, following a seminar on women and violence, everyone fears for her safety — especially those who know about her husband's controlling character. Is this a one-off domestic crime or part of a wider series of murders? What else has been simmering beneath this couple's apparently normal middle-class life? As Resnick explores deeper, he finds disturbing parallels between the couple he's investigating and his own evolving relationship with Hannah Campbell.

AN APRIL SHROUD

Reginald Hill

After seeing Inspector Pascoe off on his honeymoon, Superintendent Andy Dalziel runs into trouble on his own holiday. He accompanies his rescuers back to their rundown mansion, where he discovers that Lake House's owner, Bonnie Fielding, seems less troubled by her husband's tragic death than by the problem of completing the Banqueting Hall. Prompted not only by a professional curiosity — why would anyone want to keep a dead rat in a freezer? — but also by Mrs Fielding's ample charms, Dalziel stays on. By the time Pascoe reappears, there have been several more deaths . . .